FOREWORD

Mark Russinovich is recognized by many as the world's leading expert on the Windows operating system. His tools are used worldwide by corporations and government agencies not only to keep their IT systems running, but to perform advanced forensics.

In this book, Mark has woven a compelling tale about an imminent threat to every person, household, corporation, and government that relies on technology and the systems that we depend on. While what Mark wrote is fiction, the risks that he writes about eerily mirror many situations that we see today. Clearly, we are more and more dependent than ever on Internet-connected computer systems: it is the way we communicate, do our banking, pay our taxes, book our travel, and buy merchandise. We take for granted that these systems will always be there and are set to protect our privacy and are secure. The strength of the Internet and Internet technologies is that we are so connected. However, this strength is also a weakness—these systems are vulnerable to attack from anywhere by anyone, and with little capital investment. The Internet also facilitates maintaining anonymity, on which many of us depend, but often creates a fertile ground for bad actors. As Mark's story unfolds, we see the hacker creating superviruses hiding behind many layers of virtual disguises, which make fixing the problem even more complicated and dangerous.

For too many years, we have heard cyber-security experts saying that we need to have more security, we need to use antivirus, we need to use anti-spyware, back up our systems, use firewalls, and be vigilant about what documents we open, links we click on, and programs we execute. These and other technologies help protect a system or small network, but do not necessarily protect the overall environment that weaves through the very fabric of the Internet, touching all of us. Mark has created a unique work that is not only entertaining but a call to action as well. This is a great read and a forward-looking picture of what we need to avoid.

I hope stories such as *Zero Day* remain just that—great reads that will hopefully never come true.

PROFESSOR HOWARD A. SCHMIDT
PRESIDENT AND CEO, INFORMATION SECURITY FORUM LTD.
WHITE HOUSE CYBER SECURITY COORDINATOR

ZERO DAY

000 **ZERO DAY**

MARK
RUSSINOVICH

FOREWORD BY
HOWARD A. SCHMIDT

THOMAS DUNNE BOOKS
ST. MARTIN'S PRESS
NEW YORK

This is a work of fiction. All of the characters, organizations, and events portrayed in this novel are either products of the author's imagination or are used fictitiously.

THOMAS DUNNE BOOKS.
An imprint of St. Martin's Press.

ZERO DAY. Copyright © 2011 by Mark Russinovich. Foreword © 2011 by Howard A. Schmidt. All rights reserved. Printed in the United States of America. For information, address St. Martin's Press, 175 Fifth Avenue, New York, N.Y. 10010.

www.thomasdunnebooks.com
www.stmartins.com

Library of Congress Cataloging-in-Publication Data

Russinovich, Mark E.
   Zero day : a novel / Mark Russinovich ; foreword by Howard Schmidt. —
First edition.
      p. cm
  ISBN 978-0-312-61246-7
  1. Cyberterrorism—Fiction. I. Title.
  PS3618.U7688Z47 2011
  813'.6—dc22

2010040346

First Edition: March 2011

10 9 8 7 6 5 4 3 2 1

F
RUS

MEMORANDUM

NS rated 10

DATE:	April 14
FROM:	John S. Springman
	Deputy NSA, The White House
TO:	Roger Witherspoon
	Executive Assistant Director, DHS
RE:	Interim Report

Following the catastrophic events late last year, Congress and the President directed the creation of a confidential Committee of Inquiry. Attached is the Interim Report of the Committee. It strikes me as a bit purple in places and speculative in others, but I accept that this is an accurate and fair rendering of the events last year. The IR has been disseminated to all involved agencies. Should there be areas you wish expanded, be certain to convey that desire to me within 10 days. Should you desire redaction of any portion, I am instructed to advise that such a request must be made in writing within the same time period, and state with specificity those sections to be deleted accompanied by a satisfactory explanation of the justification.

It is clear to me now that you were perfectly correct in your initial impression as stated at our enabling meeting. The events that led to such a cataclysmic chain of events, events I wish to add from which we are still attempting to recover, began in New York City, but only by a few minutes. They might just as easily have started over the Atlantic.

WEEK ONE

MAJORITY OF COMPUTERS LACK SECURITY, REPORT

By Isidro Lama
Internet News Service
August 10

A report released Wednesday found that more than 80% of computers lack essential security software.

The overwhelming majority of PCs in homes have been found to lack essential security protections, according to a report by a leading cyber-security firm. Most home computers lack either a firewall, anti-spyware protection or current antivirus software.

"Curiously, most consumers falsely believe they are protected," said a spokesperson for the Internet Security Association. "The reality is quite the opposite."

Despite modest improvements in home security since the first survey four years ago, much remains to be done. "At a time when the public turns increasingly to computers to handle finances and to house personal information, it is leaving itself exposed to exploitation," the spokesperson added.

The situation is no better with military and government computers, according to the report. "We are significantly exposed to a cyber-attack," the report concludes, "the consequences of which could exceed our imagination."

0 0 0 0 0 0 0 0 0 0 0 1

MANHATTAN, NYC
SATURDAY, AUGUST 11
12:01 A.M.

Shhh!"

When the whisper came out of the darkness, the man stopped. A vast panel of glass covered the wall before him, displaying uptown Manhattan in a scene that might have been sold as a poster. Ambient light and the soft glow from a dozen computer monitors was all that spared the room total darkness. The logo of Fischerman, Platt & Cohen floated on each monitor.

In the hallway, the steps faded. A moment later her fingers touched his arm, pressing lightly against the soft skin on the inside of his wrist, her flesh much warmer than his. The thought of her so excited aroused him even more.

She tugged and he followed. "Over here," she whispered. He tried to make her out in the darkness but all he could see was her form, shapeless as a burka. They stopped and she came into his arms, on him even before he realized she'd moved. Her scent was floral, her mouth wet and also warm, tasting of peppermint and her last cigarette.

After a long moment she pulled back. He heard the whisper of clothing across nylon, the slight sound of her skirt dropping to the carpet. He sensed, more than saw, her form stretch on the couch. He unbuckled his trousers and let them drop around his ankles. He remembered his suit jacket; as he removed it, her hand touched his erection through his undershorts. She tugged them lower, then encircled him with her fingers.

Her grip guided him, and as he entered her, a single computer screen sprang to life behind the groaning couple. Turning blue, it read:

Rebooting . . .

After a few seconds, the screen flickered and read:

NO OPERATING SYSTEM FOUND.

The screen turned black.

BRITISH AIRWAYS FLIGHT 188
NORTH ATLANTIC, 843 MILES OFF NEWFOUNDLAND
FRIDAY, AUGUST 11
12:01 A.M.

The flight attendants were clearing breakfast in the passenger compartments as Captain Robert McIntyre scanned the dials of the PFD, the primary flight display, once again. Beside him, copilot Sean Jones sat facing dead forward in that semihypnotic posture so common to commercial pilots on extended flights.

The sound of the twin engines well behind the pilots was distant. Outside, air slipped past the airplane with a comforting hiss. The Boeing 787 Dreamliner, with 289 passengers, all but flew itself. Once the airplane reached a cruising altitude of thirty-seven-thousand feet, the pilots had little to do but monitor the instrumentation and be available should something go wrong.

The airplane could take off, fly itself, and land without human assistance. It was state-of-the-art, fly-by-wire technology, which meant the airplane had the latest in computers. The manual controls, such as the throttle and yoke, were not physically connected to anything, though they were programmed to give the feel that they were. Instead, they emitted electronic signals that moved the parts of the plane needed for control.

Computers had even designed the plane itself. So convincing was the computer construct that the airplane was approved for commercial use and had gone straight to production without a prototype. McIntyre commented from time to time that the 787 was the most beautiful and well-behaved airplane he'd ever flown. "Any plans in New York?" he asked his copilot.

Jones sat motionless for several long seconds. "Excuse me," he said finally. "Did you say something?"

"Want some coffee? I think you were off somewhere."

Jones yawned. "No, I'm all right. I get so bored, you know?"

McIntyre glanced at his wristwatch. They were still more than an hour out of New York City. "Better watch it. You'll be on record in another half hour."

The cockpit voice recorder functioned on a half-hour loop, constantly recording thirty minutes at a time, again and again. Pilots had long learned to be utterly frank only when they were not within half an hour of approach or for the first half hour after takeoff. These were the times anything unusual occurred, if at all. Once in the air, the airplane was all but unstoppable.

"I know, but thanks. 'Plans,' you asked? Nothing much. How about you?"

"Just a walk in the park, I think. I'm too old for the rest."

"Right. Tell it to your wife." Jones glanced back outside. "What's the altitude?"

"Let's see, right at thirty-seven thousand . . . Jesus, we're at forty-two thousand feet." McIntyre scanned the dials again as if searching for an error. The airplane had climbed so gently neither of the men had noticed. "Do you see anything on the PFD?"

"No. Looks good. We're on auto, right?" They'd been on autopilot since London. This wasn't supposed to happen. The plane had just come out of a complete servicing. All of the computer software had been reinstalled, with the latest updates. Everything should have been functioning perfectly. Instead, they were on an all but undetectable gentle incline.

"Right," McIntyre said. "I'm resetting auto. . . . Now." Nothing changed. After a moment he said, "Altitude is 42,400 and climbing. What do you think, Sean?"

Jones pursed his lips. "I think we've got a glitch. Shall we go manual?"

Pilots were under enormous pressure from the company never to go manual except at takeoff and on approach for landing. The computer not only flew the airplane in between but did a far superior job, increasing fuel efficiency by as much as 5 percent, a great money saver. If the pilots went manual, the flight data recorder, which kept a record of everything from preflight to postflight, would record it, and they'd have to file a report justifying their action.

"Airspeed's dropping," Jones said evenly. The autopilot was not only failing to keep the airplane at the proper altitude, but it hadn't increased power to the engines to compensate for the steady climb.

"Altitude is 42,900 and climbing," McIntyre said.

The door opened behind them and the senior flight attendant, Nancy Westmore, entered. "Are we climbing, boys? It feels odd back there."

The pilots ignored her. "Airspeed is 378 and dropping," meaning 378 kilometers per hour, well below the standard cruising speed of 945. "Altitude is 43,300 and climbing," Jones said.

"Have a seat, luv," McIntyre said. "And strap in. We're going manual." Westmore, a pretty blonde, blanched, then dropped into the jump seat and buckled up. The two had carried on an affair for the last three years.

"Bobby," Jones said, "PFD says we are approaching overspeed limit." The computer was reporting they had exceeded their normal flight speed and were approaching a critical limit.

McIntyre looked at the controls in amazement. "That's impossible! Airspeed is 197 and falling." The yoke-shaker program engaged and the stick began to rattle in front of him. In traditional airplanes, the yoke shook at stall. In the 787, the computer simulated the effect for the pilots.

At that moment the stall warning came on. "We're nearly at stall! It can't be both. Going manual . . . now."

A soothing woman's voice spoke. "Warning. You are about to stall. Warning. You are about to stall. Warning . . ."

But when the autopilot disengaged, nothing happened.

"Are you nosing down?" Jones asked, looking over, seeing for himself that McIntyre had pushed the yoke forward.

"No response," McIntyre said. "Nothing. Jesus!"

"Airspeed 156, stall. Altitude 43,750, still climbing. Holy shit!"

Then the mighty 787, cruising at over forty-three thousand feet, stalled. All 427,000 pounds of the airplane ceased to fly as the plane nosed up a final moment, then simply fell toward the blue ocean eight miles below. All three experienced a sensation of near weightlessness as the plane plunged toward the earth. Westmore closed her eyes and locked her mouth shut, vowing not to make a sound.

Behind them came a roar of passengers screaming.

As it stalled, the airplane lost its flight characteristics, which depended on forward motion through the air for control. The plane fell as an object, not as an aircraft. Without comment McIntyre pulled the yoke well back, fighting to maintain some control and keep the craft upright. Without air control, the plane could easily roll onto its back. If it did, they were lost.

Under his breath Jones said, "Hail Mary, full of grace, the Lord is with thee . . ." He scanned the PFD. "Airspeed 280, altitude twenty-nine thousand."

"Jesus," McIntyre said. "I've got nothing." The yoke was not giving him any feel. The plane was moving through space absent any control. "Engaging auto!"

Through the closed door came more screams. Neither pilot heard them.

Jones reached over and engaged the autopilot. Both men were trained that in an emergency, the autopilot had a superior solution to any they could come up with. They'd been shown example after example of pilots wrestling with airplanes until they crashed, doing the wrong thing over and over, when the autopilot would effortlessly have saved the craft.

"Patience. Give it time," McIntyre said as if to himself.

Another long moment passed. Nothing happened. The airplane wobbled to the right, corrected itself as it was designed to do, then wobbled to the left.

"Airspeed 495, increasing; altitude twenty-seven thousand, falling," Jones said. He resumed the Hail Mary.

"Mother of God," McIntyre muttered, "hear me. Disengaging auto. Setting throttle to idle!"

The airplane was now in a significant dive, and the crew could feel the buildup of airspeed as it rushed toward the sea. The sound from the passengers was now a steady desperate drone. The plane was well nosed forward. The horizon, which should have lay directly in front of them, was instead high above.

"Airspeed 770, altitude twenty-two thousand!" Jones's voice had risen an octave.

"Shit!" McIntyre said. "God damn you!" he shouted, cursing the airplane. "Reboot," he commanded. "Reboot the fucking computer! Hurry up."

Jones tore his eyes from the PFD. "Rebooting." They were under strict orders never to reboot in flight. This was a ground-service procedure. Jones fumbled for the switch. "Got it! Not responding, Bobby. It's not responding! It's locked!"

"Kill the power." McIntyre's face shone from sweat. "Hurry. We haven't much longer!"

Jones looked to his right, ran his hand and fingers down the display, found the master switch, and flipped it off. The PFD went black.

"Wait!" McIntyre snapped. "Give it a second. Okay. Now!"

Jones flipped the switch. "On!" There was a pause. The dials before them sprang to life.

From behind them came a steady roar of terror punctuated by loud noises, as luggage from the overhead compartments and laptops flew about, striking anything in their own flight path.

"Engaging auto!" McIntyre said. Nothing.

"It's still rebooting," Jones said. They couldn't know for certain either their airspeed or altitude, making reliable decisions impossible. "I estimate fifteen thousand with airspeed in excess of 836." They were nearly at standard cruising airspeed. "We're falling fast."

The nose was now well down as the 787 plummeted toward the earth. The air slipping across the exterior controls of the airplane had restored flight control, but the yoke still denied it to the pilots.

The sensation of falling was palpable. Behind the men now came a high-pitched howl neither could place. It was neither mechanical nor human. McIntyre glanced back, expecting the worst, and realized it was Westmore. He hadn't thought it possible for a human voice to make such a sound. "Quiet, luv," he said, trying to calm the terrified woman. "Please!" He turned to the front. "Disengaging auto!" In front of him, filling the entire windshield, was the blue expanse of ocean.

"It's rebooted now!" Jones shouted.

Without warning, the plane suddenly responded to the yoke.

"Oh, shit," Jones said, as the captain began to try to raise the nose of the plane. The dials were giving information now. "Airspeed 915, altitude eight thousand! Easy, Bobby, easy. Don't overdo it." If they managed to pull the aircraft out of the dive, the danger was that it would rocket uncontrollably into the sky, a situation nearly as deadly as the dive itself.

McIntyre pulled on the yoke steadily. His face was masked in sweat. His breath came out in short, labored puffs. The plane was pulling up in response to his command, but the horizon was still much too high, the space before them nothing but ocean.

"Airspeed 1034, altitude four thousand! Oh, God!"

McIntyre pulled back more forcibly on the yoke. They felt the g-forces as he compelled the airplane out of the dive.

"Airspeed 1107, altitude three thousand!"

"Come on, you bastard, come on." McIntyre pulled the yoke well back, all but certain one of the wings was going to come off.

"Oh shit, oh shit, oh shit!" Jones said. The g-forces pressed them heavily into their seats.

"Get up, get up, motherfucker." Behind the men, Westmore screamed again.

"Airspeed 1122! Altitude twenty-three hundred!" Jones said in a high-pitched voice, almost in falsetto.

"Climb, you bastard, climb!"

Suddenly the g-forces vanished as if an invisible hand had been lifted from them.

"We're climbing!" Jones said with a laugh. "We're climbing! Airspeed 1103, altitude twenty-six hundred!"

Flight 188 rocketed into the sky like a ballistic missile.

OOOOOOOOOOOOO **2**

Coffee? A Danish?" she asked with an inviting smile.

"No, thank you. I'm fine," Jeff Aiken said, considering closing his eyes until summoned for the meeting.

"Mr. Greene will with be with you any moment."

Jeff, still in a fog from his hasty trip, didn't take the time to admire what he sensed was an inviting view. The receptionist was not yet thirty, stylishly dressed, trim, obviously fit, but wearing the latest hairstyle, which made her look as if she'd just crawled out of bed and sprayed it in place.

Jeff had received the urgent call Saturday night—Sunday morning, actually—right after falling into a deep sleep, still dressed, splayed atop his bed at the Holiday Inn in Omaha, Nebraska. He'd just finished an exhausting all-night-all-day stint at National Interbank Charge Card Services. Their security system had been so porous that financial crackers, as criminally minded hackers were known, had systematically downloaded the personal accounts of more than 4 million "valued" customers. News accounts reported that the data looting had gone on for two weeks before being discovered. Jeff had tracked the information loss back more than three months and guessed it had been going on even longer.

Once he'd agreed to fly to Manhattan and negotiated a substantial fee for his time, it had taken all day Sunday to finish the security checks he'd installed on the new NICCS system. He doubted it would save the company from the ire of its violated cardholders, or federal regulators. If the company had spent a thousandth of his fee on routine security earlier, none of this would have happened. He never ceased to be amazed at the mind-set of supposedly modern executives. They still conducted business as if this were the twentieth century.

He'd arrived at the Omaha airport just in time to catch a red-eye to New York City. This would be his first trip there since the death of his fiancée, Cynthia, at the World Trade Center on 9/11, and he was almost overwhelmed by a range of unwelcome emotions. For an instant it was as if he were reliving the horror all over again. By the time he'd taken a taxi downtown, checked in and showered, he'd pushed his terrible memories aside and caught exactly ninety minutes sleep before shaving and dressing to arrive for this 9:00 a.m. meeting with Joshua Greene, managing partner of Fischerman, Platt & Cohen.

"Mr. Aiken?"

Jeff opened his eyes and realized he'd fallen asleep. He glanced at his watch: 9:23. "Yes?"

"Mr. Greene and Ms. Tabor will see you now. Are you sure you don't want some coffee?"

"Thank you. You were right. I'll take a coffee after all. Black." He smiled sheepishly. "Better make it a large."

The receptionist laughed, flashing brilliant white teeth. She showed him through the double door into the managing partner's office. "I'll get that coffee right now," she said.

The reception area had been designed in a 1920s art deco style that Jeff believed was inspired by the original interior design, given the age of the building and the exterior motif. The impression was reinforced as he entered the conference room. Dressed in brown penny loafers and wrinkled tan chinos, a dark blue travel blazer with a matching light blue polo shirt, he was accustomed to looking out of place in most corporate offices. After all, he reasoned, they hired him for what he knew and could do, not for his wardrobe. With short sandy brown hair and dark eyes, he was six feet tall and thirty-six years of age and had mostly kept his athletic build despite his work. Even catalog clothing fit him well, a girlfriend had once commented.

The pair sat at an expanse of glassy mahogany. The lawyer, Greene, was well dressed, to put it mildly, reminding Jeff of Gene Hackman in *The Firm*. That had been the mob's law firm, and Hackman had been the bad guy. The other was their IT person; she was almost, but not quite, a fellow traveler with Jeff, though her clothes had a Gap and Banana Republic look.

The well-suited man stood and introduced himself as Joshua Greene. "This is Sue Tabor, our IT manager. I thought it would save time if she sat in."

"We spoke late Saturday," Sue said as she rose to shake hands.

"Yes, I recall. Barely."

They waited as the receptionist returned with a large black coffee and a Danish Jeff had not requested. Greene waved her off before she could ask if anyone else wanted anything.

Sue was slender, of partial Asian heritage, late twenties, with jet-black hair stylishly cut in a bob. Her slender lips were a crimson slash, and she wore more makeup than he was used to seeing in offices. Beneath her shirt he detected modest breasts, but her figure struck him as all angles. Her grip was firm, but there was no denying a certain shine in her eye as she met his gaze.

Greene was perhaps sixty years old and had the look of a man who spent his share of time in the gym. Broad-shouldered, he had graying hair and wore glasses with scarcely any rim, the lenses reflecting as if made of crystal. If someone told that Jeff Greene had once played football, it would have come as no surprise. While Sue was clearly West Coast in her accent, Greene came from somewhere in the Midwest. Jeff had heard a lot of that Johnny Carson talk in Omaha.

"I don't want to waste your time, Aiken," the lawyer said, "but I'd like to give you a brief summary before I hand you over to Sue. Saturday morning one of our associates came in earlier than usual and found himself the first in the office. When he attempted to use his computer, he could not. He checked with other computers and discovered that *none* of them were working. Sue was summoned and . . . I'll let her handle that part."

Greene cleared his throat. "I just want you to understand how critical this is. We billed more than ninety million dollars last year. We're not a large firm, obviously, but we are highly respected in our field. According to Sue, we cannot access our computer system. This includes our litigation records, both current as well as archived, e-mail, and our billing records. She also suspects that everything may be lost, or lost in part. She tells me that until we identify the source of the problem, we cannot even access our backup records to determine if they've been contaminated."

Greene gave Jeff a withering look that suggested he was at fault for the situation. "In short, we are dead in the water. Our cash flow has been stopped; our attorneys are unable to adequately work on existing cases. Once clients start figuring this out, those in a position to will defect, the others will sue. We need everything back, as soon as possible. The situation is critical."

Sue spoke, eyeing Jeff steadily. "The server is unbootable. I couldn't access the system at all."

That was odd, Jeff thought. In most cases, an infected computer would still boot, even if it didn't properly operate thereafter. "What are you able to do as an office?" Jeff asked.

"The attorneys are working on e-mail through our Internet provider's backup system," she said. "Many had current files in their laptops and are using those. I've not touched our backups since I have no idea what I'm dealing with here."

"How do you handle those?" Jeff asked.

"We have nightly backups of each computer to an in-house master server. Once a week, we make backup tapes that are stored in a fireproof safe. Once a *month*, we make a second set of backup tapes, and those are stored in another safe, off-site."

"Good. We'll have something to work with. How much can you tell me about what happened?"

"Sorry to say, almost nothing. The system simply isn't accessible. Not to me, at least." Sue grimaced.

Greene spoke. "Working without computers is a real problem for us. The younger attorneys simply don't know how to do without them; they've always had access to the various legal databases and resources. I had no idea we'd become so dependent on them." He glanced at Sue, then back to Jeff. "And obviously, being denied access to our work product is a serious problem—one that will prove very costly if you fail to fix this in a timely manner. Serious enough to put us out of business, in fact.

"But my most immediate concern is the prospect of losing our recent billing records. The longer we are down, the worse this is going to get. The system was automated. Now our attorneys are using pen and paper. We need to have our automated program up and running, and we need those billing records. They are vital. As is the case with any company, our income stream is essential."

Jeff took a long pull of coffee. It was hot and bitter. "Have you considered that your staff may have the virus in their laptops, since they were connecting to their office computers?"

Sue nodded. "I thought of that. Over the weekend I warned them not to boot, but I was too late. Some had already turned on their computers, but they had no problems. I've been running virus scans and system checks on their computers and found nothing other than the usual. Fortunately, so far whatever struck us is limited to our main system. Or seems to be." She smiled wanly.

"Do you have any idea what it is?" Jeff asked.

"None, but that's not really my area. Our firewall is excellent and up-to-date. We run antivirus software and keep it current. When I say 'up-to-date,' I mean daily. I have an assistant whose first job every morning is updating everything, seeing to the patches and running system security scans. He does that before he does anything else, and he comes to work ahead of most of the associates. So you can appreciate that I'm mystified how this could happen, because it should not have."

"That sounds good. And you're right: your measures should have been enough." Faced with the fresh challenge, Jeff felt himself growing suddenly alert and energized. This was very different from the work he'd just been doing, and any solution was going to be demanding, exactly the kind of problem in which he could lose himself.

Greene interrupted Jeff's thoughts. "I've got a meeting with the other partners and need to give them something. How long, Aiken? How long will this take, and how much of our information can we get back?"

"I can't say, in all honesty. Not at this point. I'll let you know as soon as I can make an assessment."

"All right," Greene said grimly. "I'm told you're the best. I need you to prove it."

O O O O O O O O O O O O 3

Buddy Morgan, balding, fifty-three years old, overweight, returned from his coffee break four minutes early. A twenty-three-year veteran of the United Auto Workers, he had the right to select his own shift; that's why he was working now. The supervisor, a longtime drinking companion, didn't give him any grief while the new robots did what they were programmed to do.

Not like the old days, not at all. Buddy had served his time on an air gun, the last eight years of it driving three nuts home to partially mount the right front wheel of the Ford Taurus. God, how he'd hated those never-ending days.

But that was behind him. Now he had seniority. As he told his wife, June, he was nothing more than a grease monkey. The robots did all the work. His job was to make sure they stayed online.

It was a helluva system, he had to admit. His domain was fourteen of the robots, "turkeys" as he called them. Each consisted of a massive arm mounted on a squat pedestal. At the working end of the arm was the "head," complete with a "beak." This was the part that did the welding, fast, accurate, untiring. The whole "gaggle"—he was unaware that the proper word was *rafter*—was run by the master computer. He monitored a dummy terminal at his workstation, but had no control of the system. That was work for the college boys.

Buddy spent most of his shift at his station, glancing at the monitor, then up at the slow-moving assembly line, then at his turkeys, nodding and twisting in their odd dance. The area around the workstation was filled with the smell of electronic welding and a not unpleasant sweet aroma of fine oil that came from the robots. His nearest coworker was a hundred feet away, and that was just fine with Buddy. Most UAW brothers were a pain in the ass.

Buddy's job was simple enough. He walked behind the turkeys and checked the moving parts for signs of a problem. This rarely happened. Japanese-designed, the things were built in Korea and could really take it, he often said. On a regular schedule, he pulled one off-line for examination. Not pulled, exactly; he pressed a large blue plastic button that caused the robot to retreat from the assembly line five feet. There he lubricated certain points, in all just six; then he wiped the entire machine down, though that really wasn't his job, but he liked his turkeys looking good; then he pressed the blue button again, and the docile thing slid back in place.

The amazing part was that the other turkeys knew one of them was missing—something to do with the programming—and they simply assumed the job of the one he took off-line. Amazing. Really amazing. If you didn't get laid off, this automation thing was a wonder.

At first he'd been surprised such high-tech turkeys required manual oiling at all. He'd figured they'd designed that into them. His trainers explained that they had originally been self-oiling, but factory managers, in an excess of cost-mindedness, had put the robots on the floor without adequate supervision. There had been some real problems. They might be twenty-first-century marvels, but a certain number of turkeys required the presence of a human. The solution had been to design them so they had to be serviced regularly.

But for the most part, his fourteen turkeys worked untended and to perfection. They were completely silent, as far as he could tell. The only sound came when they zapped the frame of the SUV moving along its two rails, like a subway car crawling along.

Today, however, Number Eight was giving him fits. He'd pulled it off-line three times already, and his boss, Eddie, told him to quit messing with it. Take it off-line for good and let the techs fix it. The other turkeys could take up the slack for a few hours.

That struck Buddy as pretty sloppy. He would never have told anyone, not even June, but he loved sitting at his station, that monitor frozen in place telling him everything was as it should be, the turkeys, nodding and straightening, twisting this way and that, as they welded the frame of Ford's new SUV, the first of the really big hybrids. He just loved it.

But Eddie had a point. Sometimes even a turkey acted up. They could work forever, but not without some maintenance. Buddy reached Number Eight and lowered his hand to press the button. Unseen behind him, the dummy monitor at his workstation flickered. The screen reset.

Along the line, the turkeys stopped in place. Then, like soldiers in close-order drill, they pulled themselves back as if standing to attention. Buddy stopped what he was doing and gawked. He'd never seen anything like this. The assembly line was still moving, but the turkeys weren't zapping the frames. He stepped forward to take a better look.

At that moment, all fourteen turkeys spun in place in a violent, dizzying circle. Number Eight struck Buddy with its beak, sending him flying onto the assembly line, landing with a loud grunt, sprawling across the tracks.

Stunned, he couldn't move for several vital seconds. Just as he grasped where he was, the frame of a new Monument SUV moved across his neck.

OOOOOOOOOOOO 4

After Greene left the conference room, Sue Tabor led Jeff to the IT room, moving with a catlike grace. "Don't let his manner bother you," she said. "Josh is a good guy—for a lawyer, I mean—but his neck's on the line over this. If we don't recover enough data to save his hide, he'll be forced into retirement and I may be out of a job."

"I doubt that it was your fault," Jeff reassured her. "I'm seeing more and more of this sort of thing. Malware is more easily finding ways into once secure computer systems. Viruses of all kinds are simply getting more sophisticated."

Sue sighed. "I warned him last year not to go all electronic. He didn't listen. We had a small accounting department then, run by a blue-haired lady who was the firm's first hire forty years ago. Though everything was on computers, she insisted on running billing-record hard copies every night. Greene thought the size of her department was a needless expense, and so was all that paper. She was retired, her department was reduced to two, and no more hard copies. I warned him."

"There's nothing worse than being right when your boss is wrong."

Sue looked at Jeff sideways, with a sly smile, and that shine in her eyes. "Sounds like you've been there."

Jeff closed his eyes for a moment and drew a deep breath before turning back to Sue. "It shows, huh? What did you see when you tried to boot? Exactly."

"Like I told you Saturday night, I couldn't get into the system and decided immediately not to waste any more time trying. I'm really just a systems manager." Sue shrugged apologetically. "My primary job is to keep everything running smoothly and make certain there are no hiccups. Security is part of it, of course, but it's limited to updated antivirus software, patching, and a firewall. Our primary problems have been viruses associates bring in from home on their laptops, or employees opening attachments from spam. Nothing I couldn't handle until now. To my knowledge, nothing ever made it into the servers."

"Have you contacted the firm's bank?" She shook her head. "You need to," Jeff advised. "You should shut down Internet access to your account until this is solved. It's possible that's what this was all about. We can't know how much information they extracted before the system froze."

"I'm on it," she said, her cell phone already out. Near the ladies' room he watched her speak intensely; then put the phone away and go through the door. As he waited, Jeff geared himself up for what he had to do. A few minutes later Sue returned, makeup freshly applied, her lips repainted that bright crimson. "Thanks," she said. "I should have thought of that on my own. They're taking care of it right now."

"There's more." Jeff was never comfortable with this aspect of his job. He hated being the bearer of bad news. "I'm sorry to say that you're going to have to unplug all the servers and every computer from the network. We have to assume they're infected, even though you've detected nothing—which would mean that at this point they're serving as a breeding ground, propagating the worm. That means your lawyers will lose their e-mail."

Sue moaned. "Let me show you to your workstation, then I'll take care of it."

The IT Center was located in an undesirable area of the building. Windowless, with monitors, computers, and cables running helter-skelter, a dry static sensation in the still air, it was a copy of hundreds of other such offices Jeff had seen. Sue introduced him to her assistant, Harold, a short, nerdy young man wearing a Yankees baseball cap with the brim backward. He was playing a video game on what looked like a personal laptop. As they entered, he hurriedly put it away.

"What are you playing?" Jeff asked. His secret vice was action video games.

"Uh, *Mega Destructor III.*"

Jeff nodded approvingly. "I've got *MD IV* in beta. I'll burn you a copy."

The young man grinned.

Sue shook her head. "Boys."

Jeff grinned. "What can I say?"

Standing with one hand on her hip, Sue explained the system, gesturing with her free hand. "Every lawyer has a desktop PC and a laptop. This is the server room with four blade servers. We use one as our Web server, another as a backup domain controller, and so on. The primary one, with our litigation records and accounting, is the one that's down. We run a standard networking program, Active Directory, and are connected to the office PCs." What she described appeared identical to other systems on which Jeff had worked. In theory that should make this job a bit easier than it initially sounded, he thought. But in reality? Jeff was too experienced ever to expect a free ride.

"All right. I'll get started," he said, looking for a place to set up. "Which one should I use?" Sue pointed as he reached down and opened his work bag, extracting a black CD case filled with a wide range of disks, which he referred to as his Swiss army knife. As he began, Sue left to inform everyone they were now off-line for the duration, at least at the office. Harold moved a chair over so he could watch what Jeff was doing.

"It's good to get some action," Harold said with a smile. "I'm pretty bored playing games."

"Glad to have you. I'm going to need your help if we're to get this fixed." Jeff's CD included the standard diagnostic and recovery tools used by everyone in his profession, but he'd added a collection of utilities he'd picked up over time. This was the disk that would allow him to boot and provide a minimal environment from which he could work, since the computer was no longer making one available.

As he slid the disk into the server's optical drive, his first thought was that whatever had occurred here was caused by any one of the thousands of new variants of existing viruses that appeared routinely, as many as fifty a month. He hoped that it was a new version of an existing virus, set loose by some student hacker looking for bragging rights. Something like that could have crept under Sue's radar. Even in that eventuality it could still be a difficult job, but one he could manage. There'd likely be full, or nearly full, recovery because the data the company needed would still be somewhere in the server.

But once his own operating system was running, the first thing Jeff noted was that he couldn't detect *any* data on the hard disk. It was as if the disk had never had an operating system installed. Even the standard C: drive icon was missing. He'd never seen this before and he experienced a sudden chill. *How can this be?* he thought. This wasn't going to be routine after all, he realized, feeling both exhilarated and apprehensive.

Sitting down at her computer beside him, Sue frowned and said, "Call me Miss Unpopular. They act as if I put the damn virus in myself." She looked at his screen. "Getting anything?"

Jeff told her what he'd done and seen so far.

"I need me one of those nifty boot CDs you've got."

Jeff smiled, suddenly looking twelve years old. "You'll have to kill me to get it." The CD was the result of thousands of hours of hard work, and in many cases it was what made his success on a job possible. He'd once joked he planned to be buried with it. "What will you work on?" he asked her.

Sue pursed her lips. "I'm going to spin my wheels, probably— analyzing the firewall and proxy server logs, if that makes sense to you." Jeff nodded. That area had to be covered, and it would save time if she did it. "Maybe I'll stumble onto something useful. This is *not* my field at all."

"You might get lucky," Jeff encouraged her. As Sue set to work, he ran a salvaging tool that could make guesses and ignore what would otherwise look like errors. With this he had more success, since it was able to provide him a view of files and folders previously not visible.

Now able to scan through what was left of the disk's data, Jeff searched for the files that contained the core configuration of the system. What he found instead were bits and pieces of the original operating system and temporary copies of portions of program data. Though he was disappointed, he was still able to reconstruct a portion of the file system and registry with its database, which stored settings and various options for the computer's operating system. *At least it's a start*, he thought.

Next he skimmed through the corrupted registry entries. It was a bit like scanning the television guide to see what was on, rather than watching an evening of programs. He found that part of the data was overwritten, a standard means of destruction. Random symbols had been written over the existing data, making it difficult, sometimes impossible, to recover the original data. Peculiarly, though, only a portion of the original data had been overwritten. If that had been the purpose of the virus, Jeff thought, the job was incomplete.

Several explanations were possible. The most obvious was the presence of a destructive virus that had its overwriting operation aborted by a bug in the virus itself. The virus might have triggered behavior that resulted in the operating system's becoming corrupted, which had then stopped the virus and the overwriting dead in its tracks. Not very sophisticated, if that was what had happened.

A truly effective virus would never kill the driver or operating system that served as its host. That would be like a disease killing someone before it could infect anyone else. The most effective viruses were those that existed on computers with the operators never knowing any better. Before the operating system was destroyed, such a worm would be seeking to replicate and spread itself, though slowly, so as to escape detection. But in this case some part of it had nuked the system, in effect committing suicide.

Now Jeff scanned the corrupted registry file settings. Malware commonly created entries so that the operating system activated them each time the computer was turned on, or whenever a user logged in. He examined every entry that looked even remotely suspicious. When he located a reference to a program or piece of code he didn't recognize, he found the code's file and examined it further, looking to see if the file provided the product it was associated with and the company that wrote it, since malware typically lacked such information.

Then he performed Web searches to find information about the file's purpose, to see if anybody had previously flagged it as malware. Tedious and time-consuming, this formed the heart of what he did each day at work when on jobs like this. That initial flash of excitement he'd experienced waned as exhaustion began to overtake him again. Working while exhausted was typical, though. In these situations, time counted for everything. Yet so far, nothing.

Two hours later, Jeff finally got a break when he came upon a reference to a device driver that appeared suspicious. Device drivers were programs that allowed other programs to interact with a bit of hardware, such as a printer, and were attractive to malware authors because they could be leveraged to create spyware, viruses, and adware that hid from standard security protections. Most home PCs had some form of these types of malware without the owner even knowing it.

All device drivers had information that included the path to the file on the disk that contained the driver's code, so Jeff was able to locate the driver image in question without any trouble. One, ipsecnat.sys, had a name that looked similar to that of a legitimate and standard driver, but he didn't recognize it. When he examined it, the file's version information reported itself as being from Microsoft, but a Web search turned up no hits on a driver by that name. *Score one for my team*, he thought.

Reinvigorated, Jeff loaded the driver into a code analyzer that allowed him to see a human-readable version of the instructions that the computer executed. Analyzing malware at this level was a big part of his job, so he could run through the instructions in his head the same way the computer would. This way he was able to understand its overall purpose.

He read:

```
.text:00000000007B35D8 xor [rcx + 30h], rdx
.text:00000000007B35DC xor [rcx + 38h], rdx
.text:00000000007B35E0 xor [rcx + 40h], rdx
.text:00000000007B35E4 xor [rcx + 48h], rdx
.text:00000000007B35E8 xor [rcx], edx
.text:00000000007B35EA mov rax, rdx
.text:00000000007B35ED mov rdx, rcx
.text:00000000007B35F0 mov ecx, [rdx + 4Ch]
.text:00000000007B35F3 loc_7B35F3:
.text:00000000007B35F3 xor [rdx + rcx*8 + 48h], rax
.text:00000000007B35F8 ror rax, cl
.text:00000000007B35FB loop loc_7B35F3
.text:00000000007B35FD mov eax, [rdx + 190h]
```

```
.text:00000000007B3603 add rax, rdx
.text:00000000007B3606 jmp rax
```

When he finished, Jeff was thoroughly alert. The code was obviously encrypted. Viruses often encrypted themselves to make it time-consuming, or even impossible, for virus scanners to unravel the core code. The malware decrypted itself into memory when launched, which could take up to several seconds because of the levels and complexity of the encryption scheme employed. That was why a slowly booting computer was often a sign of infection.

The next three hours flew by as Jeff tried to match the encryption algorithm used by the hacker against those commonly employed by malware authors. Finally, he decided that he was looking at something new. This part of his work was like a puzzle to him, one in which he pitted his own creativity and determination against that of the hacker. In its own way it was not so different from the most difficult computer games he played except that real stakes were involved here. Knowing that kept Jeff's excitement tamped down, though he couldn't resist a mental pat on the back before continuing.

As a precaution, he set up what was essentially a "virtual" computer that allowed him to examine the virus in operation, but at a much slower pace. The virtual computer behaved exactly like a real one and, to the user, looked like the screen of a real computer displayed in a window on their desktop. But the virtual computer gave Jeff great control over the process since he was able to control execution of the malware, starting and stopping it as needed. In this way, he hoped to be able to unravel the code.

Next he dropped the code onto the disk as an unencrypted copy of the driver. Completely consumed, he lost all touch with day and night. Even Sue didn't exist as a person. She vanished from his world, though she sat next to him. He was neither thirsty nor hungry. He felt no discomfort in his body.

It often seemed to him, during a job like this, that he'd been born for this work, such was his capacity to shut out everything else. For him a computer problem was like solving a brain teaser, and he loved games. He also hated being defeated. The real world could be chaotic and violent and frequently felt, at least to him, to be out of his control. But with work he could understand a computer, even the viruses that at-tacked them. Success here was clearly defined: when he was finished, the computer either worked or it didn't.

Right now his only world was the one on the screens before him.

DEPARTMENT OF HOMELAND SECURITY, WASHINGTON, D.C.
DIVISION OF COUNTER CYBERTERRORISM
MONDAY, AUGUST 14
9:51 A.M.

I don't get the connection," George Carlton said as he leaned back in his chair, eyeing with cautious pleasure the woman seated before him.

Dr. Daryl Haugen, dressed casually in jeans and a snug blouse, paused before responding. Slender and just over average height, with a fair complexion and blond, shoulder-length hair, she was stunningly attractive. The way Carlton eyed her while pretending he was not was a reaction she'd grown accustomed to as a teenager. A computer science graduate of MIT and thirty-five years old that July, she'd worked hard to be taken for what she was, much more than a pretty bauble on a man's arm. Men such as Carlton, who acted as though they took her seriously when all they really were interested in was her butt, rubbed her the wrong way. But what she had to get across to him was too important for her to waste time getting angry over his juvenile chauvinism.

"We've come up with eight incidents so far," she said, leaning forward to emphasize her point. "The most deadly was at a hospital in New York City. The computer glitch there appears to have caused four deaths from misapplied medications. There are similar reports out of several hospitals in other boroughs."

"What about these other incidents?" Carlton leafed through the papers as if searching for something specific, then stopped in apparent frustration. "I've read your report. Frankly, I don't see a connection between any of them, and I certainly don't see a national security issue. As you know, during my tenure here we've made significant strides in combating computer viruses, especially when they target government or military computers."

Daryl sighed to herself. *Not that again*, she thought. "I can't be certain, but it looks like more than one virus. It's odd, striking like this in so many seemingly unrelated places, and being so deadly." She wrinkled her brow. "The viruses were also in systems that should have excluded them. We need to understand quickly why they didn't. We have no idea how many of them are out there, or how they spread. If they're commonly on the Internet—and this assumes we're dealing with more than one and not a single virus with different manifestations—they're going to cause a lot of trouble, not just in home and business computers but in government and military ones as well."

"Well, that's good," Carlton said.

"Excuse me?"

"I mean that they are going after computers in which my department has a direct concern," he said hastily. "Not that the viruses are good as such."

Daryl bit her tongue. She needed this fool's help.

"I'm saying that's the kind of thing we are so effective at interdicting," Carlton added, dragging his eyes away from her chest. He'd first met Daryl when she'd worked at the National Security Agency in 2000. She'd been assigned to liaison with his Cyberterrorism–Computer Forensics Department at the CIA. She'd been unexpectedly forthcoming, even providing some source data they'd lacked, which proved quite accurate. But the best part of the arrangement had been her drop-dead looks. He'd suggested drinks more than once, but got nowhere. Neither had anyone else in the department.

He'd been more than pleased when he learned that she'd left NSA and was now assistant deputy executive director CISU (Computer Infrastructure Security Unit)/DHS and head of a team at US-CERT (Computer Emergency Readiness Team), which technically reported to him at DHS, where he was now chief of counter cyberterrorism. US-CERT was expected to operate independently, alerting him only when they came upon an issue of national security. This was the first time she'd ever asked to work in the field. He doubted he even had the authority to refuse, but he was damned if he was going to acknowledge any limits to his power.

"Aren't the hospitals cooperating?" he asked, squaring his shoulders to look more forceful.

"Sure," Daryl confirmed. "But I don't know what they're holding back, thinking it's not important. The virus or viruses will have left tracks. I can't trust others to find them. That's not what they do. They just want to get their systems functioning. We need to educate ourselves quickly. The protections at one of these infected hospitals were much better than those of, say, nuclear power plants." She met his eye to see if she was making her point. "We need to know, George. We can't sit on this."

For a moment Carlton wondered what she knew, and if that was meant to be a veiled threat. "Well, of course you should go. Thanks for keeping me in the loop. Keep me posted."

He watched her retreating figure with more than a little regret and sighed. These computer types were always getting worked up over nothing. The few attractive women among them were the worst.

KELLOGG, IOWA
SKUNK RIVER NUCLEAR GENERATING STATION
MONDAY, AUGUST 14
11:43 A.M.

Barnett Favor scanned the computer screens with a practiced eye, then leaned back in his chair. He'd begun his shift at six that morning and had just finished lunch. On most days he "assumed the position," as he jokingly called it—closed his eyes and took a catnap. Either of the other two men on the shift, or the computers themselves, would alert him if he was needed. Favor crossed his hands comfortably on his stomach and closed his eyes.

The Skunk River Nuclear Generating Station was a General Electric boiling-water reactor, located on the Skunk River some forty miles east of Des Moines. It provided nearly half of the electricity of the city, while the rest of its output was distributed throughout the eastern rural stretch of the state and into western Illinois. One of the last nuclear power plants completed in the United States, it had undergone an extensive overhaul in 2005 and was now entirely modern.

In the years since the disaster at Three Mile Island, when multiple human errors had caused a partial core meltdown, enhanced reliance had been placed on computers to handle the complex decision-making necessary if something went wrong. As a result, Favor and his team had almost nothing to do with the plant operation.

Since the overhaul the station had run without incident, not that there had been many in the previous two decades of its operation. Favor had been with the company since high school and was just two years from retirement. He'd cut his teeth on an old coal-fired generating plant, discontinued when the Skunk River Nuclear Generating Plant had come on line. In the early days the operation of the two hadn't been all that different. Water was still heated and turned into steam, which ran turbines, which produced electricity. The only real difference was how that water was heated.

After several minutes Favor shifted in his seat, then accepted that he wasn't going to nod off. Instead, he decided to get himself a Coke. If he couldn't take a nap, he'd take in a bit of caffeine.

The control room of the plant looked like something out of *Star Trek*. A long, curved wall contained a wide range of gauges and dials. At waist level was a shelf the workers used for a desk. Immediately in front of them was a bank of computer screens that told the story. The men used three chairs on wheels to scoot across the floor and along the wall as they monitored the conditions of the plant. In reality, they had little to do.

Just as Favor stepped from the soft-drink machine, every computer screen in the room blinked, twice. "What was that?" he said.

Orin Whistle, who'd worked there nearly as long, looked up from the paperback he'd been reading, a blank expression on his face. "What happened?"

Josh Arnold stood up in place as if he might suddenly need to run. "Something's going on, Barney."

At that moment Favor could feel the change. The plant was tens of thousands of moving parts, each performing its specific function. The mix produced a familiar vibration and comforting background hum that changed only when one of the two reactors was taken off-line for maintenance. Otherwise, nothing ever changed.

"The turbines are speeding up," Whistle said as if to himself. "I'm resetting the control." He looked at the gauges, the amber lights playing across his face. "No change."

"Heat's up, Barney," Arnold said, touching the temperature gauge in front of him as if to confirm what his eyes told him. "I don't see why, though."

The twin nuclear piles were set to run at their standard temperature, allowing the water coursing through them to be superheated to produce the steam that created electricity. A second stream of water ran through the system like coolant from the radiator of an automobile, intended to maintain the core at exactly the right temperature. It was all self-monitoring and self-adjusting. Until this moment, Favor had considered it impossible for the reactor to increase in heat without his ordering the computer to make the change.

"Watch the pressure," Favor said. Pressure was key to being certain the nuclear core was always covered with water. The crew at Three Mile Island had notoriously failed to ensure that single necessity and, as a result, had brought disgrace on themselves and an end to new nuclear plants in the United States.

"Pressure's up," Whistle said, his face paling. "And it's rising fast."

The Klaxon sounded, repeating every three seconds. Atop the curved wall, red lights began to blink. The computer had taken them to Code Red.

"Shut it down!" Barney shouted. "Josh, call Central Iowa and inform them we're going off-line now!"

"Jesus, Barney, they'll raise hell. Half of Des Moines will go dark."

"Do it, Orin, shut it down now!"

Orin hesitated. "We've got a few minutes to figure this out, Barney. There'll be hell to pay if we act too fast."

"We aren't going to figure this out." Favor knew there was no point in delay. Trying to outthink a computer, even one making a mistake if that proved the case, was foolhardy. "The computers run things now. Tell them we're shutting the reactors down now!"

Orin typed commands on his keyboard and punched the ENTER button.

"Didn't you hear me?" Favor asked when nothing changed.

"Sure thing, Barney," said Orin, his eyes frantically scanning the gauges. "But there's no response."

Josh cupped his hand over the mouth of the telephone. "Central Iowa wants to know why they aren't getting the standard three-hour notice so they can pull juice from elsewhere."

"Tell them we'll call back," Favor said. "Orin, give it the command again. Josh, check the temperature. And turn off the damn Klaxon and lights!"

Favor had moved so he could monitor the key indicators, his soft drink unopened and unnoticed in his hand. The noise stopped and the red lights were extinguished. Several workers from other sections had filed into the room, but they stood well back, watching nervously.

"The temperature's spiking, Barney. I've never seen it this high," Josh said. "The turbines are screaming."

The men heard a high-pitched whistle. "What's that?" Orin said, his face now chalk white.

"Oh, shit," Favor muttered. "We're venting coolant. The water's turned to steam. Orin, shut the fucker off!"

"I've given it the command four times, Barney. Nothing's happening! Don't blame me."

Though a nuclear reactor is complicated, in one aspect it's quite simple. Left alone, uranium runs into an uncontrolled chain reaction. But it's not left alone. Control rods are inserted in a regular pattern through it. They absorb neutrons and have the power to turn the core cold. The plant is heated simply by raising the rods. All that is necessary to regulate heat, or shut the plant down, for that matter, is to lower the rods.

But the computers were refusing to do just that.

Favor flashed back to a key meeting held during the overhaul. The systems analyst who'd installed the computers and multiple backups had just explained to the company's operations director and his deputy that nothing could go wrong. "This system is utterly foolproof."

The deputy had learned forward and said, "Nothing's foolproof. We're dealing with a nuclear power plant. What if all your fancy systems go wrong?"

"That can't happen, sir. Not if you follow directions and update the software."

"Of course it can happen. Where's the fail-safe?"

"I don't understand." The systems analyst had looked genuinely perplexed.

"If it all goes to hell and we're facing a meltdown and don't want those boys to be stuck telling some computer what to do, how do we pull the plug ourselves?"

"I assure you—"

"There isn't one, in other words," the deputy said to his boss. "They want us to trust the computers to do it." He fixed his gaze on the analyst. "We need a mechanical switch to crash this plant, if it comes to that."

The director had agreed, and at a cost in excess of $1 million, a fail-safe had been installed. Both the director and his deputy had been forced out the following year for spending too much money on the overhaul, but the safety system had remained in place.

"Josh, Orin, come with me," Barney said now, before running to the far wall and two large red handles, much like those of a fire alarm. Above them was written MECHANICAL SHUTDOWN. USE ONLY IN AN EMERGENCY.

"Josh, yank that one." Barney grabbed the first and pulled. The handle refused to budge. Josh tried his, with the same result. "Orin, give me a hand," Barney shouted. The Klaxon and the pulsating red lights resumed. Some of the workers who'd been watching bolted from the room, making their way to exits.

"We're in overload, Barney," Orin shouted as he wrapped his hand around half of the lever while Favor took the other. "On three. One, two, three!" The men pulled. Slowly, the handle moved. It stopped some five inches out. Applying leverage to it, they forced the red handle fully down.

Favor turned to the other. Josh had managed to move the switch an inch from the wall. All three men grabbed a piece of it and pulled. Slowly the handle moved until it too was in the down position. The men stood silently, panting, waiting.

The fail-safe was a direct cable to the control rods. The levers severed the cable holding them aloft. In theory, the control rods would drop into the core by gravity, shutting down the reactors.

"Do you think it worked?" Orin asked in a near whisper.

"I hope to God it did, Orin. I sure hope it did."

Josh glanced nervously toward the door. "Maybe we should get out of here, just in case." Nodding their agreement, the others followed.

At the door, Favor turned back and looked at the elaborate control panel one more time. *How could this happen?* He wiped his bare hand across his face, which was drenched with sweat. A thought chilled him to the bone. *What if the thing isn't dead? What if it is just playing possum?*

Favor turned and walked away. Within a few feet, he was running.

BROOKLYN, NEW YORK
MERCY HOSPITAL
MONDAY, AUGUST 14
5:09 P.M.

At Brooklyn's Mercy Hospital, the fourth hospital Daryl Haugen had visited in the city since arriving early that afternoon, she presented her US-CERT credential to the IT manager. "How many now?" she asked once he'd closed the door to his office.

Willy Winfield was perhaps thirty-five years old, balding, with thick glasses. He understood the question at once. "Still four, so far. We've taken all the patients off the computers and are handling medication manually, as we used to."

"Have you figured out yet what happened?"

"Our medication software was scrambled." Winfield's tone was matter-of-fact, but Daryl could hear the heartache behind it. "Patients were given medicines and dosages unrelated to their needs. It's been a disaster and put us at considerable risk from lawsuits. My people are working on it, but we can use all the help we can get. Would you care to see?"

"Yes, I would. That's why I'm here." This was one reason why she'd insisted on getting into the field. Whatever this was, it had already shown itself to be deadly, and she needed to be on the ground to understand its true scope and impact.

They walked along hallways with confusing turns. Modern hospitals had been expanding so rapidly there was often little logic to their layout. Winfield steered right, then right again, then left three times. Some of the hallways turned off at less than right angles. Within a few turns, she was hopelessly lost.

At last he said, "Here." Winfield took her into ICU, where a young girl lay fighting for her life. She looked perhaps eight years old. The number of wires running from her body were distressing, as was the steady beep of the monitor. A nurse hovered beside the girl poised for immediate action. Daryl was anything but sentimental. As she gazed at the inert form of the helpless child, though, the objective software engineer threatened to give way to the woman who adored children and was devastated to see one in such condition. Pulling herself together, she asked, "What happened?"

"Her medication was mixed, like the others. Her heart stopped— for an undetermined period of time, since she wasn't on a monitor. There was no need . . ." The man was near tears.

Not far away a young couple watched the girl through a large window. Seeing where Daryl looked, Winfield said, "Her parents. Very nice people."

"What's going to happen?"

"We're waiting for her signs to improve before we take her off the ventilator." He touched Daryl's sleeve and gently led her away. "The doctor believes she suffered severe brain damage. She's young and strong. He's hoping she'll recover, but it's not looking good. I wanted you to see the human toll this has taken."

Daryl nodded. "I see it. I'd like to look at your system, if I could, and talk with your IT people." She forced herself to remain steady. She'd need a clear head to unravel this disaster.

"Of course." As they walked back through hallways toward the computer room, Winfield asked, "Why would anyone do something like this?"

"I have no idea."

OOOOOOOOOOOO 8

A cold drizzle streaked the cracked window. It was already fall in Moscow. It seemed to Vladimir Koskov as if summer had been the briefest illusion. He reached out and pressed the aging tape back against the pane, but it rolled away almost immediately. He could feel the cold air leaching through the glass onto his hand.

Vladimir sighed, then picked up the butt of his unfiltered Turkish cigarette and used it to light another. He inhaled deeply, then coughed as he jabbed out the old cigarette and laid the fresh one on the edge of the ashtray.

The small apartment was typical of those built during Soviet days. Of shoddy construction, rushed to completion to meet an arbitrary deadline, it was small, less than five hundred square feet, one room with a cramped kitchenette in one corner, and a bathroom with a shower. The tiny kitchen table, with room for just two, the bed, and his computers all but filled the remaining space. A path was kept clear to his workstation, with three keyboards for three computers he'd built himself and which he never turned off. He could roll his wheelchair to the refrigerator, and to the doorway of the bathroom to empty his bladder sack if Ivana was at work or shopping.

This was twenty-nine-year-old Vladimir's world. At one time the confinement, the limits of his physical existence, had nearly driven him insane. On the brink of life-ending despair he'd discovered a universe, one he could access without ever leaving this room. His portals were there on the desk and at his keyboards, on his screens, where he was the same as everyone else. It was liberating. Empowering. He had thought at one time to be an engineer, but his sudden awakening as a cripple had forced on him a fresh evaluation of life expectations. Instead, he'd taken his computer skills and morphed them into a kind of expertise that had saved him.

The new Russia was brimming with opportunity, but few ways to make any money if you were not a prostitute, mobster, or drug dealer. If it had not been for Ivana, none of this would have been possible. She'd worked one job after another, never complaining. Sometimes he found her endless self-sacrifice to be all but unbearable.

Vladimir tapped the keys and returned to the Web site he'd been browsing. He spent twenty minutes scrolling through the various forums, examining the code posted there. Little of it was fresh or unknown to him. On occasion he'd see something that caught his attention, code he thought he could use, something new and creative. But on examination it was usually rubbish, or pointless.

Code was the essence of any computer, and of the Internet, which was simply a connection of millions of computers. Code was the machination behind the curtain that made everything else work. Code turned keystrokes into words in word processing, code made images, code produced color, code created hyperlinks.

Everything on a computer screen came from code. Those who could write code at a sophisticated level were creators; a handful were, in their way, godlike, for what they wrote produced marvelous manifestations.

But there was code, and there was code. Like a child painting a tiger by the numbers, some hackers, as code writers were generally called, did little more than follow the lines created by others. These script kiddies copied and pasted this from here, added a little of that from there, and counted themselves lucky when it actually produced something that worked.

Code generated in such a way looked as childish to the skilled hacker as that child's colored picture of a tiger. Other bits were repeatedly written, to the point of being counterproductive. One section might create an action, another would stop it; then it would be created again, then stopped again, sometimes in long, pointless strings. An amazing amount of code could be written to produce almost nothing. Useless code lay everywhere, occupying a cyber universe with its clutter.

Then there were the hackers such as Vladimir. These were artists of the most rare and talented sort. Their code was lean and strong, producing results with the sparest of keystrokes. What they wrote was elegant, masterful.

The Russian had made his cyber reputation by discovering a vulnerability in Windows XP. He'd posted the details in various chat rooms to claim the credit. Several weeks later, Microsoft confirmed the vulnerability when it released a patch to repair it. Vladimir had responded by posting the details of a second vulnerability. This time it took Microsoft three months to release a patch.

In standard computer protocol, Vladimir had no business publishing the vulnerabilities. He should have given the information directly to the company. By taking the approach he had, he'd gained an initial reputation for himself, but he'd also exposed many thousands of Windows XP owners to virus attacks. By posting, he had been able to claim full credit. Had he notified Microsoft, then posted the details only *after* the security patch was released, he would have been mocked.

Vladimir's reputation had grown when he posted the first vulnerability in Windows Vista within hours of its being released. In fact, he'd discovered three vulnerabilities while examining the beta version—but by that time he was losing interest in what he considered the juvenile game of claiming credit for finding weaknesses in the software giant's programs. It was impossible to produce a complex program to serve so many millions of users and not leave *something* vulnerable. He'd claimed the one, but had quietly informed Microsoft of the other two.

Still, Vladimir's reputation had been made. He'd had no lasting desire to involve himself daily in the cyber-hacker world and had always been a private person, so with the posting of the first Windows Vista vulnerability, he'd withdrawn from regular active exposure in the hacker chat rooms and forums.

By this time Vladimir had realized he possessed an extraordinary aptitude. It took another two years to turn it into meaningful income. Now his services were much sought after, and he could pick and choose his assignments. He maintained an e-gold account—a digital gold currency created to allow the instant transfer of gold ownership between users—into which his fees were deposited outside Russia. There were over 3 million e-gold accounts and nearly 4 million ounces of gold in storage. But one of the unintended uses of the accounts was to, in essence, allow the laundering of payments.

For his immediate need, Vladimir decided no help was to be found on the Internet. He returned to the code he was writing and tried again. Still . . . something eluded him. He went back and rewrote a section, then nodded. He copied the sequence and dropped it into his test computer. It worked.

Vladimir smiled. Slick. This last was his best. Even he was impressed.

As was his habit when working, Jeff set his digital watch to chirp every two hours. When it went off, he would stand from his station, stretch, then take a walk around the offices to exercise his body and clear his head, though a part of him never let go of the problem he was grappling with. He'd drink a Coke or a cup of black coffee, use the restroom, wash his face, then return to his place.

Respectful of his dedication, Sue didn't break his concentration with idle chatter or questions about what she was seeing over his shoulder. She took her breaks at different times, always returning with the smell of cigarette smoke about her. He'd sniffed once before realizing it came from her. She'd said, "I know. A disgusting habit. I just *have* to quit."

At one point some hours into the process, Harold disappeared. It could have been the middle of the night or broad daylight. Jeff had no idea. But when Harold returned with food from the all-night diner, Jeff realized how hungry he was. He wolfed down a ham-and-cheese sandwich just as the new framework dropped the unencrypted copy of the code onto his disk. He chewed as he analyzed it.

So far, he had discovered mostly negatives. The single most troubling development had been an attempt by the virus to replicate itself. In this case, it had failed, but, he realized, in other environments it might well be succeeding. It didn't affect what he was doing today, though it could mean disaster for thousands of other businesses. But that was in the future. Right now he had to concentrate on what he was getting paid to do. As he finished the food and wiped his hands on a napkin, Jeff mentally groaned at what he saw. Even the decrypted code he'd labored so long to produce was obtuse. The cracker was using tricks that ran in the low-level environment. That meant that this approach was a dead end.

Jeff didn't realize that Sue had been gone until she reentered the room. She came up behind him and leaned down at a time when he had his screen filled with the string output. Her proximity reminded him for a moment that she was an attractive woman. But almost as quickly as the sensation came, it vanished. It had happened before when he'd been drawn to a woman. He knew the shutting down of his emotions was related to Cynthia's death, and the guilt he felt about not having done more to prevent it.

But nothing would ever change what had happened.

His BlackBerry rang, snapping him out of his gloom. "Excuse me," he muttered to Sue, as he answered.

Sue took the opportunity to examine Jeff much more closely as he listened to his caller. She'd been attracted from the start and, having watched him work, was now even more impressed. Now she could take him in as a man and liked what she saw. She wondered if he mixed business with pleasure. In her experience, most men did, given the chance.

"I'm in Manhattan too, on a system crash. I've never seen anything like it. I'm sorry to hear about the deaths." Jeff paused. "Sure, sure. That sounds good, Daryl. Maybe I'll know something by then." Slipping his BlackBerry back in his pocket, he looked up at Sue. "Sorry about that. A colleague. She's in town working on something similar."

"She's obviously dedicated. It's the middle of the night. Could it be the same virus?"

Jeff considered what Daryl had told him. "It's possible, except her virus didn't crash the system. Just caused it to malfunction in a deadly way."

"I guess we should be thankful no one's died even with all the problems we're having. This could be a lot worse. Any luck? You've been at this for some time, and I thought I worked long hours."

Jeff grinned. "It's why I get the big bucks. I may not solve the prob-lem, but they can't complain about the time I put in." Jeff's smile van-ished. "What I've found so far isn't making much sense."

"Any guesses?"

"Unfortunately, a few." Leaning back in his chair, Jeff folded his arms across his chest. "So far, whatever you contracted isn't a known variant of a virus. It doesn't look very sophisticated, since it killed itself, and in probability is a cut-and-paste job at its core. But it was plenty destructive. It wanted to replicate, which is bad news for other com-puters. It's also encrypted and deeply embedded, which is making my job very tough. From how some of the code is written, I can speculate that the author may be Russian. If true, that's not reassuring at all. The Russian Mafia is heavily involved in financial fraud through malware."

Jeff stopped and thought about the implications of what he'd just said. In recent years the Russian Mafia had hired the best software en-gineers in the former Soviet Union to create new viruses and unleashed them on the cyber world. They were making hundreds of millions a year, and the more they made, the more aggressive and creative they'd become.

"I'm surprised the virus has been so hard to find," Sue said, focusing his thoughts.

"They usually aren't," Jeff agreed. "Typically, I spend most of my time recovering information and rebuilding systems. But lately I've been see-ing more and more of this kind of thing. A cracker gets into your system to do damage, not to steal information. Not long ago a guy was caught who hired a cracker to shut down the Web sites of his major competitors. These were Internet businesses; as long as he got away with it, everyone's customers went to him."

"That's terrible!" Sue knew the Internet was used for scams, but she'd never before heard such a story. To her, the Internet should be benign, a resource to make life better, not a destructive force.

Jeff knew what Sue was feeling. He often felt the same way. "I hate to say it, but that's only one of hundreds of ways to profit from cyber-crime. In the good old days, hackers were geeks out to make a name for themselves. Now they can earn money, sometimes big money, with the same skills and malicious intentions. There are even Web sites where you can download malware. You graft on something you've cooked up yourself, and you're off and running. One guy got into a bank's system and had a tenth of a penny—that's all, just a tenth of a penny—taken from every transaction over one hundred dollars and wired into an off-shore account. The bank's computer was programmed to round pennies up, so it kept covering the shortage."

"What's a tenth of a penny?"

"I have no idea." Jeff shrugged. "I guess they break currency down as far as they can. He could have asked for a twentieth, or a hundredth."

"What happened?"

"Within four months he'd made over six hundred thousand dollars. Even then the bank's computer kept covering for him. I don't know how long it would have gone on if he hadn't made the mistake of not deleting all bank-employee accounts from his scam. See, these people knew the system, and a lot of them balanced their checkbooks to the penny. One of them spotted that the accounting system was skewing and checked the programming. He found the virus, and it didn't take long to find the crook." Jeff took a sip of coffee. That hadn't been his case, but he'd cracked one like it, and it had felt very, very good. In some ways the satisfaction he took from his work was more important than the pay.

"I'm surprised our security measures didn't stop this. They were supposed to," Sue said.

"All security systems are reactive in nature. That means the virus has a head start in infecting computers *before* it's identified and enters the log of the antivirus and firewall programs. There are very sophisticated crooks who have taken to hiring crackers to deliver viruses that steal financial information. Computer security has become much more difficult now that there's a great deal of money to be made. Russian crackers looted a French bank of more than one million dollars in 2006."

Sue shook her head in amazement.

"Since your firewall and antivirus software didn't spot whatever it is, it's something off the charts," Jeff said, rubbing his forehead, trying to ease his exhaustion away. "Something new, or something very sneaky—perhaps something targeted specifically at you. Any business makes enemies."

"I hadn't considered that." Sue shifted in her chair and pointed at Jeff's computer screen. "But you think this is Russian."

"I can't really put my finger on it. I've been able to read some of the code, and it's just got a Russian feel to it."

"Maybe somebody copied some Russian code."

"Could be, could be. But like I said, the Russians have lots of computer-savvy people, and they lease themselves out to criminal groups."

"You think something like that happened to us?"

"I can't say at this point. I see sophisticated along with sloppy work. The virus might have been after your data or bank records, but something went wrong because the code was carelessly written."

"So you think this is about our financial data?"

Jeff grinned. "I don't know. I'm just speculating here. It might also be an attack meant to create the destruction it's causing, or something gone awry. It's possible it steals information, sends it out, then destroys itself to cover its tracks. I just don't know enough yet."

Harold was long gone and no one was working in the outside offices. The building was quiet, almost as if it were asleep. "Let's get some more coffee," Sue said. In the break room she emptied the coffee machine, rinsed out the pot, filled it with bottled water, opened a container of coffee, and placed it into a new filter. She turned the machine on, then leaned back against the counter to wait. "So you still play video games," she said with an amused look.

Jeff smiled. "My secret vice. Actually, it's all related. At least that's what I tell myself. I prefer online first-person shooting scenarios. It's how I deal with stress and it's something I can do anywhere. I also like brainteasers."

"That's where your work comes in."

"Right. I hate to lose. I'll stick with a virus until I have it figured out, no matter how long it takes."

Sue arched an eyebrow. "That must get expensive for the client."

He shook his head. "No, there's a point beyond which it makes no sense to keep billing. After I've fixed the problem, though, I'll take the virus home and work on it there until I've got it." He met her eyes. "How long have you been here?"

Sue gave him her nonoffice smile. "Just over four years." Pouring them each a fresh cup of strong coffee, she motioned to Jeff to sit down at the well-used table. Placing his coffee in front of him, she seated herself, took a sip, and sighed with satisfaction before continuing, "I'm from northern California, went to UC Berkeley for computer science. I worked at Microsoft, then took a job in San Francisco before moving here. I've worked at Cohen ever since. Until Saturday, it was a good job. Greene's a pain sometimes, but as long as the system works, he leaves us alone, and Harold has no life away from work. Sadly, that makes two of us. And so you don't have to ask, my dad's white and my mom is third-generation San Francisco Chinese. Big scandal in the family. What about you?"

"I'm from Philly originally. I majored in math, enjoyed computer science, so went to the University of Michigan for my Ph.D."

Sue flashed that friendly smile again. "I have to say, Jeff, you certainly don't look like a computer geek."

He laughed. "Genetics, mostly, though I played rugby in college and football in high school."

"Then what?"

"I taught at Carnegie Mellon, but like almost everybody who isn't a suck-up, it became clear I wouldn't get tenure. I went to work for the Cyber Security Division at the CIA, in 1998."

Sue lit up. "A spook, huh?"

"Hardly," Jeff said, eager to discourage any romantic notions about his CIA work. "I worked in a crummy office just like yours, only buried in the basement at Langley. Technically I was head of a three-man team called the Cyberterrorism Unit, but my two assistants were always off doing standard IT work for the division."

"What'd they have you doing, or can't you say?"

"No, I can talk about my duties, within reason," Jeff said. "The only danger is I'd bore you to death."

"I'm listening."

"Trust me, it wasn't glamorous." He filled her in on his years at the Company, telling her he'd held no illusions when he was recruited for the position. "Government work is government work. But I figured it couldn't possibly be worse than academia. I was wrong."

Though the threat to the Internet was real enough, at that time it was considered to be largely abstract. The Company budget was allocated primarily to the traditional physical threats. When it came to computers and the Internet, the threat was generally perceived as the possible physical destruction of facilities.

As their primary mission, Jeff and his truncated team worked on recovering data from computers seized from suspects and known terrorists. But they were also responsible for tracking the use of the Internet for terrorist activities and for potential threats.

During the years of his employment, as the Internet grew and spread its tentacles into every aspect of American life and the world community, the potential for a cyber-terrorist attack rose exponentially. The safety of the Internet, and of those computers connected to it, was dependent solely on the security of each individual computer that formed part of the network.

Jeff had certainly seen the threat. He had reasoned that as more government agencies conducted both external and internal business through the Internet, as more banks came online, as nuclear power plants continued linking to one another, and as the U.S. military came to increasingly rely on the Internet and computers to conduct its operations, his unit would receive greater resources and command more attention. He'd been wrong.

The irony was that the Internet had originally been developed as a national security system. In the 1960s, the Department of Defense had been concerned about the vulnerability of its mainframe computers— back in the days when all computers were mainframes—and of its increasingly computer-linked communications system. Several well-placed ICBMs, or even one at a critical point, could potentially cripple America's ability to defend itself. The air force was especially concerned about maintaining real-time control over its nuclear missiles.

What then emerged was a government-funded system of interconnected computer redundancy. The idea was that even if several computer hubs at key installations were nuked, the system, the actual Internet, would reroute itself around them. In theory, like the multi-headed Hydra of Greek mythology, it would be impossible to defeat. It might be slow, it might electronically hiccup, but the system would function. Jeff wasn't so sure. The designers had only considered outside threats. They'd never contemplated the ultimate digital universe they'd created, or that the real threat to the Internet might well come from within.

Although the Internet had proven itself enormously popular with the worldwide community and had become increasingly vital to the lives of individuals and the welfare of Fortune 500 companies, interest in safeguarding it wasn't as high as it ought to be. Jeff was convinced that it would take a significant failure of the system or a coordinated cyber-attack to awaken everyone. Just as it had been impossible to put the United States on a proper war footing before Pearl Harbor, the same fate seemed to await the future of Internet security. No one liked being Cassandra, but he'd found himself playing that role, seen as an alarmist while his warnings were ignored.

Jeff dragged his thoughts back to the present. "'Though my primary concern was cyber-security, I knew the Internet could be used to organize and coordinate terrorist attacks," he told Sue, taking up where he'd left off. "I wore out my welcome arguing for resources. I finally decided that only a seriously mounted terrorist attack against us with significant damage against a target that mattered was going to shake the lethargy of the intelligence community."

"I guess we got that on 9/11, didn't we?" Jeff seemed to wince, and for a moment Sue feared she'd misspoken.

After a pause he said, "You'd think so, but I'm still not sure they got the point."

Sue freshened their coffee and pushed the container of skim milk closer to Jeff. "Go on," she encouraged.

Jeff prepared his coffee as he continued, "In those days I spent a lot of nights trolling hacker chat rooms looking for signs of a plot."

"Not much of a social life."

Jeff smiled. "No. Probably about as active as yours."

"I might surprise you." She pointed her raised cup toward him. "But finish the story. I'm waiting for the part about bosses not listening."

Jeff looked away. How much did he really want to say? He'd avoided the subject until now. But maybe it would be good to talk about it.

First he told her how for most of 2001, he and his team, when available, worked to retrieve information from the hard-drive disks sent to him. Seized from various terrorists or terrorist suspects by a wide range of agencies throughout the world, the disks, or copies of them, had ended up in the hands of the CIA. If British SAS captured an IRA suspect, the hard drive from his computer, or its clone, would at some point find its way to Jeff's desk. It was the same for the Mossad. Even the CIA's own meager foreign-agent force produced disks from time to time.

As is generally the case in intelligence, the individual bits of data he produced from these sources by themselves meant little. Once he plucked them from the disks, though, they were fed into a master program by his unit, where they might, or might not, assume their proper place in the database about the terrorist world. He never knew. In fact, he had no idea if anyone was routinely consulting the growing body of data his unit was compiling on the operations of various worldwide terror groups.

"So what happened?" Sue asked. Jeff saw how eager she was and wondered for a moment how she'd react to the whole story.

"I really can't go into it. Let's just say, my boss and I had a disagreement, and I left."

"There's a story there you'll have to trust me with sometime," she said mischievously. "Is that when you started your own company?"

"Yes," Jeff said, glad to change the subject. "Turns out all those contacts I made with the Company were good for something. It's been a bigger success than I ever expected. One job after another. So no complaints there." He sipped his coffee and turned to the problem at hand. "Let's get back to you. The bad news is that your records, financial as well as work product, are all but a total loss from what I can see. I keep holding out hope they'll turn up somewhere, but I don't think so."

"Is there anything you can do for us?" She looked hopeful and he hated having to disappoint her.

"I'm trying to identify the virus sufficiently so that we can be certain it's not in your nightly or weekly backup. With that information we can determine if they're clean." He held up a hand of caution at seeing her become crestfallen. "I haven't found a hint of when you picked this up, so I can't tell from the time frame which, if any, of your backups are clean. It could have been lurking in there a very long time."

Sue bit her lower lip. "I was afraid that might be the case." She thought a moment, then gave him a wan smile. "So the worst-case scenario is that our current computers are fried. Useless. Whether or not we can recover the data from the backups, I'll still have to install a brand-new system. It will kill me." She made a face at the very thought of it. "It's going to take weeks to physically put everything in place, then load and link the software, then at least a month to get all the bugs out. And we have to know how to find this virus before I can activate it with our old data so that someone doesn't inadvertently reintroduce it. I don't even want to think about that." She looked into his eyes. "Save me from it all, will you? I'll be very grateful." She drained her coffee, then yawned. "Have you noticed these marathon sessions are getting tougher and tougher, the older you get?"

"Give me a break, Sue. You're a kid compared to me."

Sue smiled. "It's been good talking, though. If I get canned, I might come looking for a job."

"It won't come to that, I'm sure," he said, though it wouldn't surprise him if she ended up being the scapegoat. It wouldn't be the first time he'd seen that happen.

"I might come looking anyway." With that, she gave him a warm smile and left for the IT Center, her short hair bouncing, lean hips swinging.

Back at the office a bit later, Jeff asked if she'd found anything useful.

"Almost nothing." She grimaced. "I examined the logs. As I'm sure you know, we're hit thousands of times a day by malware looking for a vulnerability. Some of it's generated by a living hacker, but most are by automated worms, trolling the Internet. It was a bit daunting, realizing how under assault we constantly are, but I didn't see any failure in our protection. This obviously got through, but I can't see when or how. Wish I could be more help."

"And Harold?"

"I've had him reimaging the lawyer workstations and laptop systems in the office with clean system installs of the operating system and necessary applications. He's also checking the e-mail archives and database for signs of tampering." She yawned, covering her mouth with the back of a hand. "Last, but not least, I've got him screening all the complaint calls we're getting from associates. They don't pay me enough to do that."

She hesitated as if considering something, then said, "I've been meaning to mention a string I came across in your printouts, but you were awfully busy. I don't think it's anything important, but look at this." Jeff leaned over and read:

Sh3 w!ll n3v3r l3t ur sp!r!tz d0wn
Sh3s a v#ry k!nk! g!r7

Jeff realized he'd missed the text in his earlier scan. Sometimes the clues to a cracker were in the ego parts, those sections of code about himself he couldn't resist inserting. "I never saw that. What is it?"

"Don't laugh, but I think it's leet-speak," she said, straightening up.

Leet-speak was hacker language. Malware authors often left their calling cards in their code, even if it was only for them and other hackers to see. Since this one was originally encrypted, it was obviously not meant for the eyes of security investigators.

"It's 'Super Freak,'" Sue said, dropping her arms.

"'Super Freak'? The song?"

"I think so." Sue wrinkled her brow. "How does it go? 'She's a very kinky girl, the kind you don't take home to mother.'" Sue's singing voice was surprising deep and guttural. Now that she had the words and the tune, she was really getting into the song, swinging her hips, raising her voice. "Yeah! I've still got it! Our hacker likes Rick James punk funk. He's not *all* bad."

"Aren't you a bit young to know Rick James? 'Super Freak' was . . . what? Sometime in the early '80s?"

"Rick James is classic."

Jeff looked back at the screen. "Okay, 'Super Freak.' But what does it mean? Is that the name of the virus? Or the cracker's handle? Someone who's a Rick James fan?"

"Super Freak" might be significant, then again it might not, Jeff thought. Some virus code changed hands so many times all kinds of leet-speak from script kiddies crept in. It might not be connected to the virus's author at all.

"It might be his cyber handle," Sue suggested. "You should be looking for it in any code you find. I'll see if I can turn anything up in hacker chat rooms later." She yawned again. "I'm beat." She gave him a winning smile. "I'm going to lie down for a bit. I haven't pulled an all-nighter since college." She turned and walked away toward the couch, stretching as she did.

"No problem," Jeff murmured. "I'll probably lie down a bit later myself. I've still got some juice, though, and will feel better if I can get something definite before taking a real break. Your boss will ask, I'm certain." He looked over at Sue; she was already asleep.

BROOKLYN, NEW YORK
MERCY HOSPITAL
TUESDAY, AUGUST 15
8:09 A.M.

Daryl Haugen was given full access to the IT center in the basement of Mercy Hospital, where she found the staff cooperative. They'd taken the deaths of patients personally. Winfield had dropped by several times, but she had nothing to give him. Working not far from a furnace at an unused station, it had taken nearly a day of work to unlock the code she detected in the server. Yet, so far, she'd turned up nothing useful.

She felt the adrenaline coursing through her despite the long hours. These crackers were so full of themselves, so certain they could fool everything, she went after them with a vengeance. She'd never been able to tolerate such self-satisfaction. She found it interesting that George Carlton, officially the man responsible for stopping this sort of thing, was no less egocentric. For some time she'd thought he was just pitching his department when he crowed about his accomplishments, but she'd come to realize he actually believed he was doing an effective job. *Contempt* scarcely described her true feelings toward him.

Something had scrambled the hospital medication program; she just couldn't identify it. Her staff in Virginia was on this, but thus far they'd come up with nothing useful. The more people of talent and skill she had engaged, the sooner they'd have a solution, so she'd been glad Jeff Aiken was available. He was bright, creative, and hardworking. From her experience she knew he had the knack of thinking outside the box.

Daryl had located suspect code from a corrupted registry file and was now running it through a string analyzer, a program that dumped any data values in the file that could be represented with a printable character. Many code values translated to printable characters so there was a lot of garbage, but she also saw strings the programmer had in the code that referenced registry settings and files. Programmers often left debugging code that included messages in place that would be revealed in the string output. It took Daryl a few minutes to go over the strings, which largely looked like this:

```
rX + %"/
Lep
}ccc
oaaaa_ep
LRI?9\
z_____/VK<-
XRG???
m988m
4TTTTTAWK-
999877766mv.,0A@UTTTU
hRU
8877666.,,,&&&1TU
YRIPPPF
m\.1,,,,,2TW
PPPP
FFEEEDD
```

As she scanned the text, Daryl spotted a few strings that vaguely resembled words, but weren't quite English. One grabbed her attention because it looked as if it contained *COM*, the domain of most Internet sites:

```
ABKCOM
```

But it was missing a separating dot between *ABK* and *COM* that would show up if the string were actually a universal resource locator, or

URL, such as ABK.COM. Had the programmer left out the period for some reason? Perhaps it was a mistake or an attempt to hide that it was a URL. Trying to find clues and vaguely feeling as if there was more to the snippet, she continued examining it, letting her mind take her where it would.

Intuition struck. Picking up her pen, she wrote the letters backward in her notebook:

МОСКВА

Of course! That was "Moscow," written in Cyrillic.

Moscow! Why would that be a string? She searched for other clues in the text around it but found nothing. And why would a Russian hacker want to change the medication program in an American hospital?

She shot out of her chair and began to pace. It made no sense.

Of course the hacker could have copied code originally written by a Russian. But if it was Russian, the purpose of the virus should have been financial, since that's what most Russian malware was about.

Unless this was something else.

Daryl had been a child prodigy, smart as a whip from the first. Her parents, both professors at Stanford University, had encouraged her wide-ranging interests from the time she was a toddler. As their only child, she'd received undivided love and attention. So easily had things come to her, the child Daryl had been surprised to realize how slow her classmates were, even in the accelerated classes she attended. As she moved into her preteens, she finally found her place at a prestigious academy.

Under the tutelage of a teacher from Spain, she'd discovered a natural affinity for language. Before she was twelve years old, she spoke Spanish, Portuguese, and Italian fluently. The transition into Latin and French in her teens was seamless. For a time her parents were convinced she would become a linguist, and they accepted that as her natural vocation.

But Daryl also enjoyed mathematics and computers. As each drew her increasing interest, she found herself more and more in the world of boys. When she began to blossom at age fifteen, even the geeks with whom she spent most of her days noticed, though they were too awkward and shy to do anything, a situation she thought was just as well.

The last thing she wanted was a collection of panting admirers getting in the way of her real loves, numbers and the computer.

Daryl had gone to MIT at seventeen, then done her Ph.D. work at Stanford, while living with her parents. That had been nice, seeing them as adults, as equals. She'd come to appreciate the remarkable upbringing they'd given her. As she neared completion of her graduate work, Daryl had considered what to do. She'd always wanted to get the bad guys and briefly considered applying to the FBI. In the end she went with the National Security Agency, which had a greater use for her particular skills. The NSA intercepted foreign communications to develop intelligence information and relied extensively on computers to make it all happen.

Daryl had always been most comfortable working alone, though consulting with Jeff Aiken had come naturally. In recent years she'd stayed in routine business contact with him, especially when working on a new virus.

They had met at Langley, in the old CIA, the Company, before the 9/11 fiasco and the creation of Homeland Security, back in the days when the CIA thought it knew everything. She'd been sent from NSA as part of a show committee of cooperation. In fact, none of the American intelligence agencies cooperated significantly with one another, not the FBI, DIA, NSA, or CIA. But they were routinely admonished to cooperate, so committees such as hers were created, and meetings such as the one where she'd met Jeff were held from time to time.

"See if you can find anyone there," her boss had instructed, meaning, see if she could connect with someone useful, willing to share information despite the unofficial policy against such cooperation. Jeff had been a new face so she'd taken the open seat next to him, separated by the corner of the conference table.

Jeff was a handsome man, one who took care of himself, she noticed as she waited for the meeting to start. Not at all like most of the others in the room. He placed a mug of black coffee on the coaster before him, then said, "Could you hand me the Sweet'n Low, please?"

The bowl was to her left. She'd reached over and handed him a pink packet. The moment their fingers touched, an electric shock went through her body. His hand hesitated; she was certain he felt the same thing. She looked at his clear gray eyes. He glanced at hers, then looked away. Clumsily opening the sweetener, he poured it into the mug, spilling almost as much as he put in the coffee. "I'll need a napkin. I'm all thumbs today," he'd said without meeting her eye.

During Daryl's junior year at MIT, when she was 19, she'd been heavily courted by the scion to one of America's wealthiest and oldest families. With a name embarrassingly long and followed with the number IV, he was considered the most desirable catch on campus. When her dorm sisters first realized that "Four" was interested in their nerdy roommate, they'd been envious.

Daryl had never before been courted, not like that, and found the experience interesting as a form of minor cultural ritual. Four was pleasant when he wanted to be but, she'd told her mother, not really quite smart enough for MIT. She wondered why he'd come.

"Because Dad wanted me to attend Yale," he'd told her one evening when she asked. "Anyway, I like it here, better since meeting you."

That night they'd gone to bed for the first, and only, time. In his room Four had stopped her from undressing, telling her he wanted the privilege for himself. She'd stood unmoving as he slowly unbuttoned and unzipped her out of her winter clothing. She'd observed the experience as if it were occurring to someone else, as if she were standing to the side. When at last she was down to her bra and panties, Four had pressed her to the bed, removed his clothes, then lay beside her. Then he slowly removed her bra and panties, breathing heavily as if lost in a trance.

It was January, and from the uncovered window silver moonlight spread across her now nude body. Four stopped as she lay naked and said over and over, "Magnificent. Magnificent."

The sex was better than she'd expected. Daryl could see why a woman might get excited over it, but afterward Four had been distant, as if wrapped in his own world. He called repeatedly after that night, but she'd never gone out with him again. She understood what was going on and was not flattered.

Throughout their weeks of dating, Four had repeatedly spoken of her beauty. Then he had worshipped at its altar. She had no desire to be any man's idol. From that night forward she committed herself to her work. No more dating, no more pawing. She wore baggy clothes, no makeup, and buried herself in her studies.

She counted herself the better for the experience. Four, she realized, had been full of himself, certain he was God's gift to women, to her, to the world, when in fact he was a self-satisfied, egocentric snob. She considered herself well rid of him, and from this had come her utter contempt for egocentrics.

Four had not taken rejection well. He spread stories that Daryl was a slut, that he'd dropped her because she'd cheated on him. His stories only seemed to increase the attention of the other male students, and no hiding beneath oversize clothes could conceal her obvious beauty and latent sexuality.

As a release, and because she'd discovered her aptitude for sport, Daryl played intramural soccer after moving to Stanford for graduate work. She threw herself into the game and, if not the star of the team, was taken seriously as a player. On weekends she backpacked and hiked throughout northern California and parts of Nevada. She skied at every opportunity.

When Daryl first met Jeff, she was working in cyber-security, performing virus analysis, at that time a new field. A rising star in the NSA, she'd played a major role in identifying the hackers of two high-profile viruses. Overall, though, she was bored and generally annoyed by the obvious attention of men to her physical appearance. She'd learned, however, that it could work to her advantage. As for marriage and family, she had her work and found it endlessly fascinating.

After that first meeting, she'd seen Jeff at two others. Following the third a small group had gone for coffee together. It devolved into just the two of them. Their conversation had been on the merits of the Windows operating system versus that of the Macintosh, and in such detail they'd driven the others away. Not once, she realized, had he looked at her breasts, and for the first time since they'd developed, she was disappointed. What was the point of great tits if a man who interested you didn't notice?

Over the telephone she'd once complained about it to her mom, a woman of considerable beauty herself. "The ones you don't want to notice, will; the once you'd like to notice usually won't. Get used to it," she'd told her daughter.

Daryl and Jeff had reached that point where young couples talk about themselves. She'd gone first. When it was Jeff's turn, he told her how he'd been raised by two elderly grandparents who had doted on him. "It sounds lonely," she'd said.

"They were awfully good people, and very loving. They passed before I was graduated from college. I've been mostly on my own since, until recently that is." He'd brightened, then told her about his girlfriend, Cynthia. That had been the end of any thoughts she'd had about the two of them.

After that they worked together from time to time. At one juncture he'd provided her with significant information unofficially. A few months later, she'd done the same. From then on they'd formed a fast and close working relationship, unfettered by his relationship with Cynthia.

She'd learned through a mutual friend of Cynthia's death and had, in her subsequent contacts with Jeff, noticed the change in him. Where once he'd frequently been lighthearted, now he was somber. She regretted that she'd never found the proper moment to express her condolences at his loss.

She was looking forward to seeing him, especially as she was convinced he was the one person who could help her with this virus. As for the rest, well, time would tell.

RIO DE JANEIRO, BRAZIL
RUA FRANCISCO OTAVIANO
TUESDAY, AUGUST 15
10:16 A.M.

With a touch of distaste Maria Braga watched the scraggly-haired young man enter.

The Euro Internet Café, just two blocks from Copacabana Beach in Rio, catered largely to the tourists who walked by and to certain Cariocas who didn't have a computer of their own. She knew both types at a glance. The tourists were dressed in fresh beach attire, while the locals were primarily diligent, well-scrubbed students. With six computers and one booth for international telephone calls crammed into the long, narrow room, Maria made an adequate living for herself and her daughter. In the four years she'd run the café, she'd only been robbed once.

The young man's name was Nicolau. Maria thought he was weird. She didn't like the way he looked at her, staring at her modestly covered breasts as if she were naked. She was certain he was some kind of pervert.

And he was a nerd. She could tell this guy knew all about computers. He'd probably built his own at home or, at least, bought the very latest models. From the looks of his expensive watch, he could afford it. He didn't have to use hers, so why did he?

Nicolau rarely stayed at the station more than three or four minutes. That alone was strange. He was up to something, but she had no idea what. She'd thought about charging him more—maybe he'd go somewhere else—but her fees were posted.

Nineteen-year-old Nicolau da Costa was a hacker. His father was a senior vice president with Banco Central do Brasil, while his mother ran a modest flower shop on Avenida Nossa Senhora de Cobacabana. Nicolau spent his nights at his computer playing video games or online in various chat rooms, exchanging virus code, talking endlessly about creating a virus that everyone in the world would know, but wouldn't cause enough damage to get him arrested.

He'd found it wasn't that easy. More than once he'd been on the verge of launching a virus, but had always held back. Brazilian prisons were notorious. He had nightmares about ending up in one. You never knew when the authorities might decide to make an example of someone. Even his father wouldn't be able to help.

Every once in a while, though, a job came along. This was the fifth in less than a month. He dropped onto the chair and checked to confirm that the computer was connected to the Internet. He looked back at Maria up front, then slipped his floppy into the computer and launched the code. The e-mail had told him to leave the floppy in place for three minutes. As he waited, he browsed two Web sites, then, satisfied, extracted the floppy.

Now he entered his Yahoo e-mail account and sent the following message.

Date: Tues, 15 August 10:21 —0700

He typed in the address, careful that no one was looking.

From: Riostd <riostd69@yahoo.com>
Subject: sent

rlsd code. rdy for another when u r. send $.

RioStud

At the counter Nicolau smiled as he counted out the coins for his time. Nicolau thought Maria was hot, but wondered if she had been raised in a convent. He and his friends talked about traditional girls like that, though none of them had ever met one who had been. She sure dressed like a nun.

MANHATTAN, NYC
IT CENTER
FISCHERMAN, PLATT & COHEN
TUESDAY, AUGUST 15
10:25 A.M.

Stepping outside the building, Jeff was surprised to see it was mid-morning. A slight breeze was coming in off the Atlantic and the air was clear, invigorating after the sterility of the IT Center. He walked around the corner to a deli he'd spotted earlier, where Daryl had agreed to meet him. He was looking forward to seeing her again. Quite apart from her ability to help him in his work, he'd always enjoyed her company.

For the last day the world outside had not existed for him. Nothing mattered but the pixels on the screen, accessing the operating system, the story he discovered as he inched his way toward solving the problem, the bits of information that formed together in time to crack the mystery, and the final recovery of the blocked, stolen, or destroyed data. Though this one was not solved—not yet.

Daryl was due any minute. As he entered, he realized that the deli might have been out of *Seinfeld*, with a dozen people ensconced in booths or sitting on stools. He took an end booth, placed an order for coffee, then sat drinking as he waited.

He felt bad about leaving Sue with such a mess, but he had to take a break and rest to think clearly. He glanced over at two men and one woman working on laptops with Wi-Fi and wondered how many viruses each had without knowing it. Two other men in business suits were sitting at a small table having an animated conversation. From the few words he picked up they were talking baseball. Apparently the Yankees were losing.

As a barista cleared a table beside him, Daryl Haugen entered, glancing first left, then right. She was wearing her usual garb of jeans, with a tight white blouse. He waved a hand; she spotted him, smiled warmly, and came over. Sitting across from him, she placed a half-empty bottle of water on the table, then flopped her laptop bag onto the floor. She looked stressed, very, very tired—and lovely.

There was no denying her beauty. He'd once sat in a meeting, bored out of his mind, only to realize he'd been staring at her. Her returning look had not been pleasant, and he'd been careful ever since. Still, simply being with her was an appealing experience.

For an instant he couldn't help comparing her to Sue. Daryl had a freshness, a spontaneous way of behaving, about her that was quite engaging. Sue was more artifice and calculation. The two women could not have been more different, and his response to each was night and day. He felt relaxed and open around Daryl, but on guard with Sue, making sure that he kept within the bounds of professional interaction.

"No coffee?" he asked.

She shook her head. "No. I had plenty earlier. It gets me wired if I'm not careful. How have you been? How's it going in the cold, cold world of private enterprise?"

In the years since he'd left the CIA the two had run into each other at the occasional conference. But mostly they'd exchanged e-mails and talked over the phone about difficult problems they'd encountered. Jeff was by nature a puzzle solver, while Daryl was the most gifted computer expert he'd ever encountered. Together they made a great team, but their different lines of work didn't offer many opportunities for collaboration.

"I'm doing fine," he said. "Business continues to boom. I do it all myself so I don't have to waste time with employees. It keeps me busy. My main problem is reminding myself to keep increasing my fees. Computer security is a pretty hot topic for many companies. But who am I telling? How do you like CERT?"

"It's US-CERT, and I like it a lot." She grinned and for a moment the tension in her face vanished.

In the wake of 9/11 came recognition that cyberspace was vulnerable to attack and that something needed to be done. The new Department of Homeland Security lumped together a number of previously independent and disparate groups in various agencies. Related to that, but also independent of it, in early 2003, the president issued a directive creating the National Cyberspace Security Response System and within it the United States Computer Emergency Readiness Team, labeled in government jargon US-CERT. As the operational arm of the National Cyber Security Division, its primary objective was to create a strategic framework to prevent cyber-attacks against U.S. computer-oriented infrastructure.

A different organization, known as CERT, had been created earlier, in response to the infamous Morris worm, which had brought 10 percent of Internet systems to a halt in 1988. Housed at and part of the development center at Carnegie Mellon University in Pittsburgh, Pennsylvania, it held a less audacious mandate. CERT was intended to coordinate communication among the various cyber experts to prevent future virus outbreaks, though with the advent of 9/11, the older CERT's profile had significantly increased.

But the total effect of so many organizations with overlapping jurisdictions hadn't improved America's defenses; instead, it created chaos. Turf wars intensified rather than easing, and obvious measures took months or years of discussion and debate to implement—if at all— because it wasn't clear which organization was ultimately accountable. In Jeff's view, it was all tragic and pointless. The threat was self-evident. Only those with the power to do something about it seemed unaware.

How anyone could do nothing in the face of such an obvious threat was something he could never comprehend or accept. The anger he felt whenever he thought of it burned at him, but he could do nothing more than what he'd already done and continued to do, every workday. Sometimes he wanted to scream, but he knew no one would listen. He'd just be defined as a kook and in consequence lose any effectiveness he had. This was, he now realized, one more reason why he'd made a point to stay in contact with Daryl.

"I didn't know you were a field operative," Jeff said.

She gave him a quirky smile. "I have a very competent team. Between my laptop, e-mail, and cell phone, we're in constant contact." She paused. "And I needed to see this situation for myself."

"How do you like Homeland Security?" he asked with a knowing smile.

Daryl grimaced. "The bureaucracy can be wearing, but my part's pretty good and getting better. I'm surprised anyone's got time to work."

"You're with my old friend George?"

"With? We consult one another. I don't spend any more time with him than I need to."

"How's that going?" he asked, though he had no doubt of the answer. She despised the man as much as he did.

"Did I mention bureaucracy?" She made a face. "Don't get me going, though honestly, when it comes to that group and their maneuvering for power, he's better than some I could name. It's just that I feel like I'm talking into an empty oil drum most of the time. All I hear is my own echo back. Commercial attacks are up steeply, but both he and the department don't really seem to care about that all that much. Lots of people and companies are losing information that costs them money. These high-tech crime groups in Russia are getting fat off of us, and nobody's made them a priority."

"I hear the Company ran another simulated attack last summer." Such information was common knowledge in the elite world of cyber-security Jeff occupied. He'd been waiting to ask someone in the know about it. "What was the outcome?"

She laughed. "It was like all the ones before Silent Horizon in 2005 or Operation Cyber Storms I, II, in 2006 and then Cyber Storm III in 2009. CIA and DHS rigged the tests so completely there was no way they couldn't defend. They established perimeters no real attacker would ever follow while everyone defending a system against penetration knew the attack was coming, and what the rules of the game were. It was ludicrous, but management took great comfort from the results. They're back to worrying about terrorists blowing up a computer system. It's like the old FBI chasing bank robbers while the Mafia was running rampant. DHS does what its component parts have always done. There's an extraordinary lack of imagination there." Daryl shook her head, still amazed at the stupidity of it all.

"It's got, what? More than two hundred thousand employees? That's enough manpower to do the job right."

"That's it," Daryl confirmed. "Cyber-security is so far down the totem pole we hardly count. If it wasn't for the work of the private-computer and Internet-security companies, we'd be getting nowhere." She took a pull of water. "Did you read about the airplane?"

Jeff shook his head. "I've been in a cocoon. What happened?"

"As I understand it, a British Airways flight from London to New York had an incident over the Atlantic."

"Don't tell me it was a Boeing 787?" Jeff had long anticipated such an event given its heavy dependence on computers.

"Yes, indeed, a fly-by-wire, computer-designed-and-operated aircraft."

"What happened?"

"Apparently the plane began to climb very slowly, and the airspeed dropped while on autopilot. The crew was not alerted and didn't recognize their danger until it was nearly too late. As it was, the plane stalled at forty thousand feet."

"Jesus." Jeff shook his head in disbelief. "Like the Spanair crash last year they think was caused by malware."

"Yes. They were lucky they were so high. They needed all but a couple thousand of those feet to recover."

"What happened?"

"We don't know, but I understand they were only able to save the airplane by rebooting the controlling computer in flight."

"That took nerve." Jeff was impressed. Someone had known what to do when the chips were down and had acted on that knowledge.

"More than you can imagine. They had *no* command while the computer was off-line. There is no mechanical backup to the controls. That plane fell like a rock."

Jeff gave a low whistle. "That's a bright crew to manage something like that, under those conditions."

Daryl raised an eyebrow. "They deserve a medal. But you haven't heard the best part. When they tried to reboot, the computer locked up. They had to power off. It's a miracle they got enough control back in time."

My God, Jeff thought. He couldn't imagine anyone having the presence of mind to pull off a stunt like that in such an emergency. Those men really did deserve a medal. Still, those systems should have been secure from infection, and fail-safes should have prevented the need for manual intervention. "What about the redundant systems?"

"They didn't work." She paused. "There were eight deaths. They managed to pull out of the dive that followed the stall, but the plane shot up to over fifty thousand feet before nosing down again. The autopilot was handling the roller-coaster ride, but still . . . No one in back was prepared, and most were unbuckled. Passengers were knocked around like pieces of cordwood. Five of the deaths were small children. They were thrown around like missiles. The adult deaths were from broken necks and internal injuries. One passenger is paralyzed. Many others were seriously injured."

"Welcome to the twenty-first century." Jeff ran his hand through his hair, then picked up his coffee. Cold.

Daryl nodded. "So . . . tell me what you've found."

Jeff filled her in on what he knew so far. US-CERT worked cooperatively with the Cyber Security Industry Alliance, formed by Symantec and McAfee among others, as well as with the Internet-security departments of every major corporation, and computer and software giants such as IBM's Internet Security Systems and Microsoft. It was in everyone's interest to cooperate. That was one reason she'd been willing to meet him when he told her he'd run across something unusual. As he spoke, she nodded, taking an occasional sip of water. When he told her about the words to the song "Super Freak," though, she put her water bottle down.

"I just ran into that same name this morning at Mercy Hospital," she said when he stopped. "It was spelled S-U-P-E-R-P-H-R-E-A-K."

It was as if a piece of an especially difficult puzzle had fallen into place. "I haven't seen the name under any spelling, just the disguised words from the song 'Super Freak.'"

"I was at Mercy when when you called," she said, talking more rapidly. "But they didn't lose some billing or litigation records. Like I told you, four patients were killed. The program modified their medicine records and instruction. Jeff, I think we're investigating the same virus. Did you hear about the death at a Ford assembly plant?"

He shook his head.

"I can't be certain, but it appears the plant's robot software picked up a virus that sat there, waiting. The virus took over without warning, causing the robots to perform in nonscripted ways. We think that's when the worker was knocked onto the assembly-line railing. In response, the company powered down, then unplugged the robots. Their server was fried. They installed a replacement and are reloading the software. It looks like they'd be all right except for the death, of course, and the loss of about two weeks' production. The financial cost to them will be in the tens of millions."

Jeff was puzzled. "I thought industry networks were off-line for security purposes."

"They mostly are and this one was. I talked to the IT manager again this morning. They traced the original virus to a software engineer's laptop. He was in the habit of downloading whatever he was working on, then taking it home with him. He picked up the virus there when he used the same laptop to access the Internet. When he hooked it up at work, the worm latched onto the company's software, planting the virus."

Jeff thought a moment, then said, "Back to the 787 incident. Is it possible what we're dealing with could be crafted for avionics software?"

"I don't know," she said, looking surprised at the thought. "It seems unlikely, but it highlights one of the problems we're having. We don't know what the virus is doing and what it isn't doing. For that matter there could very well be any number of incidents about which we know nothing. The world is so computer-dependent you can't always make the connection to one of the viruses when something happens."

"So what's Superphreak? Do you have any idea?"

"Not yet. I've got my team working on it. It could be almost anything. It could be a word left by a script kitty. It could even be the cracker's name." Daryl pushed away her water bottle and started drumming her fingers on the table. "It looks to me as if whoever wrote this used old code, copied and pasted to create this one. I don't think he realized the word was there. I found parts of *Superphreak* in three places."

"I think he's Russian," Jeff speculated. "I can't put my finger on it, but the way some of the code is written just has that look. And, given their track record, this could well be an economic attack of some kind by Russians."

Daryl stared at Jeff, impressed. "Good guess, Mr. Holmes. I found the word *Moscow* written in Cyrillic in the code not long before I ran into *Superphreak*."

"So that's it then." Jeff experienced a moment of elation. Russians.

Just as he'd thought. It felt good to have been right. "Do you have any idea how widespread this is?" He wasn't in a position to know, but Daryl was.

"When I left for the office Monday, we had seven reports that looked suspicious. We've picked up more than fifty since then."

Jeff was astounded. "It's spreading pretty fast. Who's working on detection and a fix?"

"I think I can safely say *none* of the private security companies are at this point, though they've been alerted and we've given them all the code we have. They report a higher-than-usual flood of former viruses and variants that require their attention. Superphreak hasn't appeared in any of their honeypots and we can't prove a connection, so they think we're overreacting. It's very frustrating. We're assuming we won't be able to figure out the vulnerabilities these things use to spread right away, or get the software companies responsible for them to release fixes anytime soon. So we were hoping to get them onto the problem immediately, but no luck." Daryl shrugged. "But even if they did respond, the problem is, as you know, that it would take weeks to come up with signatures and patches. And that's the best case. How long it takes for users to download and install them is another matter altogether."

"You should push the process," Jeff said. "You can't just leave it to agency inertia." He could have bit his tongue. He knew Daryl was doing everything she could.

"I'm trying." She looked annoyed.

"Why so pessimistic?"

Daryl glanced around the room, then leaned forward. When she spoke, her voice was subdued but firm. "Because so far we've spotted at least ten variations of the code and we aren't talking knockoffs. These were written with entirely different code, as if by a different cracker, but in the end they all do something very destructive. I have no idea how many variations there are. And not knowing gives me the willies."

Jeff thought of the airliner falling out of the sky, the hospital deaths, the man killed on the assembly line. Were these just the tip of the iceberg? Mentally, he ran through a list of other dangers: nuclear-power stations, traffic-control systems, defense networks, Wall Street. The list was limitless and suddenly he felt overwhelmed. "What else?"

"It seems to be composed of three functions. The first is the exploit code that gets the virus into the system without detection. The second is the trigger. The third is the payload itself, which causes all the damage. We've got three variants of the exploit, five of the virus, and we've just started. I have no idea how many others there are." She sighed. "Two hospitals outside of New York report their medicine distribution systems were also jumbled. We know of eleven deaths nationally so far. A small power station in Connecticut had its sluice gate turned wide open and it couldn't be closed. By the time they figured out the problem was the computer they use to control their water release and the electricity they produce, they'd lost a significant amount of reserve capacity. It will take them two years to restore it. They didn't have backup software and are running manually now. It's almost laughable, but they had to recall a retired worker to show them how the system works without a computer. A nuclear power plant in Iowa had to do a mechanical shutdown to prevent a meltdown. This next one's been kept out of the news so far, but Tucson International Airport lost its air traffic control system. Fortunately, it was during a slow period and there were no incidents. More and more is coming in every hour, but you can see why I'm not sleeping well."

Until now, Jeff realized, he'd been focused on his client's narrow problem. He'd not seen it as part of an expanding, and dangerous, reality. Daryl was scaring the hell out of him, and he experienced a surge of anxiety and fear he'd not felt since those last days before 9/11. "What's the potential?"

She paused, then said, "Anything's possible. It looks as if we're just seeing the surface. Here's what's frightening me." Jeff felt another chill shoot through his body. If Daryl was frightened, then this was even bigger than he feared. "First, we can't detect the virus coming in, and that's going to be a tough egg to crack. We've got to get the signatures written, the patches prepared, then out there, and I don't think there's enough time. Second, a single signature isn't going to work. The variants are too different."

Jeff nodded, took a sip of coffee, then explained what he'd learned, and what he didn't yet know. When he finished Daryl groaned. "This Superphreak, if that's the cracker's cyber handle, could be a Chechen. Or he could be a gun for hire and working for almost anyone. The Russian mob, to name just one." Neither of them said anything for several minutes as they absorbed what they had learned. "I've got more," she finally said. "There are other propagation methods besides, or in addition to, the worms. My team is reporting they've found three of the variants that spread through the address book of each computer they touched, and several of the ones we've looked at are polymorphic or metamorphic, so they look different each time they replicate. That's what I was getting at before."

"One I found wanted to replicate," Jeff confirmed. "The system went down so fast I doubt any of it got out, but that was its intention."

"What if every variant is self-replicating?"

Jeff sat back in his chair. "I hate to bring up more bad news, but have you considered this? Whoever is spreading this virus might be still at it. They could be sending new variants out every day. I'm sorry to add to your misery, but you need to get CERT and DHS serious about this."

Daryl threw up her hands. "I'm only one person with a small team. We've had six directors heading up DHS cyber-security since it was created. Almost none of them have lasted so much as a year, most only a few months. They have no clout in DHS, and if they're in the driver's seat when the attack comes, it could end their career."

"This is all very familiar, isn't it?" Jeff asked. He'd worked long enough in the government system to know what she was up against.

"I'm afraid so." Daryl's beautiful face was creased with worry. "We're trying to get the industry interested. But we're way behind the curve on this. We have no idea how many variants there are, or how many others are coming out. I lay awake last night imagining the harm that will come if we're only seeing a small portion of the Superphreak viruses."

"Take it easy. We're probably overevaluating, and it's not as bad as we fear."

Daryl wasn't buying it. "Look at the body count already! Superphreak, if that's what's causing this, is already the most deadly virus ever unleashed, and *it's just starting*. That's why I'm in Manhattan. There are dead people here because of this thing. We have no idea of the long-term harm Superphreak can cause." She paused, then leaned across the table, her blond hair falling forward. "Let me tell you what I think. What we need to do is to stop this at the source."

"How?" Despite himself, Jeff knew she was right. He'd had the same thought late the night before, but hadn't wanted to admit it until she'd said it aloud.

"Find the cracker in his home, get distribution stopped at the wellspring, then learn from him or his computers exactly how many variants there are. If we had *that* information, I could rush through the fix and the antivirus changes, and we could stop this thing in its tracks."

Jeff smiled. "You have a black-ops team that does that?"

"Hell, no," Daryl said grimly, "but we sure as hell need one."

Exhausted as he was, Jeff wanted nothing so much as to go straight to his hotel room, but there was no denying this. It had to be done.

Two blocks to the west he located a subway, bought a MetroCard, then rode the train downtown. The car was clean, cleaner than he recalled from his summer of weekend trips here that ill-fated year.

For two years, Jeff had been in a serious relationship with Cynthia Wheel. They'd lived in the same complex just outside Richmond, Virginia, and had met at the gym they shared. Petite with raven hair, she'd been a vivacious and bright young woman. It had been easy to settle into the life of an old married couple with her, without ever actually "doing the deed," as she was fond of saying, especially when naked and about to suggest another bout of sexual play.

Jeff felt a real sense of loss when, in May of 2001, Cynthia's company, ARM—Account Resources Management—of Richmond, Virginia, had transferred her to Manhattan. Jeff helped her pack, then drove her to her new apartment. "We won't let this be the end of us," she assured him just as he prepared to leave. "I promise." She'd kissed him sweetly on the mouth, stepped back, flashed her winning smile, and said, "Wish me luck."

In the months that followed, his routine was consistent. He began recording the long hours he normally gave the CIA gratis and left the office at 1:00 p.m. every Friday, to take the shuttle flight to New York City. After spending the weekend with Cynthia, he'd return home late Sunday. In August, she'd flown to see him twice, complaining of the sweltering heat in Manhattan, but by September she was thrilled as the days turned cooler with the prospect of autumn.

That August Jeff had received a disk originally seized from the ruling Taliban by one of the rival Afghan groups. He'd cracked into the disk within minutes of receiving it and saw at once that, despite its provenance, it was not Taliban. It had been prepared by a group called Al Qaeda, "the base."

Dredging up a vague memory of Al Qaeda, Jeff remembered it was one of a number of terrorist groups on the radar screen of the Company, though it held no significance to him. He checked the terrorist database to which he routinely contributed and was brought up cold. Led by an enormously rich and shadowy figure, Osama bin Laden, Al Qaeda might not be the biggest or best-known terrorist group, but it tended to target Americans with deadly results.

For the next three days Jeff gleaned information from the disk, then carefully analyzed its contents, a role beyond his purview. Checking the master database several times, he found a dozen recent entries that seemed connected.

Next, he drafted a time line. On one side of the program he listed information by date, to analyze the data flow. On the other, he listed events in the order they were to occur. He could scarcely believe what he was seeing. He printed the program, sketched an analysis, then buzzed his boss's secretary and asked for a meeting as soon as possible.

For the next two hours Jeff reviewed his information, tearing it apart as a critic might. The stark facts remained. Only an idiot, someone too blind to see the obvious, could fail to see what he'd uncovered. With dismay, he realized that was a good description of his boss.

George Carlton was a burly man of average height, turned soft by two decades in government bureaucracy. His sallow skin had become excessively sensitive to daylight over the years and he now burned quite easily. When he came into the office after a weekend in the country or at sea, his face would shine a bright red.

Carlton had begun his career as an FBI desk agent, moving into middle management from there. Then, for reasons never fully explained, he took a position with the CIA as manager of the Cyberterrorism–Computer Forensics Department. The move was unusual, but on paper, at least, it seemed a good fit. At that time computers and their use for terrorism was not a high priority, since there'd been no documented case of a foreign terrorist act within the continental United States, either against the supporting computers of the Internet or by using its resources. With the additions of other functions, including the Computer Science Group and its obscure Cyberterrorism Unit, Carlton's area of power and presumed expertise steadily grew.

He was a born bureaucrat, adept at evading responsibility for errors while garnering praise for work he'd not performed. He made few enemies over the years, which served him well. But the lack of attention his department received was the greatest boon to his career. Prior to 2001, little was expected of him in the twilight world of counterterrorism in which he'd found a niche. Though he would have preferred an airy corner office on the second or third floor, he was content with his location, far from any window and deep within the center of the ground floor.

Shortly after 4:00 that afternoon Jeff was ushered in, carrying with him the proof he hoped his supervisor would find persuasive. Carlton didn't rise as he gestured for Jeff to take a seat in front of his desk. "What have you got?" A bad boss is typically characterized as hostile, rude, and dim. Carlton was never, or at least rarely, rude; he'd been in government service too many years to be overtly hostile; and he was not stupid. For the next ten minutes Jeff laid out what he believed was going to take place on September 11, less than two weeks away.

Carlton listened with diminishing enthusiasm, then asked to see the time line. He spent a full minute examining it before commenting, "I'm confused about something. Just where do these supposed targets come from? The Statue of Liberty, the Pentagon, the World Trade Center, the White House, the Capitol, the Sears Tower, the Golden Gate Bridge, the Washington Monument." He looked up. "Mount Rushmore? I suppose I can see the logic of the Pentagon, the other government buildings even, but Mount Rushmore? I don't get it."

"I admit listing all of them as possible targets is speculative, but it's speculation based on text," Jeff said. "Those names came from various communiqués. They're not only after what could be called hard targets, structures connected to our government and military, but also after our economic infrastructure and landmarks." Jeff's mouth was dry and he found the words difficult to form. "They're very into symbolism. And Al Qaeda's targeted the World Trade Center previously. Their purpose with those truck explosives was to topple one of the buildings into the other, taking them both down like dominoes."

Carlton snickered. "They were wrong, weren't they? In fact, Al Qaeda isn't all that effective, if you look at their track record. And they certainly seem to prefer the Horn of Africa. It's difficult to see them posing a genuine threat to us from . . . where are they? Afghanistan, of all places."

"It's all there," Jeff insisted, pointing at the documents he'd assembled. "Most of it, at least. Enough." Though he was struggling to contain himself his voice rose a bit as he said, "We need to do something."

Carlton looked at him sharply. "Have you any idea how many threats a day are processed by the Company? Each one is given a score. If I pass this one higher up, it will receive, I'm telling you categorically, the lowest-priority score that exists."

Jeff's heart sank. "You can't just sit on it," he said in near desperation.

Carlton paused. "I'm not going to sit on it, as you put it. But we need more information or no one will act. I'm going to hold on to this for a few days. Don't be concerned. There's plenty of time yet. In the meanwhile, see if you can get me something with meat on the bones. But be assured that either way I'll pass it along in time."

Driven by a mix of frustration and fear, Jeff skipped his trip to New York City that weekend, and the one after, each time telling Cynthia that as much as he wanted to see her, he was buried by a pile of work and wouldn't be able to relax even if he did come. With a passion born of desperation he worked eighteen hours a day, every day, pulling his two assistants from their IT assignments and instilling in them his own sense of urgency as he put them to work on the project. Accessing real-time chat rooms and other sources previously identified as Al Qaeda communication channels, what emerged was a terrorist plan on the fast track. Collecting intelligence wasn't his job and shouldn't be necessary: what he'd already done should have unleashed the enormous resources of the Company.

By Tuesday, September 4, after preparing a far more comprehensive presentation of what he considered to be a highly credible threat to

America, Jeff went directly to Carlton's secretary. "This is urgent. Will you see to it George gets this at once? He's expecting it." She'd smiled stiffly and taken the file.

He didn't like leaving it that way, but given the nature of his relationship with his boss and the bureaucracy of the Company, his hands were tied. It wasn't how he wanted to handle it; it was how he had to handle it if he wanted anything positive to happen.

Back in his office Jeff continued with his relentless schedule, sleeping on his couch, washing up and shaving in the restroom. Carlton e-mailed him that he'd forwarded the file to the appropriate teams, but despite his effort and long hours, nothing more of consequence emerged. Beside himself with anger and frustration, he called Cynthia in Manhattan on Friday, September 7. ARM's offices were at the World Financial Center, just across the street from the World Trade Center.

"I need you to do something for me without my going into detail," he said, knowing Cynthia would instantly grasp the time for questions was later. "I want you not to go into work next week. Stay home, or better yet, leave the city." The target date might get moved a day or two, so he didn't specify Tuesday. "Can you work from home or, better yet, visit your folks?"

"Wow. Pretty short notice." Her voice was steady and he felt reassured she'd do as he asked.

"It's not just important. It's vital."

"Vital, huh?" From the beginning Cynthia had been impressed with Jeff's serious and sober nature. Only when she finally grasped the full extent of it had she seriously begun to consider him for a husband. Her confidence in him and his judgment had continued to grow as they'd dated. "As in 'life and death'?"

"You could say that." Jeff fought off the sudden urge to tell her everything. He'd kept it inside for so long he was about to burst. But he couldn't. He just couldn't. It wasn't so much that he was worried that he was wrong, but scared of the panic he could set off. She had to act on his warning and he was considering what he'd do next if she didn't, but his serious answer seemed to sober her. "Okay. I'll visit my folks. Won't they be surprised?"

Jeff breathed a sigh of relief. "Thank you. Thank you. Make it all week, please. I want your promise that you're leaving the city tomorrow morning. And no matter what, you won't go to work next week."

"Okay, I promise. Cross my heart, hope to die." Cynthia was perplexed by the entire exchange. Was there a threat he couldn't mention? Clearly that was his message. It couldn't have been at her personally or he'd have said so. Given what he did for a living, that meant the threat was of a broader nature. The only thing that came to mind was a terrorist attack. Jeff was in a position to know about such things. And she also knew, from what little he'd told her over their time together, that most threats came to nothing. She had confidence in her country. Jeff was just being cautious and she loved him all the more for it. The worst part was, she could say nothing to her coworkers, not without getting Jeff fired or even indicted.

Jeff was a sober man, not given to extremes. If he told her that she needed to leave town, she was prepared to take his word for it. She considered her alternatives. None were appealing. She wasn't about to drive to Albany and check into a motel for the week. Still, she'd promised, and a promise made was one to be kept. She decided to work from her home all week and arranged to have what she needed brought to her, claiming she was deathly ill and highly contagious.

Shortly after speaking with her, Jeff made a mental note to call Cynthia on Sunday, then attempted to meet with Carlton again, but was told he had no opening until the following week. Frantically, Jeff took to prowling the hallways near Carlton's office and intercepted him on his way to a meeting. "Do you have any word yet on my report?" Jeff asked, keeping pace with his superior.

"Yes," Carlton said, giving him a pointed look. "They're giving it due consideration."

"There's more information that seems to nail next Tuesday down as a date and confirms a number of the targets including the Capitol, the White House, and the Pentagon."

"I told you, I passed it along." Carlton all but rolled his eyes. "Now I've got a meeting, Jeff. It's been taken care of. Move on. You know these Arabs. They couldn't organize a conga line." With that, Carlton ducked into a conference room.

Jeff knew it was pointless going over Carlton's head but he tried anyway. He knew he was making enemies, understood that he was effectively ending his government career, but he didn't care. This was too important.

When everyone of consequence had gone home on Friday, he was left with nothing else to do but continue working throughout the weekend and into Monday with his team. Following a thirty-six-hour stretch, vainly searching for another bit of concrete proof, totally consumed by his work, Jeff lost track of time and never called Cynthia.

And so it went uneventfully all day Monday when, out of the blue, one of Cynthia's college roommates called and suggested breakfast at Windows on the World at the World Trade Center the next morning. She knew Cynthia was about to become engaged and wanted to hear all the details. Cynthia left her apartment that morning to meet her, excited at the prospect of sharing her private hopes and dreams with the woman who had once been her best friend.

In Langley, Jeff was distracted by his cell phone, which rang, rang, rang. Digging around in his clothing, he pressed a button.

"Something terrible's happened." Cynthia's voice was strained, as if she was about to cry. "I stayed home, like I promised. I did. Then Karen came to town and we went to breakfast then . . . then . . ."

In the background Jeff could hear pandemonium. "Where are you?"

"Windows on the World, the restaurant at the top of one of the Towers."

For a moment Jeff heard and felt nothing. His body turned numb. When her voice returned, it was from far away.

". . . felt something a little bit ago. The whole building just shuddered, and I thought we were going to fall over." Her voice was quivering. He could tell she was struggling for control.

"Get out, Cynthia. Get out now!"

"I already tried!" Now she sounded panicked. "Everyone says a plane hit us! I can't get out, Jeff. There's fire all below us. There's no way out. No way. I'm really scared." She paused. When she resumed, her voice was strangely calm. "I called to tell you that I love you, just in case."

"Go to the roof!" Jeff insisted. "They'll bring helicopters to evacuate you." He gripped the telephone fiercely in his sweaty hand, trying with his voice to will her into action.

"It's jammed up there. You can't get on top. We tried earlier." Her voice was desperate. "Oh, Jeff. This is what you mea—"

They were cut off. Jeff tried to call back, but her cell phone had no service. He snapped on the television set in his office and saw the burning Towers. His team crept in a few minutes later. "We didn't want to disturb you. You'd know soon enough," one said.

The other stared at the screen, transfixed. "Nobody listened to us."

Jeff kept calling Cynthia without connecting. The three were watching as each Tower in turn fell in a great white, billowing cloud of pulverized concrete. There had been no helicopter evacuation.

Jeff sat motionless. The cell phone snapped in his hand, the battery flying out and clattering onto the floor. His rage was almost more than he could stand. He wanted to kill Carlton and, in a flash, saw himself killing the director and all of senior CIA management too.

He shot to his feet and glared at his team, wanting with all his power to strike at them, as if they were the cause. Managing to control himself, he slumped back into his seat, the rage turning on himself, for not calling Cynthia, for not saving her, for not doing enough to save anyone. He should have made someone pay attention.

His assistant was right. No one had listened.

OOOOOOOOOOO14

Captain Vandana Shiva lifted the binoculars to see if he could spot the offshore facility at Nagasaki as yet. He knew it was early, but he never entirely trusted computers and the Global Positioning System on which they relied. He'd begun his forty-one-year career as a seaman aboard a traditional Indian dhoni. In his mind that had been real seamanship, just the crew and the small boat against the ocean and wind. It had required skill and courage, and it was nothing like what he did now.

An uncle had liked the young Shiva and, lacking a son, financed his education. He'd done well and subsequently risen steadily in the merchant service until reaching the culmination of his career three years earlier when he'd been given command of *The Illustrious Goddess*, the largest supertanker ever built.

With a crude-oil cargo capacity of six hundred thousand DWT, or deadweight tongue, there had never been a ship of this size in history. More than a quarter of a mile long and nearly the width of a football field, it plied the oceans at a respectable eighteen knots. Because it drew more than twenty-six feet, few harbors in the world could accommodate the vessel, so it nearly always docked at an offshore oil facility where its enormous load of 4.5 million barrels was pumped by undersea pipe to an onshore storage facility and refining plant. This single ship contained enough energy to support a small city for one year.

Managed with a spare crew of just forty Filipino seamen, *The Illustrious Goddess* was only possible because of computers and modern technology. Both were needed to design and build her, both were essential to allow her to operate at sea. The ship had been controversial from the start, but her Hong Kong owner had insisted that she be the largest supertanker ever built. So huge was the vessel that it could not steam in the English Channel nor could it pass through either the Suez or Panama canals. But she was entirely suited to load her cargo off the coast of Saudi Arabia at Ras Tanura, the largest such offshore oil facility in the world, then make the passage to Japan and back, at great profit to her owner.

A ship of this size had had problems from the first. Initially she'd had an unplanned vibration that was finally identified as coming from improperly designed gears. At some expense that had been repaired. Then there'd been problems with the sides of the vessel when the ship wasn't fully loaded. They'd found it essential to maintain a proper balance of crude oil and sea pressure to prevent dangerous cracks from appearing in the structure. Next came a problem with navigation. So immense was the vessel that it had been necessary to include the earth's rotation when calculating its route.

The primary problem, though, had been control. She was pushed through the seas with just a single enormous screw, also the largest ever built. On most major ships two screws were considered essential to allow the ship to be properly steered and stopped in an emergency. But for reasons of cost, this ship was fitted with just one. During test trials it had proven extremely difficult to turn the ship from its course once it was at speed. Even worse, at slow speeds it couldn't be turned at all. Nor could tugboats budge the ship when it was fully loaded.

On top of that, the ship just wouldn't stop.

That was an exaggeration cited by critics of the owner for pushing the envelope to this extent, but in truth the ship was hard to stop indeed. Even with the propeller in full reverse, with the ship's inertia it took twenty minutes and many miles to bring it to a halt.

All of this caused Shiva great concern. It meant every move of the ship had to be carefully scripted. It meant always thinking far ahead. It meant that smaller vessels had to get out of its course because he had no way to keep the ship from striking them. He was certain that *The*

Illustrious Goddess had sunk small fishing vessels more than once when steaming near a coastline.

To perform his duty meant depending entirely on the computers to get it right. No expense had been spared in creating the finest software system a British company could design.

It also meant worrying all the time, which was why he was scanning the horizon for a glimpse of the Nagasaki offshore facility. The engines should go to "dead slow" any minute as *The Illustrious Goddess* began to reduce speed for the docking, but the ship had to be maneuvered into exact position before he lost much headway. Once the vessel slowed to a crawl, he wouldn't be able to dock her if she wasn't properly aligned.

But what bothered Shiva most of all was that technically even major storms were supposed to be of little concern as the loaded ship unnaturally rode the heaviest waves with scarcely any effect. To Shiva, that was wrong. The sea was the master, always. A ship of this size was arrogance; it showed a contempt for the ocean, and from that could only come a great harm.

"Sonny," Shiva said. "Do you have it on radar?"

Sonny Olivera glanced up. "Yes, Captain. I've got it."

"Well, I don't. There's a haze blocking it from view. Renato, shouldn't the engines be at dead slow?"

The helmsman, Renato Arroyo, scanned the dials. "I think so, Captain. Any second now."

Three minutes passed with no change. "This is cutting it close," Shiva said. "What does the GPS show?"

"There's no alert, sir. All's normal," Olivera said.

The ship continued plowing through the choppy seas as if in the middle of the Indian Ocean. "This isn't right," Shiva said finally, his seaman's instincts telling him something was wrong. "We should be slowing by now. How far are we out?"

"Fifteen clicks, sir," Olivera answered, his voice no longer unconcerned.

Shiva considered the situation. The engines should have gone to reduced speed at eighteen kilometers. "Check the computers."

After a moment: "Normal readings, sir."

Shiva began to sweat. They were well overdue to reduce speed. Aimed straight at Nagasaki harbor and land, they were going at eighteen knots. But if he went to manual, could he pull this off? He could slow the ship, but he doubted very much he could make the turn and bring it to a halt within the prescribed circle for the offshore facility to do its job. He'd never done it before and was certain he couldn't do it without a computer. But what choice did he have?

"Take the computer off-line. We're going manual. Helmsman, dead slow."

"Yes, sir," Olivera answered, glancing nervously at his captain.

Shiva felt no change in the ship. "Sonny? Are we manual yet? Hurry!"

"Captain, the computer is locked." Olivera looked up in a panic. "It won't take a command!"

"Try again."

"No change, sir." Olivera's voice rose. "It won't accept a command!"

Shiva could see the offshore facility now, shimmering in the distance. Behind it was the mainland and the city itself. He began to sweat profusely. If he turned off the computer, he wasn't certain he could command the ship. Even on manual the commands were sent electronically. Nothing was connected directly by wire or cable as in the old days. There was an override system, he knew, but he'd never used it before.

"Captain?" Arroyo's voice was urgent.

Being in command meant Shiva had to command. That was the single truth he'd been taught over the years. Right or wrong, the captain gave orders. "Turn off the computer."

"Sir?" Olivera said in disbelief.

"Hurry! Turn it off. We have to go manual."

A moment later Sonny said, "It's off. It wouldn't take the shut-down command, so I had to kill the power."

"Dead stop, Renato," Shiva ordered.

"Dead stop, sir." Arroyo took the control in his sweaty palm and rang the command.

The engines continued throbbing unchanged.

"Do it again," Shiva ordered, fighting to remain calm. The offshore facility was looming far too close on the horizon.

Arroyo sent the order again. Nothing.

"How far are we out?" Shiva asked, willing himself to remain calm. The captain must never panic.

"GPS is down with the computer off, sir," Olivera answered.

"Hard to port!" Shiva ordered. If he couldn't slow the ship, he needed to head it in a safe direction.

"Hard to port, Captain," Arroyo repeated as he spun the wheel. "Sir! Nothing. I've got no control. It's just spinning in place!"

The Illustrious Goddess continued at 18 knots like an arrow straight at the offshore facility and the port beyond. Shiva estimated the distance at under ten kilometers. Even if he had control, he couldn't stop the ship in time.

"Full reverse!" Shiva ordered.

Arroyo moved the control. "Full reverse, sir."

Nothing. The engines continued as before. The ship plunged ahead without alteration.

"Turn the computer back on. Reboot. Hurry, Sonny, hurry!"

A long minute passed. "The computer's frozen, sir. It's locked."

"Do it again and keep doing it until we have control."

"Captain, we're almost there!" Arroyo screamed.

Desperate, Shiva radioed the offshore facility and the port that he had no control over the ship. A small Japanese naval ship came out and signaled frantically for him to stop, but he could do nothing.

One mile out the computer was still locked and steering was unresponsive. Shiva sounded the horn as warning, over and over. The deep, resonant blast reverberated like the voice of God as the ship moved across the ocean, but it did no good except to draw a crowd of workers on the facility to the rail and members of his own crew to the deck.

The massive ship passed the floating facility with fifty feet to spare, though they cut several oil lines and crushed at least one small tender tied to a moorage.

Shiva could now see the port. "My God," he muttered. "Sonny, you still can't get the computer up?"

"No, sir. It just locks, over and over." Olivera looked up from his screen at the reality beyond the windshield. His face was dripping in sweat. "What's going to happen?"

Four minutes after rushing by the offshore facility, *The Illustrious Goddess* roared into Nagasaki harbor, smaller ships scattering in every direction. The enormous ship made the sound of an onrushing locomotive until it struck bottom more than one hundred yards out, but with its mass plus the surge of the engines continuing without respite, the ship plowed ahead as if nothing had happened. Like a mammoth battering ram it streaked across the harbor, then struck land, continuing almost without letup until two-thirds of the ship was out of the water. The sounds of twisted and torn metal were horrifying.

Crossing the port, the massive ship killed six men who'd been too slow to move.

Shiva and his disbelieving crew were knocked to the deck by the force of the impact. A deep moan came from within the ship. The ship's screw continued to turn and turn, the water behind it boiling into a chocolate-colored froth. Out of water, without the pressure of the ocean, the sides of the ship ruptured, and 4.5 million barrels of oil began surging out.

O O O O O O O O O O O O 15

Jeff's decision to form his own computer-security company when he left the government had been logical and, for the most part, satisfying. His involvement in the events leading up to 9/11 were known to only a few within the Company, who certainly had reason not to brag about his discoveries. The veil of secrecy over his work at the CIA also prevented him from going public with the details, though he'd come to accept that it would have done no good if he had.

Instead he plunged into the world of cyber-security, where he believed he could do some good. He knew the government was where he belonged, but it was too mired in bureaucracy for him to be effective. Perhaps he could attack the problem from the private sector and make a good living at the same time. From his experience, the level of security for most computers, even those for otherwise quite sophisticated businesses, was paper-thin. Their security programs weren't updated routinely or even activated, and patches released for vulnerabilities were often not installed.

In the worst-case scenarios, viruses propagated at an alarming rate. SQL Slammer, a virus released in early 2003, doubled every 8.5 seconds and infected 90 percent of vulnerable hosts within ten minutes. It was responsible, directly and indirectly, for shutting down thirteen thousand Bank of America ATMs.

A more recent high-profile example was the Conficker worm. It was originally launched by as-yet-unidentified hackers in late 2008 to serve as a general-purpose platform for malicious activity ranging from spamming to denial of service attacks. By constantly updating to use increasingly more sophisticated update, propagation, and rootkit techniques, it had managed to infect an unknown number of computers with estimates as high as 15 million.

Every year, every few weeks in fact, more and more viruses were unleashed, and increasingly they were searching for ways to steal money. One-third of the U.S. workforce was online, while millions more banked in cyberspace. Internet crime had outgrown illegal drug sales, netting more than $120 billion annually. There'd been nearly two hundred major intrusions into corporate computers, exposing more than 70 million Americans to financial fraud. This included everything from dates of birth and Social Security numbers to credit-card numbers and passwords. Ford Motor Company had had the records of eighty thousand employees stolen online.

Worse, the numbers were likely far greater, since so many individuals and companies had no idea their systems had been hacked. The government was largely unconcerned, or unknowing, for the DHS research budget for cyber-security had been cut to just $16 million.

Basically, it is so damn simple, Jeff thought. Viruses found their path into computers in two ways. They could enter through a vulnerability in an application or within the operating system itself, or they could inadvertently be downloaded by the computer user, who was tricked into manually running the virus, believing it was something it was not.

Regardless of the method for contamination, the virus would make its way freely into thousands of computers undetected before one of the security companies' honeypots, computers left online with no protection, attracted the virus. Thereafter, it could take several hours to several days for an antivirus company to create a signature and deliver it, known as a rollout, to their customers. Once loaded, antivirus software prevented the virus from executing, so the user with the program installed was safe against the virus, no matter how the contamination occurred. The antivirus software on customer systems usually checked for the updates once per day, though automatic updates were often never turned on by owners.

When a virus that exploited a new vulnerability was discovered, the antivirus company also notified the software vendor whose product contained the vulnerability so it could prepare a fix, known as a patch. To create, test, and make the patch available, the vendor would take anywhere from a few days, in the most critical cases, to weeks or even months, for vulnerabilities that were less critical.

In both cases the patch was rolled out to customers over a period of days. It could be months before most customers installed the patch, and many companies or individuals never installed it at all. When a particularly risky vulnerability was identified, vendors sent security bulletins to customers advising them to manually download and apply the patch rather than wait for the automated update.

The security companies were always playing catch-up. A new risk existed for a minimum of a few days to weeks. The system, if that's what it could be called, left a surprisingly large number of computers susceptible, even to viruses that had long been identified.

The situation was magnified because most home users didn't possess a security system, and if they did, they let its license expire, leaving the system exposed. Government computers were no less vulnerable. It was well known that the Chinese had obtained an enormous amount of U.S. national security data by entering computers believed to be secure. Other governments were doing the same thing. It was cheaper, and more effective, to hire hackers to work the Internet than to recruit, train, and support spies or to pay traitors.

Because of all this Jeff had no lack of work, particularly since his reputation preceded him into the market. Increasingly, however, he was seeing malware that traveled under the radar, destructive code that insinuated itself into computers without detection. It wasn't necessary to open an e-mail or even to neglect your antivirus software. All you had to do was connect to the Internet and the malware found you, if you had a vulnerability.

The truly destructive viruses, those that stole financial records, destroyed systems, and such, were more often like subterranean trolls. They were unleashed by their creators, or by someone working with them, and flashed across the core of the Internet, seeking a way to enter a computer by exploiting a vulnerability, an error or pathway inadvertently left open in one of its programs.

The viruses were always there, permanent, relentless. They never tired, never became frustrated, required no fresh direction. As they pressed their electronic nose to the security wall of each computer, they probed for that little mistake written into a program that allowed them to gain entry, undetected, undeflected by firewalls or antivirus programs.

These worms descended to the depths of the computer, burrowing down and existing like a living parasite, planting themselves within the operating system. They were designed to resist detection. To mask themselves further, they worked slowly at replicating clones, sending out new versions of themselves to seek new computers at an all but undetectable rate. They were a cancer on the Internet and on every computer they entered. They grew, spreading their electronic web into every space they could find. This was the future of all serious malware, one increasingly concealed from detection by a cloaking technology known as rootkits.

Yet years after the tragedy of 9/11, the FBI was claiming that Al Qaeda and other terrorist groups lacked the ability to attack America's cyber infrastructure. They didn't say the system was safe. No, they said that the terrorists didn't have the ability to exploit it—yet.

Bringing his thoughts back to the present, Jeff stepped from the subway station onto the sidewalk and stopped.

He blinked his eyes at the sudden light, trying to take it all in. The sight of nothingness where the World Trade Center had once stood, dominating the landscape, stunned him.

To his right, still erect and fully functioning, was the World Financial Center. Except for broken windows and some concern about foundations in the weeks after the attack, it had emerged unscathed. Account Resources Management was up and running after a six-month hiatus in upper Manhattan.

The company lost three employees that day: Cynthia and another coworker attending a meeting near the top of the North Tower, plus one who was arriving late for work and was struck by debris from United Flight 175 when it hit the South Tower. There had been a memorial service, but Jeff had been too overwhelmed with grief, loss, and culpability to attend. For the same reason, he'd not gone to the service the family held in Cookeville, Tennessee. Now, though, his anger was all on himself, and his burden of guilt was almost more than he could bear. He simply could not face it.

He walked at a steady pace around the enclosed site. With each step he found the enormity of the devastation overwhelming. To see it on television and in pictures was one thing. To be here, to see it like this, was something else entirely.

From time to time he came upon memorials, some official, most impromptu, commemorating the loss of one group or another. At the poster of three Brooklyn firefighters raising the American flag over the rubble that terrible morning, Jeff stopped.

What was the point in walking? What did he think he was accomplishing?

Jeff gazed into the gaping chasm. Cynthia's body was never recovered. Whatever there had been of her lay there, before him. He closed his eyes and wept.

ISTANBUL, TURKEY
SEFAKÖY DISTRICT
ISTANBUL TECHNICAL UNIVERSITY
TUESDAY, AUGUST 15
3:11 P.M.

Like most of the other students, Mesut Elaltuntas worked on his own laptop at the university computer-science center. The university had an excellent computer program, which was why he went there. They provided this room on campus where students could access the Internet with their own computers, since many of them didn't have Internet access at home. The room might have been on any college campus anywhere in Europe or America, except here in Turkey the air was thick with the fog of cigarette smoke.

Elaltuntas scrolled down the list of Web sites produced by his Google search. He was already familiar with several of them and knew they were of no use to him. Others weren't related to the code he was searching for. He'd already used one that suited his purpose; now he wanted another very like it. He pursed his lips and continued to scroll.

At first the idea of constructing new viruses had seemed simple enough. He'd designed a few himself and considered releasing them, but the arrest here in Istanbul of the cracker with the screen name Coder had made him cautious. Coder had bragged to everyone in various chat rooms how easy writing virus code was and how you could make money at it. Now he was in jail. Sure, his real name had appeared in newspapers and on television around the world, but that wasn't the kind of fame Elaltuntas sought.

But right now he needed a new base virus code. He already had the code for turning systems off and on. When he'd been given it, he'd had no idea what it did, but he'd spent some time studying the code and was now certain. At first it had scared the hell out of him, but once he realized that he was covering his tracks in ways that hadn't occurred to Coder, he'd been thrilled at the possibilities. Someone was up to something big and he was a part of it.

Elaltuntas needed to place that code into a virus with a proven record of exploitation. His employer paid a flat one hundred euros for each new virus Elaltuntas produced, but added another hundred if it had a larger than average degree of exploitation. Elaltuntas didn't know how his employer made that determination, but he'd been paid the extra hundred often enough these past weeks to figure his employer knew how to do it.

There! StopHackers.com. Crackers posted their virus codes in many places, but Elaltuntas had learned that Web sites that claimed to be fighting malware were actually a great source for the code. He suspected they actually existed for the purpose of disseminating it. It was posted right there on the Web site. Anyone could help himself.

Now that he'd copped the most obvious viruses and knew the remaining common viruses and their variants, he'd already used the best. Finding something for which a security patch didn't yet exist was his dream, but he'd settle for a new virus or variant of an old standby that looked to have fresh access.

StopHackers.com was a new Web site to Elaltuntas. He scrolled through the boilerplate that the Web master had lifted from similar sites, then entered a chat room discussing various viruses at length. He found a lot of chatter about a new one out of Manila, home of the Lovebug, called Doomer. It was a network worm, which meant no attachment had to be opened for it to enter a computer, and gained access by exploiting a vulnerability in Windows XP. *Excellent.* But the best news was that Microsoft had yet to announce a patch. That meant he would likely have at least a month of smooth sailing, and an extra hundred Euros in his account.

None of this bothered him in the least. Since he'd been a small child, he'd enjoyed breaking things. Too often he'd been caught and punished. Now, on the Internet, he could smash the biggest of things and never be caught. He found it thrilling.

Elaltuntas copied the code, then dropped it into his own cracker file. He studied the new virus for a few minutes, but didn't understand it. The inventor had been clever. Mentally shrugging, he searched for the point where he could insert his new code so that it rode piggyback into computers along with the virus. *Shit!* He went back to the Web site and read the entries in the chat room carefully. Thirty minutes later he found what he was looking for. *Stupid! I should have spotted that on my own!* Back into his own file, he pasted his own code into the location—tailor-made, it seemed, for just such an addition.

Let's see. He customized the code he'd copied to infect an unattended computer, then downloaded the virus. The girl who owned it, Melek, had asked him to keep an eye on her laptop while she went out for lunch. He'd smiled and agreed. A few seconds later the worm announced it had successfully dropped itself on the target. It had taken. *Excellent.*

Back at his own computer he sent an e-mail from his Yahoo account.

Date: Tues, 15 August 15:56 —0800

He typed in the address.

From: Wiseguy <wsgy17@yahoo.com>
Subject: new code

hve the code inserted in new doomer. it tests. is attached. when will u send money? do u wnt more?

Wiseguy

Elaltuntas attached the new file and watched the Yahoo e-mail account go through its virus scan with some amusement. He hit RETURN

TO MESSAGE and sent the virus. He'd check back later that day for his answer. Then he spent the next twenty minutes searching for another virus for his new code to piggyback on, certain he'd have a use for it.

Melek returned to her computer. *"Saðol,"* she told Elaltuntas with a smile. He smiled back. She'd never know how she'd just thanked him for what he'd placed into her computer, not unless she was secretly controlling a nuclear power plant.

MANHATTAN, NYC
IT CENTER
FISCHERMAN, PLATT & COHEN
TUESDAY, AUGUST 15
6:09 P.M.

Jeff walked to the law firm's building from his hotel, enjoying Manhattan in the early-evening hours of a late summer day. He passed joggers, restaurant owners setting up chairs and tables outside, office workers rushing for home or to join someone for a drink and conversation. Picking up a double latte and toasted bagel, he crossed the marbled lobby, then took the elevator to the law firm's offices on the twenty-second floor.

He entered the IT Center quietly in the event Sue was asleep but found himself alone. Jeff took his place and inserted the driver in the virtual machine. To see what the driver was doing, however, Jeff needed to use a kernel debugger. He set break points so that the machine would stop when it reached points where Jeff believed he might be able to study the driver's operation.

Going this far was both good and bad. Good in the sense he hoped to produce something useful; bad in that he was forced to go so far searching for answers. But something important was eluding him, perhaps more than a single something. The only truly good thing about all this he could point to was that Daryl was at least as fully engaged and she had far greater resources than he did.

The system ran a moment; then Windows hit a break point and the

debugger stopped the virtual machine, putting it in a form of electronic suspended animation. Jeff read the script, then entered a *g* for
"go" to allow the driver to continue. A few minutes later he reached his
fourth break point. Examining the standard Windows-system data
structures on the screen, Jeff noticed that the driver had made modifications to the control flow of several functions used by applications to list
the drivers loaded on a system. He launched a device-driver listing diagnostic tool, but saw no sign of the driver he was studying. The driver had
intercepted the utility's query and stripped the driver from the list before returning the data.

"Shit," he muttered under his breath. *The bastard's using a rootkit.*

Once rare, rootkits were becoming increasingly common in malware,
since they allowed malware to be hidden from security tools. With a
sinking heart he understood now what he was up against. Part of the virus, or another one altogether, was hidden from him.

Rootkits weren't limited to malware. In 2005, Sony had released a
range of CDs that were designed to prevent excessive duplication. The
End User License Agreement accompanying them was not complete in
that it failed to inform customers that the CD was installing a rootkit
onto their personal computer. More than 2 million CDs were shipped
with the rootkit, promptly dubbed malware by computer experts who
detected its presence. More than half a million customers innocently
placed the hidden code deep within their computer's operating system.

The affair turned into a fiasco for Sony. Early attempts to delete the
rootkit disabled the computer's ability to play any CD and, worse, caused
the computer to crash. The rootkit was also not very well written. Hackers soon found they could attach viruses to it, using Sony's own software
to cloak them from detection. Sony was forced by a public uproar to
recall the CDs and make a removal patch available, but the harm to the
company's reputation was done. A major international corporation had
publicly been branded with employing hacker code. The long-term consequences were incalculable.

Jeff ran a rootkit detection program, then cursed again. There on
the screen was unmistakable evidence of the rootkit. He'd seen the
behavior, now he had confirmation. As a cloaking technology, rootkits
worked by hiding files, registry keys, and other objects in the system in
the kernel mode of Windows. When a user ran a standard detection

program to see what programs were operating, the rootkit had many ways to remove the program it was concealing from the list being generated. In this case, the program being cloaked was the virus.

The next step was to run a number of advanced security tools, searching for evidence of code that would activate the rootkit at each booting. It came up empty. Then Jeff dumped the service-table contents, studying them carefully. Each should point at addresses within the Windows kernel, but within minutes he found two that did not. One of the intercepting functions was part of the ipsecnat.sys device driver that he had been studying. Now he knew which driver implemented cloaking. *At least now I can see if I can disable the cloak and expose whatever it's hiding*, Jeff thought. Opening a command prompt, Jeff entered the hidden directory.

The sophistication of this rootkit was troubling, he realized, especially when compared to what appeared to be the cut-and-paste construction of the part of the actual virus he'd examined so far. The rootkit was lean and cleverly fabricated. Jeff paused for a moment to reflect. What the malware was suggesting to him was at least two creators. That might be significant; then again, it might not. A basic cracker might have created the virus, then found the slick rootkit to hide it. He couldn't imagine anyone skilled enough to build this rootkit unleashing such a hack job of a virus. He wouldn't be able to resist cleansing the code. *What if they're working together?* he thought, wondering what the implications of that might be.

Jeff took a moment to text Daryl, informing her of the rootkit. A few minutes later she responded with a single word: "Shit!" *No kidding,* Jeff thought, before turning back to his work.

Next he stepped instruction by instruction through the driver, trying to discern the goal of the virus, without luck. Then it occurred to him there might be more than one, so he examined the assembly language he'd generated earlier. This was extraordinarily time-consuming. Long, exhausting hours dragged by as he threw himself into the brain-taxing exercise. When he could go on no longer, he slept on the couch rather than return to his hotel. At some point Sue returned. Harold appeared and began bringing them food at regular intervals, though Jeff couldn't have told anyone what he ate if his life depended on it.

One of the major problems he was up against, Jeff realized, was that he couldn't tell what kind of external influences were normally in-volved in this suspect driver's operation. Perhaps the driver had a helper program or some other external stimuli that caused its payload to trigger. Or it might have been something within the virus code it-self, even a standard mechanism in the computer's operating system. So far he'd found nothing to tell him why the virus had been unleashed nor anything to hint at what the purpose had been beyond simple de-struction.

Was this a financial operation launched by Russians? Or had it been a simple shotgun attack meant to cause immediate widespread destruc-tion? He simply couldn't tell. He was burrowing deeper and deeper into decrypting the driver, but still lacked the answers he sought to tell him how the virus actually ran when it was "live."

Just when he thought he wouldn't be able to restrain himself from picking up the computer and throwing it across the room, Jeff came across something that promised to be interesting. Even though the driver had decrypted much of itself, when it launched, it still left pieces of itself encrypted. With some effort he coaxed the driver into executing cer-tain code sequences that decrypted more of itself.

The newly decrypted code sequence referred to another driver with a more sinister name, bioswipe.sys, that it expected to be able to ex-tract from itself and execute. However, the second driver wasn't in the driver file he had, nor in the corrupted installation when he went back to look for it.

BIOS, or the Basic Input/Output System, was the code programmed into the computer itself that started the computer and was responsible for reading the initial part of the operating system code from the first sector of the hard disk into memory and executing it. Modern computers had BIOS that could be "flashed" or reprogrammed with new instruc-tions. Computer manufacturers sometimes made BIOS updates avail-able that fixed bugs or improved the computer's start-up performance.

But a virus that knew how to reprogram the BIOS could erase its contents, making the computer unbootable. Repairing such a computer was tedious and sometimes even impossible. Part of this virus was miss-ing, he realized, either because it had already been deleted or because it wasn't part of the variant installed on the law firm computer. Still, the sheer scope of this attack on a system with all the standard safeguards in place was astounding and underlined the enormity of the problem he faced.

Sue took a break, then returned, freshly scrubbed, munching on a candy bar. "Still at it, I see? Did you read about that ship in Japan?"

"No. What happened?"

"Its computer guidance and navigation systems failed. The ship slammed into Nagasaki, killing some people. I saw a video. The harbor is just filled with crude oil. There's speculation it was a virus of some kind. What do you think?"

"It's possible, but there's no way of telling if it's what we have here."

"Okay, expert. What can you tell me?"

Matter-of-factly, Jeff walked her through what he'd uncovered.

"I'm confused," she said, wadding up the candy-bar wrapper and pitching it toward the trash basket, missing by a foot. "Does it want to steal our financial information? Destroy our records? Or destroy our computers?"

"Good questions all. The answer is, I don't know." Jeff frowned. "I've seen no evidence of stealing information, but it both destroyed records and destroyed computers. It's malicious and destructive but, from what I can see, it's got no clear purpose."

"What triggered it?" Sue looked every bit as confused as Jeff felt.

He shook his head. "I don't know."

"Can you find it in our backup? I'm under a great deal of pressure here. Clients have figured out we've got a problem and are threatening to leave." Her face was creased with concern.

Jeff hesitated. "I should be able to locate what I've found here. But it's like proving a negative. If I find it, then the backup records are tainted and of no use. But if I don't find what I've got here, that doesn't necessarily mean something else isn't buried somewhere. I have no sense of how much I've discovered, and I'm almost certain to have missed something. I'm beginning to think there're at least two viruses here. And I'm dealing with cloaking. A great deal could still be concealed from me."

"But if you find nothing, that's a good sign?"

Jeff understood Sue's need to get this problem solved. Her job likely depended on it. He wanted to sound encouraging, but experience taught him otherwise. Cautiously he said, "Yes, as far as it goes. You could make a copy of the backup, I'll check it for what I've learned. If it seems clean, or if I delete the evidence of what I've learned here, I might disable the viruses, allowing you to boot up and see what you've got."

Sue brightened. "I like the sound of that."

"Don't get your hopes up too far. That's going to eat up a lot of time with no guarantee. I'd feel better if I knew more."

"If you crack this too late to do us any good, what's the point?"

Jeff hesitated. "There may be clues in the calling cards the cracker's left in his code. If we know more, maybe we can determine if the backup is secure before putting in all that time."

Sue stared at him a moment, then seemed to reach a conclusion. "'Super Freak.' My guess is, that's our key."

O O O O O O O O O O O 18

MANHATTAN, NEW YORK CITY
CENTRAL PARK
WEDNESDAY, AUGUST 16
7:36 A.M.

Jeff placed his foot on the cement bench and methodically began his stretching routine. Beside him passed a steady stream of runners, circling the Central Park Reservoir, one of several jogging paths in the park. When ready, he set out along the Lower Track, which followed the old Bridle Path. This was the course he ran many years ago when in Manhattan because of its forgiving soft dirt and its sheer beauty. He ran steadily, passing a few slower runners, yielding to others. His course took him beneath three lovely cast-iron bridges, and from time to time he caught a commanding view of the park in its late-summer glory.

Jeff Aiken had been born the youngest of two sons. His memories of his parents dimmed with each year as they and his brother were killed in a two-car accident when Jeff was six years old. He'd been spending the weekend with his paternal grandparents and remained with them thereafter in their Philadelphia home.

Joe and Wilma Aiken were adoring surrogate parents, though they were already quite old when they assumed the obligation of raising their surviving grandson. Wilma tended to the house while Joe was active in the Elks and his Masonic lodge. Jeff's grandfather died when Jeff was a sophomore in high school, and his grandmother passed when he was an undergraduate. Since then he'd been largely alone.

His shoes struck the soft earth with a steady, nearly hypnotic rhythm he found comforting. Perhaps the only aspect of his work he disliked was how it tended to keep him shut up in offices and away from his time in nature, running alone.

Jeff didn't find it odd that he was drawn to running. Loving though his grandparents had been, he'd had little in common with them. Feeling alone, he buried himself in books, then in mathematics, and finally in computers. Embarrassed by the elderly couple with whom he lived, pained to discuss the tragic death of his family, he'd made few friends during his teens, fewer in college. He'd long since resigned himself to a solitary life. His world with computers added a satisfying, though sterile, dimension to it.

Meeting Cynthia had changed everything. For a brief time he'd seen himself as part of a larger family, with a future that included children of his own. The pain of her loss had been almost more than he could bear, piled as it was on top of the loss of his parents and brother, then of his grandparents. The survivor's guilt he felt from not being in the car with them when his immediate family had been killed—added to his guilt at failing to embrace the unconditional love of his grandparents, and at failing to save Cynthia—was nearly overwhelming. But he saw no alternative to the course his life was taking, to carry on alone, to do his best, to make sure he did what he could so that others never had to go through what he had, even if his ability to help was limited to the world of computers.

His shoes slapped the dirt as he sank into the pleasant nothingness of the run.

MANHATTAN, NYC
IT CENTER
FISCHERMAN, PLATT & COHEN
WEDNESDAY, AUGUST 17
11:08 P.M.

Sue Tabor entered the office, then glanced at Jeff Aiken asleep on the couch, exhausted after a long stretch of work combined with his run. Should she go ahead and do it? Shrugging, she went to her computer and opened Google. She could no longer really contribute anything to his search, and she'd decided to follow the only specific clue they had. She typed into the box *Super Freak*. Time to learn what the name meant to the Internet.

"Do you mean: *superfreak*?" the Web site asked.

Sue glanced at the count. Just over 4 million hits. This wasn't going to work. Still, she scrolled through three pages of entries just to be certain. It was all Rick James in one form or another.

She deleted the space between the words and hit ENTER for *superfreak*. Now she was down to 195,000 hits, but it was just more of the same. Rick James.

She entered *super freak code*, followed by *super freak virus*. She spent an hour going through the various hits with no results.

Undeterred, she sought out hacker groups and began scanning entries for the name Superfreak or Super Freak. Nothing. But what else did she have to do? Two hours into her search, in her third hacker forum, she spotted the word *Superphreak. Yes!*

Sue backtracked on the thread, but the name didn't appear again. Someone using the name Dante had mentioned Superphreak in a discussion about security code in the e-mail program Outlook Express. But there was no information about this Superphreak, no hint of who he was or what he was up to.

Checking, she found that the site had an open chat room, so she entered under the handle Dragon Lady. As luck had it, Dante was in the thread. She typed:

> Posted: Dragon Lady @ August 17
> I have a question for Superphreak. How do I contact him?

Sue waited, biting her lower lip. Was Dante still in the thread? Maybe he'd gone on to something else. It might be days, weeks even, before he returned to this chat room. Five posts appeared over the next fifteen minutes, then:

> Posted: Dante @ August 17
> I cn pass mesg myb. Wht do u wnt?

Sue's heart was pounding. For an instant she considered waking Jeff up, then decided against it. She forced herself to concentrate, then typed:

> Posted: Dragon Lady @ August 17
> Looks like he does really good work. Have him contact me.

She gave the Yahoo e-mail address she used when she was forced to register one on Web sites. She watched the chat room for another half hour, but Dante didn't make another entry.

Just in case, she went to each of the forums she'd visited earlier and posted this message:

> Posted: Dragon Lady @ August 17
> I like your work. Contact me ASAP.

Again she listed the Yahoo address, then sat back in her chair.

Without giving it any thought, she crossed her fingers. *Okay, fat's in the fire.* On the couch Jeff stirred, then lay motionless. The sound of his deep sleep overwhelmed the all-but-silent-whir of her hard drive kicking in.

HELSINKI, FINLAND
KRUUNUNHAKA DISTRICT
THURSDAY, AUGUST 17
11:43 P.M.

Oddvar Thorsen lit a cigarette, blew smoke toward the ceiling, then stared back down at his screen and read again:

> Posted: Dragon Lady @ August 17
> Looks like he does really good work. Have him contact me.

Someone was looking for Superphreak. That was interesting. For a moment he wondered if the poster was even a woman, let alone an Asian woman. He thought about Lucy Liu in that movie with Mel Gibson, *Payback*. Now that would be hot!

He considered for a moment if the query was of any value to him, then copied the e-mail address and dropped it into his Thunderbird e-mail "To:" box.

> Subject: lady looking
> Dragon Lady at dlady1312 @ yahoo.com is looking for you. Sys u do gd work. Know her?
> Dante

Superphreak was peculiar. Kind of surly and more than a bit arrogant, he acted as if he were the only one who knew anything about code. Thorsen might hear back, or he might not. He wondered once again what this was about, not that it mattered to him. But since he did work with Superphreak from time to time, and it was always best to stay on someone's good side, he'd sent him the heads-up.

Thorsen turned back to his specific problem. He was being paid to speed up the load time of certain encrypted codes. Even with newer and faster machines, start-up times were noticeably slower once a computer was infected. He'd been instructed to fix the problem, but was making little progress. He took another pull on his cigarette and turned to the work.

Two hours later his computer pinged. Thorsen opened Thunderbird.

Subject: RE: Lady looking
Date: August 18 01:38 AM
To: Dante
u know hr? Wht does she wnt?
Superphreak

OOOOOOOOOOOO 21

Trying not to nod off, Jeff focused on Sue. Since midafternoon, she'd been working on an untainted stand-alone server. With her work CDs, she'd rebuilt the firm's standard operating system, then made a copy of the last nightly backup, before installing it into the server.

Jeff had spent fourteen hours searching through the copy of the nightly backup, seeking out the same signs he'd found in the melted-down server with the virus. He'd found no sign of a rootkit, no indication of a virus. The backup had appeared free of any malware, but he'd reminded Sue that not finding a virus didn't mean it wasn't there.

Harold watched them both with keen interest. He'd been responsible for seeing to the creation of the backups, so had decided to stick around to watch what happened. He'd called home to tell his mother that he'd be late and was standing just behind Sue as she said, "Jeff? It's ready." When Jeff didn't respond, she nudged his shoulder. "We're ready. Unless you'd rather get your beauty sleep."

Jeff blinked, then rubbed his eyes. "What time is it?"

"Almost midnight. It's Thursday, in case you've lost track."

"Right. Give me a minute and I'll be right with you." In the restroom, Jeff scrubbed his face hard with a dampened paper towel. He looked up at the mirror and for an instant was startled by what he saw.

Strain and exhaustion were written all over him. He laughed to himself as he realized he felt just as bad as he looked.

When he returned, Sue pointed to the coffeepot. "It's fresh. Harold went out for sandwiches earlier, if you're hungry." She watched as Jeff poured himself a cup of coffee. "We're set to go."

Jeff picked up half of a chicken sandwich, then walked to her screen. He was impressed with all the work she'd put into this and with her effort to get the law firm up and running. He wondered if Greene appreciated her dedication. "Cross your fingers. I've been searching for elusive code almost from the start, and the bastard's used at least one rootkit that I know of."

"What else can I do? At worse we risk the new server and some of my not so valuable time. It's not connected to anything. No harm, no foul."

Harold stood beside Jeff, looking on with concern, and Jeff gave his fleshy shoulder a light squeeze. Sue glanced up and gave them a wan smile. "Here goes." She clicked the mouse to boot the restored system and held her breath. When it came up, she logged in. Nothing happened for a moment. The screen seemed to hiccup, turned blue, and read:

Rebooting . . .

After a few seconds, the screen flickered and read:

NO OPERATING SYSTEM FOUND.

Then the screen turned black.

"Shit!" she said. "Shit! Shit! Shit!" She stood up and glanced around the room as if looking for something to throw. Finally, she slumped back in the chair.

It was as bad as Jeff and Daryl had feared. This virus was one of the toughest he'd come across. His standard approach wasn't going to work. He and Sue might get lucky—it was still possible—but with a sinking heart he realized this was all a small part of something much bigger. They were far more likely to sink into an electronic abyss than find their way to success.

"I guess . . . ," Sue said finally, "I guess we could try a copy of the monthly backup next."

"Like that'll do any good," Harold said, before he slunk out of the room.

WEEK TWO

WEEK TWO

"WE ARE LOSING THE MALWARE WAR"

David Lynch
Cyber Security News Alert
August 17

Security software companies are not keeping up with the release of computer viruses, according to a report released this week by the Cyber Security Consortium.

"Make no mistake, we are at war and we are losing," said Edith Hedberth, director of the CSC in Washington, D.C. "Malware is being released at a rate faster than our ability to counter it."

According to the report, the Internet is the new home of organized crime and is a hotbed for financial fraud. In the midst of what Hedberth described as a "virulent attack," no security software can offer complete protection. None, in fact, can guarantee so much as 90%. "They are all reactive and malware is increasingly sophisticated," she added.

Financially motivated cybercrimes are increasing at a dramatic rate, costing Americans tens of millions of dollars each year. "We hope this is a wake-up call, but are not optimistic," Hedberth concluded.

MOSCOW, RUSSIAN FEDERATION
DMITROSVSKY ADMINISTRATIVE DISTRICT
FRIDAY, AUGUST 18
2:07 A.M.

Vladimir Koskov was twenty-one, and deeply in love, when he and nineteen-year-old Ivana were returning from the theater as he described the future he envisioned for himself. These were exciting times in Russia, and it seemed to his fertile mind that almost any career path was available to him.

They had met at the university, where Ivana was majoring in computer science and taking a course Vladimir was teaching. Though skilled with computers, her interest in them had waned and she'd turned to languages, but they continued to see each other. By that night, they had been a couple for two years.

As they laughed and joked, Chechen rebels, in reprisal for the Russian president's latest crackdown in Chechnya, detonated a car bomb just off Red Square, striking at the late-night crowd. Ivana was walking beside a building wall, with Vladimir between her and the full force of the blast. She recalled only a blinding, silent white light and what seemed to her the heavy yet gentle press of Vladimir's body against her own. Waking in a hospital four days later, undamaged except for a temporary hearing loss, a doctor informed her, "You were one lucky girl, Ivana, to be walking with a gentleman."

Vladimir had been both lucky and unlucky that night. Lucky, in that thirty-four people were killed by the explosion while another dozen were seriously maimed. He was the closest to the Lada to live, but not without a cost. There, he was unlucky. The blast threw him against Ivana, and the pair of them against the wall. He had just leaned over to kiss her, turning slightly, and took the full force of the explosion on his back. His spinal cord was all but ruptured just below his waist.

When Vladimir swam back to consciousness, he learned in quick succession that Ivana had lived and was expected to recover with no permanent injuries, and that he would never walk again. The same doctor who spoke with Ivana said, "I know you don't consider yourself fortunate, but you are. The others are dead and have no life at all. You will live, and unless you choose to climb into a bottle of vodka, you can have a good life. It may not seem like that today, but it's true."

Vladimir didn't agree. His life was over. Ivana wouldn't stay with a cripple. His plans were destroyed. There were no more dreams.

But he'd been wrong, though for one long year he'd done everything he could to make his dark vision a reality. He'd drunk bottle after bottle of cheap vodka, called every friend and every member of his family vile names to drive them from his life. In many cases he'd succeeded, as he wallowed in a pool of debasement.

But Ivana was made of tougher stuff. No matter how hard he worked to drive her from his life, she stayed. She pulled him from despair and gave him life. Two years after the explosion, they were married. The next year she found their apartment, where they'd lived ever since. Life hadn't been easy. She'd worked all manner of jobs to support them, finally finding steady work as a translator.

Vladimir had long ago given up being bitter over his fate, though he couldn't avoid bouts of self-pity that overwhelmed him from time to time. He'd slowly learned to live by burying himself in the hacker world he'd discovered on the Internet. He acquired computing skills that gave him a worldwide reputation among those who did such things and regained some of the self-respect he'd lost in the accident.

Later, he learned to earn a modest but growing income, about which he was enormously proud. He'd become so skilled at writing code he'd been recruited by more than one of the new Russian computer companies, but in each case he'd declined good pay to remain his own man. He might be trapped in a wheelchair, but in his work he was free. To be employed by a corporation was to throw away his most important freedom for a paycheck.

Now, as he did from time to time, he reached over and laid his hand on the FireWire drive on his desk. He kept all his work in it and either took it with him on those rare occasions when he left his computer or hid it. It was too valuable to risk. The information there was his private gold mine.

Vladimir took a final pull on his cigarette, then crushed it into an ashtray. Time to go back to work. He lit another cigarette as he entered one of the chat rooms where he was a regular visitor. He knew perhaps a dozen hackers well from this one room. They exchanged problems, sought solutions, bragged about successes, but most of all they discussed hacking and the latest developments.

He opened his IRC chat client, then entered the h@xx0rd chat room. Six hackers were signed in and listed along the right pane of the window. A few of the names he'd heard of here and there—just script kiddies. A few were chatting, but often some who were signed in just sat and watched. Some of the names might be IRC bots, programs that monitored chat, which was no surprise, especially since the chat thread was about Internet security. That was the principal subject of the hackers who spent a lot of time there.

> Ulysses: prblm is that when I try t close bdcli100.exe it crashes
>   casng server t crash :\ tried in 2 box's now
> Saintie: you could close bdcli only using exit command in top
>   shell there
> Ulysses: thanx ☺
> Saintie: hxdef is simple, d00d, u hve t configure your inifile and
>   run .exe file, that's it but u shld know many rootkits are
>   working on NT kernel only if u just download hxdf archive
>   in download section, unpack it to some directory and run
>   main exefile it should disappear from your explorer or
>   whatever u use t manage your files, that's the correct
>   functionality, so try it and see where it works or not
> Xhugo: Thanks for all the sweet information here. I am looking

for information on detecting rootkits. Pointers
welcome ... Read the SecurityFocus articles, but want
more ... ☺ know!

A detailed description of rootkits and the means for implanting and detecting them followed. It was nothing new to Vladimir. The chat turned to computer security.

Xhugo: Don't be a fool! They can't fix all the holes ... there is
            always a way ...
Dante: Its not open like it used to be but at least any h@ck3r
            wntng to pwn the inet ...
Xhugo: They're all scum ... beneath me ... they cause trouble
            and it just closes down t openness net should have.... If
            it wasn't for all these cr33ps there'd be no need t tighten
            down the hatches.
Saintie: They're destroying it, d0Od ... can't you see? ... are u
            people stupid! ... the webs just another way t make
            money ... that's what its all about ... it's about filthy
            lucre ... they deserve what they get, and I give them
            plenty, believe me ...
Xhugo: j3rkov and sp@ts got shut down ... they gt taken in by a
            hunnypot ... the server looked wide open ... looked like
            a financial server too.
Dante: yeah, they're stupid shits too! ... I told them ... I heard
            they go p0wnd ... they were able to trace them down ...
            how dumb is that?
Pere: ouch! Not the way it used to be ... that's for sure ... you
            can't get into certain sites ... not anymore ... the time
            you could guess at passwords and user names is over ...
            secure firewalls and patched systems everywhere ... I'm
            working harder at this all the time ...
Superphreak: Don't be such idiots ... course you have to work
            at it ... u thnk they're going t just gv it away? ... nothings
            really secure, nothing will ever be secure ... u can gt into
            anything if u want t and spend the time ... u can steal
            money, turn systems off, turn systems on ... only thing

different is not everyone can do it anymore . . . newbieZ R
out of game . . .

Vladimir took a drag on his cigarette, glanced up at his poster of a
bare-chested Rick James with dreadlocks, then continued typing.

And there's people who pay for it . . . pay very well. Anyone know
Dragon Lady?

FAIRFAX COUNTY, VIRGINIA
FRIDAY, AUGUST 18
9:51 P.M.

George Carlton retired to his den, splashed brandy into a snifter, and took a sip. At his leather easy chair he removed a Dominican corona cigar from the humidor, cut the tip, then lit it with a lighter that emitted a blue-and-gold flame like a miniature blowtorch. Setting the lighter down, he pulled on the cigar, then took a longer sip of the brandy.

Carlton and his wife, Emily, lived northwest of Alexandria, Virginia, some two miles from the Beltway, not far from the Ivy Hill Cemetery. Their house was one common to the area, with a decent though not extravagant expanse of yard thick with overgrown trees and a hedgerow between each plot.

The Carlton family was American blue blood. The first documented ancestor, William, had come to the British colony of New York to serve on the staff of General William Howe in early 1777. He'd proved popular on the social circuit that consumed the interests of the British officers during that first winter of occupation. In general, his staff work was adequate and his American career was marred only by an aborted field command. A less senior officer took the blame for the debacle, and Carlton was transferred to England, where he was soon well wed. But within twenty years he had spent the family into the poorhouse. His oldest son, also named George, with no realistic prospects in Britain, emigrated to the United States.

For three generations the Carlton family prospered in America.

They were connected by marriage, schooling, or business to most of the new country's families of influence. But in the period following the Civil War, the family's wealth began to decline. Carlton's grandfather, Edward, had invested heavily in the stock market following World War I, and for a time it appeared the Carltons would be restored to their former luster, but the weekend he would have received a warning to get out of the market in late 1929, he was on his yacht with his sixteen-year-old Cuban mistress, and the family lost nearly everything. Edward took the honorable way out, though he botched his suicide, which he'd tried to mask as a boating accident.

Carlton's father, another William, served under "Wild Bill" Donovan in the American OSS during World War II, providing invaluable staff work. As a reward he was selected to be one of the five most senior officers in the newly created Central Intelligence Agency after the war. He and the fifth director, Allen Dulles, got along well, but when Dulles was forced to resign following the Bay of Pigs fiasco, William Carlton's career went into eclipse. He retained just enough influence before dying of lung cancer to see that his son, George, who had gone into the FBI following his graduation from Yale, received a favorable appointment with the Company. The transfer had been more than unusual and raised a few eyebrows, as the FBI and CIA were rivals and rarely exchanged staff.

With a stellar family name and widespread connections, Carlton's career should have flourished. Though the family had retained their Nantucket summer cottage, his father had been compelled to sell the surviving family estate in Maryland after the suicide of his father. The fact was, the Carltons were broke.

George Carlton had sought a wife with one concern in mind—to marry well and restore his fortune. A family name, especially in America, counted for nothing without the money to go with it. The woman he chose, Emily Langsdon, was a bit horse-faced with an overbite, but she had a fine figure and her pedigree was impeccable. Her family was, reputedly, so wealthy as to be beyond comment.

George's awakening upon his return from a honeymoon he had financed by mortgaging the Nantucket cottage was brutal. He'd told Emily that it was his duty as her husband to assume management of her finances. She'd agreed. He soon learned why: there was almost nothing to manage.

While Carlton came to learn that the Langsdon family was wealthy indeed, the details of the wealth were devastating in their effect on him personally. Emily's father had fallen out with his father many years before. The grandfather had seen that his granddaughter lacked for nothing, that she was properly educated and traveled, but Emily's father was omitted from the will and all but eliminated from the Langsdon Family Trust.

Emily would inherit no property and had but a single trust fund herself, containing a mere $500,000. It was managed by the family financial administrators. She received the income from it in an annual check. Upon her death the fund would revert to the Langsdon Family Trust and not go to her surviving spouse or children, if any.

It was, Carlton thought, a gruesome way to manage a family. It had come as an enormous shock. During the years of their childless marriage, Emily had been good about financing her luxuries from her own income, but the burden of supporting them had fallen to Carlton and his government salary. Had they lived a modest middle-class life, this would have proven more than adequate—he'd done reasonably well in the CIA— but neither of them had come from middle-class lifestyles. They moved in circles that required more than they had, and over the years Carlton had been driven deeply into debt.

His move to Homeland Security had been motivated in part by a substantial increase in salary, as well as by a falling-out with his director. Regardless, he had found a way to alter his financial position to the positive. Almost like a miracle, if he believed in them.

Carlton coughed once, sipped brandy, took another puff on the cigar. Things were looking up to such an extent that he was considering dumping Emily, who'd been such a disappointment. If the cash flow continued as promised, he'd be living beside warm water and sipping drinks with umbrellas by year's end. He could think of half a dozen young things he'd rather have with him, rather than horse-faced old Emily.

MOSCOW, RUSSIAN FEDERATION
ARARAT PARK
SATURDAY, AUGUST 19
12:11 P.M.

It was a beautiful day in Moscow.

Ivana wasn't working this Saturday and insisted her husband leave their cramped apartment and take some air. "You need to be outdoors," she said. "Away from this smelly place. You need to see some normal people, *real* people, and stop spending all your time on that computer talking with electronic messages."

To pull Vladimir's wheelchair backward out of the apartment had taken some effort, since he'd had new equipment delivered the previous day. With nowhere to put it he'd instructed that the man place it in the cleared path out the door. Before they'd done anything, however, he'd insisted on getting his external drive and taking it with him.

"If we had a fire," Ivana said as she stacked boxes, "you'd be trapped here. We can't keep living like this."

At twenty-seven years of age, Ivana Adamov Koskov was a petite, dark beauty. Like her mother—indeed, like most traditional Russian woman—she was a pessimist. If anything could go wrong, you could count on it. Life was to be endured because there was no alternative. The one bright spot in her life had been her love of Vladimir Koskov. Their short early years had been filled with hope.

The bomb had nearly destroyed them. Though she had emerged essentially unscathed, her beautiful Vladimir bore terrible scars and had been crippled for life. The day Ivana was to go to the hospital and move him into the apartment she'd rented, her father, Sasha, had taken her aside.

"What are you doing?" he asked, the smell of vodka on his breath.

"Getting Vlad, of course," she said haughtily. She had long since stopped listening to her father. "We have an apartment now."

"You can't be serious about this." Ivana's father was a veteran of the ill-fated Soviet war in Afghanistan. He'd seen, and once intimated that he'd done, terrible things. Since his discharge from the military he'd been adrift, never really settling at any job, despondent if not embittered, turning increasingly to his bottle. She'd watched her mother slowly retreat with resignation into the role of enabler for her father until she couldn't bear to watch it any longer.

"I love Vlad, Father," she said. "He is a good man."

"He is a cripple! What future can you have with such a man?"

"His body is crippled, but his mind is whole. I love him for who he is. Please, you're in my way."

"You're nineteen years old," her father pleaded. "Don't throw your life away like this."

"Vlad needs me. He can't live alone and he has nowhere to go. I'm late. Please, Father, I must do this."

That had been eight years before. Her father had never accepted the situation, but at family gatherings he was always cordial if not friendly to Vladimir. His drinking was no worse, though, and that at least was something.

Ivana had arranged for their neighbor to help her, and with great effort the pair of them managed to get the wheelchair and her husband down three flights of stairs since the elevator wasn't working. Vladimir had stoically sat in place, unable to help, resigned away from his computers to his role as an invalid.

But Ivana had been right. The weather had turned, and it was a glorious Russian summer day. Vladimir had forgotten the beauty of the vast sweep of the sky overhead, the smell of the trees and flowers, the familiar sounds of the city. For the first hour Ivana just pushed the chair to give him a full taste of the city. Finally, they reached Ararat Park in the heart of Moscow.

Families from across the city were gathered here. Most were enjoying picnics, while others were content to walk and enjoy the beauty. From a vendor, Ivana bought their lunch. She found a shaded spot beneath a tree set on a small hill from where they could watch the people.

As a couple with a small child passed them, Ivana said, "Perhaps we should have a baby."

Vladimir laughed. "What? And put it in the sink?"

"We'll have a bigger apartment soon."

"Maybe. But why would you want to bring a child into this world? You don't really think anything will improve, do it? You aren't that stupid." He watched her as he spoke. He often tried to bait her like this.

Ivana looked up. "A baby would make me very happy." Vladimir's body was scarred and much of it was useless, but in her mind's eye Vladimir was the same young, strong man to whom she'd given herself so willingly. He was handsome still, she knew, handsome enough to have turned the heads of more than one woman since they'd left the apartment.

"Maybe later. When we can afford one, when we have enough room. I can't work with a crying baby all day, you know."

"I'll see to it that doesn't happen. Anyway, you said you were making a lot of money these days."

That was true. More and more work was coming Vladimir's way. He was even paid in hard currency, and in the new Russia, hard money opened every door. Parked in an e-gold account out of the country, his money was growing. So what if he didn't know who was paying him? A cloud passed over Ivana's face.

"What's the matter?" he asked a bit nastily. "I thought you were happy."

"It's nothing."

"It's my work, isn't it?"

Ivana looked at him. "What if State Security is eavesdropping? You could be arrested. And me as well!"

Vladimir laughed harshly. "I'm doing nothing illegal."

"You're very secretive about it for something that isn't wrong."

"I'm not secretive. It's . . . complex, that's all. It would be pointless for me to try and explain it." He tapped her head, striking once so hard she jerked back, out of reach. "Anyway, it's nothing for you to be concerned about. It's my business."

"But what *if* State Security is listening in?"

Vladimir snorted. "I'd like to see them try. All my communications are encrypted so they can't eavesdrop. You worry too much. Just like a woman."

Ivana was close to tears. After a few moments she persisted, "They have resources."

Vladimir rolled his eyes. "They are idiots! They aren't smart enough to catch me."

"Catch you at what?"

Vladimir lit a cigarette. "Never mind." He reached down into the pocket beside his wheelchair and pulled out his MP3 player and headset. Within seconds he was listening to Rick James, his eyes closed, his head moving to the beat. Ivana could no longer stand the music.

She turned away, her face covered with tears. Maybe her father was right. Maybe she was throwing herself away on a bitter, secretive man. She stood up and removed her outer clothing to reveal a new bathing suit Vladimir ignored. She spread a blanket and lay back to bask in the sun.

A few feet away, an elderly woman caught her husband admiring the view and poked him in the ribs as she glared at Ivana. "Slut!" she said.

What if he was lying? Ivana thought. What if State Security stormed their apartment? A chill spread across her body at the thought.

ooooooooooo 25

Twenty-two-year-old Miguel Estrada stood across the street from the outrageously pink Del Rey Hotel in central San José and watched the gringos with disgust. *They're turning us into a nation of whores and pimps,* he thought.

It was lightly raining, as it often did this time of year in San José. Estrada stood under a canopied doorway with several others, waiting for the rain to stop. In front of the Del Rey Hotel, American, Canadian, and German men laughed drunkenly, clutching lewdly at the buttocks of the prostitutes working as waitresses. It was all Estrada could bear to watch.

He'd read that government officials were cracking down on the sexual traffic for gay men and children, but from what he could see, nothing was being done about traditional prostitution. And in the open like this! Something needed to be done, or Costa Rica would be perverted beyond recall.

The rain stopped, and people began moving away. Estrada walked another block, then turned to his right, entering a doorway beneath a sign that read in English FLAMINGO MASSAGE. Gloria, the regular counter girl and the owner's current girlfriend, was sitting at the counter. "Hello, Miguel. Rosa will be out in a few minutes. Have a seat."

The spare waiting room was empty so Estrada sat by the door. He glanced at the same garish travel posters he'd seen countless times before. Four minutes later, a loud American in a florid shirt with a grin on his face emerged from behind a curtain. "You take care now, honey," he said to Gloria as he walked out, ignoring Estrada. A few minutes later Rosa emerged. Spotting her boyfriend, she came over and tried to kiss him.

Estrada turned his face away. "Don't. I know what you do back there."

Rosa was twenty-six years old, with a Nordic look not uncommon to native Costa Ricans. She and Estrada had been dating for three months. "What do I do you don't like?"

"You know."

"I give massage, Miguel. That's all. I'm not a *puta*. If you don't like it, don't come around."

He sulked for a moment, then said, "I need to use the computer."

Rosa glanced at Gloria, who was reading a magazine. "Why don't you use the one at home? You spend all your time on it anyway."

Estrada smirked. "Not for this, trust me. It will only take a minute. Please."

Rosa shrugged. "Hey, Gloria. Miguel wants to use the computer for a minute, okay?"

Gloria glanced up from her magazine. "Sure. Don't get caught."

Miguel walked passed Gloria into the office. The computer was on and connected to the Internet. Slipping a disk from his pocket, he sat down and inserted it, clicked RUN, then waited three minutes as instructed. When he was done, he removed the disk and returned to the waiting area.

"Okay. When will you be home?" he said to Rosa.

She shrugged. "I don't know. Later sometime. See you then." Again she tried to kiss him and again he turned his face.

As Estrada walked out, Gloria said, "You should get a new boyfriend. That one's trouble." She placed a piece of chewing gum on her wet pink tongue and pulled it into her mouth.

"He's cute," Rosa protested, who preferred a boyfriend without a job, as they were less trouble. "Anyway, if I didn't support him, he'd starve. He's too skinny as it is."

"How was he?" Gloria said, meaning the customer.

Rosa laughed as she lit a cigarette. "Quick. We're going to need more condoms."

FAIRFAX COUNTY, VIRGINIA
SATURDAY, AUGUST 19
9:51 P.M.

George Carlton had been with the CIA for eleven years in 1999, when he was given the opportunity to travel to the Middle East.

Company policy was that when managers reached a certain level and possessed a specified tenure, they should travel. The idea was to broaden horizons and give them the chance to put faces to the names they saw in so many reports. The more personalized the operation of the Company was, it was believed the more likely managers would exercise caution when making decisions that could impact lives. These junkets, as they were called at Langley, were much sought after, since they required no real work. They were, more or less, extended vacations at taxpayer expense.

In November of that year, Carlton had flown directly to Paris, where he spent several pleasant days. From there he flew to Madrid, then on to Rome. At the American embassy, he was reacquainted with Meade Gardner, the senior State Department adviser to the American ambassador for the kingdom of Saudi Arabia. They had belonged to the same fraternity at Yale; not Skull and Bones—neither of them had been so fortunate—but Delta Kappa Epsilon. The association had served Carlton well over the years, though not as well as he'd anticipated when he'd been initiated.

Following the various introductions, the pair had retired from the smoke-clouded salon to the patio overlooking the embassy garden.

Amid fragrant Cuban cigar smoke and cognac they had reminisced. Twice divorced, Gardner was currently "between marriages" as he put it. Tall and angular, he was, in Carlton's opinion, a bit pompous—but the two had been roommates and good buddies for a time. "How do you like Riyadh?" Carlton asked to be polite. Through French doors, a quartet played Brahms softly.

"Disgusting," Gardner said, slurring the word a bit. He'd downed more than his share of Scotch since the pair met. "The Saudis are an arrogant bunch. They know they've got us by the short hairs and make no bones about it. If they turned off the spigot, it would be back to the Stone Age for us. It gives them clout and that's something they understand. Revolting people, just revolting."

Carlton didn't disagree. He had no love of Arabs. "What about your social life? It must be awkward in a Muslim country."

"You've got that right." Gardner made a face. "Everything's tied to one of the embassies. They house us Westerners in our own compound, and until a few years ago I hear it was pretty good. Booze, parties, babes away from home the first time. A little bit of home in the Muslim desert. But the Wahhabi mullahs objected and the religious police were allowed to crack down. Now it's as sterile in the compound as it is everywhere else in Riyadh. Five million Arabs, the men horny as hell. You ask me, they're all a bunch of perverts. They can't even see a woman unless she's a sister or wife. I can't stand a culture that puts its women in bags. A few strip clubs and brothels would set things right, if you ask me."

"Still, all that money," Carlton mused. "It must be interesting at times. It surely isn't all doom and gloom."

Gardner grimaced. "Oh, I suppose. The embassy parties sound more like board meetings at times. They're swimming in dollars, I tell you. They hardly know what to do with them. But they're accustomed to being thought easy marks, so they're careful as hell. They've got so many Western-educated men these days, they prefer partnerships to outright investments."

Carlton hid his interest, but an hour later he'd managed to receive an invitation from Gardner to join an American delegation of computer representatives to Saudi Arabia, though Carlton had been scheduled for Ankara, Turkey. The State Department was sponsoring the

trips of certain business representatives in hopes a few would land con-
tracts with either the Saudi government or some of the businesses
headquartered there. Carlton would travel in open cover, meaning he
would use his real name and passport, but his credentials attached him
to the delegation of Applied American Computing Solutions, Inc., from
Dallas, Texas. The owner of the company was the sole representative of
his firm, but he enthusiastically added Carlton to the trip when he
learned he was honoring a favor for the American Saudi ambassador.

They'd sat together on the nonstop from Rome to Riyadh two days
later. Peter Houser of AACS was a bit short and had gained a substantial paunch and lost most of his hair while prospering selling software.

"I was lucky," he admitted shortly after takeoff. "I didn't know
software from hardware, but I figured computers were the coming
thing and bought a well-run company. For the most part, I've just
stayed out of their way." He gazed out the window as the plane banked
over the Mediterranean. "You're not a spook, are you?" he'd asked
unexpectedly.

Carlton had almost smiled. Instead, he'd eyed the man as he replied, "You never know."

Two thousand feet above sea level, Riyadh was a sprawling traditional
Arab city with a distinctly modern heart. The Kingdom Centre, the tall-
est structure in the city, was a massive building of modern art more
suited for Brasília than the Saudi desert. The temperature was a balmy
eighty-two when they stepped from the airplane at King Khalid International Airport.

Houser announced that this was his first trip to the "Arab world," and
his curiosity was untouched by the slightest hint of anticipation. "Sooner
this part's over, the better," he said as he walked, his carry-on firmly
clenched in his hand. His next stop, he'd told Carlton, was Cairo, where
he was looking forward to seeing the Pyramids. "Can't see one damn
reason in the world to be here, of all places," he said, using his free hand
to gesture about him, then winking at Carlton, "unless I get a contract of
course."

The fourteen-strong delegation was met by a State Department public
affairs officer and ushered through passport clearance before boarding
three heavy-duty vans. Houser remarked that the glass seemed unusually
thick as they pulled away from the curb. "No need for concern," the

young officer said, "but there have been some attacks and caution is always in order."

Houser met Carlton's eyes with an expression that said, *What am I doing here?*

The drive to the Al Faisaliah Hotel in the Olaya district consumed an hour of Carlton's life he would never get back. During that time he formed the conviction that Riyadh should be placed high on the list of nuclear targets. If an exchange of such weapons ever occurred, it seemed to him the powers that be should take advantage of the opportunity to rid the world of this eyesore. Everywhere he looked he saw backwardness; never a smile on a single face. It was as if night had descended over the city even during the glare of daylight.

That afternoon he stretched out on his bed, took a nap, then dressed and wandered down to the hotel bar, only to discover the hardest drink being served was tea or something called a mocktail, fresh fruit juice served with Arabic coffee. The hotel itself was gorgeous; situated on the highest ground in the city, it offered a spectacular view of an uninspiring expanse of buildings, at least in Carlton's opinion. At seven that evening the delegation was taken to the American embassy for a reception.

The embassy struck Carlton's keen eye as a deceptively designed fortress. A modern structure designed to blend in with older buildings, it was elegant and state-of-the-art, for which he was grateful. Perhaps two hundred were in attendance. Traditional Arab dress was as common as Western-cut suits. With just a handful of exceptions, the only women were Western and their evening dress was far more demure than what he'd seen in Paris, Madrid, or Rome. It was like attending a cocktail party in Salt Lake City, he decided—except for the Arabs.

Most of the Arab men were wearing a *thoub*, the familiar flowing robes of the desert, with the red-and-white-checkered *shumagg* banded with a black *ogal*. Perhaps a third of them wore a formal, dark-colored, gold-edged *bisht*, a sort of cloak, over a dazzling white *thoub*. The few non-Western women were, he gathered, from India and Asia. He wondered which of the Arabs were in business.

Shortly after eight o'clock Carlton was approached by a middle-aged Saudi of average height, with startling fair skin and jet-black hair. He'd noticed the man earlier, as he was perhaps the most elegantly dressed of the Arabs and moved with an almost catlike grace.

"Allow me to introduce myself. I make it a practice to meet everyone I do not know at these affairs. I am Fajer al Dawar." Carlton took his hand and gave him his name, briefly mentioned his cover story. "Computers? You don't look like a computer type to me."

Carlton smiled. "I'm management. I don't know that much about them in detail. And what do you do?"

"I'm president of the Franco-Arab Chemical Company."

The men visited for perhaps five minutes before Fajer moved on. Part of Carlton stirred. He felt instinctively that this was the sort of man he'd hoped to meet, someone in a position to make all his dreams come true. Carlton wanted desperately to talk to him longer, but there was no way to manage it in such a setting and Fajer certainly hadn't seemed interested. So later that night, after Carlton had gone to his room at the hotel, he was surprised to see an envelope slipped under his door. Opening it he read:

> *Mr. Carlton,*
> *Please join me tomorrow evening for a private dinner at my home.*
> *I will send my driver for you at eight. Tell no one.*
> *FAD*

Carlton was stunned. It was as if the man had read his mind. He breathed a sigh of satisfaction. His first impression had been correct. He considered going to the business room and searching the Internet for Fajer's name and that of his company, but decided better. Saudi Arabia was a virtual police state, and he couldn't expect that even a harmless Internet search would go undetected. Better not to take the risk.

The next day he could scarcely keep his focus on the tour. More than once Houser commented on how distant Carlton seemed. They were taken to the Masmak Fortress, the citadel in Old Riyadh, and the National Museum that afternoon, which, as far as Carlton was concerned, was more than enough.

That night Carlton dressed in his best suit and exited the main entrance shortly before 8:00. Standing immediately outside was too obvious, so he moved to his right and stood near a pillar perhaps fifty feet away. His first year with the Bureau, he'd been assigned to surveillance.

He'd been one of a two-man team following members of foreign delega-
tions. It had been boring in the extreme, but his partner had taught him
every shadowing technique, every camouflage method known to man.

"We look at motion, mostly," he'd told Carlton through cheap cigarette smoke. "We're conditioned to be hunters and react to moving
prey. The best way to hide is to not move."

There were no shadows. Carlton didn't want to appear obvious, so
he stood motionless in demi-shadows between the pillar and the wall.
Six minutes later a heavy, black Mercedes pulled up and stopped in
front of him. The uniformed driver came to his side and said quietly,
"Mr. Carlton?"

"I am."

"Please?" The driver gestured to the now open rear door. Carlton
entered to find himself alone. Unconcerned, he was carried across the
largely darkened streets of Riyadh, but his curiosity was at fever pitch.
Forty-five minutes later the car entered the gates of a vast compound
on the outskirts of Riyadh. Carlton stepped from the car and found
Fajer, dressed in a Western suit, waiting to greet him at what was the
entrance to his home. "I'm so glad you could come. It will be just the
two of us, if you don't mind."

"Of course not. I must say I was very surprised to receive your kind
invitation."

"You told no one?" Fajer asked with mild concern.

"I did not."

"Excellent. I knew I could count on your discretion. Please. This
way."

The house reminded Carlton of the movie *Casablanca*. He sensed it
was vast, but there was no one to see but his host. The architecture was
Moorish, the rooms oversize with arched ceilings. The dining room
into which he was led was large enough for a banquet, but the vast
table had just two place settings, at an end. Fajer gestured to pillows
and the men sat.

"Red or white?" Fajer asked as dinner was served. A waiter hovered
with a wine bottle wrapped in a brilliant white napkin.

"White. Thank you."

"The rules against intoxicants are relaxed in my home." Fajer held
up his glass. "Cheers."

"Cheers." Carlton was a bit overwhelmed and willed himself to be cautious. This could turn out to be the most important meeting of his life, or not. He mustn't let his expectations form his interpretation of what was about to take place. He must ground himself in reality.

A succession of servants brought course after course of the most exquisite meal Carlton had ever enjoyed. A mix of French and Middle Eastern cuisine, it was done to perfection. Carlton kept the conversation carefully neutral and praised each course. Following a cloyingly sweet dessert, the only dish that disappointed Carlton, Fajer suggested port and cigars. "I want to show you my garden."

Outside was balmy, the sky overhead a velvet black. The men strolled slowly along a pathway that wove through the carefully manicured plants, subtly lit by lights rising no higher than their ankles. "Despite its name, my company is international in scope and not limited to chemicals, though we are one of the largest chemical importers into the kingdom. I'm assuming you've never heard of it?"

When Carlton shook his head no, Fajer explained how he'd assumed command of his father's company following Cambridge. "These are difficult times for any business," he said, "as I'm sure you know. Key to the success of an international company is information. You understand?"

"Of course. Knowing what is real and what is not, what is coming, is vital in most human endeavors."

"Please, let us sit." They sat on a carved bench beside a gurgling fountain. "Mr. Carlton, I have great respect for America and for Americans, as I have for our British friends. Though I do business with the French, I must confess that I have never understood them. No one in the world, in my opinion, has better information than the CIA." Carlton felt his heart jump. "Information, after all, is their business. You must learn all kinds of things not necessary to America's national security, but information that could be of enormous help to someone in my position."

Carlton maintained a poker face as he said, "What are you saying? And what's this about the CIA? Spies, aren't they?"

"Come, Mr. Carlton. We are both adults. I have my sources. You are the deputy director for—what do you call it?—the Company. A man in such a position is important, and very valuable to someone like me."

Carlton took a pull of his cigar, blew the smoke out, then had a sip of the port. He drew on the cigar again before speaking. "Actually, I'm a manager, hardly a deputy director, but you have the rest right."

Late the next morning, Carlton boarded his plane for the flight to Athens, sitting once again next to Houser. "Didn't see you last night," the man said.

"Had a touch of the flu, or perhaps it was just fatigue from all the traveling."

"Well, you didn't miss much. I can't wait to get out of here." Once the plane was well over the Mediterranean, Houser leaned close and in a conspiratorial voice said, "Did you get what you came for?"

Carlton thought a moment before answering, "I'd say so, yes."

ARLINGTON, VIRGINIA
US-CERT SECURITY OPERATIONS
SUNDAY, AUGUST 20
8:01 A.M.

Daryl Haugen entered the restored redbrick building through the side entrance, swiping her access card at the door. Inside, she stopped at the security desk, signed her name, logged the time, and presented her identification to one of the three uniformed DHS guards. She'd come straight from her morning workout, having only taken time to shower and change into casual clothes before coming to her office.

"Thank you, Ms. Haugen," a stone-faced guard said.

Daryl smiled, passed through the security scan, and set off for the elevator. All three men watched her retreating figure with mute approval.

The Lee Building had been constructed just before World War I. In its day it was state-of-the-art, featuring larger windows than previously used and massively thick brick walls since no steel support was used in the construction. Housing various private, state, and finally federal agencies of declining significance over the decades, it had undergone a major renovation in the 1980s and now was the location for her Computer Infrastructure Security Unit, or CISU.

Since discovering Superphreak, Daryl's staff of twenty-three variously skilled Internet and computer experts, most of whom she'd hired herself, had been on twelve-hour shifts, seven days a week. All previous assignments and holidays were canceled. Priority one was to understand the Superphreak viruses, identify their variants, determine the scope of their contamination, and organize a defense. Six of her staff were assigned to work directly with the private CSIA, Cyber Security Industry Alliance. The objective was to get everyone involved on the same page.

Since the CISU occupied the entire top floor of the Lee Building, someone could stand at one end and view every workstation and every member of the staff in a single glance. Daryl had seen the arrangement in a Tokyo office and grasped its improvement over individual offices and cubicles. She'd installed the new arrangement the first week after her promotion.

"Team leader meeting in five minutes!" she shouted as she stepped off the elevator. In the break room she filled her cup with coffee, grabbed a cinnamon bun for breakfast, then went directly to the glass-enclosed conference room. Setting her laptop down, she plugged it in and booted as she ate her breakfast.

Two team leaders entered over the next two minutes, each carrying a laptop and sheets of paper. Neither looked as if he or she had slept in the last three days. The third and final one to enter closed the door as Daryl began.

"Mercy Hospital in Brooklyn has four deaths so far, perhaps more to follow. From what research I've been able to do, there have been other hospital deaths. There are many incidents out there that just may be a result of the virus we're chasing. A British Airways flight all but crashed over the Atlantic, some passengers were killed. It's being blamed on a virus in the plane's computer. Now I don't want to sound like one of those TV shows, but I need answers. If this virus is the cause of all this, and potentially more, there will be panic. We can't afford that. The panic could end up killing more than the virus itself. We don't have time for idle talk. What have you got?"

The question was directed to Oscar Lee. Average height, lean with bright dark eyes, he jokingly claimed the building was owned by his father. From Berkeley, he'd followed the same employment path as Daryl and was recognized for his overarching grasp of viruses and his ability to coax outside agencies to help. She'd made him responsible for coordinating the effort with CSIA, since he already headed the team that liaisoned with them.

"The vendors aren't on board yet, but I've convinced a few people here and there to give this some time," he said, sounding weary and nervous. "So far we've got three rootkits identified. The first appears to have been released back in June. They conceal at least twenty-seven viruses, with different functions. We haven't determined what all of them are as of yet.

"Many of the variants are either missing an exploit code or have one that we haven't been able to identify. Those that do are mostly trying to use a variety of old exploits that work only against unpatched systems. The vendors report a surge in numbers of old viruses. We do have three that are exploiting a single zero-day vulnerability in Microsoft operating systems." *Zero day* was a term used to identify software bugs for which no fix exists, that aren't widely known, and that malware authors use to spread their viruses.

"Jeez," Michelle Gritter muttered quietly. At twenty-three, she was the youngest of the management team, and the only woman. Pudgy, though not unattractive, she was a chronic nail-biter. She moved her left hand to her lips.

"Anything else?" Daryl asked.

Oscar shook his head. "Isn't that enough?"

"Michelle?"

The young woman lowered her hand before speaking. "We're attempting to establish the scope of the contamination. As of a few minutes ago we have 964 referrals of malware containing the word *Superphreak* from end users. We're working on it and have managed to determine these referrals are primarily generated by six versions of the virus."

"I don't like the sound of that," Oscar said, shaking his head. "How many are out there hidden by a rootkit nobody's detected"

Daryl said, "It's our job to find out." She could see the concern written on the faces of her team. She'd hoped for better progress but knew the reality would be like this. Turning to the remaining team leader, she said, "Tom?"

Tom Gentry was the oldest of the group at thirty-one. Almost entirely self-taught, he lacked the academic degrees of the others but possessed a near genius understanding of computers. Daryl relied on him for his innovative thinking and his accumulated knowledge. His team was responsible for preparing the solution to the Superphreak virus.

Tall and gawky, he was always uneasy in meetings, and today was no different. Shifting in his chair, he gulped down a big sip of coffee before speaking.

"Obviously we need to have a way to identify the viruses so signatures can be prepared, then we need signatures that work for each of the variations. Superphreak is the recurring figure we are focusing on, but we can't rule out that the word might not appear in some variations."

Michelle spoke. "You mean there could be Superphreak viruses without the name?"

"Sure," Tom said, reaching for his coffee cup again and nearly knocking it over. "Someone else certainly knows more than I do at this point, but from what I've seen, the only really sophisticated part of the viruses are the rootkits. The viruses in general are of mixed quality and from a number of sources, some old, some brand-new."

"How about distributing signatures?" Daryl asked.

"Oscar's companies are probably our best bet for that. I think we're going to need a bunch of them." Tom wrinkled his forehead and looked her directly in the eye. "I just don't see how we can do all this, boss."

"The security vendors tell me they aren't getting any of them in their honeypots," Oscar said, seconding Tom's concern. "They're devoting their time to this wave of old viruses going around. We sitting at this table can see the train barreling down the hill, but we can't get out of the way or even get the rest to pay attention."

The room was silent for a long moment. "Do we have a sense that these are all the result of a single hacker?" Daryl asked.

Tom cleared his throat. "I'd say not. There's more than one person involved, that's for sure."

"Are these scattered hackers just jumping on a bandwagon? Or is this orchestrated?" Daryl asked.

Oscar hesitated. "I don't know if *all* of them are working together, but some of them must be. You know, boss, I have an idea. You can bet they use the Internet to communicate. They might even be in chat rooms." Daryl nodded agreement, irritated she'd not already thought of that. "They're sure to have left a trail."

"You've got a good point," she said.

Encouraged, Oscar said, "Maybe we can coax some of them out of their hole. You know how crackers like to brag. Maybe we can locate a few of these people and fool them into giving us some of the answers we're working at finding the hard way."

Tom brightened. "I like that."

"So do I." This just might be the shortcut Daryl had been hoping for. "See to it, Oscar. Find me three or four people good in chat rooms and forums, and let's see what they come up with. Let's keep it up, folks. We're not lying down for this thing."

PARIS, FRANCE
5ÈME ARRONDISSEMENT
GRAPHISME COURAGEUX
MONDAY, AUGUST 21
7:44 P.M.

Michel Dufour stared out the window and wondered once again why he was still in Paris. Every friend of his was either vacationing in the south or traveling abroad. Paris in August was dreadful. Hot, dirty, the streets filled with loud tourists, the waiters surly and sarcastic.

He sighed. What was there to do? The deadline loomed and could not be moved.

Pauvre Michel, he thought, *poor Michael*. Repeating the phrase his older sister had used to mock him as a child whenever he felt sorry for himself, he swiveled from the window and returned to his monitor.

He typed for several moments, then confirmed he was into the Internet access at a cybercafé he knew, one of a dozen around Paris he used. He wasn't about to leave any trails leading to the office. Next he opened a send box and typed:

Date:	Mon, 21 August 19:45 —0700
To:	RioStud <riostud69@yahoo.com>
From:	Xhugo49 <xhugo49@gmail.com>
Subject:	$$$

Money snt. Attached is doomer. Release, not from your home or work, ASAP. Confrm when done. More t cum.

Xhugo

Dufour glanced at his list, considered for an instant if it was worth his time to copy and paste, decided it was not. Instead, he opened another message box.

Date: Mon, 21 August 19:47 —0700
To: MgEst109 <MgEst109@racsa.co.cr>
From: Xhugo1313 <xhugo1313@yahoo.com>
Subject: $$$

Money snt. Attached is new doomer. Release but not from home or work. ASAP, then confrm. More t cum.

Xhugo

Dufour stretched, grimaced, opened another send box, then typed:

Date: Mon, 21 August 19:49 —0700
To: DanteHell <DanteHell@earthlink.com>
From: Xhugo49 <xhugo49@gmail.com>
Subject: problem

Load time still too slow. Must reduce by half. Hurry.

Xhugo

The Finn was full of himself. Always promising work he couldn't deliver. Thought he was hot stuff with code. That should fix him. Dufour took a long look at his work list, opened another e-mail send box, then typed:

Date: Mon, 21 August 19:51 —0700
To: Wiseguy <wsgy17@yahoo.com>

From: Xhugo2009 <xhugo2009@msn.com>
Subject: great!

Doomer works very well. Gd job. Kp it up. Will pay 1,000 euro bonus
for similar clean work with no existing patch. Want 10 more like last
one ASAP. Sugst u open egold account for transfers.

Xhugo

That was almost it for the night. Dufour dug through the papers
strewn about his desk but couldn't find another fresh list. He reminded
himself that he had to get better organized.

Then his fingers found a scrap of paper. Oh, yes. One more for the
night, then some wine and Yvette. He started to type *xhugo49 @ gmail
.com*, then decided he was finished with that e-mail address.

Date: Mon, 21 August 19:54 —0700
To: Superphreak <sprphrk@au.com.ru>
From: Xhugo1101 <xhugo1101@msn.com>
Subject: status

New product with u code works very well. Have snt money to u
egold account. Confrm u recve. We r on schedule.

Xhugo

MANHATTAN, NEW YORK
HOTEL LUXOR
EAST THIRTIETH STREET
TUESDAY, AUGUST 22
12:09 A.M.

A package, delivered by courier, was waiting at the front desk for Jeff when he returned to his hotel. Thanking the clerk, he rode the elevator up, all but asleep on his feet.

In his room he tossed the package on the desk, stripped off his clothes, then stepped into the shower, where he scrubbed himself top to bottom. Running the hot water over his body until his fingertips were puckered, he smiled briefly when he glanced at them, recalling how he'd called them "old" fingers when he'd been a child, wondering if his grandparents' age was catching. He toweled off, then slipped on the hotel bathrobe, feeling if not reborn than at least much better.

Jeff sat at the desk, fingering the package. What he wanted most of all was sleep, but he'd promised Daryl he'd do what he could to help. And, he had to admit to himself, no matter how tired he was, sleep might not easily come when what he was finding on his client's server was emerging as his worst nightmare. For years he'd complained to any-one who'd listen about the lack of real Internet security. Now it ap-peared that a cyber-attack might well be upon them. From what Daryl was telling him, the attacks linked to Superphreak were broadly tar-geted, meaning the cyber-assault was widespread and aggressive.

He had no complaint about his actual client. In other circumstances a man like Joshua Greene would have been ranting at him every day, thanks to the enormous pressure he was under. Instead, Greene seemed satisfied with dropping in on them two or three times during his work hours. "I'll take care of him," Sue had said that first day, and apparently she had.

Jeff had spent this entire day in a copy of the firm's monthly backup, trying to prepare it for Sue's booting. He'd found more than he had with the daily backup, but had no way of knowing if he'd cleaned out enough.

He'd located two rootkits in the law firm's computers but still had no idea how many virus variants there were and what triggering devices they were using. He hoped Daryl, with her much greater resources, would come up with something on that.

In the case of his client, Jeff had decided that one of the viruses was designed to destroy financial records stored by SQL Server, one of the more popular databases used by midsize businesses. If this same payload was in the Social Security Administration records, or company pension records, or in the computers that controlled Wall Street, when the trigger kicked in, the damage would be incalculable. His sense of frustration and despair increased with each new discovery.

His work at the firm was about finished, though, one way or another. Sue was going to attempt a boot again later that night. He'd been too exhausted to stay for it. He'd find the results out soon enough.

Something like this had been coming at them for years, and for too long he'd felt like the lone sentry to realize it. Not that long ago a hacker had detected an exploit in the Excel program and had the nerve to offer it on eBay, in essence selling potential access to every computer online with a copy of Excel. How many was that? Ten million? Fifty million? With so many cloned programs and illegal copying, there was no way to know. Each one represented a doorway through which any cracker could send his malware. And the guy who'd discovered it sold the knowledge over the Internet as if he were peddling a used Ford!

Jeff had visited Web sites where anyone could download rootkit and other virus code. The creators were just giving the technology away. Any novice hacker with a rudimentary knowledge of viruses could now cloak his programs or discover a new, nastier virus.

Security firms named variants with letters of the alphabet. Some viruses had so many variants they wrapped around the alphabet three times. One virus alone was known to have two thousand versions.

The Sober worm, one of the most proliferative ever released, actually communicated with its creator. The guy wasn't a dunce. The worm checked specified URLs on certain days to search for instructions on what destructive act to commit. The thing was, the URLs didn't exist. The creator knew the ones he'd planted in the virus. When he was ready to give it instructions, he created the URL on the day he wanted to tell it what to do. How did you stop something like that? Jeff thought.

The number of businesses harmed by malware was increasing every month. The public only read about it when ABC, CNN, or the *Financial Times* was struck. Though thousands of new viruses or variants of old ones were released every year, the great harm was coming from the ones seeking financial gain. You could now hire people to write malware to make you a profit, and plenty of unscrupulous people were taking advantage of that.

If it wasn't this time with Superphreak, Jeff thought, then soon enough such an attack would be mounted and bring the Internet, and a significant number of the computers connected to it, down for the count, requiring that everything be rebuilt from scratch. Billions of dollars' worth of information would permanently be lost. Businesses and operations necessary to maintain the nation would stop in their tracks. Countless tens of thousands would be thrown out of work; companies would fail. The cost to the nation and to the world's economy was all but incalculable. It would be what had happened to Fischerman, Platt & Cohen but on a worldwide scale.

Once the system was rebuilt, there could be no certainty the virus, or some variant of it, could not worm its way into the new system. The price to be paid for the current complacency was likely incalculable. Jeff couldn't contemplate it without bile rising in his throat. But, on his own, what could he do about it? And even when he'd had access to the powers that be, fools such as Carlton hadn't taken him seriously.

Jeff logged onto his laptop as he tore open the package from Daryl, revealing an external USB hard drive. He unfolded and read her hastily scribbled note:

*These are copies of disks we received late yesterday and today. Each
has Superphreak and each has a rootkit, as you predicted. They are
getting easier to find thanks to you. Each does something different.
Three more deaths have been reported. I'm scared.*

Jeff grimaced. He was scared himself. His ICQ icon blinked and the
laptop chirped. He opened the instant-messaging system.

DOO7:	Did u gt CDs?
JA33:	Yes. Jst startng.
DOO7:	Paswrd is Rubicon. Weve ID'd 3 rootkits. We nw hv 8 diff functns so far 4 the cloaked viruses.
JA33:	Wht r thy?
DOO7:	Cnt tell. Sum seem related to $ recrds, othrs t admin functions, sum t industry contrls. Thy seem intended jst t jam things up.
JA33:	What am I lookng for?
DOO7:	These are t ones we couldn't identify. See wht u can learn.
JA33:	I'll try.
DOO7:	Thks

Jeff hoped that her confidence in him wasn't misplaced. If her entire team couldn't identify what she'd sent, he doubted that he could.
For two hours he worked on the disk and made little progress other
than to cover familiar ground, though he was getting faster at it. Finally, his attention was drawn to the time stamps on a number of files:
Date modified: 09/11. The dates were off nearly a month. Odd.

Curious, he ran another forensic tool, then stopped cold as he read
the results. That was it. It had to be. The trigger to the viruses was the
date!

Jeff stood up and began pacing the room. Had he missed a changed
date on the law firm's computer? How many other infected computers
had the wrong date somewhere in the software?

Then there was the date itself. It might be a fluke. Or perhaps Superphreak was using the date as a trigger to make a point.

Which raised still another issue—could all the Superphreak viruses be time-triggered? Was that something they'd missed? Could that be what happened at the hospitals? At the Ford plant? To the airplane?

Jeff's heart was racing as he called Daryl. After several rings her sleepy voice answered.

"I've just come across something unusual on those CDs." He told her about the modified dates, hearing the apprehension in his own voice.

"The trigger is the date 9/11?"

"I'll check my client's computer in the morning. Your team should follow up too."

"Of course." Daryl hesitated. "Jeff, what if—"

"I know," he cut her off. "I've already considered the possibility that we're actually dealing with Arab terrorists. But let's not get ahead of ourselves. Let's first see if it really is the trigger."

No sooner had he disconnected than his cell phone rang.

"The monthly backup crashed and burned," Sue said, sounding weary. "Just like the other."

FORT DUPONT PARK, WASHINGTON, D.C.
WEDNESDAY, AUGUST 23
6:31 P.M.

George Carlton eased his BMW down the narrow, two-lane road, then pulled into an isolated picnic area. He sat there idling for five full minutes before switching off the ignition. It had been at least a year since he'd last used this drop box, and he was certain no one had followed him.

He'd had no idea how useful working surveillance for the Bureau would be. In fact, he wished he'd paid closer attention to his seasoned partner, because playing the part of the fox instead of the hound was daunting. It *seemed* simple enough to drop off a disk with information, but he knew how easy it was to fall into patterns.

During his time Carlton had played a small role in catching a Soviet operator working under embassy cover who'd returned to the same drop box too often. He'd been so predictable that the Bureau had set the location under surveillance, no longer bothering to follow him to the site. They'd had no trouble catching the American traitor who provided the Soviet operator with information, visiting the same drop box. From what Carlton knew, they'd turned the traitor into a double agent for a good two years, during which time he gave false information to the Soviets, before deciding his usefulness was gone and they had arrested the Russian, rolling up a spy ring.

So when Carlton had initially set up his locations with Fajer al Dawar, he'd insisted they be employed in an unpredictable rotation. It had gone as smoothly as he'd hoped, and Carlton intended for it to stay that way. Still, during the years of their association, as he preferred to think of it, he always experienced a bit of angst whenever he dropped off a disk on the way home from work.

At their first meeting in Riyadh years ago, Carlton had given Fajer a Hotmail address for contacting him. "Only use it once," Carlton had cautioned. "When we meet next, I'll have a more secure system for communication worked out," certain that Fajer was impressed with his caution and expertise.

They'd met for the second time in New York City four months later. Fajer was attending various business meetings on behalf of the Saudi government, as Carlton understood it, and requested that they meet, bringing along his first contribution of information. Carlton had stayed at a cheap hotel on Broadway where they'd allowed him just to flash his driver's license so he could register under a false name and pay in cash for two nights. He'd told Emily he was away on business, and though such trips for him were rare, she'd not so much as lifted her nose from her Sidney Sheldon novel.

In the end, Carlton had left it to Fajer to come to his small room. Better to risk that then to travel about the city, have the bad luck of someone spotting him, then have to answer questions.

Fajer had arrived on time, dressed in a Western suit and unaccompanied, as Carlton had requested. They'd shaken hands, and as they sat facing one another, Carlton said, "Forgive the hotel. I was able to use cash and a false name."

"A wise precaution." Then came a round of courtesies that Carlton bore patiently. Finally Fajer asked, "Do you have something for me?"

"Yes," Carlton said, patting his jacket pocket, "but I want to go over some of the terms again."

"Of course. You've had some months to reconsider my proposal. It is only natural that you would have questions." Fajer smiled, a man accustomed to being in complete command of every situation.

"The use of this material is entirely commercial, as you said?"

"Absolutely. And you control what it is you give me. If you are concerned the information could have any other use, withhold it. I will never know."

"I ask because I am not a traitor."

"Of course not," Fajer assured him. "We are both honorable men. There is no question of that." Fajer pulled a cigarette from a packet and held it up in question. Carlton nodded agreement, though he was in a nonsmoking room.

After returning from his junket, Carlton had scoured the Internet for everything he could find about the Franco-Arab Chemical Company—Franco-Arabe Chimique Compagnie, or FACC, as it was better known. Fajer was all but impossible to find, identified only as the company's Saudi owner. The name of the company, Carlton discovered, was a bit of a misnomer. While at one time it had apparently been the primary importer of various chemicals into the Saudi kingdom, it was now primarily an importer of oil-production equipment, computer-related electronics, and electronics in general.

Carlton had applied himself in determining just what kind of information would be of use to such a company, while being the most profitable for him. At home, he'd conducted extensive Internet research on Saudi Arabia and oil to learn what was in the public domain, then at the office he'd accessed databases available to him and compared the two. He'd found several strategic reports prepared by the CIA he thought Fajer would want and downloaded them. Using a laptop he bought just for this purpose, he vetted the material at home, reducing it to bullet points with short generic summaries, which he printed on standard stock paper he was careful never to touch. That way, should the information get beyond Fajer, its original source could not be identified. Between reports to the Saudi, Carlton planned to keep the laptop in his bank deposit box.

That winter Carlton had surprised Emily with a week's vacation in Aruba. They'd never taken a holiday in the winter before, and she'd been thrilled. While she lost money at one of the casinos, he'd established a numbered offshore bank account for himself, one he could access and control via the Internet. Since returning home he'd been cautious never to access it with one of his own computers or those of the CIA or Homeland Security. As an added level of security, all payments from Fajer were wired to a GoldMoney account he'd established. From there it went to Aruba. The money was as untraceable as twenty-first-century technology made possible.

During that hotel room meeting Carlton had said, "In case I didn't make it clear when we first met at your lovely home, I have no interest in this unless it is very profitable." Fajer had nodded his head. "Here is the information from two Company reports you might find of interest." Carlton handed him a manila folder.

"And here," he continued, giving Fajer a printed sheet of paper, "is the account into which you are to wire the money. If it is enough, we will meet again." He'd then briefed Fajer on the various drop boxes he intended to use. "Our personal meetings must be infrequent. None is even better. I mean no disrespect, but each time I see you increases the likelihood I'll be detected."

Fajer nodded as if impressed. "I understand and agree, though from time to time a personal meeting may be necessary."

"The American government views the release of commercial data the same way it would if I were behaving as a spy."

Fajer pursed his lips. "I wasn't aware of that. We must be very careful, in that case. There is much more at risk here than your career. Why not simply e-mail the material to me?"

Carlton had considered that very idea. He'd checked with Jeff Aiken of his Cyberterrorism Unit on Internet security, someone whose expertise in this regard he trusted, and though he'd understood e-mail was usually easy to trace, efforts could be made to conceal it. He decided that was too complicated for him and not worth bothering with. Besides, he understood that the NSA programs monitoring e-mail were highly sophisticated, and he was certain his messages would be spotted. No, the old proven methods were best—except hereafter he'd leave the material on the less bulky disks.

"The drops are safer," he'd answered. Fajer had not pursued the matter.

Those two initial reports had garnered Carlton $50,000. Over the years, Carlton had taken in half a million dollars from Fajer, transferring data to him on average just twice a year. The money had made possible his new car and better vacations. He'd also paid off his personal debt, being careful to do so slowly. Only now was he in a position to start piling up the money. With a bit of luck, Carlton was of the opinion he'd be retiring early from DHS. And since most of his assets didn't legally exist, a divorce was likely in the cards.

He'd only met with Fajer twice since that 2000 meeting in New

York City. The last had been in Arlington, Virginia, the previous June. This time Fajer had taken a modest hotel room, and as before, they met indoors.

Following the exchange of the usual pleasantries and the information Carlton had brought, Fajer had crossed his legs, taken a long moment to light an elegantly thin cigarette, then said, "I have an associate in Paris. The relationship between us is very complicated, and you'd have to be an Arab to understand it. The bottom line, as you Americans so delightfully say, is that I have a family obligation with this person I must fulfill. I don't like it, but I have no alternative. I hope you understand."

Carlton felt a tingle along his spine. He'd been trained in the art of espionage, what was then called tradecraft, and could not view his relationship with Fajer without considerable suspicion. Their arrangement had gone on much longer than he'd initially thought it would, so long he'd become accustomed to the idea that it would continue unchanged for another few years. Now he wondered if it had all been a setup, aimed for this very moment.

"This associate is engaged in the use of computer viruses to obtain financial information. He then draws money from those accounts."

"Theft."

Fajer looked in pain at the word. "I assure you this is as unpleasant for me as for you. What I require is quite simple. I must know if the government is alerted to an extensive network engaged in planting code on a large number of computers. That is all."

"The government is a big place."

"Of course. I mean within your province. No more."

"For how long?"

Fajer shrugged. "I'm not an expert on these things, but as I understand it, the worms, if that's the right word, are being quietly planted now. Once enough are in place, then at a predetermined point they will all be activated at once. I have explained that I can only assist this one time."

"Does anyone know about me?"

Fajer looked horrified. "Of course not! My word of honor! It is assumed that someone in my position has contacts. I was just asked to use them. This unpleasantness repays an obligation, and I will be considerably in your debt. You've been very helpful to me these last years, and I've come to regard us as friends. I wouldn't do anything to jeopardize that. If there was any other way, you can be assured I'd do it."

Carlton took time to retrieve a bottle of water from the minibar and open it. He took a sip, then said, "I don't know . . ."

"My personal guarantee to you will be one million dollars, half to be paid now, half when the operation is finished, sometime before the end of the year." Carlton was motionless. "In addition, you will be paid five percent of what is collected."

"How much will that be?"

Fajer smiled. "I have no faith in such a figure. It seems too ridiculous. I asked the same question and was told your share would be no less than fifty million dollars." Fajer stopped, stubbed one cigarette out, then elegantly lit another.

Fifty million dollars! Carlton's mind raced at the possibility. He could retire at the end of the year, begin his new life. But did he trust Fajer? Was he hearing the truth? An Internet financial scam seemed plausible enough, but it was very different from what they'd been doing. It was outright theft, and if a den of thieves fell apart, who knew how it would end?

"Are you quite certain I'll be kept out of it?" he asked. Risk, his broker often said, was directly associated with return.

The Arab placed his hand to his heart. "On my honor."

Carlton willed himself to slow down, to think this through, but he found his mind a fog. *Fifty million dollars!* He couldn't get past the number. "I can do this."

"Excellent," Fajer said, smiling. "We will continue with the drops as before, and I still desire the kind of information you've been providing. There is no change in that, but I ask you to set up an electronic mail system for contacting me in the event you learn something definitive on this other business. I will leave it to you."

That had been just over two months ago. The first half million was safely in his Aruba account, invested in a balanced portfolio. Carlton stepped from the car and walked to a picnic table where he sat, as if lost in thought. Instead, he surreptitiously scanned the area to be certain he was not being observed. Satisfied, he walked to a tree as if to urinate. As he stood there, he slipped the disk into a hole. A few minutes later he was on the highway, expecting to be home within the half hour.

LONDON, UNITED KINGDOM
SOUTH LAUREL ROAD
THURSDAY, AUGUST 24
7:09 A.M.

Brian Manfield awoke with a start.

He'd slept with his window undraped so that the first rays of the rising sun flooded the small room with light. He hated alarm clocks, though one was set on the stand beside his bed. He reached across the naked back of the young woman and switched it off.

In the bathroom Manfield turned on the shower and, as he waited for the water to warm, urinated at great length in the toilet. Finished, he climbed into the shower, where he washed and shaved. Six feet two inches tall, weighing 185 pounds, Manfield was fit and worked to stay that way. With thick dark hair and deep blue eyes inherited from his mother, he was exceptionally handsome. After toweling off, he slipped on a robe he'd acquired at the Carlyle in Manhattan, then went to the kitchen for his usual breakfast of fruit, toast, marmalade, and tea.

Outside was one of those sparkling days London sees too rarely. He carried his breakfast onto his balcony and ate standing up, taking in the expanse of the old city. He loved London. He'd spent most of his adult life here and couldn't imagine living anywhere else.

In the kitchen he carefully washed the dishes in the sink, then set them to drain. Back in the bedroom he meticulously dressed in a startling white broadcloth shirt with striped tie and a nearly black Anderson &

Sheppard suit from Savile Row. Finally, he slipped on the black bank-er's shoes he preferred.

Caroline Bynum stirred in the bed as he slipped on his gold Rolex. Not yet twenty years old, born with more money than God, she was crazy about him, still in the early bloom of the relationship.

"Caro," he said quietly. "I have to leave now. Take your time. Lock up when you go, there's a dear. I'll call later today when I'm free." The young woman gave a grunt, then lapsed into deep sleep. Manfield smiled, took his cell phone from on top of the dresser, and slipped it into his jacket pocket.

It was just a ten-minute walk to his office. On such a beautiful day, he never considered driving or taking a taxi. Arriving five minutes early, he greeted the receptionist, then went straight to his office, where he perused the *Financial Times* as he had another cup of tea. Then he checked his e-mail, dashed off four replies, and settled in with the newspaper.

Special Applications Security, or SAS as it was known, had been created twenty years before by two former Special Air Service opera-tives who selected the name for its meaningful initials. Five years ear-lier they'd sold the lucrative international company to Lanson Security, one of the UK's oldest security companies. SAS had, however, been largely untouched by the transition. The company specialized in secu-rity measures and hardware for private companies and small govern-ments worldwide. The former manager had been named president of the company and business had gone on as before.

Manfield had worked at SAS for just over three years and was con-sidered the company's brightest star. He spoke five languages, which had proven helpful to the company in recent years, and was adept at blending in with various cultures. He traveled on average eight times a year for the company, his usual trip lasting two weeks. Though he could present and pitch the latest offerings in terms of security gates and twenty-first-century technology, he was most skilled with small weap-ons and was inevitably dispatched when an order for such was in the offing. More than once his consummate skill with the German HK MP-5 submachine gun had resulted in a larger-than-expected order. He boasted he could write his name with a burst of automatic fire from fifty yards, then did so.

Except that the name he wrote was not really his own. Brian Man-field was born Borz Mansur in Grozny, Chechnya, to a British mother, a devoted Communist, and Chechnyan father, at that time a general in the Soviet army. Until the fall of the Soviet empire, Borz had lived in the Soviet Union, attending school in Moscow while living with his parents. When Dzhokhar Dudayev declared Chechen independence in 1991, Borz was eleven years old, so his father had sent mother and son to London for safety. Borz's father had then flown to Grozny, where he'd promptly sided with the rebels against the Russian army.

When Russia invaded in 1994, General Mansur had organized the ongoing resistance after the occupation and had directed guerrilla operations from the Caucasus Mountains. Three times he left to seek help from various affluent Muslims, once managing to reach London for a brief visit with his wife and son, whom he decided to take back with him.

In 1996, following a period of phony negotiations, the Russians once again invaded the country. This time Borz took part in the fighting, where he proved adept at night ambushes and the assassination of Russian officers. With his perfect Russian and European looks he would don a Russian uniform, then strike terror behind the lines. Shortly before hostilities largely ended that August, Borz's father was killed, betrayed by the Russians, who violated a peace parley.

Borz returned to London, where he resumed his formal education. At the same time, his mother directed that he anglicize his name. Now in his thirties; he knew no one who was aware of his past. For all appearances and purposes, he was Brian Manfield, the perfect English gentleman. If people noticed that he never ate pork sausage, or if they believed they'd seen someone looking like him emerging from a mosque, they thought nothing more of it.

At three that afternoon Manfield called Caro. "Are you up yet?"

"Of course, silly. Been up for hours. I want to see you."

Manfield chuckled. "Soon enough. How about a drink at six, then some dinner?"

"I know what I want to eat, and it's not dinner."

"Save it for dessert. I will."

WEEK THREE

INCREASE IN CYBERCRIME DRAMATIC

By Ursula White
Global Computer News Service
August 24

LAS VEGAS—In a speech to computer software providers, Michael Elliot, president of Internet Security Alliance, said that cybercrime is the greatest threat to American prosperity since the depression of the 1930s. "Effective software to stop it in its tracks is vital for any company," he said, adding, "Sadly, even companies that believe they are protected are running computer systems wide-open to incursions."

Speaking to a gathering estimated at 4,000, Elliot related several stories of looting by cybercriminals, one in excess of $1 million. Malware specially crafted to obtain financial information from home and company computers is on the increase and "is more effective all the time." One Fortune 500 company had many of its financial records encrypted and was required to pay a ransom of $100,000 for the key to restore the files.

Today's cybercriminals have abandoned widespread attack against corporate firewalls for the specific targeting of individual computers which will likely hold sensitive financial information. "The sky's the limit when it comes to cyberfraud," he said in conclusion. "We live in a cyber world at our own peril."

MOSCOW, RUSSIAN FEDERATION
TVERSKOE ADMINISTRATIVE DISTRICT
FRIDAY, AUGUST 25
4:06 P.M.

Ivana Koskov listened intently to her earphones, then said into the microphone, "The port terminals must have a significantly increased capacity on the Pacific Coast in order for us to . . ."

Listening to her steady voice was Boris Velichkovsky, the managing director for resource development and logistics for Yukos Oil and Gas Company, the largest oil company in Russia. He'd once served as deputy Soviet ambassador to the United Nations and preferred this method of translation in business meetings, where the various translators sat in another room, separated by a one-way mirror. One was assigned to each foreign speaker in attendance and was responsible for both translating from Russian into the foreign language, and from the foreign language back into Russian.

Ivana was highly proficient in English and Italian and was working hard on her French. Next would be Spanish, of which she had only a rudimentary understanding. She'd been hired for this job shortly after the former Yukos CEO, Mikhail Khodorkovsky, had been sentenced to nine years in prison for tax evasion. It was widely understood that his true crime had been to build the enormously wealthy Yukos from the corpse of the old Soviet Union, then fail to cut in the Russian president and his minions. Now he was paying the price.

Ivana had never met Khodorkovsky. Few in the company ever spoke of him. It was as if he'd never existed. But that was Russia, she'd told her husband. Czars, Party chairmen, presidents, it was all the same. The powerful all seemed to vanish in the night, to disappear as totally as if they'd never existed at all. Ivana's mother had told her of working in the old Ministry of Propaganda, cutting photographs of the vanished from archived newspapers.

Now the Texan was speaking. She seamlessly switched into Russian, glancing at her watch. It would soon be five. She couldn't see this meeting lasting much longer. Velichkovsky would want to start the eating and drinking soon enough. Only after everyone had been lubricated with bottles of vodka would the real haggling and deal making take place. This was, as Velichkovsky had once told her with a lecherous grin, just so much foreplay.

This had also been the same time he'd suggested a significant promotion would be hers if she'd just join him on a foreign trip and see to his every need. His last traveling mistress had done well for herself, he'd pointed out. Ivana had been firm in her rejection and expected to be punished, but he'd just laughed, patted her good-naturedly on the back, and called her his *хорошая девочка*, his "good girl."

The years of marriage to Vladimir had been demanding, far more demanding than her young heart had ever imagined. In many ways her father had been right in his advice, and she'd come to understand he'd spoken out of love for her rather than a dislike of Vladimir. She'd labored at one menial job after another, usually two or three at a time, to support them. Finally, she'd taken a job cleaning the offices of Interport, Inc., one of the new American companies that had set up business in Moscow.

The company, concerned with security, had supervised all the cleaning and maintenance staff with one of their own, a good-natured third-generation Russian Jew from New York, named Annie. "Actually it's Anastasya," she'd said when they first met, "but only my grandmother calls me that."

Over the following months, the two women had grown quite close. Annie came to respect Ivana and her self-sacrifice enormously. "You can't keep cleaning rooms," she told her. "You'll turn into one of those stooping old women." When she'd learned that Ivana spoke fluent Italian and Spanish and had studied English in school, she'd immediately switched to English and, when talking to her, drilled Ivana repeatedly whenever she mispronounced a word. Within six months she announced, "You're good enough to interpret if you want. I could recommend you."

"Oh, no. I make too many mistakes." The thought of the better pay as an interpreter excited her, but she was self-conscious of her remaining errors when speaking English.

"Don't be silly. You should hear the cow they're using now."

The new job had lasted less than a year before the American company closed its doors, deciding the cost of doing business in Russia was more than it wanted to pay. By then, Ivana's English was nearly colloquial, and she'd been recommended for the job at Yukos.

Ivana considered herself lucky. Her petite, firm body still reflected the years of ballet training she'd put in before giving it up for Vladimir. If her smile was reluctant, it could be dazzling in effect. Though a pessimist by nature, she viewed herself as a realist. Russians had never had a break. It was their fate. To expect anything different was stupidity. The best they could hope for was a small niche of comfort and a measure of uncertain security.

Though the cramped apartment and the often noisy building was beginning to wear on her, Vladimir gave her the most concern. She marveled at how he'd managed to crawl out of his hole of despair and find a new life for himself with computers. These past months he'd started making significant money, and she was sure they'd be moving as soon as she could find a suitable apartment.

But the more success Vladimir enjoyed, the greater his ego had grown. At times she considered it to be out of control. He could be unbearable in his arrogance. Then there were his employers. She knew he'd worked for a time with the Russian Mafia, but she was certain he'd stopped. Yet when he'd been offered a job by more than one legitimate company, he'd refused them all. When she'd suggested her speaking to Boris Velichkovsky on his behalf, he'd become enraged and accused her of sleeping with her boss. She'd stood her ground and forced him to apologize for the remark, threatening to leave him until he did.

But she could tolerate his arrogance. She saw it as a form of compensation for his disability, and she could continue to stand it, if only they had a child. For all the negatives of life, even in the so-called New Russia, what was the point, she'd told her mother, of living if you didn't have a family?

PARIS, FRANCE
18ÈME ARRONDISSEMENT
FRIDAY, AUGUST 25
9:06 P.M.

Fajer al Dawar checked his appearance in the mirror at his suite in the Paris Ritz hotel. Forty-five years old, of average height and build, he took great pride in his jet-black hair. His unusually fair skin was also a source of satisfaction to him, but he never spoke about it to his swarthy brothers. He ran a comb through his hair, patted a lock into place, then laid the counts down as he once again admired his figure in the new Armani suit.

As CEO of the Franco-Arabe Chimique Compagnie, Fajer made trips to Paris two or three times a year. At home he was a Muslim traditionalist, with two wives, though in the West he only spoke of his first. When he'd married, his father, from whom he'd inherited his enormous fortune, had taken him aside to talk. "An Arab of means should have the four wives the Prophet has promised, but no more. The first should be a woman you can hang on your arm in the West, but who also accepts her place. With the other three, you are free to choose as you wish, for no one will see them but your family. My advice is to marry once every ten years. That way you always have a young wife for your bed and to bring you children. Because they are so far apart, you will not have the jealousy problems others who are less careful in their planning face every day, to their regret."

Fajer believed his father, though he also despised him. The first son of the second wife, Fajer had seen the philosophy of wife-taking in action, and though, from his experience, it didn't work quite as well as his father had indicated, it was one of Allah's gifts to man. In all, his father had fifteen children, six of them sons. Fajer's mother had existed in the shadow of the first wife and taught Fajer from the first that she and he were but second-class family members. She had filled him with an anger he'd learned to conceal, but was the source of his ambition.

While in Riyadh, Fajer was publicly a strict Muslim, but those demands dropped away, though not without some ambivalence, the moment his private jet left Arab airspace. He enjoyed his Irish whiskey and the freer lifestyle of France, and he enjoyed enormously the statuesque blondes, available by the score at what was to him little cost.

As he rode the elevator down to the hotel lobby, Fajer considered once again his mixed feelings. He honestly did not know if he could survive without these periodic trips that served as a release from the orchestrated, oppressive life in Riyadh. As he'd come to recognize them for the safety valve they were in his life, he looked to his uncles who had never gone to the West. Each of them seemed to him a bit odd, even mentally ill. Could it be true that to submit to Allah, as Fajer had been taught, was ultimately not possible? Not, at least, and keep your sanity? Perhaps this was a symptom of the West's current subjugation of the Muslim world, something that would change when the new Muslim age began. But such was not his lot, and for that he was grateful, if torn. The pressure would build in the weeks leading up to these trips, but knowing he would soon step into his Lear made it bearable. Now he was here and he hadn't felt this lighthearted, this free, since his last trip.

To assuage his guilt, Fajer told himself these excursions were necessary. He had to present himself as he did to conduct business in the West. He had to act Western, had to fit in with foreign businessmen. If he took pleasure from the experience, he should not condemn himself for it.

In the lobby bar of the Paris Ritz, Fajer found his brother Labib al Dawar waiting, engaged in polite conversation with a British businessman Fajer had met once. "Join us," the florid-faced Brit said as he approached.

"Thank you, but Labib and I have an engagement." Fajer smiled at his younger brother, who looked as if he needed to be rescued. The businessman accepted the inevitable and excused himself.

"What was that about?" Fajer asked.

"Money. What else? They think we Arabs carry gold bars around in our pockets," his brother said.

They stepped into the late-night air. It was much cooler now than it had been during the day. Fajer thought for a moment that no city on earth was more beautiful than Paris at night. Darkness masked its few shortcomings as a metropolis, and the city was lit as if for a Hollywood production. The driver opened the door and the two men stepped into the black Mercedes. The heavy car pulled away from the hotel, hesitated, then merged with traffic. A moment later it descended into the same tunnel where Princess Diana had died.

Labib was the second son of their father's fourth wife. In Saudi families the sons of different mothers didn't usually bond, but their mothers were cousins who had often visited one another during their childhood. Labib had always looked up to his older brother; when asked to join him in this venture, he'd been thrilled to be included.

While Fajer handled the company's affairs in the Kingdom, as Saudi Arabia was known, Labib had established the corporate presence in Paris. He'd lived here now for six years and had grown quite comfortable among the French. His wife loved Paris, and their son was thriving in school.

Though Fajer looked very much like their father, Labib, at age thirty-seven, closely resembled his mother. An inch shorter than his brother, he was slender, with a nearly effeminate grace. He'd lost his fourth finger on his left hand in a camel-riding accident with Fajer when they were children, but otherwise was a perfect Arab specimen. He'd earned a degree in computer science at Harvard and had originally worked with his brother as IT manager for the company in Riyadh.

Close as they were, the brothers were different in many ways. Fajer tended to the ostentatious when in the West, and his sexual appetite was nearly insatiable. Labib preferred to live a quiet life, with one woman, and avoided all overt displays of wealth. But they shared much in common. Both hated their father, despised the corrupt Saudi ruling family, and believed the future of the Arab world lay in a return to the old ways and a restoration of the caliphate as the world's dominant power. Both of them wanted nothing so much as the destruction of America to make that possible.

"And how are things, little brother?" Fajer asked in Arabic. The driver was Polish, so they could speak frankly.

"I believe we will get the contract."

"Not that. The other."

Labib glanced at the driver a moment. "It has gone as planned so far. I see no problems."

"There are always problems, or, at the least, there is the unexpected."

"Fresh code is going out every day. We've confirmed replication. It's really only a question of how far it spreads before activation, and that we can't discover in advance without tipping our hand."

Fajer smiled. "I can hardly wait until the day comes. I will be home in the Kingdom. I suggest you return as well. We will be safe there. Nothing else?"

"No." Labib stared out the window.

Fajer could sense his uncertainty. "Tell me. Is it the Russian?"

The idea had been spawned high in a remote valley in the Hejaz Mountains near the western coast of Saudi Arabia. There Fajer had long maintained a traditional tribal settlement of about eighty people. Several times a year, especially during the torturous summer, Fajer flew by helicopter to this remote region and lived in a tent, as had his forebears. Here he renewed his ties to the earth and to the traditional ways of his tribe.

These included slaughtering a goat or sheep. He'd learned to cut the throat in the prescribed way, to drain the blood as specified, then to skin the animal before turning it over to the women. He found he took great pleasure in killing.

One of the elderly men, a fighter from the old days, had spoken to him one night about the blade and how a sword or knife were the only true weapons for any desert Arab. Firearms were used of necessity, but a true Arab warrior fought with the blade, close to his enemy where he could see the life drain from the body of the slain.

Fajer had been deeply moved. Later, the old man had given him a knife, a *shafra*, of old construction. "It has taken the blood of many infidels," the nearly toothless man had said as he pressed it into Fajer's hand. "You must use it in jihad."

The handle of the *shafra* was of white pearl, the seven-inch steel blade turned down in Arab fashion. It was meant to be worn in a sheath in the small of the back as a reserve or secret weapon. The next morning, Fajer had donned the knife. Now he was never without it.

He was so moved by his many experiences at this desert encampment that he had selected a future wife from among the people. Though she was not yet ten years of age, when the time was right, he would wed his third wife in a traditional tribal ceremony, planning to leave their children among her people, wanting them to be raised free of the temptations and contamination to which he'd been exposed as a child.

Eight years earlier, Fajer had taken Labib to the settlement for the first time. Beside a dying fire, within the comfort of his people, staring into an ebony sky with stars sparkling like tiny diamonds, Fajer first shared his vision of the future.

"We have turned away from the Prophet, the Merciful. Our punishment has been to see our people seduced by the West. The greatest curse ever given us has been oil. Because of it the West has conquered and divided us. Otherwise they would have left us at peace."

"I understand. We are but two men. What can we do?" Labib had asked.

It was the first moment it had occurred to Fajer that his brother was with him. He had felt alone until this moment. "The Prophet was but one when he began. With two, we can level mountains. Tell me of this education you have from the American university. I know very little about Americans."

The brothers had talked far into that night and several nights to follow. During the days they had hunted wild game and flown their falcons. "This," Fajer said more than once, "is the life we Arabs were meant to live."

But the men had done nothing but complain until the attack on the World Trade Center. Fajer had called his brother and told him to turn the television to CNN International. They were talking by telephone as they watched the two towers fall.

"*Allahu Akbar!* Allah is greater!" Fajer had exclaimed. "Allah be praised!"

They had been convinced that this was the beginning of something great and watched the news each day with anticipation. But as the Americans had driven the Taliban out of power in Afghanistan, then invaded Iraq, as they had harassed the followers of Osama bin Laden around the world, Fajer had lapsed into a deep depression. The West was winning again. The previous summer the two brothers had met in the Hejaz Mountains, where Fajer had expressed his loss of faith.

"Osama cannot do it alone. The American forces are too strong. We are weak, and getting weaker. It has all been for nothing."

Labib then spoke to his brother about thoughts that he had long kept to himself. "It is true that the West is corrupt and evil. But it is also true America and its allies have an enormous industrial base capable of overwhelming us in battle. Their one great ability is to build weapons, and their single greatest strength is their absolute willingness to use those weapons against anyone they consider to be an enemy.

"In the last half century they have expanded their industrial base far beyond what it once was. They have pursued their policy of creating one world under their polytheistic, hedonistic rule. To accomplish that, they have connected their means of production worldwide, but nowhere is that connection more firm than within the United States. Banks, manufacturing, national defense, government—*everything* is linked through computers, and the computers are connected through the Internet." Labib explained how this worked, then told his older brother his idea.

Fajer had slowly become excited, then ecstatic. "Can it truly be done? This is not just idle talk?"

"It can be done. What we cannot know in advance is how devastating it will be. But if we plan it carefully, I believe we can cause enormous harm that will shake Western beliefs. I think we can do enough damage so that the antiwar sentiment in America will grow sufficiently to change their course of action. We can put them on the defensive, cause them to withdraw from the lands of the Prophet, the Merciful. It will be the beginning of the great Muslim Restoration."

"Then we must do it, little brother. We must do it!"

And so they had, keeping their effort almost to themselves as they did not trust others.

"It is not the Russian, not directly," Labib said finally. "There is something else."

"Yes?"

"We monitor certain sites for signs that we have been discovered. It is passive monitoring so we give nothing away."

"Very wise. You have found something?"

"Yes. A message was posted asking for information by anyone about a hacker known as Superphreak."

Fajer had not heard the name previously. "Yes?"

"That is our Russian."

Fajer's eyes lit for an instant. "How could anyone know that name?"

"It must be in the code."

"I don't understand."

"When hackers create new code, they often use bits and pieces of old code that have worked in the past. They see no reason to reinvent it. I think our Russian took old code that had his cyber name in it, without knowing it, probably."

"I thought he was ordered to leave no trail," Fajer said.

"He was."

"He's been very careless."

"Yes," Labib agreed, "careless. But it is too late to stop it. The act is already in motion. What is done, is done. Even if we were to agree to stop or delay it, we cannot. If it is beyond our power, it is beyond anyone else's too."

Fajer considered that a moment. "I suppose. Tell me all you learn as you learn it."

"Of course."

○○○○○○○○○○○○34

As Jeff waited for his laptop to boot, he thought back on his work for Fischerman, Platt & Cohen. He'd been at it now almost two weeks, and from his point of view he had nothing to give them. He'd learned a great deal about the two viruses that infected their system, but his attempts to find and boot a clean image had been a failure. He knew more since the last effort, but he could give neither Sue nor Greene any assurance that he could rid the contaminated backup files of either virus, or if he did, that a third, or fourth, wasn't still lurking somewhere in the data.

He was conflicted about what to do next. On the one hand, the firm needed him to be successful, and the information he was learning and passing along to Daryl might be vital in helping other companies under similar attack. It might even prove useful in thwarting further ones.

But that wasn't what Greene was paying Jeff to do. He'd spoken earlier with the harried lawyer, and the man had presented a pretty unpleasant picture of what was taking place within the firm. Work wasn't getting done, clients were jumping ship, a few of the newest hires had already resigned, and no new work of any kind was being signed. Worst of all, the cash flow had all but stopped. Unless Jeff could present a realistic prospect of recovery, he felt he had no business collecting any more of his fee. If he stopped, however, the firm would go under because no one else could do a better job.

And this had another component, one he'd rather not admit to. Memories he'd long suppressed were crowding his consciousness, breaking down the barriers he'd erected around him. In many ways the work at the New York law firm was similar to what he'd done at the old CIA. He'd worn his failure to avert the 9/11 disaster, and save Cynthia's life, like an invisible yoke around his neck, and now that same sense of failure was weighing down on him again, threatening to derail the pathetically small sense of emotional security he'd won for himself since that horrific day.

I can't go through that again, he thought, *I can't fail this time too. Maybe I can't save the company that hired me, but the help I'm giving Daryl might accomplish something I wasn't able to do before. This is much more than just another job*, he suddenly realized. Buoyed by the understanding he was given something rare in life, a second chance, Jeff turned to his work with renewed energy.

Once the computer was running, Jeff sat at the desk in his room and launched a search for hacker chat rooms, recognizing several from his search earlier that week and even some from back to his CIA days, when trolling hacker chat rooms had been his late-night "hobby." He scrolled through the various chat rooms, searching for the words *superphreak* and *kinky*, or any other reference to Rick James. Nothing.

Then, shortly before eleven o'clock, he entered the h@xx0rd chat room. He'd glanced at the chat room a time or two before and knew that foreign hackers liked it, but hadn't previously seen anything that interested him. This time, though, as he scanned down the page, scrolling as needed, he was pulled up short. He read:

Godder: Hw mch?
Dante: I'm nt gettn rich, u know . . . few thousand Euros . . .
Godder: For u stuff? Seems like a lot . . .
Dante: I'm nt laughing.
Godder: Wht d thy py t most for?
Dante: I speed up loading time. Othrs sell packages and triggers.
Godder: What kind of triggers? I've gt sm of thos . . .
Dante: Clock related bt sum othrs 2 . . .

Godder: Wht packages:
Dante: U know . . . like sp@ts . . .
Godder: Who's he?
Dante: He's nt bin around fr . . .
Saintie: He's down now . . . too much heat . . .
Dante: . . . awhile. Thanks. Don't b stupid Godder. Wht kind
          packages d u think I mean? All kinds . . . Nastier t
          better . . . Thy like it bad . . . as in BAD . . . One guy's
          makng a killing with rootkits . . . But thy dnt want
          nomore. . . . Superphreak's gt a lock on that market . . .

Jeff felt the hair on his neck bristle.

Godder: I've got some stuff like that other . . . Where t?
Dante: Give me an address n I'll snd it.
Godder: Send me an email fr u at TheGodGuy666@hotmail.com.
          I'll snt It to u.

After that Godder disappeared, as did Dante. Jeff considered posting a message but decided against it. Better to watch and learn. He
opened his ICQ and saw Daryl was online. He typed:

JA33: Y arn't u n bed?

There was a long pause before she answered.

DOO7: Wt a sec.

Then she wrote:

DOO7:   Srry. Hd t finish sumtng. Wht's up?
JA33:   No luck. Thnkng abt tllng t guy I cn't help him.
DOO7:   If u cnt who cn? H'll b sht out of luck.
JA33:   Still, I feel gulty gttng paid.
DOO7:   Cum bck t work fr gov. I nvr feel guilty whn I gt my chck.
JA33:   Jst spnt tme n cht rm and read sum weird stuff.
DOO7:   Like?

JA33:   Thr ws 1 gy tllng anthr abt sllng pckgs and trggrs. Gttng
         good $ fr t.
DOO7:   Any nme we knw?
JA33:   Superphreak. He's hndlng t rtkits, slick bstrd.
DOO7:   Gv me t site. I'll put smn on it fulltm.
JA33:   h@xx0rd . . . Wht's up w u grp?
DOO7:   Same thng where we r, only mor of t. Wve fnd svrl tht r
         wpng bios fr dell and hp, kllng thm dead, dead, dead. Wv
         also gt vriants tht r deltng all data on a systm's dsks,
         rmvng trcs of itslf thn kllng oprtng systm. Nsty.
JA33:   Wht abt t sec comps?
DOO7:   No 1 prblm. Thy're bsy w whtvr. Wve gt a fw folks hlpng
         bt nt engh.
JA33:   I dn't lke any f ths.
DOO7:   And u wndr y lm up?

0 0 0 0 0 0 0 0 0 0 0 0 0 **3 5**

Fajer al Dawar lit yet another cigarette, then moved to the balcony of the Ritz suite. From his coat pocket he removed a prepaid cell phone. He had committed the number to memory. As he listened to the ringing, he thought back to the moment he had found jihad.

The man called Yousef al-Halim leaned over to exit through the doorway of the house in the center of Old Town in Peshawar. The city was not only the capital but the largest in the North-West Frontier Province in Pakistan. Strategically located at the foothills of the Khyber Pass, the city played a major role in the historical route of invasion into the Indian subcontinent. With the American presence in nearby Afghanistan and its ostensible support by the Musharraf government in Pakistan, Peshawar was an important military post. From here, periodic searches for Osama bin Laden and his supporters were launched.

Yousef had spent a week in Karachi before moving north, then a restless month in Rawalpindi, which was much larger than Peshawar, more nervous every minute thanks to the heavier and more aggressive military presence there. Here in Peshawar he'd obtained his new identity papers, then finally made contact, only to be told to wait.

Outside, Yousef dipped his hand into the water trough and scrubbed his face vigorously. Wiping his face with his sleeve, he glanced up at a brilliant blue sky. This close to the Tora Bora mountains, you could all but feel the sky pressing down. The air was still pleasant, but had a cold bite that had not been there when he'd first arrived.

It was late October. Winter would soon be coming, and with it the snow that would lock the mountain passes in their white vise. He had to move soon or he'd be forced to turn back.

Yousef's stay in Peshawar had not been totally unpleasant, not at all. The city had been conquered and occupied over the millennia by Moguls, Persians, Hindus, and Arabs, to name but a few. Each had left behind a bit of its culture and tradition. The people were of such diverse lineage they considered themselves to be a separate tribe from the rest of Pakistan. With the various cultures had come a certain laxity toward the teachings of the Prophet, though. Bars operated freely, and a local brewery produced a quality beer. Brothels were discreetly located but commonplace, though the quality of the women was not to his standards.

Since the Russian war in Afghanistan the city had been all but overrun with Afghan refugees, with the United Nations and nongovernmental organizations running the camps and providing services. Many of the Afghans had returned home, but thousands had stayed on, their homes long since destroyed. The Taliban who still waged war against the American-backed government in Kabul recruited among them, and Yousef had seen small bands of young, bearded men making their way quietly toward the nearby mountains almost weekly.

Yousef had taken to saying his prayers as the Prophet had decreed and spent most of each day in one of three traditional tea shops. There, amid the samovars and colorful china teapots, with the hookahs making the air thick with the heavy smoke of tobacco and occasionally hashish, he passed his time in thought, observation, or reading. He had come to believe that he had been reborn as a Muslim in this place and was more committed to jihad than ever.

Every ten days he changed rooms so as not to attract attention, but slowly his tea shops dwindled to just these three, which he rotated daily. He was surprised at the vitality of life here in Peshawar. Technically they were all Muslim, but the difference in culture from his native land was striking. The streets had a vitality that was lacking in Saudi Arabia.

For that he blamed oil. The resultant wealth drained the people of their natural course, causing them to turn away from the practices of their fathers.

Yousef noticed one of the young, lean men with suspicious eyes enter, move quietly through the crowded, smoky room, then take a lone chair in the back corner. He'd seen his type before. Fresh down from the mountains, they delivered a message, ordered supplies, or led recruits to a mountain camp. Such men had something of the predator. The vigorous life in the mountains and the strict diet left them slender and hard.

At midafternoon Yousef found himself waiting, as he did every afternoon at this time. Within a few moments he heard the call of the muezzin from atop the nearby minaret. *"Hayya la-s-saleah. Hayya la-s-saleah,"* the voice sang to all who would hear: Hasten to prayer. Yousef set down his cup of tea, took up his rolled prayer rug, and went into the street, where he joined the other good Muslims. He spread his rug and knelt.

When prayer was concluded, he returned to the tea shop, rolling his prayer rug. The lean man he'd seen earlier approached and in a quiet voice of command said, "Follow me." Yousef looked after the man a moment, then tossed a few coins on the wooden table and followed. He was led to the poorest quarter of Peshawar, then up an alley and into a small house. The man led him through the first room, through the second, then across a small courtyard. There he paused before a doorway and gestured for Yousef to enter. When he did, he found his effects from his room. "Wait," the man said, then turned on his heel and left.

That night Yousef was brought bread, dates, and hot, sweet tea by an aged woman dressed in black. Almost before he'd finished the meager meal he was overcome with fatigue. He lay on a goatskin and slept as if he were dead.

Before dawn the next morning the young man returned. "Bring just the rucksack. Leave the rest," he ordered.

Yousef quickly finished his morning tea. "Where are we going?" he asked, when he really meant, Am I being moved again? Or is this it?

"To the mountains. No more questions."

Outside were four young men. The air was bracing. Yousef fell in behind the young men and was led off with the others. By midday they

were out of the city and well into the countryside. They walked in silence, with the leader, who told Yousef his name was Omar, calling a
short break every two hours. Two of the others were, like Yousef, from
Saudi Arabia. A third was Egyptian, while the fourth was from Syria.
Omar instructed them to tell the others nothing more about themselves and to use a name other than their own.

Omar rarely spoke. When he did, he selected his words carefully.
His eyes were a startling light blue and his teeth were bright and even.
That first night the men rested at a farmer's house and were served by
his wife and young daughters. They slept on one side of the small house
while the family slept on the other. They were up before dawn; after a
quick breakfast of sweet tea and flat bread, they were on their way again.
That night, then the next two, they slept at campsites. The nights were
frigid. The men huddled together for warmth.

The farther from Peshawar they traveled, the more traffic fell off. By
the third day, they no longer saw military vehicles. By the fourth they
were well into the foothills of the mountains, climbing higher with each
step. Yousef's feet were covered with blisters, but he said nothing. The
young Syrian was bleeding through his tattered canvas shoes. No one
complained.

That night, their fifth, Omar led them to a camp well off the trail
they'd been following. Here they were welcomed, their feet were
treated, and they were given a full meal. "We will rest here a few days,"
Omar told them. "Remain to yourselves."

"A few days" turned into ten. Each day was colder than the previous.
On the fourth, heavy clouds filled the sky, threatening rain or early
snow. About thirty were in the camp, herdsmen with only a few women
to prepare meals and clean. One of the locals told Yousef their winter
settlement was down in the valley and they would leave for it at the first
sign of snow. He was the only one who spoke to any of them.

On the tenth night, after the evening meal, Omar gathered the five
and introduced them to a stern newcomer named Muhammad. "We
will divide into two groups tomorrow. You four," Muhammad said, gesturing at the others, "will go with me. Yousef will remain with Omar."

Omar and Yousef left with the others at first light, but soon split
away. They went to the right, while the others took the left fork of the
trail. "Go with Allah," Omar told the men as he took the hand of each.

Yousef said and did the same. That day the trail wound ever upward, snaking back and forth, often running along rocky walls rather than out in the open. It was exhausting, and for the first time Yousef was concerned that he was not physically up to his pilgrimage. But he could not stop now, would not, and pressed on no matter how tired he became.

He and Omar slept in five camps in as many nights. These were military encampments now, hidden in caves or tucked away in narrow ravines. The lean, ragged men carried with them AK-47s and watched the sky closely for aircraft.

"But we don't always see them," Omar explained when he asked what they were doing. "Often the American planes are so high they are invisible, like evil spirits, and their bombs are among us without warning."

Yousef licked his dry lips. "Does it happen often?"

"Often enough. If you are here for long, you will see."

With each camp the living conditions declined. It was colder, the men dirtier. But everywhere Yousef was moved by the extent of the commitment he saw, the willingness of fellow Muslims to fight the infidel.

They were so high in the stark mountains he lost his appetite and from time to time experienced nausea. Omar pressed him to eat the rice and goat meat that constituted their basic meal, but he could not. When Yousef believed he could go no farther, Omar took him aside. "You've done well. This is difficult even for me and I spend most of my time in these mountains. Just one more day. We will cross over the pass in the morning, then descend all day. Before nightfall, God willing, we will have reached our destination. So rest, my brother, you have earned it."

Yousef was too tired to take it in. He lay on his side, his nearby meal untouched, and was at once in a deep sleep. The next morning they left while it was still dark. They had come so far, they were in the clouds, and the cloying mist turned his clothes wet and heavy, drawing the heat from his body. But the pass was less than two hours away, and as they descended, the clouds seemed to disperse and the sky overhead was that azure he'd become accustomed to in Peshawar.

They joined three others, young men who laughed uneasily and scanned the sky incessantly. Before noon the trail led them downward.

With each passing hour, Yousef felt better. When they stopped for a midday meal and heated tea, he ate with vigor. Omar smiled.

It was nearly dark when they finally entered a narrow canyon. The three fighters who had come with them smiled warmly at seeing old comrades, exchanging embraces and news. Omar led Yousef to a fire set at the mouth of a nondescript cave, one like thousands they'd passed on his journey. Here, about the fire, were several women, the first Yousef had seen in two weeks, and two men, both a bit plump from lack of exercise and too much food. Omar squatted and spoke to one, gesturing toward Yousef. The man nodded and gave instructions.

When Omar returned, he said, "You will eat and rest tonight. Tomorrow you will bathe and prepare yourself."

Yousef nodded. At last.

Following afternoon prayer the next day, Yousef was finally escorted deep within the largest cave he had seen since entering Tora Bora. He'd been bathed, then dressed entirely in clean clothes provided to him. His hair and beard had been barbered.

Outside he'd heard a generator running, and inside he spotted cables laid along the floor. Omar had explained that all of the fuel had to be carried in so the generator was only run an hour or so a day as needed.

Some two hundred feet into the cave, after several turns, they were stopped by two armed guards. Omar explained that he would leave now but would see Yousef outside afterward. A few minutes later, Yousef was led into the presence of Osama bin Laden.

The room was located at the far reaches of the cave and had been made larger over time. It was lit by bare bulbs, with a number of unlit lamps for when the power was off. There was a desk, carpets, and pillows. The room was heavy with the smell of incense and kerosene.

Bin Laden was reclining on pillows, his lanky body stretched out like that of a snake warming itself in the sun. Unlike the others outside, his clothes were immaculately clean. His beard was whiter than in photographs, and his eyes were deeply sunk within his skull. He looked tired but otherwise quite fit.

Bin Laden extended his hand and Yousef kissed it. "Sit," bin Laden said, gesturing at a pillow.

Behind him Yousef sensed rather than saw the presence of the guards. "Fajer al Dawar, your history is not unlike my own," bin Laden said. "Why have you come so far and at such risk to see me?"

"I wish to serve Allah. I wish to destroy the Americans, to rid our people of their corrupt king, to free us of the yoke of oil. I seek the restored caliphate, to see us once again the people Allah wishes us to be!"

"So. We have even more in common. Will you have tea?"

The men were served hot tea and spoke for nearly two hours. Most of the time bin Laden did the talking, explaining his long-range plan to continue striking at the economic foundations of the West. "Their great weakness is a love of money," he said. "Because of that we will bring them to their knees."

For Fajer it was as if he were visiting the Prophet Himself. He had never been more deeply moved by any experience. The time passed as if it had been but minutes. Before he realized it, he was again kissing bin Laden's hand and bidding him Allah's blessing.

Back outside it was already dark. In the distance he heard thunder. Omar approached. "The Americans. They are trying to hit the last camp at which we stayed."

"Did they succeed?"

"We will know tomorrow. We leave at dawn. How was your meeting?"

Fajer, now once again Yousef, clutched the names and e-mail addresses he'd been given in his hand. He needed to find a safe place for them. "Good, Allah be praised. I am truly ready now for jihad."

Away from the fire, Fajer raised his eyes to the stars overhead. How long would it take to establish the caliphate? A decade? Five decades?

Fajer did not know but believed that he had this day taken an enormous first step to achieve it. The time of the West was coming to an end, and with it a Muslim rebirth such as had not been seen since the days of the Prophet.

The very thought brought tears to his eyes.

OOOOOOOOOOOO 36

Daryl's team-leader meeting was well under way. Her coffee was cold and her bear claw lay all but untouched in its napkin. Almost nothing she'd heard from the start sat right with her.

"You're telling me the scope of this thing is growing daily?" she said to Michelle.

"Hourly, boss." Michelle Gritter's team was working on determining the extent of the virus. "And the more we learn about Superphreak, the more variants we locate, the more we understand how much we underestimated it. It's been out there for months."

"Tom," Daryl said, turning to look at the man whose team was charged with developing a solution, "what have you come up with? No more depressing news," she said, holding up a warning hand. "I need some answers."

"The closest thing to good news I've got is that nearly all the Superphreak variants are tied to September eleventh as the trigger," Tom said, sounding anxious. "The ones that aren't, at least so far, are event triggered, but not until *after* September eleventh."

"So we're relatively secure for two more weeks?"

Tom hesitated. "Except for computers with the wrong date in the internal clock like you had at that law firm, the New York hospitals, and the Ford plant. I read that the Skunk River Nuclear plant emergency shutdown was caused by a computer glitch. A blogger who says he's an employee there claims it was caused by a date-related virus."

Tom glanced at his notes, then cleared his throat before continuing, "There's some indication that the virus itself is causing these date changes. A couple of the samples we've obtained trip over their own cloaking mechanisms and alter the system's clock.

"And, of course, we're not secure from those viruses triggered by non-date-related events. Our concern is that we're missing something. We're depending on the date and the cyber handle of *Superphreak* to identify these viruses. We have no way of knowing if these are just a part of an overall effort. We're assuming they identify everything this group is doing, but we don't know that. We could very well be concentrating on something that turns out to be the tip of an enormous iceberg."

Daryl's mind raced. "Oscar, does CSCIA think this is a cyber-attack being launched by a group?"

Oscar Lee, responsible for coordinating CISU/DHS's effort with the various cyber-security vendors, was usually great at his job, but like the other team leaders, this time he was coming up short. "Boss, I can't really say they're on board with this thing. It's like I told you, Superphreak's not showing up in their honeypots. They think we're overreacting. Besides, they're dealing with fresh waves of variants of old viruses. It's overwhelming them. They've got a nasty virus that's blocking automatic update systems in computers, and they're giving it priority."

Daryl realized she'd heard this before but it hadn't really registered. "You're saying this virus is avoiding honeypots?"

"It looks that way."

Daryl gritted her teeth. "Okay. I'll call the director again and see if I can't get DHS more active. At our last meeting, Oscar, I had you put people on chat rooms. Anything there?"

"Some, not enough. I was planning to e-mail you a status report after lunch."

"I'll look for it."

Tom cleared his throat.

"Yes?" Daryl said impatiently.

"Boss, I think I have an explanation for Oscar's problem with the vendors' honeypots."

"What's that?"

"We've taken several of the Superphreak viruses apart. Pretty crude in some places, really slick in others. Anyway, they're set up to avoid the IPs of the security vendors, including IPs of many of their stealth honeypots."

The table sat in stunned silence for a long moment.

Daryl leaned forward. "You're telling me this virus actively *avoids* the honeypots?"

"It sure does. Like I said, slick."

A sound like a moan came from around the table. It was going to be hell getting anyone really interested in this. Daryl closed her eyes for a long moment. *This is so very, very bad*, she thought.

European headquarters for the Franco-Arabe Chimique Compagnie occupied the upper floors of an enormous glass tower in La Défense, a contemporary business district on the outskirts of Paris composed of a cluster of towers more than thirty stories high. Considered ultramodern architectural gems by many and eyesores by others, they could be seen from central Paris on clear days. Sculptures and fountains abounded in the plazas, and entryways were decorated in colorful mosaics. There, in a corner office with a southern exposure, Labib al Dawar spent most of each workday.

But increasingly he left early and drove to the discreet offices of Graphisme Courageux across town. With just eight employees, it was located in a converted residence that legend said had been built for the mistress of King Louis XVI's finance minister. Labib believed he could not have found a better location for this particular office, situated three short blocks from the busy rue Mouffetard. His young employees mixed freely with the many students of the Latin Quarter, and by design nothing about the company drew attention. Six of the employees actually performed graphics work. Only Labib and Michel Dufour, from their single office facing the alley and separated from the front staff by a locked door, were engaged in the work of Allah.

Grandson of a *pied-noir* and an Algerian woman, Dufour had thrown himself into the jihad with total commitment. His assignment had been to recruit and coordinate the various worldwide hacker networks they were employing. It was important that the viruses they distributed not be traced to this office, or to Paris for that matter. Dufour pulled together the three components for each virus package they unleashed. These he first placed into Labib's computer, for the Arab had given himself the honor of actually assembling each virus before passing them back to Dufour for distribution. Never before in his life had Labib found such satisfaction in his work.

When he was not in contact with his hundred-odd hackers, Dufour was transferring payments and monitoring various Web sites and chat rooms for signs the cyber jihad had been detected. It was he who'd spotted the posting by Dragon Lady searching for Superphreak.

"Bonjour," Dufour said, as Labib entered the office from the rear. So separated were the two functions of the office that Labib was certain the other employees had never seen him. As an increased security measure, his strict rule was that he and Dufour speak only French. Besides, the man's Arabic was so heavily accented Labib could hardly understand him.

"How many today?" Labib asked, as he sat at his workstation.

"You have two new *noirs.*" They never used hacker language in the office, even though Labib was certain they could not be overheard. *Noir,* or "black," meant a rootkit. *Rouge,* or "red," was the trigger, while *blanc,* "white," stood for the portion that wreaked the destruction. A *boîtier,* or "package," referred to the entire device, as Labib had come to consider the malware he had had Dufour unleash.

"Excellent." The Russian did superior work. Not like a lot of the crap the others often tried to pawn off on them.

"And there are fifteen new *rouges* that look okay. You should see the ones I refused."

When his brother Fajer had expressed displeasure with the Russian, Labib had been both defensive and guilty. He knew that Dufour had made it clear to the man that they only wanted clean code, and he'd not delivered it. But Labib had been careless as well and not checked the product as carefully as he should have, Dufour only stumbling across *Superphreak* in a code the previous week. Until then he'd thought the code was free of such clues.

At the time it had seemed a crushing reversal, but Dufour had persuaded him it likely meant nothing. "It will probably not be detected, and if it is, how will it get to anyone? Certainly not in time to stop *le déluge*," as he called the looming attack.

Labib had agreed, and as they'd employed an ever growing number of crackers from whom they acquired bits of malware, other security problems had come up, which lessened the impact of this first one. Still, he'd instructed that the Russian not provide any code other than his *noirs*. In fact, Labib regretted that they had ever released any virus without the cloaking rootkits, but he'd not known they existed until Vladimir had asked if they were interested.

The problem only emphasized their dependence and vulnerability. For their long-term goals they must find a way to do all of this alone. Only then would they be truly secure.

For the next three hours Labib cobbled together a dozen *boitiers* using the two new *noirs* while mixing in the fresh triggers and destruction codes they'd received. He'd long since given up making certain every virus they released did what it was intended to do. Dufour had persuaded him that certain wreckage would come from the sheer numbers of the viruses.

Labib also cursed the amount of time this had all taken. He and his brother had intended to unleash the cyber-attack in conjunction with a physical attack by Al Qaeda. On three separate occasions Fajer had sought to make contact with bin Laden, but to no avail. When he'd finally succeeded in meeting with him in his own personal hajj, he'd come away with the names and means of contact for a wide range of operatives. But as they'd sought to coordinate with those in the highest levels of Al Qaeda's operations, one by one the men had been killed by the Americans. Finally, with great reluctance, Fajer had instructed Labib to go ahead.

"If we wait any longer, the Americans will have taken over both Iran and Syria. We cannot delay. Allah is with us," he'd said with passion.

And so Labib had placed into motion his carefully laid plans. As he and Dufour had begun to implement them, he'd been forced to reconsider his objectives. But he remained satisfied that he could wreak havoc on America in his own way. He would cost them billions, destroy systems it would take years to reconstruct, shake faith in the nation, cause disarray in its military, and force a reexamination of its activism in the Middle East. The cyber-attack would be no less devastating to Europe.

Labib attached a *blanc* to a rootkit with satisfaction. He was certain that within weeks the United States would be withdrawing from Afghanistan and would abandon its plans for Iran and Syria.

"Try this one," Dufour said, handing Labib a disk. "The hacker claims it will destroy Nasdaq's records." Then he reached back to his desk. "And here's the information your brother wanted."

"What information?"

"On someone with the handle Dragon Lady."

MANHATTAN, NEW YORK
MIDTOWN
HEMINGWAY HOTEL
WEDNESDAY, AUGUST 30
6:57 P.M.

Sue Tabor gave a deep, throaty laugh as she sat up and reached for his groin.

"Not again," Joshua Greene moaned. "I'm only flesh and blood."

"Hush," Sue said. "I've got some ancient Chinese sex techniques I want to show you."

Greene laughed. "You're about as Chinese as I am English."

"Hey! You don't know. Maybe Mom passed along a few things I've been holding back."

"Right. Let go of that. I mean it. I want to talk."

"That's not what you wanted a few minutes ago."

"I need to recharge. For God's sake, Sue, I'm not some young stud. Let it alone. Tell me what's going on with my records."

"Spoilsport." Sue sat back onto the pillows, her breasts rising like tiny mounds. "If we're going to talk, look up here and not at my tits." She reached onto the nightstand and lit a cigarette.

"Right." Greene pulled the sheet up to cover his growing stomach. He was always self-conscious in the nude, but especially so with Sue, whose body he considered to be perfect.

"It's been three weeks. We've lost a third of our accounts. I'm getting resignations. We'll be closing our doors at this rate. Can you give me any hope?"

She looked at him, then solemnly announced, "I'm pretty sure I can get you up again."

Greene laughed. "Not that, though I'd be grateful. But we're screwed if you or this Aiken guy don't come up with something very soon."

"Yeah. I know." She sat back and turned serious. "I've tried three boots so far and all were failures. We were struck by viruses with very sophisticated cloaking devices, making them very difficult to remove. The good news is we still have the backups."

"It may be too late," Greene said, "given the speed with which the firm is falling apart."

"Josh, I'm really sorry." Sue leaned closer and placed her hand on his chest. "I can't help but blame myself. You've been great not to make my life miserable over this."

Greene shrugged. "Aiken says it wasn't your fault. No security system could have stopped the virus. I've not been able to sell that to the partners, but I believe it." He seemed to hesitate.

"There's something else?" Sue asked. She'd always been impressed with Greene's ability to be involved with her while keeping the business aspect of their relationship clear. In her experience that was quite rare.

"It's not important. Really." Greene smiled weakly, clearly wanting to avoid saying more.

"What's not important?"

Greene sighed. "I've been ordered to fire you."

Sue looked into his eyes for a moment. "I see. You thought you'd get your blow job first, *then* tell me? You bastard!" Flipping over, she stabbed her cigarette out in the ashtray, then flung the sheet off her.

"No, no, it's not like that. Well, maybe a little, I guess. It's just . . . the partners insist I do something. I told them it won't improve a thing to get rid of you, but they don't see it that way."

"So I'm out of a job?" she said, standing beside the bed with her hands braced on her hips.

"I'm not supposed to tell you."

"Oh, I get it. *First* I fix the problem, then you can me! Is that the plan?" She sat on the edge of the bed.

"Yeah, I'd say that's about it." He reached for a breast. She bumped his hand away with her arm. "What difference does it make? I don't have to do it now, and anyway, it doesn't look like any of us are going to have a job before long."

Sue breathed out. "I guess not." She'd seen this coming, now that she thought about it. What else could the firm do? With the failed third attempt to reboot, she'd understood her job was on a short leash.

"And I'll let you resign, give you a good reference. You can trust me."

Sue lay back across the bed. "You know what I think?"

"No."

"No more hotel rooms. I like it better in the office."

"That's out of the question."

"Then how about the garage? On the hood of your BMW?"

"No, no, no. I told you, I've rented this room for the entire month."

"Yeah," she said in mock seriousness, "who's the boss here?"

"You are."

"Then get down, boy. My turn. And get your car washed for next time."

MOSCOW, RUSSIAN FEDERATION
DMITROSVSKY ADMINISTRATIVE DISTRICT
WEDNESDAY, AUGUST 30
7:02 P.M.

Ivana Koskov removed the *shchi* from the table, then set in place the *kuyrdak* her mother had brought by her office late that afternoon. She emptied the bottle of water into Vladimir's glass, then opened a fresh one before joining him, their heads nearly touching as they ate the rabbit stew. The food brought back pleasant childhood memories, and she wondered again if she shouldn't make more of an effort to learn to cook her mother's dishes.

As he ate, Vladimir smoked a cigarette, taking puffs between bites. A smoker herself, Ivana thought nothing of it. On the wall near his computers was a poster of Rick James with the bulbous Afro and bulging biceps. In the background their stereo had started a random selection of James's songs, including his hit "Super Freak."

Ivana had long ago grown tired of Rick James, and especially of "Super Freak." For Vladimir it was either feast or famine. He'd go months without his music, then in a frenzy it would be all she'd hear for days. He usually used his headset so it wasn't so bad. Still, she wished his taste would move on.

When they were finished, she cleared the table, wiped it clean, then set out two saucers and cups for coffee. "Vodka?" she asked. Vladimir merely nodded, then wheeled his chair backward and spun it into the bathroom to empty the bladder sack that was tied to the side of his leg.

"I think we'll have that new apartment in a few months," Ivana said. "I talked to the manager today and he all but promised."

Vladimir grunted. She heard the water run as he washed his hands. Thank God he was a clean man. Living in clutter was bad enough; if it had been dirty as well . . .

Vladimir returned to his place at the table, then downed a shot, followed by the hot coffee as a chaser. He leaned back, emptied his lungs, then picked up his cigarette. "Maybe I should give Boris a little something to move us up. I'm more than ready to get out of here." Lately, he complained endlessly about their cramped quarters.

"I don't think anything less than one hundred euros would help."

"That's okay."

"Then I'll try it." Ivana was pleased to see his commitment. "I must say the splendor of our first place has worn off."

They laughed. "Maybe you could keep this as a storage room for your extra equipment," she suggested, and they laughed again.

"It's better suited for that than an apartment," he said with a grin.

Ivana smoked quietly, punched out her cigarette. "Do you want to tell me how much you've got? I don't want to start a fight, but it's hard to plan not knowing." His elusiveness and his obsession with his work ate at her. This was the first time she'd been able to broach the subject without his responding with anger.

"I've only saved it up as a surprise. It's just over twenty thousand."

"Euros? Not dollars?"

"Euros."

"You *have* been doing well." She picked up his package of cigarettes and lit another. After inhaling, she released the smoke. "This work you're doing . . . how long will it last?"

"I don't know. Not much longer, I think. They seem to be on a deadline but I don't know what it is."

"What *is* it you're doing?" For months now Ivana had been certain he was working for the Russian Mafia again. She had feared for their safety, and his surly manner of late hadn't helped a bit.

"It would bore you."

"Tell me anyway." Vladimir hesitated, then explained about the rootkits, growing excited as he did. "They hide things in computers?" she asked when he stopped.

"That's it. There are simple ones and complex ones. I've been building more complex ones every week. It's really intriguing work."

"And you aren't doing this for the Mafia?"

Vladimir laughed heartily. "Those people? Of course not. It's out of Europe, I think."

"Where?"

"I'm not certain. They're very secretive. I'd say France, but maybe Belgium. My contact writes English like a Frenchman sometimes."

"Or Quebec, or North Africa. Don't they speak French there too?"

"Sure, but they don't have any money. But he could be anywhere. I'd have to spend a day tracing back one of his messages and even then it might not work. I don't care, anyway. His money is good." She sipped her vodka. "What?" A dark expression had crossed her face.

"You're . . . you're telling me the truth, aren't you?"

Vladimir stared at her for a long moment, the anger starting to well up. He pushed it down savagely, then in a steady voice said, "I've told you what I'm doing. I'm not lying, Ivana."

"Good. Then we are safe and I can breathe again." It seemed to her in that moment that the life for them she dreamed of would actually happen. She'd have a baby and everything would be perfect.

OOOOOOOOOOOO 4 0

Brian Manfield rolled one of the dice in the palm of his hand. Four. He went to the fourth taxi in the queue and asked the driver if he spoke English. The Pakistani nodded his head. "Say a few words if you would, mate," Manfield asked. "Just to be sure."

"Yes, I speak good English." The accent was thick, but Manfield understood him.

"Right then. Load my luggage." The other drivers ahead had exited their vehicles and were agitated, vigorously complaining that he hadn't taken the first taxi, but Manfield ignored them. The driver shot back a quick answer that satisfied no one as he moved to open the trunk. Manfield waited on the curb, discreetly scanning the area as the driver placed the luggage into the trunk, then climbed into the taxi as soon as the Pakistani did. He gave the name of the modest hotel where he'd be staying as the car pulled away from the curb and drove out of JFK International Airport.

They drove through Queens and Brooklyn in silence, then crossed the Manhattan Bridge onto the island. The going was slow after that, but before five o'clock Manfield was checked into his hotel. He showered, changed into running shoes, tan chinos, a polo shirt, and a dark blue windbreaker. The day had been crisp enough, he thought, that he wouldn't draw any attention, especially at night, with the jacket.

Outside he took in the city, realizing how much it reminded him of portions of London. He entered the subway, exiting at Inwood, where he walked four blocks. The address turned out to be a small store. The aging sign outside belonged to the former owner and read SWENSON'S SPORTING GOODS. A bell over the door sounded as Manfield entered.

The dark-skinned man in his midthirties behind the counter looked up. "We are just closing, sir." He was slender, with a well-trimmed beard. On the surface the accent was British, but Manfield recognized it at once as Egyptian.

"I won't be long," he said pleasantly. "Perhaps you have a package for me?"

The man took another look at his customer. "I don't understand."

"Omar said you were holding something for me." Manfield always felt silly with these games, but at least once in the past they had saved his life.

The man blinked, then replied steadily, "You mean my cousin Muhammad."

"Perhaps you are right, though I now recall his name was Abdul."

"*Allah Akbar,*" the clerk said quietly. "Just a moment." He retreated behind a curtained doorway while Manfield moved closer to the front door, where he could watch equally the rear of the store and the street. A moment later the man returned with a package wrapped in heavy brown paper, tied with twine. "Here."

Manfield hefted the package and nodded. "Thank you." He turned and went out the doorway without another word. Two blocks away he entered the McDonald's he'd spotted earlier and pressed his way through the crowd to the men's room. He waited nearly five minutes until the handicapped stall was free, then entered and secured the door. Inside, he spread several layers of paper across the seat, then sat and carefully opened the package. Inside was a cell phone, which he unwrapped and placed into his left front jacket pocket. The small envelope he slipped into the inside pocket of the jacket.

Next he opened the dark plastic, rectangular box. Inside was a Boker ceramic lock-blade knife with a titanium handle and a drop-forged, two-inch blade. It was small enough to pass as a simple pocket-knife any man might carry. He snapped the blade open with just his right hand, closed it, then snapped it open again. Perfect. Closing it, he slipped the knife into his right front pants pocket.

Also in the box was a .380 Astra Constable, the Spanish version of the better known Walther PPK. Made without alloys, the weapon was surprisingly heavy for its small size, a characteristic Manfield approved of as it meant less recoil. He removed the pistol, checked it for balance, confirmed it was empty, then dry-snapped the hammer three times to test the trigger pull in double action. Smooth and light. Someone who knew his business had reworked the trigger.

Beside the pistol was a six-inch-long silencer, the size of a roll of half-dollar coins. He placed it into his left front jacket pocket beside the cell phone. Two empty metal magazines were also in the box along with the supply of Remington 102-grain Golden Saber hollow-point ammunition he'd requested. It had the best spread characteristics of all .380 ammunition and was the most lethal.

Manfield slipped bullets into each clip, filling them to capacity. Placing one in his right jacket pocket, he inserted the other into the butt of the pistol. He worked the slide once, releasing it to feed a bullet into the chamber with a sharp snap. He lowered the hammer, then removed the magazine and replaced the bullet now in the weapon, then placed the magazine back into the gun. Confirming that the safety was off so the weapon was ready for immediate use, he inserted the pistol inside his pants at the small of his back.

Next he rewrapped the box, tied the package with string, then unlocked the door, delivering the stall to a ten-year-old boy dancing on his feet.

Manfield smiled. "All yours." He buried the package in the wastebasket so it didn't show, then left the McDonald's, glancing at his watch as he did: 6:13. He walked steadily back to the subway, confident he still had plenty of time.

MANHATTAN, NYC
FISCHERMAN, PLATT & COHEN
THURSDAY, AUGUST 31
9:08 P.M.

When Sue Tabor was sixteen years old, she'd lost her virginity to a summer boyfriend in a small park not far from Chinatown in San Francisco. She'd been visiting her grandmother and had decided this would be her best opportunity. She knew no one there, so no one would talk about her back home in Roseville. Leaving soon for college, she refused to be the only virgin freshman there.

In college, Sue had learned discretion and the advantages of sustained relationships over one-night stands. When she'd moved into her career, she'd discovered the value of sleeping up. She couldn't care less what her coworkers thought. She liked to screw, she'd once told a girlfriend, so why not screw someone who could do her some good? In her world of computers, attractive women were rare so she'd had little competition. And she had no complaints.

Joshua Greene was a case in point. Though nearly thirty years her senior, he'd proven a surprisingly robust and satisfying lover. Separated from his wife of twenty-five years, a separation for which Sue refused to hold herself responsible, he'd turned to his young IT manager with a fierce ardor. The more she'd insisted on sex at the office, the more passionate he'd become.

Sue had learned early on that sex with a young woman, especially one with exotic looks, was quite enough for most middle-aged men.

But if she threw in a few things their wives had long ago stopped doing and added a bit of excitement, they were hers, much harder to get rid of than to keep.

She'd been about to land her next substantial pay raise when this Superphreak bug had struck, ending all prospects. Greene had promised to find her a good job elsewhere regardless of the outcome, but she knew word about what had happened would spread and there would be some hesitation in hiring her. Managers would wonder if she couldn't have done something to prevent the contamination or at least fix it sooner.

The most intriguing part of the last two and a half weeks had been Jeff Aiken. She'd never pressed enough to move beyond their professional relationship, but couldn't help wondering what it would have been like had she done so. For a man so knowledgeable with computers, he was surprisingly fit and handsome. She'd seen a flicker of interest, but he'd taken it no further.

Not that there'd been an opportunity. Greene had spotted her interest from the first and dropped by several times a day. She didn't want to risk that job recommendation in the event this turned into a disaster. People were going to ask why Fischerman, Platt & Cohen had gone out of business, and her name was bound to come up.

Anyway, there was plenty of time. She had Jeff's card. And lots of other fish were in the sea.

It had been a difficult day. She'd made copies of the partially cleansed copies she'd twice tried to boot and had Jeff step her through what he knew about Superphreak, explaining to her the methodology he was following. She'd spent the last three days reworking the copy of the last daily backup, searching for signs of the virus. But she'd decided it was largely a waste of time. She just didn't know enough. She'd only tried because there'd been no other productive work for her.

Sue had checked her e-mail and found her Superphreak posting had generated more than one hundred messages, but none that helped her and none from Superphreak himself. The man was apparently Russian, as Jeff had surmised, and was a sort of geek god when it came to viruses. She'd asked questions of some of those who'd e-mailed her, but in the end it turned out no one really knew all that much about Superphreak except that he appeared in certain chat rooms from time to time.

She spent days in those rooms but he'd not reappeared. She'd posted a few more messages for him to contact her, with no positive results. "Dante" had been equally elusive, and Sue feared that her first message had driven the men underground.

Harold left the office at six thirty while Sue was returning to the backup. Two hours later Greene entered the IT Center, coming up behind her, then cupping her breasts with each hand. "Guess who?"

"I don't have to guess," she'd said. "No one handles me like you do. What's up?"

" 'Handles'? Is that what you call it?"

"What else? They aren't doorknobs."

"Sorry," he said in a little-boy voice.

Men can be such children, she thought. "Now, don't get that way. I didn't say I didn't like it." Sue stood up and put her arms around him. They kissed. "Like I said, what's up?"

"Me, for one. You about done here?"

"I think we're about 'done' permanently."

"That bad?"

She sighed. "I don't know. Jeff's pretty discouraged. Looks like we got hit twice by the mother of all viruses."

"Shit!" He looked as if all the steam in him had vanished.

"You can say that again. I'm almost finished for the day."

"Me too. How about the Hemingway in an hour?"

Sue nodded. "Pick up some Chinese, will you? I'm starving."

"Sure." Greene gave her that hound-dog look of need.

She patted his arm. "Later. And don't start without me."

Twenty minutes later she was ready to leave. She decided to polish her résumé the next day and would tell Harold to do the same thing. Maybe Jeff would come up with a miracle, but she wasn't banking on it. As she left the offices, several associates were hard at work. These cases had recently been started; all of the files had been in their laptops when the firm had been struck. They shot her unpleasant looks as she passed by. She guessed a few of them had sent out their résumés already.

Outside, Sue breathed in the night air as she glanced at her watch. Greene would be waiting. She stepped off sprightly, walking three quick blocks before stopping just outside the hotel to remove the keycard and to take a mint from her purse. As Sue placed the candy into her mouth, she felt a sharp pain against her right ribs.

"Don't make a sound or I'll cut you." The voice was British. "Over here."

In the alleyway, she braced herself. "Take my purse. I don't have much—"

"Shut up. Let's go to your room. Act like we know each other if the clerk's at the desk."

"What do you wan—?" The knife went deeper into her, enough to cause a wave of nausea to sweep through her.

"I said, shut up. Don't speak again. And remember . . . we're friends."

Manfield's information had included her driver's license photograph. He'd waited nearly three hours for Sue to exit the office building. He'd followed the woman, assuming she was on her way home. In the event he was mistaken, he had her address. When she'd stopped almost in front of the hotel and removed a plastic keycard, he'd realized she wasn't going home just yet. Since she lived in the city, he concluded she was meeting a lover. He couldn't risk her spending the night, so he'd had no choice but take her. He wanted this job over with.

MANHATTAN, NEW YORK
HOTEL LUXOR
EAST THIRTIETH STREET
THURSDAY, AUGUST 31
9:31 P.M.

Jeff ate as he watched cable news. No mention of the Superphreak virus, but it was bound to get into the media eventually. He wasn't convinced that would be bad. Getting the public involved sometimes had a way of speeding up patches.

He opened ICQ, saw Daryl was online, and typed:

> JA33:   Is thr any pln t leak t media?

There was a short pause.

> D007:   Hello t u 2. I hdnt gvn it any thot. Wht do u thnk?
> JA33:   We arent mkng nuff headwa. I cnt see any hrm. Wht do u thnk?
> D007:   Less I go off reservtn it wn't b my cll. Th secrity vndrs knw abt it alrdy. At sum point I'd think 1f thm wud issue prss rls.
> JA33:   I ws jst thnkng we cld gt mre rsorcs t bear if th pblc ws invlvd, + it wld pt heat on t vndrs. r thy coprtng yt?
> D007:   Its stll prtty lw n t totem ple so fr. I kp tryng. Rtkts mean mny vrss arnt detectd.

JA33:   Any nw dvlpmnts I shld knw abt?

D007:   More BIOS wipes, prmrly Dell and HP. Thy trnd th mchns
           to anchr wghts.

JA33:   How about chat rms?

D007:   Sphreak name sumtim bt no help. I dnt hv nuf staff t d t
           as mch as Id lke.

JA33:   Hv u pstd ny mssgs t sphreak?

D007:   We tlkd bot tht n dcdd gainst t. t wld alrt hm. He'd chng
           hs pttrn. No one knws mch abut t gy. We fond sm psts fr
           spreak frm otsde.

JA33:   Wh?

D007:   Smn usng t nme dragon lady. Mean nythng t u?

Dragon Lady? Someone Chinese?

JA33:   could b lmst anbdy bt ths isnt cmmn knwldg yt. th IT
           mngr at t frm is prt Chinese bt sh ddnt sy nythng t m abot
           pstng. Wht do u thnk?

D007:   Id sy sphreak hs bn tippd off alrdy. If sh hsnt tld u
           anythng it cus sh ddnt lrn anytng.

Jeff made a mental note to talk to Sue about it in the morning.

D007:   NYC tomrro. Will call to meet w u if ok.

JA33:   Snds good. Anytng els?

D007:   I think wer scrwd.

MANHATTAN, NEW YORK
MIDTOWN
HEMINGWAY HOTEL
THURSDAY, AUGUST 31
10:19 P.M.

The Hemingway Hotel had undergone a complete restoration in the 1970s, a time of considerable labor strife in the Big Apple. As a result, much of the work had been shoddy. The hotel had been sold twice since then, and it was a chore to keep the place looking good. The latest owners were contemplating whether another remodeling would be better than repairing as necessary. While they dithered, certain necessary improvements had never taken place, such as the installation of security cameras.

There was no clerk, no one at all at the front desk, as they walked stiffly through the lobby to the elevator bank. Sue punched number 4, unable to think of anything else to do or anything at all to say. In the elevator she began to sweat profusely, droplets running from her armpits. Stepping off the elevator, Manfield and Sue Tabor moved down the hallway toward room 416. At the doorway they stopped and he whispered into her ear, "Open it right now, Sue." She'd never been more frightened in her life. That he knew her name, that this wasn't a random act, terrified her. The pain of the knife was dulled by a thick layer of fear.

Sue slipped the keycard into the slot, then pulled it up sharply. When the light switched green, the man turned the handle. In they went, in a quick rush. Greene had removed his jacket, shirt, and undershirt, and he was standing by the bed wearing only his trousers, looking toward the television set. "What the . . . ?" he stammered.

Manfield pushed Sue into Greene so hard the pair fell back against the bed. Drawing his pistol, Manfield said, "Quiet now. If I have to make any noise, I'll kill you both. Tell me what I want to know and nobody gets hurt." Gesturing with the gun, he motioned for them to sit. They sat on the edge of the bed.

"If you want money," Greene said, attempting to take charge of the situation, "I've got—"

"Shut up!"

"—plenty right there on the desk . . ." Greene stopped and stared at the barrel of the gun, the energy draining out of him.

Manfield moved slowly to the desk and glanced down. With his free hand, he pocketed the cash without counting it.

"Who are you?" he said to the man.

"Joshua Greene."

"What are you to her?"

"Why . . . we're . . ."

"Yes, I can see that."

"He's my boss," Sue said, understanding what the Brit wanted to know.

"Ahh. I get the picture." Better and better. "Sue, lie on the bed, facedown. Pile the pillows over your head. And don't move. You"—Manfield indicated Greene—"come over here." Greene hesitated, looking at Sue for an anguished moment. "Now."

Sue lay across the bed, rolled uneasily onto her stomach, then crawled up the bed, inching her way slowly. She pulled the pillows to her, then piled them over her head, feeling very young. *How does he know my name?* she thought. *What does it mean?* From a distant childhood memory she found a prayer and began to say it to herself.

Greene rose, then crossed to Manfield.

"Over there," Manfield said, indicating the floor in the corner. Greene walked slowly, like a man condemned, as if each step was one of the last he'd ever take.

When Greene's back was turned, Manfield put the automatic away and brought out the knife, snapping it open one-handed. "I have a few questions. I'm sure you'll tell me what I want to know."

On the bed Sue made a small sound, perhaps a sob, muffled by the pillows.

WEEK FOUR

ROOTKITS PROLIFERATING AT DISTURBING RATE

By Arnie Willoughby
Internet News Service
September 1

Nearly one-quarter of all malware located in the Windows operating system is found to be stealth rootkits. This is the result of a recent survey by an alliance of cyber-security companies. "Rootkits are the fastest growing segment of malware," said Arliss Scarbrough, the alliance director. "Rootkits are generally not detected by existing antivirus software. They implant themselves deep within the kernel of the operating system."

Infection rates are reportedly increasing by 100 percent each month, and at this rate rootkits will soon represent the majority of malware present in computers. "Rootkits can be used to cloak any type of virus and make it very difficult to detect and remove the malware. This is an especially disturbing evolution in cyber-security," said Scarbrough, who advocated increased financing for rootkit detection software.

O O O O O O O O O O O 4 4

MANHATTAN, NEW YORK CITY
CENTRAL PARK
FRIDAY, SEPTEMBER 1
10:05 A.M.

Just north of the Pond, Jeff and Daryl sat at a picnic table. He placed her portion of the ravioli in front of her, along with the plastic utensils, as she set down their coffee and two unopened bottles of water. Jeff peeled the top from his coffee and blew steam from the hot brew as Daryl took her first taste.

"Hmm. Good," she said. "I was getting sick of bagels and rolls all the time." Jeff nodded in agreement. He'd felt the same way, which is why he'd suggested the impromptu picnic. Watching Daryl relish her first bite, he felt pleased with himself for remembering that both of them were more than the sum of their work, even though in the back of his mind he'd hoped that fresh surroundings might inspire fresh insights.

They ate and sipped coffee in silence for a few moments longer, then Daryl said, "Do you think our Dragon Lady is your IT manager?"

"I'm curious myself. I'll know in a bit. I haven't been in touch with her since we messaged last night."

"Let me know anything she's learned."

Jeff nodded as he took a bite. He glanced up and his eyes fell on a couple spreading a blanket in the morning sun. The air was cooler but still more summer than fall. Scattered about were other couples and individuals out walking, talking on cell phones, listening to iPods, tossing Frisbees. He wondered for a moment how different their lives would be in two weeks if he and Daryl failed. Would the machinery of this great city grind to a halt? Would the power grid collapse? He could scarcely imagine every catastrophe that was possible.

Returning his attention to Daryl, Jeff asked, "Why are you back in the city?" He'd been idly wondering about that since hearing from her. "I thought you had an important government agency to run?"

"I'm following up on something here." Putting down her fork, she added, "And I wanted to see you." Realizing how that sounded, she tacked on, "For a reason."

"Other than my good looks, you mean?" Jeff said, with a grin before realizing he was actually flirting with her. He'd always found women so complicated, far more complex than the most difficult computer problem. Even gentle Cynthia had thrown him for a loop every so often. But Daryl, he was finding, wasn't all that difficult. Her mind worked very much like his did, and she was no more geared toward failure than he was. They were on the exact same wavelength, in his view. He was completely comfortable with her. Sure, she was drop-dead gorgeous, but since she didn't make much of her looks, Jeff realized he hadn't either. Now, though, with the sun highlighting her golden blond hair and a smidgen of tomato sauce accentuating her full lips, her beauty was hard to ignore.

She smiled. "That, too. But there's something we need to do that you won't want to."

"So you figured to pitch it to my face?" He pushed aside his unexpectedly amorous train of thought, wondering what she was up to.

Daryl hesitated, and for a moment Jeff felt a chill as the warm feeling he'd had vanished. "Fly to D.C. and meet with George Carlton. I'll go with you," she added hastily, taking that moment to touch him briefly on the arm.

Jeff felt a tight grip on his throat. "You're not serious, are you?" His voice sounded foreign even to him.

Daryl pursed her lips. "I am." She leaned forward and spoke quietly. "Nearly all the triggers are date-related, and we're ten days out from the event. And we've got zilch. I've sent so many messages, made so many calls, cornered so many people, I've worn out my welcome. There is nowhere else I can go at this point so it has to be him. Carlton is the chief of counter cyberterrorism at DHS. If he wants to, he can wield a lot of clout. I'm being ignored and the security vendors are way behind the curve on this one. If he can get even one of them moving, we can spare a lot of people a lot of damage."

Jeff's face turned rigid. "There's nothing I can say to him that you can't." The very thought of seeing Carlton face-to-face caused Jeff's bile to rise. "And he's not going to listen to me. We've a track record in that regard, you'll recall."

"I know you don't believe this, but I think George respects your work," Daryl argued, looking intent. "I've sensed it in how he's mentioned your name the time or two it came up. I personally think he feels badly about not listening to you."

Jeff gritted his teeth as he spoke, trying to hold back his anger. " 'Feels badly'? He damn well should. A lot of people died because of him."

"Maybe. But things were so bad in those days, I doubt he could have stopped what happened. Really, Jeff. He was your boss, but only a very small fish at the CIA. His superiors would have still been studying your report while the planes flew into the Towers."

Jeff raised his voice. "We don't *know* what would have happened. He could have told someone, at least! He could have done more! At the very least, he could have *tried*!"

Daryl looked around to see if anyone was paying attention to them, then turned back to the conversation. "We all could have done more, except maybe you. But we have to focus on the here and now. You've seen this virus firsthand, in far greater detail than I have. Between the two of us maybe we can get him at least to lean on the vendors. They're the ones with the resources to counter this." Determined to get Jeff to see her point, Daryl refused to back off. She was desperate and willing to do just about anything to get him to join her in what she saw as their last hope.

"Excuse me." Jeff rose and made his way to the nearby public men's room. Inside, he scrubbed his face with cold water, fighting back the tears. Pulling out a handful of paper towels from the dispenser, he rubbed his face nearly raw. He stood quietly and drew several deep breaths, releasing them slowly. *Who am I really mad at?* he thought. *Carlton? Or myself?* The answer still wasn't clear to him. After nearly ten minutes, he returned to the table.

"There's this," Daryl said, as if he'd never left. "My team has determined that the Superphreak virus propagation avoids IP addresses owned by software security vendors. Think about that, and the effort that's gone into creating it. It's also one of the reasons why the vendors aren't giving this priority."

Jeff's voice was steady as he said, "I agree, someone's put a lot of thought into this."

"There's more." She was speaking so quietly he almost couldn't hear her over the background buzz of conversation and traffic. "It only targets U.S. and European computers."

Jeff was stunned. "The rest of the world is excluded?"

"Yes." Daryl bit her lower lip and seemed to struggle for self-control.

"My God," Jeff whispered, almost to himself. "They're after the West then, not just the technology. It really is an attack." There was nothing left to discuss. "You win. I'll go."

"Good." She pushed the remainder of her food away. "We're on the noon shuttle flight and are meeting him at three."

Gaullist protesters marching in opposition to Arab immigration had all but closed the routes into central Paris. Labib had decided it was pointless to try to drive to his office. He'd called to tell his secretary he wouldn't be in. Most of the staff, she told him, had done the same thing.

Labib dressed casually, left his car parked outside his house, then took a taxi as far as he could into central Paris. Once he reached the closed streets, he began walking, staying off the main arteries, clogged with demonstrators. It was a beautiful late-summer day. The morning air was invigorating, though he knew the city would by afternoon be sitting in a stifling heat.

Weaving his way down side streets and alleys, he reached the back entrance to Graphisme Courageux nearly two hours after leaving his house, where he found Michel Dufour hard at work.

Dufour nodded as Labib entered. "The front staff never arrived."

"The French. I'll never understand them. Where are we?"

"Just a moment. Let me finish this." Dufour continued typing as Labib dug a bottle of water out of the small refrigerator they kept in the office. He sat at his desk and waited. Finally Dufour stopped, turned toward him, and said, "Do you want an overview of the attack?"

Labib nodded.

"I've kept a rough count and believe we have dispatched more than two thousand variations of our core *boîtier*. I'm launching something like five to ten a day and will keep sending them out through the tenth. A significant number are self-replicating, and that increases the numbers considerably."

This was even better than Labib had dared to hope.

"In addition," Dufour continued, "I've paid to have the new attacks of old *boîtiers* increased. The purpose is to keep the security companies too busy to pay attention to ours. About two weeks ago we launched a *boîtier* that blocks automatic updates."

"Is it working?"

"As you know, we can't be certain, but my sense is that it is."

"What else?"

"As for our own *boîtier*, I've been spending more effort to have them encrypted and compressed. Some variants are encrypted with the activation time or codes that will be automatically published on compromised Web sites. That makes them much more difficult to decipher and should buy us enough time. I wish I'd thought of it sooner, like the *noirs*. I wish every *boîtier* had one."

"What is done is done."

The reality of the cyber jihad had never reached the level of Labib's dreams or expectations. As he had once described it to Fajer, it would ideally have been unleashed on an unsuspecting West along with a major Al Qaeda attack against physical infrastructure or targets with symbolic value. But that had proved impossible to coordinate.

The lost years had not proven all bad, though. More and more Westerners were going online, depending on their home computers and the Internet to conduct business and banking. Over those years more and more banks had turned to electronic banking, since it greatly reduced their costs and increased their profits. In theory, a bank of the twenty-first century had no need for a physical office and needed precious few real employees. The profits of such an operation would be enormous, and banks throughout the United States and Europe were racing one another to be the first.

Computers and the Internet were one of the primary means for the expansion of Western culture and were instrumental to its military and economic dominance in the world. They were the means of the most powerful attack on Islam, perverting and tempting Muslims everywhere, launched since the days of the Prophet. Those who said Muslim extremists would never destroy an Internet they too relied on for communication and the spread of propaganda didn't understand what was at stake. The Internet would be rebuilt in time, but in the meanwhile, the inflicted damage would be incalculable.

The military of the West depended more and more on computers and the connectivity of the Internet, as did Western civilian governments. In the United States nearly every government function was tied to the Internet. Social Security and the Fed, to name just two, could be accessed from the Internet. The list was almost endless, which was why Labib had elected to take a shotgun approach rather than to target specific organizations. He'd ordered a series of viruses crafted that could potentially infect every computer in America and every function tied to the Internet. He was trusting that technology would plant the electronic seed of his jihad everywhere.

The objective was to infect and destroy as much of the information and technology of the West as possible, all on the same day.

When Labib had finally devised the cyber-attack, separating what he could actually accomplish from fantasy, he had flown by helicopter and met with Fajer high in the Hejaz Mountains at the remote camp of members of their tribe. They'd consumed a traditional Arab meal consisting of *al kabsa* (rice cooked with chicken in a pot), dates, *hawayij* (a spice-blended bread), followed by *al haysa*, a sweet dessert, while watching traditional dance, performed by the unmarried young women and girls of the tribe. Fajer had pointed out one of the girls, about ten years old, a fragile beauty with doelike eyes and a luminescent face. "My future wife," he said. "I will keep her here so she is not contaminated by luxury."

Labib thought the idea of raising a wife to form was disgusting but said nothing. Though the Prophet allowed four wives, Labib knew from personal experience that the consequences for all were not necessarily good and thought his brother knew this as well. Labib loved his wife and would never take another.

Late that night, as the camp settled into the evening, amid the smells of smoke and camel dung mixed with the sweet fragrance of cedar native to the region, the brothers sat by a dying fire as Labib told Fajer what the two of them would do for Allah.

"We will launch our cyber jihad in coordination with an Al Qaeda attack that will make the World Trade Center seem as nothing. We will destroy billions of dollars in assets, cripple the Internet on which the Western world depends, unleash floods, shut down—even destroy—power plants, including nuclear ones. Airplanes will fall from the sky. Millions of computers will be permanently destroyed, including those containing the records of pensions. The loss of key data will be incalculable. Faith will be shattered. Anger against their government will be greater than ever before. It will cause more damage than the first attack did. The West, the United States of America, will suffer a great defeat. Faith in Western technology will be crippled.

"In the Muslim world, those who have been mesmerized by false prophets will turn away, while our true brothers who have been tempted by the West for too long will rise up. In Iraq, Iran, and Syria, those fighting the infidel will be emboldened. It will take years to recover from this, years of retreat for the West. It will end with a new caliphate."

Fajer's eyes had blazed with fervor and Labib had never felt closer to him, or to Allah.

But now he knew some of what he had planned would not happen. There would be no Al Qaeda attack and he could not estimate in advance the full extent of the harm he would cause on September 11. He was certain it would be substantial; it might even be crippling.

Yet this was only to be the first attack. Already he and Dufour were planning a follow-up, which they would unleash before the United States had recovered from the first. Their assault from this time forward would be relentless and unstoppable.

The rear door opened and Fajer stepped in, neatly dressed in a dark charcoal Armani suit. Labib had had no idea his brother was in Paris. He grinned and stood up, taking his older brother into his arms. *"As-salaam alaikum."*

Fajer smiled. *"As-salaam."* He released his younger brother and greeted Dufour. "How goes it?" he asked in French.

"Excellent, I believe. We are in Allah's hands," the young man answered.

"Good." Fajer found a seat. He could not remember when last he had felt so confident, so certain. Earlier that week he'd alerted George Carlton to look for any government knowledge of, or concern over, the name *Superphreak*, spelled with a *ph*. He'd received no alert and was feeling better about the security of the jihad.

"Infidels already die for Allah." Fajer smiled warmly. "And many, many more will soon follow."

OOOOOOOOOOOO 46

DEPARTMENT OF HOMELAND SECURITY, WASHINGTON, D.C.
DIVISION OF COUNTER CYBERTERRORISM
FRIDAY, SEPTEMBER 1
3:14 P.M.

As soon as he returned to his office, George Carlton regretted the half bottle of red wine he'd indulged in over a late lunch when he realized whom he was about to meet. He popped a breath mint and willed himself to be more alert.

In the years since 9/11, Carlton had experienced no guilt over his decision to sit on Jeff Aiken's report. He'd always considered it too lurid and imprecise to have had any impact on his superiors. It would only have raised questions about the kind of operation he ran in those days, and nothing would have happened in response to it anyway. Look at that FBI agent in Phoenix. They'd ignored his repeated reports about Arabs learning to fly commercial airplanes but not wanting to practice takeoffs or landings. He'd been lucky not to get fired.

Only after he was at DHS did Carlton retrieve the report one afternoon and read it in detail for the first time since he'd received it. He'd been chilled by its prescience. In detail it had contained many inaccuracies, though it was difficult to say that the suggested targets hadn't actually been intended, just not carried out. Of particular note was that Jeff had identified the operation as Al Qaeda.

To think that 9/11 would have been thwarted if the CIA and the FBI had actually acted on the report was fantasy. They'd had other information just as reliable and from sources better known to them, Carlton knew, and had done absolutely nothing. Passing the report up would have been pointless.

And, of course, once the attack actually took place, making certain no one who mattered knew about Jeff's report had been vital to Carlton's continued career. Jeff had assisted him in that regard by resigning, rather than going to his superiors.

Not that his superiors would have wanted to know such a report even existed. Carlton was sure there had been others—the Company was, after all, a big operation, and its primary mission was gathering information—and they'd all vanished as quickly as had Jeff's.

No, all in all, Carlton felt no guilt over his actions. The federal bureaucracy was what it was. He'd have been a fool to have done other than what he'd done. Which didn't make this meeting any easier. He knew Jeff had lost his fiancée in the Towers, and he'd dealt with him enough in the aftermath to know how emotional he was on the subject. But he liked seeing Daryl and welcomed almost any opportunity to meet with her. In fact, the more seriously he considered divorce, the more often he found his fantasies turning to the Scandinavian beauty.

Carlton smiled at the couple waiting for him and extended his hand. "So good to see you, Daryl. You're lovely as ever. And Jeff . . . What can I say? It's been too long."

Daryl rose and shook Carlton's hand, while Jeff ignored the offer. Carlton looked at Daryl as if to say he understood. "This way, please. Can I get you anything?"

Carlton's corner office was spacious and elegantly appointed. His recent improvement in fortune had let him indulge himself a bit. The Persian carpet was a case in point. He'd spent $30,000 on it, though he'd told staff it was a gift from his wife, who everyone assumed was rich, but it had the effect on visitors he'd sought and had become a symbol to him of the life he soon expected to be enjoying.

Just through his door Carlton hesitated, thinking about holding the meeting from behind his enormous desk. He decided to use the small, intimate, in-office conference table instead. "Nothing then?" he said as they took chairs around the table.

Daryl was stunning as always, dressed today in a trim business suit with a brightly colored floral scarf at her neck, which set off her skin tone to perfection. Jeff, as always, was dressed as in tan chinos, Rockports, a polo shirt, and navy travel blazer. He looked much older than the last time Carlton had seen him. Carlton wondered if time had been as hard on himself.

"I'm all ears," Carlton said, beaming at Daryl.

"I'll get right to it then," Daryl said. "Time is valuable and we both appreciate your agreeing to meet on such short notice. On August eleventh, CISU estimates several hundred computers nationwide were immobilized by various types of malware. There were a number of deaths. You'll recall the auto worker and hospital deaths I spoke to you about two weeks ago."

"I do." Carlton assumed his serious demeanor.

"There were more than one dozen others, all in hospitals. I sent you a list of the activities adversely affected."

"Yes, some accounting records, software in hospitals, air-traffic-control problems in New Mexico, I think, and some dams. Are those are the ones you mean?"

Jeff felt his skin crawl from merely being in Carlton's presence. Coming here was a mistake.

Daryl nodded to Carlton. "And it was Arizona, though that's not important. My team has been following up and we have a much better picture of what took place. I've asked Jeff to come because he's the most knowledgeable on the Superphreak virus. It caused the computers—"

"Excuse me? *Superphreak?*" A jolt such as he'd never experienced before shot through Carlton's body.

"That's right. Does that mean something to you?" Carlton struggled to regain his composure, then shook his head. "We've concluded that most, perhaps all of these viruses," Daryl continued, "were at least in part the creation of a hacker with the cyber handle of Superphreak, so that's what we're calling all of them. It's in the report I filed with you last week."

A report you never read, Jeff thought.

Carlton smiled and nodded. He struggled to focus on what he was hearing, but could not. In his head, all he could hear was a sound like the crashing of enormous waves. "Proceed, please," he managed to say.

Daryl looked at him oddly. "Jeff knows Superphreak better than anyone and I'll ask him to tell you about it in a moment, but for now my team has been able to identify four hundred and seventy-eight separate attacks by Superphreak, all occurring on August eleventh. We have reports of hundreds more that could be related, but we're not including them unless they're identical in operation or the word *Superphreak* has been found."

"None since August eleventh? That's encouraging," Carlton said hopefully.

"I'm afraid not," Jeff heard himself say. "It's the opposite, in fact." For an instant he wanted to strike the man.

"It sounds as if the danger has passed," Carlton countered. "If I'm not correct, you're describing a date-activated virus."

Daryl said, "Yes, but in nearly every case we've determined that the date in some part of the affected computers was off by one month. They actually read September eleventh."

For a moment Carlton felt no sensation at all in his body. It was as if he were being prepped for an operation, and the anesthesia had been released into his bloodstream. Only the day before he'd planted in Fort Dupont Park a copy of Daryl's latest report, which he hadn't bothered to read.

Daryl was still speaking. ". . . that all the infected computers are to be triggered on that date. We've drawn the obvious conclusion but have no proof. We've been focused on learning about it, deciding its scope, and persuading the vendors to act."

Carlton cleared his throat. "If I recall correctly, you believe this is a Russian hacker, interested in financial gain."

"Not quite," Jeff corrected. "In fact, we've found no hint of a desire for financial gain. Financial and other records are targeted, but the effect is destruction, not theft. And Russians are well known to hire out to all comers." He stared at Carlton to make certain he'd made his point. This was meaningless but he'd promised. "I learned from Daryl just this morning that Superphreak is programmed to avoid the IP addresses of security vendors and is only targeting U.S. and European computers. The viruses are also employing very sophisticated rootkits. I've been working nearly three weeks on Superphreak and I still don't have a handle on it. In my case, the computers were infected with two viruses, one cloaked, both very destructive. One was meant to erase all data, the other to destroy the operating system. The second succeeded before the first was finished, but I haven't been able to rid the system of the viruses."

"We need signatures and patches," Daryl said. "To get them we need the vendors to take this threat seriously."

"They aren't cooperating?" Carlton raised his eyebrow.

"Not particularly. Their honeypots haven't turned it up because it's ignoring them, and the rootkits are hiding them from detection on their customer systems." Daryl paused and looked closely at Carlton to be sure he understood the significance of what she was saying. In a firm voice she said, "I need you to lean on them."

"I don't know how much influence I can have, if US-CERT is having no effect."

"It can't hurt, George, and we haven't much time."

"What about other agencies? The FBI?"

Daryl nodded. "The increase in computer-related incidents hasn't gone unnoticed. I understand a report was placed on the president's desk two days ago. He's referred the matter to the FBI and asked for a detailed report next month."

"That's it then," Carlton said.

"It's not enough, George. This is all happening so fast there isn't time for this kind of leisure in responding. Clearly they don't understand the extent of this thing or the president would not have asked for a report; he'd have demanded action. You know how this works, we all do. They'll want to prove everything is connected and not random. They'll require solid evidence, not indicators. They'll be more concerned with covering their backs than with dealing with this hot potato. And the FBI is hardly the right agency to deal with this kind of threat."

"Who is, in your opinion?"

"The Division of Counter Cyberterrorism. That's you, George. That's why we're here."

Carlton was sweating now. He licked his upper lip. For long seconds he remained motionless. All he could think was *Superphreak!*

Jeff leaned forward. "You're not going to sit on this too, are you?" Daryl looked sharply at him but Jeff paid no attention to her; his eyes focused on Carlton like lasers.

Carlton drew himself up. "I've never sat on anything important. Despite what you think, Jeff."

Jeff laughed, the sound coming out more like a sharp bark. "You make me sick! I gave you the World Trade Center Towers as targets, the Pentagon, for God's sake! I gave you the names of five of the hijackers and you did nothing!"

Carlton seemed to recoil. "It's true, but you gave me a lot of unrelated information as well. But that's not the point. I passed the report up. I can't be held responsible if no one believed you."

Jeff shot to his feet. "You son of a bitch!"

Daryl stood up, taking control. "Jeff! Leave this room now! I'll take care of this from here."

Jeff stood immobile, then abruptly turned away and walked stiffly out the door. Carlton leaned back, removed a handkerchief, and wiped his brow. "Thank you. I thought he was going to assault me."

"But he didn't," she said. "Are you all right?"

Carlton drew a deep breath, still staring at the closed door, then slowly released it. "Yes. You see how emotional he can be, though."

"I don't want his anger to temper my message," Daryl warned. "I need for you to lean on the security vendors, to get as much of the government moving on this as possible."

"You think it's that serious?" Carlton struggled to regain some composure. He was finding it impossible to get his mind on track.

"I think in eleven days we're going to wish to God we'd done something more. You can be absolutely certain people are going to ask questions. At the least, we need to show that we did everything we could."

"Yes, yes," Carlton hurried to reassure her, "I understand and agree. I'll see to it at once. Today, in fact."

"Thank you." Daryl gazed at Carlton, who'd behaved oddly for most of this meeting, and wondered if she could trust him. "I'm going to see to Jeff now. He's in no state to be left alone." She rose. "I guess I asked too much bringing him here. I apologize for that outburst."

"It's all right. I respect how he feels. I just wish he could see my position."

A grateful Daryl shook Carlton's hand, then left his office. For once, he didn't check out her ass the minute she turned her back to him.

Carlton staggered over to his desk. His mind was whirling. *How could I be so stupid?* he thought. Frantic, he replayed his last conversation with Fajer. He had to act, had to do *something*!

Jeff wasn't outside Carlton's office or in the lobby. Instead, Daryl found him leaning against her car in the parking lot, staring in disbelief at his BlackBerry.

"Are you all right?" she asked.

Jeff looked up at her, stunned. "I just received a message from the IT manager's assistant at the law firm in New York. Sue Tabor was found murdered this morning. She was in a hotel room with the firm's managing partner. They'd both been tortured."

MANHATTAN, NEW YORK
HOTEL LUXOR
EAST THIRTIETH STREET
FRIDAY, SEPTEMBER 1
5:33 P.M.

Brian Manfield spent the day in two different movie theaters. He'd found them to be as safe a refuge as there was when on a mission. Movie theaters were dark, with a large room to disappear in. They also had several exits; the police would have to be certain the man they wanted was inside to cover them all.

And he liked American hot dogs. He'd been told the very best were sold at baseball games, but he'd never attended one. He found it difficult to believe any could be better than those he'd enjoyed that day.

Manfield's mind had not been on any of the movies that played across the screen, though. Instead, he'd relived the experiences of the previous night. Extracting the information from them had not been difficult. Threat alone had been sufficient to learn everything they knew. Once satisfied, he'd slit both their throats before taking a shower.

They were long dead as he dressed, making certain no blood was on his clothes. The hallway had been clear when he'd left the room, and there was no security camera to avoid. A clerk had been at the front desk, but Manfield had turned his face and was on the street within a moment.

He finished his third hot dog of the day and wondered what they put in them. They had to be unhealthy, but he didn't care. Wonderful. He glanced at his watch. It was time.

Outside, the city was beginning to slow from the bustle of the day. He walked eight blocks to the Hotel Luxor, glad to stretch and get the exercise, then positioned himself in the shadows of the alley across the street, checking first to make certain he had the alley to himself. Removing the pistol, he screwed the silencer onto it, then slipped it into his right jacket pocket. He had a good description, but it could apply to any number of men. He'd need to be certain first. From here he could cover both directions to the hotel. He hoped the man would be back soon.

There was much to do and, as always, little time in which to do it.

OOOOOOOOOOO 48

MOSCOW, RUSSIAN FEDERATION
DMITROSVSKY ADMINISTRATIVE DISTRICT
FRIDAY, SEPTEMBER 1
6:38 P.M.

The two-bedroom apartment was spacious and well lit, with a southern exposure. It was new, and empty of all furniture, which only heightened the sense of size. It was everything Boris had promised.

"It will be like living in a gymnasium," Ivana said.

The building manager who was showing it to them smiled agreeably.

From his wheelchair, Vladimir said, "It will fill up fast. My stuff will take up an entire bedroom."

"Everything is to European standards," the building manager said. "High-speed cable in every room. It's all very modern." He was a short, unshaven man, the kind of "new" Russian who'd secretly become rich in the last decade.

Down a hallway they heard laughter. "It seems a bit noisy," Ivana said.

The man shrugged. "Not so much. We do have a few lighthearted types, but it is not an issue. They are reasonable. You will find this as quiet as any such building in Moscow."

"When is it available?" Vladimir asked. If he wanted silence, they would have to move to a dacha in the country.

"Now, of course. Today. I will need your decision and the deposit if you decide to take it, before you leave. I have others scheduled to see the apartment later."

"Perhaps we could have a moment to talk in private?" Ivana said.

"Of course. I'll return in ten minutes."

Ivana walked about the open space, stepping briefly into each room. "What do you think?" she asked her husband, who was sitting in the middle of the living room in his wheelchair.

"It will do. It's expensive, though."

"You said you wanted more room. You said you have the money. I can keep looking, but this is the first suitable place I've found in six months."

Vladimir said nothing as he fumbled a cigarette out of a package and lit it. "I'd like to take it. I don't think I can stand our place any longer. I feel like I'm suffocating there."

Ivana thought of the rent, more than she made in an entire month. She couldn't possibly make the payment on her own. "Can we afford it? Really?" She still wasn't certain her husband was telling her the truth.

"Yes," Vladimir said irritably. "I wouldn't say take it otherwise. Why don't you listen to me?"

"And what if State Security comes crashing in some night? What then?" Her grandfather had vanished in that very way. It had been the worst night of her life, one that came back to her again and again in her nightmares. She'd watched her grandmother wither away and die the following year.

"That won't happen. I'm not working for the Mafia. How many times must I tell you? I'm not breaking laws."

"You have. You used to brag to me about it."

"That was a long time ago. It was stupid of me to do that, and I don't think there were laws about it then anyway."

"But you were glad to do it. I remember how you told all your computer friends. Then I learned hackers used what you learned and ruined computers or stole records. It was terrible. It's like you are a burglar or something. I want an honest life, Vlad. After all I've done, haven't I earned one?"

Vladimir lit a cigarette. "Yes, you have. Believe me, I've told you everything." Ten minutes later he counted out one thousand euros into the sweaty hands of the manager.

MANHATTAN, NEW YORK
FISCHERMAN, PLATT & COHEN
FRIDAY, SEPTEMBER 1
8:33 P.M.

Jeff and Daryl said little on the shuttle back to New York City. Daryl had taken a window seat and stared morosely into the early-evening sky. Jeff withdrew into his own thoughts, trying to make sense of the murders.

Torture suggested someone wanted information. What could an IT manager know that would be of interest to anyone? Or the managing partner of a law firm? It made no sense, unless it was a psychopath. Difficult as it was to believe such people existed, he knew they did.

He couldn't help but wonder if the murders were connected to Superphreak in some way. No one killed anyone over a virus, but this was no ordinary virus. The idea struck him as ridiculous, yet plausible at the same time, causing him to feel even more disoriented.

As soon as the plane landed, Jeff called the IT Center directly at Fischerman, Platt & Cohen. He'd tried several times before boarding with no luck. This time Harold answered. He was clearly distraught and could scarcely speak, but managed to convey that he was still working his way through backups.

"I'm going to the law firm," Jeff said to Daryl as they walked toward ground transportation. "Want to come?"

"If you think I can help."

"I do. And I'd like you to come." He could use the emotional support, he realized.

Traffic as they entered the city was heavy as it made the transition into the weekend. The feel of Manhattan was different as night descended, it seemed to Jeff. Or perhaps that was due to the murders. Suddenly, his world seemed darker than it had been since 9/11. With a certainty that startled him, he grasped the connection. What had begun that terrible day in 2001 was continuing; events that had cost him so much then were now poised to engulf his world again.

He placed a hand on Daryl's shoulder, which seemed thinner and more vulnerable than ever. "We need to be careful," he warned her, seated with him in the back of a cab.

She turned to face him.

"There may very well be a connection between Superphreak and the murders."

Daryl looked at him as if he'd just slapped her. The car bobbed as it hit a dip, then droned as it crossed a bridge with a metal surface. Jeff held her gaze. "I don't believe this is simply about hackers. It's clear to me it's something much bigger." Her eyes grew round as she took in what he was saying.

A few moments later they arrived at the offices of Fischerman, Platt & Cohen, taking the elevator to the IT Center. Perhaps three associates were at their desks. Otherwise the office was darkened and empty. Compared to when he'd first arrived, it seemed all but abandoned to Jeff.

They knocked, then entered. Harold was there, his young face set with determination. He looked up from his computer screen with watery eyes. "Any luck?" Jeff asked. He'd expressed his condolences by telephone earlier when he'd asked Harold to stay over that day.

"Yeah. I think I've located it." Harold looked tired, but determined to do all he could to help. He'd had a crush on Sue. She'd been smart, knew computers, and treated him like an equal. Her death left him feeling empty.

"Good. Show me, then let us get to work." When he introduced Daryl, Harold waved at her without interest. "How are you doing?" Jeff asked as Harold typed, even though he knew Sue's young assistant had been devastated by her murder.

"I'm glad you gave me something to do. Sue always ran the show here and gave me instructions. I was lost." He looked at Jeff. "I guess I should be looking for a job or something."

"Probably. How's the firm taking the losses?"

"Pretty bad. Things weren't looking so great, now this. Some people . . ." Harold's voice trailed off and he stopped typing. Jeff placed a comforting hand on his shoulder. "Some people aren't so nice, you know?" Harold continued, his voice wavering. "They said, 'Good,' when we got word, as if Sue and Mr. Greene had it coming for messing up. I just hate them!" Harold finished typing while choking back tears.

"Go home, Harold," Jeff said, squeezing his shoulder. "Get some rest. Thank you for your help. I know how much Sue valued you and what you did. Try and remember the good, okay? It will help a little."

The young man nodded, looked at Daryl in farewell, then gathered his knapsack and left.

"What are we doing?" Daryl asked, as Jeff sat at the monitor.

"I'm trying to find out what got Sue killed."

Harold had left the computer open in one of the chat rooms Sue had visited. But Jeff found that he couldn't really concentrate. Always in the past he'd been able to put from his mind any concerns he had. In fact, he'd buried himself in work after Cynthia's death primarily to block the pain.

But he found he was still stunned at the murder of Sue Tabor and Joshua Greene. He'd liked Sue. She'd been attractive, bright, and dedicated. He'd even come to like Greene, though it was now more apparent why he'd dropped by the IT Center so often. Still, he'd never pressed Jeff unreasonably for results as his clients often did. He'd seemed to understand the enormous job with which Jeff had been tasked. He was horrified at the thought of both of them tortured and murdered. Neither of them had deserved what was done to them.

The extent of the evil he and Daryl were confronting threatened to overwhelm him. Memories, both real and imagined, of Cynthia and the awful death she'd suffered crowded his mind. But when he turned toward Daryl, the sight of her quietly working at Harold's computer, her attention totally focused on the screen in front of her, had an unexpected calming effect on him. *She's right*, Jeff thought, *and she's exactly the person I want by my side.* Turning back to his own screen, he gave it his full attention.

His time on Sue's computer was both tedious and unproductive. If Jeff had thought anything would jump out at him, he'd been mistaken. Shortly before midnight, Jeff and Daryl left the law offices. Daryl suggested they eat but Jeff shook his head. "No. I'm not hungry. I'll join you if you want, though."

"I'm not really hungry, either," Daryl said.

Both of them were resisting feeling defeated, in over their head. "Let's walk," Jeff said. Instead of taking a cab, the couple strolled to the Hotel Luxor, which Jeff had picked because it was only a few blocks from where he'd be working. The night was pleasantly cool after the closed space of the IT Center. Servers had this habit of warming every space they occupied, and their constant electrical workings charged air in ways that were unnatural. It was good to be outside again, and Jeff wondered for a moment if he wasn't throwing his life away working in closed rooms.

At the hotel he held the door for Daryl, then collected his key from the night clerk, who'd been reading the paper. The pair rode the elevator to his room.

Across the street Manfield spotted them at once. It had been a long seven hours to wait. He hated stakeouts but they were, he knew, essential to success. The street had been quiet for more than an hour before he'd noticed this particular man. As Manfield watched the man enter the hotel, he was nearly certain he was the one. The man had done all right for himself, Manfield allowed, as he waited for them to take the elevator. The blonde with him was quite a dish.

When the couple vanished through the closing doors, Manfield rushed across the street, ran toward the elevator, stopped, then muttered to himself. Spotting the night clerk, he behaved as if he'd just had an idea. "Listen," he said, as he approached the counter, "wasn't that Jeff Aiken I just saw? We were supposed to meet for drinks, but I was late. He'd mentioned he was staying here, so I tried to catch him."

The clerk was elderly, with a thick thatch of white hair and pale blue eyes. He'd been a doorman here before his legs gave out. "I couldn't say, sir. Would you like me to check if your Mr. Aiken is a guest?"

"Would you?" Manfield said with a warm smile. "That would be great."

The clerk checked the computer. "Yes, he's a guest."

"Wonderful! What room and I'll just pop up?"

"Oh, I can't give you the room number, sir."

"But I already told you," Manfield protested. "We're old friends and I just missed him for drinks. He's expecting me." It had worked in the past and there was no harm trying.

"I'll be glad to call him if you like. You can speak and make whatever arrangements you want."

Mansfield turned pensive. "Well, I'd hate to awaken him at this hour if I was wrong. He can be quite a bear."

"Perhaps you'd like to leave a message then?"

"No, no. I'll just give him a ring first thing. Perhaps he'll have time for breakfast. You've been most helpful."

As Manfield left, the clerk stared after him, wondering what that had been all about. Certainly not what the man with the English accent claimed. He considered calling the guest and informing him, but the man was right about one thing. People hated being awakened at this hour. Instead, he turned back to his racing form.

UNITED FLIGHT 914
SATURDAY, SEPTEMBER 2
12:47 A.M.

George Carlton stretched out in his first-class seat and stared at the back of the seat in front of him. It had been a hectic day since his disturbing meeting with Jeff Aiken and Daryl Haugen. First he'd attempted his emergency phone number to Fajer al Dawar. The Saudi had insisted on his accepting it, and Carlton had repeatedly refused before relenting. He'd distrusted having the number at all, feared any direct connection, but had finally settled on memorizing it. Until now, he'd never used the number.

That afternoon he'd paid cash for a prepaid cell phone, then bought long-distance minutes. He'd called Fajer and had after several attempts been forced to leave the cell phone's number and a message that the man call him at once. Then he'd stayed away from his office, pacing in a shopping-mall parking lot, waiting on the return call.

Their conversation had taken place late that afternoon and had done nothing to resolve Carlton's concerns—though candidly, he had to admit his reluctance to speak frankly over an open line probably made that impossible. But there just had to be a plausible explanation other than the one he'd concluded. Finally, he'd insisted on a face-to-face meeting, telling the Saudi it was most urgent.

Fajer had replied, "I'm only too glad to meet with you. But you must understand, I am in Paris now on business. I cannot possibly get to the

United States for another month at the earliest. I assure you there is no need for concern."

"Then I'll come to you," Carlton had answered. "I'll call this number when I touch down tomorrow. Be certain you answer it."

A hectic few hours followed as Carlton instructed his assistant to contact the travel office and arrange his priority departure. The young man had been surprised at the request since from what he could see his boss never did anything on impulse. "What do I say is the reason?" he'd asked.

Carlton had given this only cursory thought. "I must meet with my European counterpart at once. Set up a meeting first thing Monday morning, but I'm leaving tonight. I don't want to meet suffering from jet lag."

He'd then spent half an hour poring over reports, searching for some justification for this abrupt trip. He finally located one that might make the case. In any event, he didn't abuse travel privileges. His boss might not like it, but Carlton figured he could sell it if it came to that.

On the airplane sleep wouldn't come. He'd had two double Scotches since takeoff but they'd had no effect. Only now, as Carlton turned his head and stared into nothingness, did he realize he'd neglected to tell his wife he was leaving the country.

MANHATTAN, NEW YORK
HOTEL LUXOR
EAST THIRTIETH STREET
SATURDAY, SEPTEMBER 2
12:59 A.M.

There had been a moment when Jeff and Daryl left the law firm, as they'd walked those few blocks to the Hotel Luxor, when Daryl knew she should have taken a taxi to her own hotel. She'd waited for him to say something, to thank her for her help, to arrange to meet the next day, but instead he'd walked to his hotel talking the entire time about what he'd just learned. She'd meant to say good-night, but for the first time since they'd met, she sensed, on some emotional level, he needed her to stay.

"Now we know Sue was 'Dragon Lady,'" Jeff said as they stepped onto the street relieved at last to have some concrete information. "I traced her back two weeks to her first posting with it. She'd put up more than a dozen since the first, listing an e-mail address for Superphreak to contact her at."

"What came of it?" Daryl asked.

"Nothing, from what I can see. There were a lot of crackpot replies but only a handful read as if the writer had had dealings with this Superphreak guy."

"What did they say?" she asked, hoping this was good news.

"He's supposed to be some kind of hacker legend. A few years ago he found two vulnerabilities in Windows Vista shortly after it was released. He posted the details before Microsoft learned of them, so it was months before they released the patches."

"That's not protocol. He was supposed to advise Microsoft."

Jeff snorted. "Sure, but by publishing earlier he gained credibility with the cracker community as someone who doesn't go totally by the rules. Since then, though, he's become pretty reclusive."

Despite herself, Daryl found herself intrigued by the hacker's obvious brilliance. *Why can't people like that use their brains for the common good?* she thought. "What do the hackers say about him?"

"He's Russian, so we had that right. And he's a genius in writing certain viruses."

Daryl grimaced. "That's no surprise."

"Lately his specialty has been rootkits." Since Jeff had first confirmed Sue had made indirect contact with Superphreak, he'd had an idea and decided now was the time to approach Daryl with it. "You know, it's occurred to me that if we could talk to him and convince him, by hook or by crook, to give us all the rootkits and variants he's written, we'd be weeks, even months, ahead of this. The vendors could do a rush job on signatures and patches."

"Then I've got good news for you. We've got a name." Daryl was grinning.

"How?"

"My team has been hard at work tracing the usage of the word *Superphreak*. We didn't have much luck in an open search but got lucky in the NSA's archives of closed hacker forums and chat rooms. We found a key post from several years ago when a hacker was chatting with Superphreak and called him Vlad. Then we searched for a Vlad and came up with over a dozen, but only one of them with a post related to the same technical data discussed in Superphreak chats. His last name was in the e-mail address in the forum posting: vkoskov@zhtskky.ru. There was only one hacker forum posting using this account, but our search found it, which is why they say that everything you ever did is somewhere on the Net. After that it was simple."

"I would think he'd have been more careful," Jeff said.

"This was several years ago. I don't think he was giving security much thought then. His name appears to be Vladimir Koskov, and I have an address for him in Moscow."

"Do you think it's valid?" Jeff wanted to believe this was their first real break, but it seemed too easy, too simple.

"Probably." Daryl nodded. "Or at least I think it's where he was living when he registered that first e-mail account."

Jeff paused a moment. "Someone should pay him a visit."

"I've already made the request, but it will be weeks before I get a response through channels, and even then it might not be a positive one. They have to go through the embassy in Moscow, and I'll be told they have better things to do."

"We don't have weeks!" Jeff exclaimed. "Hasn't anyone figured that out yet?"

"Sure. You and me. That's about it. And the people we work with."

At that moment they reached the Hotel Luxor. They entered the lobby, where Jeff retrieved his key, and she went with him upstairs, all without either of them acknowledging what they were doing.

"Drink?" he said when they entered the room.

"Yes. Bourbon, if you've got it."

Jeff opened the minibar, dug around, then produced a bottle of Jim Beam. "I can get ice, if you'd like."

"No need. And I'll drink it from the bottle, so forget about a glass."

He laughed, handed her the small bottle, then dug out a beer. He popped the top, held it out for a toast. "To getting this asshole." She smiled wanly and they drank. The beer tasted good going down, and for a second he considered drowning himself in an ocean of pilsner. But he knew that was no answer, having drunk his fair share in the months after Cynthia's death. And for the first time since this while ordeal began, he had some good news to hang on to, maybe even act on. Suddenly, he was also aware that a beautiful woman, one to whom he was very drawn, was sitting there with him in his hotel room. And he was happy about it. He sat in a chair beside the small breakfast table and looked directly into her serene face.

"I haven't missed the fact that you're here in my hotel room," he said, finally understanding that though Cynthia was still with him, she was now only a memory, albeit a lovely one no one could ever take from him. She'd been perhaps the most practical person he'd ever known, and he knew that she'd approve of where he found himself now.

Daryl sat on a nearby armchair, sipped her drink, and said, "I thought maybe you figured there was a cord connecting me to you, or something."

"It's the 'or something.'" He drank again, his mind back on their immediate problem. "I was thinking about what you said before, about backtracking to find out the identity of Superphreak. I bet that's how they found Sue Tabor. I traced the e-mail address she used, and it was registered in her name with the law firm address. There's so much on the Internet now if you know where and how to look."

"Of course. With that, they could have found a photo, even located some bio information on her."

Jeff nodded. "'The Internet: Friend or Foe?'" he intoned. "Sounds like a bad evening-news segment."

Daryl gave a small smile. "So you really think that whoever is in back of this avalanche of viruses killed her? There are dozens of people working on this."

"Sure, but her they knew. And all they need to do is just slow things down. There isn't a lot of time left, remember? They wouldn't know how important she was to our effort, but if they're of that mind-set, where's the harm in killing her? What do they have to lose? And she was the one asking about Superphreak. No one else was."

Daryl shivered. "It gives me the willies, if you're right. This means they have assassins available to kill people."

"If I'm right, it looks like they do. But we can't know that for sure."

Daryl took another pull on the bottle. "Okay, killing her *might* make some sense, but why kill her boss? He was just a lawyer, for God's sake! You start down that path, where does it end?"

Jeff shrugged. "Because they were together."

"You mean he got caught at the wrong place at the wrong time?"

"Probably." Jeff thought back to his meetings with Joshua Greene. The man didn't deserve his fate. "Consider what we've discovered up to now. We have dozens of variants, most encrypted and buried within operating systems protected by rootkits. So far nearly all of them are triggered by the date September 11. And look at all the targets, including the ones we know and the possible ones. We're talking Wall Street, banks, the Fed, Social Security, to name a few. How about the power grid? You know how sensitive it is to tweaking, and it can be down for *weeks*, months even. You mentioned a nuclear power plant crashing. And there has to be a whole lot more I haven't even thought of. Not to mention that response systems require using the Internet, and systems that route the Internet might be killed off."

Despite himself, Jeff found his anger rising. "For me the deciding point was when you said that the variants were targeting IP addresses for the United States and Europe. Given that, plus the number of people who must be involved, this attack is every bit as real as flying planes into buildings. The potential loss of life and economic meltdown is tremendous. It's what they were after on 9/11. They didn't pick the World Trade Center by *accident*. They knew how much disruption it would cause. It's as if they're after what makes Western civilization what it is."

Daryl nodded. "We've become so dependent on computers the Western economy would grind to a standstill if what we think is true. When computers only replaced what we did by hand, it wasn't so bad. You can always go back to doing it manually. Those hospitals I saw were forced to return to old procedures. They don't have enough staff to handle all the paperwork, and no one working there now remembers how it was done. They had to reinvent the system and made a lot of mistakes in the process."

"But in too many cases, computers are doing things we *can't* do by hand," Jeff pointed out. "You've got computers instructing other computers. We can't replace that with a human being. And once we rebuild, we'll still be stuck with an Internet system, and a host of computers, we can't trust."

Jeff finished his beer and opened another, but with a shake of her head Daryl refused another bourbon. "If you transfer what's happened to Fischerman, Platt and Cohen to any number of similarly sized businesses," Jeff said, "not just us but the world will go into a depression unlike any we've ever previously experienced. I can't imagine the level of unemployment and the resulting social implications."

"It could be the zero day to end all zero days," Daryl agreed. "This time, we don't really know how extensive this'll be, until zero day."

"And it's been going on for months, at least. Have you ever *heard* about an operation of this scope before?" She shook her head again. "Let's face it, we aren't even in the position of the little Dutch boy putting his finger in the dike. We can do all we can for the next ten days and a cyber Apocalypse will happen regardless. There are so many variants, with such a high level of sophistication, we'll never solve this, not in time." Jeff's face hardened as he made his decision. "We've got to get to the source so we can start on the countermeasures."

"Koskov?" Daryl said, her eyes opening in disbelief. "But we aren't secret agents. I wouldn't know how to go about it. I've sent my request. That's all I can do."

The two stared at each other while a feeling of sadness bordering on despair slowly crept over each of them. Wordlessly, Daryl reached out to Jeff. He took her in his arms and held her tightly. This had been a long time in coming. He kissed her lightly on the forehead for the first time. His lips moved down her cheek. Then their lips met. He felt her stir and they kissed more deeply; it was as if a wall between them had suddenly vanished, as if they were one. She gripped him fiercely and the tenderness turned to passion. He ran his hands along her body, and then she murmured, "Get the light, Jeff. I'm really very shy."

OOOOOOOOOOOO52

Two hundred and seven hours to go, Fajer al Dawar thought. After so long, so many frustrations, and so many disappointments, not much time was left until all the work would be realized. *"Allahu Akbar,"* he muttered.

In these long months since he and Labib had launched their cyber jihad, Fajer had found himself increasingly torn asunder. The part of him that he thought of as Arab relished his role as warrior for Allah. The destruction of the West was the holy goal of all Arabs, he believed. The Prophet had decreed that Islam would, by force of arms, be the one true religion of the world. America and the West were the only significant obstacles to accomplishing that. And they were weak. Like an infant dependent on its mother's breast, the West now fed on computers and the Internet. Take them away and they'd be helpless.

Fajer would show them that Arabs were strong, that there was no God but Allah. For all his personal wealth and power, he was secretly certain that Westerners despised him. The women he bought pretended enthusiasm, but he knew they looked at him with contempt because he was an Arab and a Muslim, just as did the men with whom he did business. Without his money the West would condemn him to the most menial of places. Soon, very soon, he would set all that right.

George Carlton stepped off the plane at Charles de Gaulle Airport and punched in Fajer's number. *Answer, you bastard, answer!*

"*Oui?*"

"I've arrived. Where do we meet?"

"How was your trip, George?"

"Fine, just fine," Carlton grunted. "Where do we meet?"

"You know the Notre Dame Cathedral?"

"Of course."

"Take a taxi to the left bank of the river, immediately opposite the cathedral. You will see a small park just east of the famous Chat Noir cabaret. I will be seated there awaiting you. Say in one hour? And do not be so agitated. There is no reason. You have wasted a trip to a most beautiful city. Perhaps after you have had some rest, I can show you the sights."

Carlton clicked off the phone.

It seemed to Fajer that fall would come early to Paris this year. He sat on a bench at the small park and smoked a Habana cigar as he waited for the American. The triangular park touched the street beside the Seine. On the other two sides the expanse of grass and trees touched three-story apartment buildings, with two narrow alleys running away at an angle. Notre Dame loomed just across the river. Fajer wondered idly how it would look remade as a mosque.

Carlton had been useful over the years, but never so much as in these last few months. Until two weeks ago, Fajer and Labib had known with certainty that no one in the U.S. government who mattered had detected their jihad. The information had allowed Labib to launch ever more sophisticated malware into the electronic maze of the Internet. He'd been willing to risk creating a far larger pool of hackers than he'd originally contemplated; today ten times as many viruses and variants were in the ether as they'd intended, all thanks to George Carlton.

Fajer had not been surprised at the ease with which the American had been seduced and bought. His experience in business was that all Westerners were for sale. It was merely a question of finding the price or that lever unique to the individual. It wasn't all that difficult. With government officials, it was even easier.

All and all, Fajer was pleased with Carlton, but this sudden meeting was troubling. Two weeks before the American had passed on information that told him US-CERT was targeting their viruses. Fajer had been agitated at the news, but Labib had assured him it made no difference at this point. Still, it was disturbing.

Two Frenchwomen walked by Fajer on their way to work and he eyed them appreciatively. He had to admit the women of Paris had a certain grace and fashion sense he'd never seen elsewhere. It was as if the women in London and New York aped their French sisters.

Fajer wondered for a moment what it would be like in Paris on September 12. Though the bulk of the attack was against the United States, many of the viruses also targeted European computers, and of course the entire structure of the Internet would be under attack. Would he notice anything from this same bench? Would there be chaos in the streets? Or would the damage be confined to office buildings and financial institutions? He'd planned to be home in Riyadh for the event but now reconsidered. Why deny himself the pleasure of witnessing disaster firsthand?

A taxi pulled to a stop fifty feet away, and he saw Carlton climb out. Paying the driver, Carlton looked about, squinting in the morning sun, spotted Fajer, then walked toward him. The man was still wearing the suit he'd flown in and had not shaved. He looked angry.

Fajer stood as Carlton approached. "Good morning," he said, extending his hand.

Carlton ignored it and dropped to the bench. Fajer joined him.

"Did you have a good flight?"

"No," Carlton almost shouted. "Tell me what's going on, Fajer! What have you got me into?"

Americans, Fajer thought with disgust, *always in a rush*. "I've already told you. You supply information from time to time and are well paid for it."

"What about this Superphreak you're concerned with? What's that?"

Fajer examined his cigar for a moment. "It is part of the financial operation I told you about last summer."

"How?" Carlton glared at the Arab.

"Are you telling me the name is now of interest to your government?"

"I'm telling you nothing. I'm *demanding answers*."

"I already told you. It's distasteful, but I'm compelled to fulfill a family—"

"Cut the bullshit. This is an operation, isn't it?"

"Operation? I don't know how you are using the word."

"As in a 'mission,'" Carlton said, nearly as if talking to a child. "You're involved with people planting viruses on the Internet, viruses meant to cause harm, not collect financial information. It's some kind of attack, isn't it?"

"Tell me what you know." Fajer had not expected this, not now, not when he and his brother were so close. He could not imagine what had roused this man's suspicion.

"No, Fajer, you're going to tell me," Carlton demanded. "I told you once but I don't think you were listening. I may be a little bent but I'm no traitor. I'm getting reports about the planting of a massive number of viruses in computers all over America. They've all got the name Superphreak in them, and that's the same name you're suddenly interested in. I insist you tell me what's really going on."

Fajer drew a discreet, calming breath. "It's as I told you. The man who created these things apparently uses that name. I have only just learned about it and thought it a more effective means for you to detect this financial business I told you about."

Carlton looked about them out of habit. "I'm no fool, Fajer. You're destroying me." Carlton realized he was sweating and fought the urge to run his bare hand across his forehead.

Clearly the American knew more than he was letting on. The Arab dropped his cigar to the ground and stepped on it with his shoe. "Come with me. There are too many eyes for this to take place here." He stood and began walking through the small park into one of the two narrow alleys. Carlton reluctantly followed, hesitating before entering the confined space. "What else is it you know?" Fajer demanded.

Carlton glared at the man. "These viruses. They've got the name Superphreak, all right. What you didn't tell me was they're triggered to go on September 11. Does the date sound familiar to you?"

"My God!" Fajer said, feigning shock. "The idiots! My friend, I know nothing about this. I think it's someone's idea of a bad joke. The people doing this are Arabs, I've made no secret of that. One of the computer experts writing the code surely picked that date for its symbolic value, but these are not terrorists, I assure you. They are simply thieves. You can relax. Everything is fine."

For the first time since his meeting with Daryl and Jeff, Carlton felt doubt. Could Fajer be right? Was that all this was? Some Arab hacker filled with a bit of zealousness had picked 9/11 just to make a point?

"I told you," Fajer continued smoothly, "that the code is being planted in thousands of computers and will be triggered to execute at the same time. As I understand it, a virus that is not functioning is harder to detect, so they want them all to launch on the same day. Some zealot picked that date for its irony. You know how young men can be. I'm sorry it has caused you this needless worry."

Carlton struggled to remember what he'd been told and what he'd read. "These viruses—they destroy financial records, they don't steal them."

Fajer pursed his lips. "They've sent out a great many. I suppose some might have interacted with certain computers in a destructive way or more might have been destructive in application, but I assure you that is not their purpose. They are not meant to destroy the computers."

Now it came back to him. How could he have forgotten? He'd been a fool for ever trusting this slick Arab son of a bitch. "What about airports?" Carlton demanded. "And dams? These Superphreak viruses are interfering with them, and that has nothing to do with finances. How do you talk your way out of that?"

Fajer sighed. "I don't, my friend, I don't. You should have just taken the money." With that he drew the *shafra* from the small of his back and plunged it deeply into Carlton's stomach as if punching him, then pulled it across his midsection with savage force. He watched the American drop to the ground with scarcely a sound, move his mouth like a fish out of water. Carlton's eyes slowly rolled up as he struggled to breathe, lying in a growing pool of red.

"You should have taken the money and kept your mouth shut. No one would have known. And there is nothing you could have done to stop this." Fajer wiped the knife on Carlton's clothes, then put it away.

Fajer's cell phone rang. *"Oui?"* The Arab listened, then gave rapid instructions in English. By the time he'd finished, George Carlton was dead.

MANHATTAN, NEW YORK
HOTEL LUXOR
EAST THIRTIETH STREET
SATURDAY, SEPTEMBER 2
9:05 A.M.

The sun had already been up for some time when Jeff awoke. In the bathroom, he washed his face quietly.

Returning to the bedroom, he sat at the desk chair, where he could see Daryl clearly. In this time of exhibitionist tattoos and body piercing, with the supposed equality of the sexes, it seemed to Jeff that many women were just mimicking drunken sailors on shore leave in their expressions of independence. One of the consequences, he believed, was that men of his generation, and those of the one coming up, seemed no longer to respect women or hold them in the esteem they once had.

He'd always admired Daryl's fine mind and hard work as a professional. He'd been aware of the chemistry between them from the first moment they'd met. But since Cynthia's death he'd been hollow, unable to react to any woman in an emotional way. Sure, he'd had relationships, but his heart wasn't in any of them. He'd thought that part of him had died with her. Now he realized that it had not. His attraction to Daryl had been so gradual, so natural, awareness of it seemed to have snuck up on him like the first breath of spring after a particularly harsh winter.

Daryl lay now with her head on a pillow, her face turned toward the morning light entering through the blinds. She looked as calm and innocent as a five-year-old child taking a nap. Her elegant, lean body was stretched out, only partially covered by a white sheet. Her right breast rested against the bed; the other was half-covered by the sheet in a provocative manner, as if a photographer had posed her. Under the cover was the rise of her hip, then the delicate line of her legs. It was a breathtaking sight.

Daryl licked her lips. "You're staring at me," she said without opening her eyes.

"Maybe."

"No maybe about it. You're embarrassing me."

Jeff crossed his fingers. "I'll stop."

She rolled on her back, then kept turning until she stopped on her left side. Her back, Jeff decided, was as beautiful as the rest of her. "Promise me something," she said, her voice soft and low.

"Anything." He uncrossed his fingers.

Daryl jerked her head toward him and opened her eyes. "Careful what you say there, dude."

"Anything."

"It's pretty simple, actually. Don't worship me, okay?"

Jeff laughed. "You mean like a goddess or something?"

"More like an object of beauty or something. Okay?"

"I see," Jeff said, though he wasn't sure he did. "All right then, to me you are a hag. We need to turn out the lights to do it or put a paper sack over your head. Better?"

She grinned. "Perfect. Don't look, I've got to use the bathroom."

Jeff closed his eyes, then peeked the moment she stepped off the bed. Amazing.

Once Manfield was satisfied Jeff Aiken and the blond woman weren't coming back out anytime soon, he'd gone to his hotel and slept five hours. He'd returned to his position at six that morning, where he waited patiently. It had been a risk, he knew, but he'd been too exhausted to maintain the watch any longer. He was reasonably certain his target had not left while he'd been gone.

"Now what?" Daryl asked. She was scrubbed and dressed, though in yesterday's clothes and still felt grubby. "Go to the police?"

Jeff had considered that at some length. "I can't think why. Would you believe our story of cyber terrorists attacking the United States, unleashing assassins to murder computer programmers and managing partners of law firms?"

She couldn't help but laugh a little at the description. "When you put it like that, I guess not. So what do we do?"

"Eat. I've done enough thinking on an empty stomach. Maybe we'll come up with an action plan over an old-fashioned American breakfast."

"Meaning?"

"Coffee and bagels haven't been doing me much good lately. Time for some bacon and eggs. I know just the place."

Officer Jerry Kowalski moved to the corner of the intersection as far from the dirt and dust as he could manage. The overtime for covering street construction was welcome, but he hated the noise and grime. He was wearing old shoes and an unofficial pair of trousers close to the official blue of his standard uniform. Better they took the beating than the ones he wore on duty.

He idly wondered if he could get away with wearing one of those surgical masks that people wore in Japan and Hong Kong. He decided he'd look stupid, and his uncle, the sergeant, would ream him out good, and the union would bump him to the bottom of the overtime list. As his uncle often said about the force, "Better not to stand out."

The jackhammer started up again and he slipped in his earplugs. Noise. And dirt. What a mess.

Then, across and down East Thirtieth Street, for the third time he spotted the same guy hanging out in the alley. His partner had told him not to ignore his instincts. "If you're drawn to something, there's a reason. Don't talk yourself out of it," he'd say, then tell Jerry to stop staring at the babes and, for a change, try looking for illegal activity or scumbags up to no good.

In Jerry's opinion this guy really stuck out. For one, he was neatly dressed in a blue windbreaker, tan pants, and very white sneakers. Not the typical alley cretin living out of his shopping cart. For another, though he moved from time to time, he was pretty cool about it all, trying to be discreet without being obvious. The guy had to be up to something.

The first time Jerry spotted him all he'd seen was some subtle movement where it shouldn't be. It was as if he was waiting for someone. *Yeah*, Jerry thought, *waiting in a skanky alley for his date*. Something was going down for sure, though just what he couldn't decide.

Across the street from the alley was the Hotel Luxor, and Jerry figured that someone in there had something to do with why the guy was waiting. With nothing better to do he'd run down in his mind the possibilities. The guy could be a process server in a divorce action or lawsuit; that struck him as pretty logical. The guy was dressed too neatly to be a panhandler, but upon reconsideration, he was also dressed too neatly to be a process server. Those guys were usually pretty ratty.

He could be a jilted boyfriend—that was the one Jerry liked best. The guy was waiting for his girlfriend to get off work so he could corner her and have a few words. Or, Jerry thought, maybe she was shacked up with some guy and what the man in the alley had in mind was something other than a few words.

Just then the doorman opened the doors and out of the hotel walked a stunning couple. The blonde was lovely, while the guy looked as if he could be a model or something. Both were trim, fit, looking the way everybody secretly wanted to look.

Across the street the guy in the alley stirred, and Jerry's eyes went straight to him. Alley guy started across the street, not looking as if he were moving fast, yet covering the distance to the other side quickly, moving to intercept the couple. Jerry froze for a second, not certain what he should do. He spotted the guy slip his right hand into his jacket pocket.

"Don't be a spectator," his partner was always telling him. "You want to watch crime, watch *Law and Order* on TV." Jerry moved toward the couple, not even realizing that as he did so, he placed his hand on his gun.

Alley guy was picking up his pace and Jerry could see he was angling to reach the sidewalk just behind the couple, his hand coming out of the pocket now. Jerry felt the hair on the back of his neck stand up and his skin prickle. A man in an alley, a couple, people walking back and forth on the street. Nothing was odd about the movement itself, Jerry saw it a thousand times a day on patrol, but this was different. He knew it. Jerry drew his weapon.

Jerry himself was almost across the street, about thirty feet in front of and to the left of the laughing couple. Alley guy was maybe twenty feet away from them, still in the street but almost to the cars parked along that side. His hand was in view now and Jerry saw the pistol with the big nose on the barrel. A silencer, he knew, never having seen one in action before, but the entire gun looked just like one with a silencer they'd shown his class at the academy.

"You!" Jerry shouted. "Drop that gun! Freeze!"

On the sidewalk, Jeff heard the officer and turned toward him. The uniformed man was pointing his gun behind them, yelling at someone. Jeff looked and saw a man just reaching the parked cars, a gun in his hand. The man turned toward the cop and Jeff heard three pops like subdued firecrackers, sensed rather than saw the officer struck with bullets. Then the officer's gun fired in a loud explosion, then fired again, and again and again as he tumbled onto the pavement, landing on his back.

Jeff pushed Daryl forward without thinking. "Run! Run!" he said as the pair broke into a sprint down the street, then around the first corner.

Jerry felt the bullets striking him across the chest like heavy blows. Alley guy had been incredibly fast. Jerry cursed himself for missing him. The only bullet he'd fired that was even close was the first, but he knew it had gone high and wide. The others had gone into the cars or pavement as he lost his balance and fell. *Shit!*

The cop had come out of nowhere. Manfield had seen him standing watch over the construction site and assumed he was some kind of traffic officer, which, in England, were always unarmed. Even if he was armed, Manfield had decided that with the noise and traffic it was unlikely the cop would even see what he was up to. If he did, it would all be over before he could respond.

Spotting the couple coming out of the hotel, Manfield had focused only on them. His instincts told him to kill both of them, but the man first, since he was the target. He moved across the street as quickly as he dared, drew his weapon, then heard the cop. He couldn't believe the man had actually been watching him. Spinning, he'd shot him three times in the heart, saw him topple over, then had taken off after the running couple, ignoring the gunshots in his direction as they weren't even close.

At the corner he turned and saw they were already well down the street. He looked back and saw the officer flop over on his back. He was talking into a communication device of some kind. At the construction site, the workers had stopped; it was silent. They were staring straight at Manfield and pointing.

Pursuing the couple meant drawing the police to him, and a running gunfight in midtown Manhattan made no sense. Manfield ran back up the street, then disappeared into the alley. Along the way he wiped, then ditched, first the pistol, then his windbreaker. Emerging on the other side, he flagged down a taxi. "Trump Tower," he said, then sat back in the seat and watched for trouble.

Fifteen minutes later he paid the driver, then entered the lobby of Trump Tower. There he drew out his cell phone and punched in the numbers. After several rings a man answered. Manfield quietly explained what had just happened. He listened, then turned off the phone and put it away. He walked the five blocks to his hotel, ridding himself of the knife and the cell phone along the way. In his room, he showered, changed, then checked out.

Outside, Manfield walked three blocks to a taxi stand. There he drew out his single die and rolled it into the palm of his other hand. Four. He went to the fourth taxi in line. "Driver, take me to Newark Airport."

"Certainly, sir," the dark-skinned man said as he got out to place Manfield's luggage into the trunk, ignoring the shouting of the other drivers. As they sped off, Manfield sat back in his seat and replayed the events of that morning, wondering where he had gone wrong. It was the police officer, he decided. He'd made the assumption the man was incompetent. That had been his mistake.

On East Thirtieth Street, Officer Jerry Kowalski sat on the curb, still sucking in air when his uncle, the sergeant, arrived. "What the fuck happened?" he demanded. Jerry told him.

Afterward the sergeant said, "Shit! Fifteen years I been a cop and never fired my piece once. You're on the force—what?—two years and you're in a gunfight. And you didn't hit shit, you know that?"

"Yeah, I know." Jerry didn't need to be reminded.

"At least you did something smart."

"What's that?"

"Your wore your fuckin' bulletproof vest like I told you, that's what. You struck two cars. Before you leave today I want a report. The owners are gonna be screaming about this."

0 0 0 0 0 0 0 0 0 0 0 5 4

AIR FRANCE FLIGHT 19
SATURDAY, SEPTEMBER 2
10:03 P.M.

At the ticket counter, Jeff paid to be upgraded to business class, since first class was closed. The flight left Newark at seven thirty that evening. Two hours out, they had dinner and shared a bottle of wine. Having talked it through before takeoff, they had nothing more to do until they reached Moscow. Daryl was in the window seat, covered with a blanket, her head wedged between the seat and the wall, sound asleep.

Jeff looked at her tenderly, realizing that he was more concerned for her personal safety than his own, or the fate of the world, for that matter. Was he right to bring her along? But was leaving her behind any safer? He just knew he couldn't bear the thought of losing her.

Jeff booted his notebook and for a few minutes tried to lose himself in *Mega Destructor IV*, but it was useless. His current world was too real for him to find release in one of fantasy.

He went online and checked the news. He could no longer consider any disaster without wondering if it was the Superphreak virus. A chip-manufacturing plant in Taiwan had shut down overnight. No deaths, but management wasn't commenting on the cause. An entire office building in downtown Austin, Texas, had lost all power. More than thirty people had been trapped in elevators and had to be manually extracted. The building was evacuated by using the emergency stairs. A commuter plane had crashed in Kansas with seventeen dead. Which, if any, of these was Superphreak? How many others had occurred Jeff didn't know about? How many had died?

Then a *New York Times* article caught his eye. Until now he'd wondered why no one was putting this all together. He and Daryl had the advantage of being on the inside, but it had been more than three weeks since the attacks started. The failure of the U.S. government security agencies to come on board was inexcusable, but how hard could it be for the media to start connecting the dots? Or at least to ask the right questions?

And there it was. Using the local computer-related hospital deaths as a hook, the reporter wrote about a series of unusual incidents nationwide. These included some Jeff already knew about but several he did not, including the apparent destruction of a Midwest bank's database, the unscheduled shutdown of two more nuclear power plants, and the loss of several significant Internet routing systems.

"A source within the White House," the article said, "confirms that the president has already directed that a national security assessment report be submitted to him as quickly as it can be prepared. The source would neither confirm nor deny that the many incidents are related nor comment on another report that they are part of a coordinated effort directed against computers worldwide."

That, at least, is something, Jeff thought as he closed the computer, put it away, then leaned back in his seat. *They still haven't put it together but are starting to.* When someone finally did, Jeff couldn't help but wonder how much damage the reaction itself would cause.

He listened to the engines for several minutes, then glanced over at Daryl again. *This is crazy,* he thought for the hundredth time since hearing the shots. *We're not secret agents.*

Earlier, once they'd been satisfied no one was chasing them, Jeff had grabbed a taxi and had them dropped off at Central Park. He'd found a large open field, and from there, convinced he could see anyone approaching, trusting the outdoors rather than a closed space, he and Daryl had discussed what to do.

"Do you think we should go to the cops?" she asked, even though, when she'd suggested this earlier, in Jeff's hotel room, they'd dismissed the suggestion. But bullets fired from an assassin's gun now gave weight to what then had seemed a far-fetched scenario.

"No. They wouldn't believe us. We might be detained as witnesses or even suspects, and there's no time to lose right now. If we don't put a stop to this, no one will. There's simply too much at stake to take such a chance."

Sue's face was tight with anxiety. They stood in silence for a long minute.

"Do you think the cop is dead?" Daryl finally asked. "What happened to the other man? The one who was chasing us."

Jeff shook his head. "I don't know about the cop. He went down. The other guy ran to the corner, but it didn't look like he chased us past that."

"Who do you think he is?"

"The same guy who killed Sue and Joshua Greene."

Daryl nodded. "Me too. But why us?"

"Sue and Greene were tortured. Sue must have told him who was helping her."

"Maybe we should get a gun. I mean, if it's up to us to defend ourselves."

"In Manhattan? And, trust me, I'd be more a threat to us with a gun than anyone else. I've never so much as shot one." He scanned the park and saw no one approaching them.

"You should warn Harold—that's his name, right?"

"Good thinking." Jeff called the IT Center and reached Harold, who'd had no trouble accepting the need to disappear. He'd told Jeff he was already considering it and had just the place.

Daryl sat on the grass. Thirty feet away, a young couple were helping their child learn to walk, clapping with pleasure every time he managed three or four steps. Jeff started working his BlackBerry with his thumbs. "I've got us on a flight to Moscow, leaving from Newark tonight. You got your passport?"

Daryl looked at him with excitement. "Never leave home without it. Are you thinking what I think you're thinking?"

"Our problem isn't that someone's trying to kill us. Our problem, Daryl, is that in nine days Muslim terrorists are going to unleash an enormous, sophisticated attack on the Internet and the United States.

And we're the only ones in a position to do something about it. If you've got a better idea, I'd like to hear it."

Much had happened since Jeff had first set foot in that Manhattan law office. In some ways it was a lifetime. He'd gone from a significant, if relatively mundane, job to realizing that his life was on the line, though he was still just a small part of the solution to a much bigger and more important problem. But there was more. He finally understood where he'd gone wrong in the weeks and days leading up to 9/11. He'd been too passive, too trusting. He'd looked to others for solutions.

Now he understood he should have raised holy hell. When Carlton had ignored him, he should have gone up the chain and kept going up until someone listened. If that had not been possible, he should have gone public, no matter what the risk to his career.

He'd known he was right and he'd known what needed to be done. If nothing else, a public disclosure of what he'd found might very well have frightened the terrorists off, caused them to delay their attack. Who knew what would have happened then?

That was the true source of his anger, he realized. Some part of him had always known he'd sold himself short and, in so doing, had doomed more than three thousand people, including the woman he'd loved.

That was all changed. No more would he sit back and play the guilt-ridden victim.

And there was Daryl. She was risking everything without a second thought. His feelings had come on him slowly, but what he'd thought no longer possible was now a reality. He had to do this, for both their sakes. And for the sake of the three thousand he'd already failed.

"Let me make some calls." Daryl pulled out her cell phone and began with her office. Satisfied that they were now safe, Jeff led her to a sidewalk vendor as she talked. Buying black coffee and doughnuts, he laughed at the absurdity of it all and the sudden realization that getting shot at in real life was nothing like being one of the shooters in the video games he played. This was for keeps.

By noon Daryl tucked away her phone. "I've got my team on it. I've told them I'm going to be traveling this week, trying to run down Superphreak. They think I'm joking. I've got some odd news too." Jeff raised his eyebrows. "I couldn't reach George Carlton. I wanted an update on where DHS is on this. They told me he left the country yesterday in a rush, something about an appointment in Paris."

Jeff wrinkled his brow. "What do you think?"

She shrugged. "I left a voice mail for his assistant, telling him I'd be out of touch for a few days, asking them to please take some action on Superphreak, not that it will do any good. The guy had taken the weekend off, which tells me everything I need to know about how urgent they think this is."

Exasperated, Jeff said, "What about the vendors?"

"No real change. We told them again it was avoiding their honeypots, and a few said that they would look at generating some signatures for the samples we have, but that's way too little way too late."

Jeff sighed. "I checked the temperature in Moscow. It's colder than here. We should do a little shopping while we can. And get some cash. Credit cards don't work everywhere."

They'd made it to Newark with time to spare. At an airport hot spot, Jeff booked them into the Moscow Metropol Hotel for three nights. "Gotta love the Internet," he said as put away his laptop.

Waiting to board, Daryl said, "How are we going to find Superphreak?"

"You've got an address. We'll give it to a taxi driver."

"Okay. Let's say it's that easy. We find him, then just ask him to turn over the viruses he's created? That doesn't sound like much of a plan."

"We can always pay him."

Daryl brightened. "Money's good. That might work." Then with a sinking heart she added, "If he's not a fanatic or something."

"That's possible. But he's a Russian and I'll bet he's a gun for hire."

"Unless he's Chechnyan."

Jeff frowned. "Yes, there's always that."

OOOOOOOOOOO 55

Brian Manfield marveled at how he could use his British passport to enter Russia. For a moment he recalled how he had infiltrated Russian lines in Grozny, first as a dirty-faced waif, worming his way close enough to use his knife, then later dressed as a Russian soldier on guard duty. Now he stepped off an airplane and handed the authorities a piece of paper, and they stamped it and all but gave him the keys to the city. Amazing.

Somewhere, he knew, was a file under the name Borz Mansur, presumably with a grainy photograph of him as a gawky teenager. But no one in Russia had any reason to connect him with the distinguished British representative of SAS, London.

The trip had been exhausting. He'd taken Czech Airlines from Newark to Prague, then flown from the Czech Republic directly to Moscow. With luck this Russian business would be quickly over and he could go home.

Outside he took out his die, then put it away and got in the first taxi in line. He wanted to do nothing to attract the attention of authorities here in Moscow. Airport security watched for anything out of the ordinary. He stuck with English in speaking to the driver: "The Golden Ring Hotel. You know it?"

"Oh, yes, sir! Very nice hotel. You will like. Very pretty womens stay there in bar." The driver had not shaved in three days. He was middle-aged, with a dark complexion. "I can give you name of special one. Very nice. College girl, looking to meet handsome English gentleman."

"No, thank you."

They drove for a few minutes, then the driver said, "Nice boys and young men too."

"No, thank you. I'll keep the offer in mind."

"Here," the driver said, never taking his eyes off the road. "Take my card. You call me for anything, anytime, okay? I make your stay very good indeed. Very special."

Manfield glanced at the card as he moved to put it into his pocket, intending to toss it as soon as he checked in. Stopping, he read the name on the card. Vakha Dukhavakha. A Chechen. "How are you, my brother?" Manfield asked in Chechen.

With astonishment the man met Manfield's eyes for the first time in the rearview mirror. "I am good, Allah be praised," he answered in the same language.

"Praise be to Allah, my brother."

The car sped along the wide Moscow street toward the city center. Finally, Vakha said in Chechen, "You look the perfect English gentleman."

"We are all two faces in this world, my brother."

"Yes," Vakha agreed, his voice sounding sad. "If I can help you, only say the word."

Manfield thought. He'd taken the first taxi. Then the driver turned out to be a Chechen brother. The odds of that were not so long. Many of the taxi drivers in Moscow were Chechen. Should he be suspicious? At times Allah handed you a gift. A few minutes later the taxi pulled up before the Golden Ring Hotel.

"I must check in," Manfield said. "Wait for me." He handed the man some of the rubles he'd acquired at the airport.

"I will wait. Keep your money, my brother," the driver said, waving the rubles off. "I will be there." He indicated a spot just down the street.

As Manfield checked in, he said to the clerk in English, "I'm expecting a package."

"Yes, sir. Just a moment." The young man returned with a wrapped box the size of a laptop. "Here you are, sir. It arrived earlier today."

In his room Manfield washed, then changed into casual clothes. He opened the package and removed the pistol. This time it was a Russian Makarov .380, the Soviet equivalent of the German PPK. Included was an extra magazine, already full. He checked the automatic and found a bullet in the chamber and the magazine filled. In the package was a folding knife with a single four-inch locking blade. This one was Swiss and a bit larger than he was accustomed to, but of high quality.

A message on a slip of paper was written in Russian. "No photo available. The name is Vladimir Koskov, late twenties, in a wheelchair. Destroy all computers." Finally there was the fully charged cell phone, which he turned on. He placed the items into his pockets, memorized the address, then tore up and flushed the message.

Thirty minutes after arriving, Manfield left the hotel, spotted the taxi, and entered the backseat. He gave the driver an address. "Drive carefully. I wish to attract no attention."

"I understand."

MOSCOW, RUSSIAN FEDERATION
DMITROSVSKY ADMINISTRATIVE DISTRICT
SUNDAY, SEPTEMBER 3
6:21 P.M.

Ivana Koskov was satisfied with the bedroom. She'd been able to buy a new IKEA bedroom set and was thrilled. They finally had enough room for her things and a bed big enough for the two of them. Vladimir had suggested twin beds, but she was determined to continue sleeping with him. In the corner of the room was an unoccupied place where she mentally placed a baby crib.

Their old living room furniture was to be delivered the next day, so that room was still empty. She'd carefully written their new address on tape that she'd placed on every piece of furniture and on the boxes containing their odds and ends so there'd be no mistakes. She trusted her father, but had no idea whom he'd bring to work with him the next day. Her father was staring out the window. "You can just see the river from here," he said.

Ivana went into the small, second bedroom. She had bought a proper workstation for Vladimir and earlier, with a cousin and her father, had moved his main computer. Vladimir would be moving in this night, and tomorrow she and her father would finish moving in the rest of his computer equipment.

Once he was set up here, there was no rush to move anything else from their old place. She had the week. Her best friend from work, visiting family in St. Petersburg, had lent her an aging Lada to help with the move. Ivana's plan was to be completely installed in the new apartment by the end of the next weekend. She was thrilled at the idea.

Even Vladimir was coming around. Having his own room in which to work was too inviting. Ivana was certain that the change in environment, the more open space, and a baby on the way would bring back the young man she'd always loved with such devotion.

"You've done well," her father said.

Ivana smiled. "Thank you. I found it, but Vlad is paying."

The man grunted. There'd been no vodka that day, and for that she was grateful. Tonight would be different, though. "Let's get your man then. We'll finish up his things tomorrow while you are at work."

"Thank you . . . Grandpa."

"*Ded*? What are you talking about?"

Ivana touched her stomach. "It was confirmed Friday. Don't tell Vlad. He doesn't know yet."

"Grandpa! I like the sound of that." His eyes grew warm. "Have you decided on a name if it's a boy?"

MOSCOW, RUSSIAN FEDERATION
METROPOL HOTEL
SUNDAY, SEPTEMBER 3
6:33 P.M.

Jeff had been surprised at how much the Metropol Hotel resembled the office building for Fischerman, Platt & Cohen. As he examined the art deco motif, he decided they'd been built around the same time and had been influenced by the same architectural style. The coincidence was eerie. Yet the building could not have been better located. It was across the street from the Bolshoi Theater and just a short walk from the Kremlin, not that they'd have time to take in the sights.

In their room they showered and changed, discussing plans as they could.

"I'm for just going to the address tonight," Daryl said. "If it's a business, or someone else is living in the apartment, we might as well find out. Then we can start fresh in the morning."

"I agree." Winging it like this held a certain excitement, but he couldn't help second-guessing his decisions. Events were sweeping them along. It was reassuring to have Daryl's steady presence. He didn't think this was something he could do alone. "We don't have much time. Ready when you are."

Jeff had dressed in gray running shoes, dark wool slacks, a long-sleeved wool shirt, and a lined black leather jacket he'd bought in Manhattan. A pair of gloves was tucked into the jacket's pockets, along with a black watch cap. Daryl came out of the bathroom and laughed. The only difference in their attire was that her leather jacket was a dark brown, and instead of a watch cap, she had a scarf folded into her jacket pocket.

Downstairs the couple asked for a taxi with a driver who spoke English. It was apparently not an unusual request, as the doorman merely gestured and one of the waiting cars pulled from the line and drove to the entrance.

As they slid into the backseat, Daryl asked the driver, "Do you know this address?" She handed him a slip of paper. The man glanced at the paper, nodded, and drove off.

"I can't believe we're here," Jeff said, watching the trees and buildings whip by outside the car.

"It is surreal," Daryl agreed. "Let's think about what's going to happen if we meet Superphreak. Any thoughts on how to handle the approach?"

Jeff shook his head. "We'll just have to play it by ear. Some things you just can't plan ahead for."

MOSCOW, RUSSIAN FEDERATION
DMITROSVSKY ADMINISTRATIVE DISTRICT
SUNDAY, SEPTEMBER 3
6:56 P.M.

Manfield instructed Vakha to stop one block short of his destination. He paused before getting out. Having the taxi waiting for him when he finished was inviting. The last thing he wanted was to come out of the building with someone in hot pursuit and nothing to do but flee on foot. Russia might no longer technically be a police state, but it remained a heavily policed one.

But keeping Vakha here meant exposing him to information he'd rather the man didn't have. Still . . .

"Wait," Manfield said. "I will likely be ten minutes or so. Do nothing to attract interest, but watch where I enter and move closer when the ten minutes are up. Allah be with you."

"And with you," the driver said.

Vakha Dukhavakha had been born in Moscow of Chechen parents. His father had served in the Great Patriotic War and been swept up in the army purges that followed victory. Released at Stalin's death, he'd remained in Moscow for the remainder of his life, a bitter, angry man.

An only son, Vakha inherited from his father an absolute hatred of the godless Communists. Vakha had watched the collapse of the Soviet Union with emotions bordering on ecstasy. In the years since, he had, from time to time, been of service to the so-called Chechen Mafia in the city. This Englishman masking his true Chechen self was intriguing, obviously up to something. Vakha had instinctively offered him his assistance. Brothers could do no less for one another.

He eased the car forward.

Manfield found the apartment building without difficulty. Not trusting the elevator, he decided to take the stairs to the third floor, passing the open door of the concierge without being observed.

The stairway was ripe with the smell of boiled cabbage, potatoes, and onions. It brought back a wave of childhood memories, when he'd lived happily in Moscow with his mother. The steps creaked loudly and he dismissed any thought of approaching the door silently. The target would be accustomed to the sounds of foot traffic outside. What would attract his attention would be the sudden absence of sound, especially in an unexpected way in the hallway.

As he reached the third floor, Manfield hesitated only a moment before walking directly to Vladimir Koskov's door, while placing his hand on his gun.

Vakha watched as another car stopped outside the same building the Englishman had entered. A slender woman got out, followed by an older, heavyset man. Russians. She removed the wiper blades, put them into the car, then locked it up. Both of them went into the building without hesitation.

The moment they disappeared, a taxi turned the corner behind him, drove down the street past him, then stopped at the same place. Another couple got out of the car, foreign and handsome. They gave the driver money, faced the building as if uncertain about what to do, then went inside.

Curious. The Russian couple might very well live there or be visiting. But the foreign couple was too much of a coincidence for Vakha.

The moment the couple was out of sight, the taxi drove off. Vakha engaged the gears and slowly moved his taxi even closer to the building.

Vladimir Koskov thought the old apartment looked naked, even with the various moving boxes stacked here and there. The place was still crowded, but without his primary computer and monitor, it was as if the major part of the apartment had already been moved. It was like an enormous chasm.

How many years had he worked here? For how long had this cramped space been the center of his world? More than he could recall offhand. He couldn't remember ever seeing this little room so empty.

Vladimir was organizing what was left for the next move since Ivana had promised he'd be up and running in the new apartment that night. The rest of this would come over the next day, and he could get completely set up then.

He had prepared a sketch of the small bedroom that would be his new office, drawing where everything would be placed. He had to admit that having more room was going to be nice.

He lifted his head. Someone had been walking outside and stopped. He heard a knock at the door. Many times, most in fact, Vladimir didn't answer the door. But this was moving day; it might be Ivana's cousin, or even her father, without a key. Vladimir wheeled his chair to the door, leaned well forward to reach the handle, and turned it.

"We'll take the stairs," Ivana said to her father. "The elevator is too unpredictable."

Sasha grunted his agreement and led the way up the stairs, his daughter immediately behind him.

Jeff paused at the open door just inside the entrance, assuming this was the concierge, or whatever it was the Russians called the downstairs occupant. He reasoned whoever it was likely served as some sort of spy for the police, especially for matters out of the ordinary or involving foreigners.

Beside him, Daryl shook her head and pointed to the elevator. She tugged his sleeve and headed toward the doors. At the elevator, she punched the button; the doors crept open, as if they had been waiting for them. They stepped in and pushed the button for the third floor.

"No need to bother anyone," she said to Jeff quietly. "Besides, the concierge might call ahead, and we wouldn't want that."

"You're right. There's a lot to this secret-agent stuff. I wonder if there's a book I can access online?"

Daryl rolled her eyes.

Once the handle turned and the door opened even a crack, Manfield kicked it as hard as he could. The door struck the footrests of the wheelchair and bounced back at him, nearly slamming shut. Manfield threw his body against the door, pushing it and the wheelchair back until the door was open all the way.

State Security! Vladimir thought, frozen in place. He sat wide-eyed then reached for the wheels of his chair as if meaning to move. Before he could speak, Manfield pressed the muzzle of the gun against the young man's chest and fired once.

Vladimir let out a sound as if he'd been punched hard in the chest. His mouth opened to cry out but no sound came.

There'd been no silencer, which had distressed Manfield, so this was the best he could do. Pressing the barrel of the gun against the body had muffled the sound of the single shot, but not the way a silencer would have.

With his foot Manfield closed the door behind him, shoving the dying man and his chair aside, and made his way to the computers, noting at once the large open space in the middle. One of them had been moved. He spotted the boxes and realized that the man had been moving.

The way this had played out, Manfield didn't have much time. The Russian neighbors might mind their own business and ignore the muffled shot, but someone could just as well call the police militia. He had to work quickly.

Manfield seized the first computer tower and yanked at it, struggling to free it from its cables, trying to decide how best to disable it permanently since he couldn't easily get at the hard drive. He looked about the room and found a heavy screwdriver. Setting the tower down, he braced it with his foot and pried the side loose. Inside were various printed boards. He jerked one out, then another. These he set on the floor and snapped into the case pieces. Taking the heavy screwdriver, he stabbed at anything inside that looked substantive.

He stood and stilled his breathing. He heard nothing. Satisfied, he turned to the next tower.

Sasha recognized a gunshot. "Stop!" he said, freezing in his tracks on the last step before the landing of the third floor.

"What was that?" Ivana asked.

"A gunshot."

"My God! Vlad! They've come for him!"

Her father stepped back and reached for his daughter. He was unarmed; neither of them could do anything about what was happening in the apartment. His concern was for her safety.

Ivana tore from his grasp and bolted up the last step onto the landing. "Ivana! No!" her father cried. "Stop!"

Instead, the young woman ran to the door and pushed it fully open. A man across the room was struggling with the computer, but what drew her eyes was Vladimir's lifeless body, slumped to the side in his wheelchair, a large patch of blood spreading across his chest, running down toward the floor.

"Vlad!" she cried out. "Vlad!" Rushing to the chair, Ivana took her husband's head into her arms.

Across the room, Manfield had freed the second tower and thrown it to the floor. He was attacking it with the screwdriver when Ivana rushed into the room. He drew his gun, glanced at the sobbing woman holding the dead man, then turned his attention to the tower. He fired into it, once, twice, three times, the shots sounding like enormous explosions in such a small area. He turned to the woman, and a burly older man appeared in the doorway.

Manfield knew he was out of time. He'd done what damage he could and had killed the target. He bolted for the doorway, pointed the pistol at the man, then, when he did not move, shot him once, pushed his body aside, and climbed over him as he scrambled out the door.

In the hallway Manfield turned to his right to run from the building when the elevator doors opened. For an instant, he saw the same couple he'd tried to kill in New York. He couldn't imagine how they'd managed to make it to this very place in Moscow so quickly, or why they were here. It was like seeing an apparition, and it momentarily stunned him.

Manfield had no time but he had a bullet to spare, so as he reached the stairs, he aimed the gun at the couple and snapped off a shot. He sprinted down the stairs and a moment later was in the street.

Vakha pulled the car to a stop and Manfield jumped into the rear seat. "Away from here, brother! Quickly!"

Vakha pressed the accelerator and sped off.

Fajer and Labib were approaching the final week of jihad, and Fajer could hardly contain his excitement. Soon he would be rewarded for his time and money, and America brought to its knees.

Apparently content with the condition of her hair, the lovely Hungarian he'd been watching stood, the subdued light striking her body to perfection. Fajer was certain she'd studied the pose—and was glad she had. She moved slowly toward him, then his cell phone rang.

"This is Greta," the voice said. "I have news."

Greta, oddly, was the name of an English- and Russian-speaking Chechen assassin Osama bin Laden had given Fajer. The man had come highly recommended, and though he'd missed one of his targets in New York, he'd killed the most important one. He would be calling from Russia. The assassin spoke in English, the only language they had in common. Fajer wondered for a moment if the whore spoke English and decided she did.

"Go ahead."

"The man is no longer a problem. He had three computers. Two are destroyed. But he was moving, and the third was gone. I believe it is at his new apartment. Is it important?"

Fajer thought about that for a moment. The woman sat on the side of the bed, smiling. He took her head with his free hand and lowered her face to his groin. She understood at once. He almost hissed as she took him in.

"I prefer you disable it as well. Can you reach it?"

"I can try. If I can manage it without great risk, I will."

"That will do."

"There's something else."

Fajer listened carefully, forcing himself to concentrate as the woman skillfully performed her service.

"Interesting," he said when Greta was finished. "In that case, finish them or destroy the computer. Both, if you can, but one or the other for certain."

Fajer dropped the cell phone to the floor and cursed his own weakness as the whore moved her head up and down, up and down.

MOSCOW, RUSSIAN FEDERATION
DMITROSVSKY ADMINISTRATIVE DISTRICT
SUNDAY, SEPTEMBER 3
7:14 P.M.

Are you all right?" Daryl asked, pushing open Jeff's jacket as she leaned toward him. She sounded frightened even as she struggled to stay calm.

Jeff held his hand against his shoulder. The bullet had creased the flesh and it was starting to bleed. It stung like hell, and of course, the new jacket was ruined.

"It just hurts. You're certain it was him?"

"Absolutely," she said breathlessly. "He wasn't shooting at me, so I had a better look."

The shock of being shot suddenly washed over Jeff, and he collapsed to the floor.

"He's gone, he's gone," Daryl murmured, as she helped Jeff to his feet. Almost embarrassed by his near faint, Jeff shook his head hard and gave his complete attention to Daryl, who was still looking at him with great concern. "He ran down the stairs, after he shot you. And that man over there too, I think," she said, indicating Sasha, lying splayed in the hallway.

Sasha was still breathing, but his life was draining out. At the doorway appeared a hysterical young woman, standing as if torn between two terrible choices. Jeff was holding his shoulder, blood seeping between his fingers. No one spoke.

Finally, the woman threw herself across the man lying in the hallway and sobbed uncontrollably, muttering words of endearment in Russian. Jeff looked into the apartment and saw a man in a wheelchair, dead. *Could he be Superphreak?* he thought. *Or was Superphreak the dead man in the hallway?*

"Vladimir Koskov?" he said.

The young woman looked up from the now dead man, as if seeing them for the first time. She said something to them in Russian, something dreadful, as if she'd uttered a curse.

Daryl answered. "We don't speak Russian. We came to see Vladimir Koskov. We mean neither him nor you any harm. What happened here?"

The young woman switched to English. "You are not State Security?"

"No. We're Americans. We're looking for Mr. Koskov."

Ivana, tears running down her face, looked into the apartment. "He is dead." She looked at Jeff. "The man shot you? Why?"

"He tried to kill us in New York City yesterday," Jeff said. "And now here. We don't know why."

The woman looked around and gathered herself. "We must leave, unless you wish to be arrested. The militia will be here any moment and they will arrest all of us. It is their way. Hurry!" She rushed toward the stairs, Jeff and Daryl following.

In the lobby, a small group had gathered. Spotting Ivana, they asked questions all at once. She rushed through them, telling Jeff and Daryl to hurry, then ran into the street. She opened the door to her car, ignoring the continued questions, and told the couple to get in. In the distance they could hear the clarion sound of a police car. They jumped in and Ivana pulled away from the curb.

Vakha saw the three pile into the car and asked, "What do I do?"

"Follow them," Manfield said. He could not believe his good fortune. The only witness to the shooting and the couple he was to kill all in the same car. Allah was truly on his side. "And don't lose them. This is important."

The woman drove the Lada like a maniac, weaving down narrow

streets, then breaking out of the residential blocks onto Tverskoy, heading toward the Kremlin.

"Who are you?" Ivana demanded.

"My name is Daryl Haugen. This is Jeff Aiken. We're Americans."

Jeff moaned beside her. The pain was suddenly much more intense. His face was pale and sweat now beaded his brow.

"You already told me that," Ivana snapped. "You are American agents?"

"No," Jeff said, grunting in pain. "I'm a private computer consultant."

Daryl hesitated. "It's complicated. I do work for a government agency, but Jeff and I are in the same line of work. I'm not an agent like you mean." Daryl began dabbing at Jeff's forehead with her scarf.

The car made a sudden turn to the right, shooting passed the Bolshoi Theatre. "What's going on?" Ivana shouted. "Tell me or get out of the car!"

"We think Koskov—"

"My husband."

"I'm sorry," Daryl murmured, cutting her eyes toward Jeff. He nodded his agreement that Daryl should continue talking to the young woman. "But we think your husband created special viruses and sold them to very bad people. And they've killed him because of it. Now the same man is trying to kill us."

"Viruses?" Ivana slowed down, but was still going faster than the rest of the traffic, as she wove back and forth between cars. Horns honked, drivers raised their fists, some cars were forced to swerve away. "I warned him about that," she said quietly. "He was always so secretive about his work. What kind of bad people?"

"Terrorists. Muslim terrorists." Jeff could scarcely believe his own words. This was all so unreal. He lifted his hand and looked at the blood for an instant.

"What would they want with viruses?" Ivana asked.

"These are very sophisticated ones," Jeff said. "And very special. They destroy computers."

"Vlad wasn't like that," Ivana insisted. "He used to be, but not anymore. He told me he's been building viruses for a European security

company to test against their software. They kept asking for more sophisticated ones, so he said he built some very tough viruses, with encryption and cloaking characteristics. He said they were very pleased."

"They lied to him," Daryl interjected. "They're using the rootkits he
designed to launch an attack against America and Europe. It's going to
hurt, even kill, a lot of people if we don't stop it."

"Vlad is dead. So is my father. I can't help you." Ivana's face was set
as she made another sharp turn, the tires squealing as the car leaned
violently to the side.

The sudden movement made Jeff's shoulder throb. "Easy," he cautioned.

"What do I care? My husband and father are murdered. What do I
care?"

"We've lost people we cared about too," Jeff said. "Other people are
dead and more are going to die if we don't stop this. Your husband was
used. His work has been put to a very, very bad purpose. You can't leave
it like this. You just can't." As he spoke, Ivana placed her hand on her
stomach. *Could she be pregnant?* Jeff wondered. Maybe that was the
way to get through to her.

"Think of the future," Jeff said. "Did your husband keep records?"

Ivana was now crying, her face streaked with tears. "He kept all his
work in an external drive."

"The police will be at the apartment by now," Daryl pointed out.

"Not there," Ivana said, shaking her head. "We were moving. The
drive is at our new apartment." Ivana swerved the car left, then right,
her jaw clenched shut.

Jeff thought. "As long as you have it, you're in danger. That's why
they killed your husband; it's why they'll keep trying to kill you and anyone else around it. Give it to us. They'll know we have it, and you'll be
safe. Please," he added, his voice hoarse with desperation, "the lives of
thousands depend on you."

Ivana started to tell them to go to hell, then placed her hand over her
stomach again. She paused to think. "There is an expression that should
be Russian. Perhaps you know it. 'The enemy of my enemy is my friend.'
So I help you."

MOSCOW, RUSSIAN FEDERATION
DMITROSVSKY ADMINISTRATIVE DISTRICT
SUNDAY, SEPTEMBER 3
7:37 P.M.

Excellent," Manfield said as the car they were following came to a stop. The taxi driver had been skilled in keeping up.

Vakha eased his car to a halt, then sat idling as they watched Ivana exit the Lada, followed by Daryl and Jeff. With Ivana leading the way the three entered one of the newer apartment buildings that had sprung up about Moscow in the last decade.

"The same as before," Manfield said. "Ease up to the front. I won't be long. Thank you, my brother."

Vakha grunted, then watched the assassin exit his taxi. Once again he wondered what he was up to. A Chechen who looked and behaved like the perfect English gentleman. There was a story in that, but Vakha was sure he would never learn it.

The man paused at the Lada, looked inside momentarily, then entered the apartment building. Vakha engaged the clutch and crept slowly toward the front entrance.

With every passing moment Ivana's despair gripped her more tightly. In a few short minutes she had lost her father and husband, the two most important men in her life. She'd seen how the gunman had looked at her, had noted the muzzle of the weapon paused for an instant on her heart before swinging to her father. She'd nearly died. She wished she had.

The doors to the elevator opened on the ninth floor. "This way," she said to the Americans. At her new apartment she fumbled with her keys before opening the door, turning on lights as she entered.

Not even an hour ago Ivana had stood here with her father filled with dreams and hope. Now it was all gone. At least she'd told him about the baby, she could be grateful for that. She tried to take some solace from his having died knowing that.

"It's in there," she said, indicating the small bedroom that was to have been Vlad's office. "It's in a box, I think."

Jeff squeezed Daryl's shoulder and went to find the external drive. He needed to do something about his arm soon. Blood was dripping on the floor.

Daryl looked about the stark apartment. It was growing dark outside and the city lights sparkled through the large living room window. "I'm so very sorry for all that's happened."

"This was to be our new home. We'd worked so hard to afford it. Now . . ."

"I understand." Daryl did. She looked at the young women warmly. "Thank you for helping us. You are doing a great service to the world."

"The world?" Ivana said bitterly. "What do I care for that? My world is all but dead."

One-handed, Jeff dug an external drive from the bottom of one of the boxes. He looked for another, then carried it into the living room.

"We need to do something for you," Ivana said matter-of-factly. "You're bleeding everywhere." She went to the kitchen, knelt, and dug around, returning in a few moments with bandages and tape. "Here. Take that off."

Daryl helped as Jeff removed his jacket. Ivana tore the sleeve above the wound, dabbed away blood, placed a large bandage across the wound, front and back, then taped it in place. "This will hold you for a bit," she said as she finished. "You should see a doctor, but if you do, he will know what this is and report you."

"Thank you. I'm sorry to ask, but is it possible to boot the computer to confirm the information is here?" Jeff asked. Daryl gave him a withering look. "I know the timing isn't good, but I need to be certain. I wouldn't want to come so far and not leave with the information."

"It's there," Ivana said. "Vlad told me he kept all of his work in the external drive. It was an old habit with him. And he only had one."

"I think we should go," Daryl said, then turned to Ivana. "You must have family you can go to. Your mother?"

"Ahh!" Ivana said, putting her hands to her lips. She had not thought about her mother once. "My poor mother! Someone will have called her from the building, if only to warn her the militia might come." She took out her cell phone. "I need to call."

Manfield stepped off the elevator on the eighth floor. He'd seen the address on the boxes at the apartment and noted it along with the apartment number. Once the Lada had stopped here, he'd known where his targets would be.

He checked the door to the stairwell. It did not lock from either side. Excellent. He went up the final flight of stairs two at a time, slipping a fresh magazine into the pistol as he did. This would all be over in the next few minutes, and he was glad. He had missed the couple in New York and that bothered him. He was still puzzled at how the American couple could have come here, to the very place he had been sent, but reasoned they were after the information he was being ordered to destroy.

On the ninth floor Manfield eased the door open and saw the hallway was clear. He placed his hand on the Makarov. *Now*, he thought. *Now.*

The assassin stepped into the hallway and began examining the doors for numbers, moving with athletic grace, humming softly to himself.

Ivana spoke intently into her cell phone, fighting back tears. Jeff took Daryl aside and whispered, "I'd really feel a lot better if we knew the drive actually has the information."

Daryl nodded. "So would I, but this isn't the time. We can confirm it at the hotel. If it doesn't, we come back here and check the computer. Okay?"

"I guess." Jeff hefted the drive. This entire situation was ludicrous.

Twice now he'd narrowly escaped death at the hands of a brutal mur-
derer. In New York, with its violent reputation, he hadn't been certain,
but in Moscow there was no doubt. The man had murdered two people
just seconds before attempting to kill him. If that bullet had been just
a few inches to the left, he'd have died in that elevator. *But I'm committed to this*, he reminded himself. *This time I'm not going to let anyone
down, especially myself.*

Ivana was still talking to her mother, the words coming out between sobs. Daryl, who was standing beside her, looked to Jeff as if to
say, *Be patient.*

Jeff thought for a moment. Were they safe? Did the killer know
about this place? Had they been followed? The way the young Russian
had driven it didn't seem likely, but he couldn't be certain. What he
wanted, desperately, was for him and Daryl to be gone, out of Moscow,
out of Russia, home, in America.

In the hallway he heard loud voices.

Manfield was moving steadily down the hallway when he heard the
group get off the elevator, laughing loudly at some joke. He turned to
see them clearly.

There were five men, out to celebrate from appearances. Two were
holding bottles of vodka by the neck as if wringing a chicken. Others
had unopened bottles tucked into the pockets of their jackets. Three of
the men wore old army field coats. Veterans.

Manfield hesitated, then decided to stall until they had entered an
apartment. He knelt as if to tie a shoelace.

Ivana took the cell phone from her ear and turned it off. "Neighbors are
with my mother. She already knew. She thought I was dead, too, so I'm
glad I called. I must go."

"We have to go too," Daryl said.

Ivana opened the door, then reached for the light switch. Outside, a
group of men she'd seen before in the building were approaching,
laughing boisterously. She stepped into the hallway, then to the side so
Daryl and Jeff could leave the apartment.

At that moment Ivana spotted Manfield behind the men, moving slowly toward her, his piercing blue eyes glued to her. She started to speak, but nothing came out. Daryl and Jeff moved into the hallway, which was suddenly crowded as the drunken men reached the doorway. One eyed Ivana and Daryl appreciatively. One said something in Russian.

Jeff followed Ivana's gaze and spotted Manfield. "Run!" he shouted. He turned to his right, pulling Daryl with him, but came up against one of the revelers, who took offense. Pushing Jeff hard against the wall, he spoke in an angry, guttural voice, smelling heavily of vodka, his eyes bloodshot and watery.

Ivana was petrified. She could not take her eyes away from the man who had murdered her husband and her father. She knew he wouldn't hesitate to kill her and her unborn child.

Manfield was still moving slowly toward her, waiting for the group of men to move and give him a clear shot. Then he heard the American call out and saw the pushing match with one of the Russians. He didn't want to shoot, didn't want a massacre, since that would only heighten the militia's attention, but there was no choice. He raised the pistol and aimed at Ivana.

A second Russian had joined in and shoved Jeff hard too. The external drive clattered to the hallway floor. Daryl was trying desperately to separate the men, explaining in English that it was all a misunderstanding, that they had to stop this and leave them alone.

The moment Manfield fired, the men moved as a group and bumped into Ivana, who went down. The sound of the pistol in the hallway was deafening. The men turned toward the sound and spotted the weapon. Ivana was on the floor, masked from Manfield by a forest of legs.

Those holding Jeff turned their drunken attention to the shooter. Amazingly, Daryl thought, not one of them ran or even moved as if to run. Instead, angry and growling, as a single body they advanced on the man with the gun, shouting accusations in Russian. She turned to Jeff, who crumbled to the floor.

"The drive," he gasped. "Get the—"

Instead, Daryl tried to pull him up and away from the group, away from danger.

On the floor, Ivana held her hand to her head, feeling a sharp pain, trying to stop the flow of blood that was streaming from her temple.

She staggered to her feet, her free hand finding the external drive. She grabbed it as she stood up, swaying, her vision a misty pink.

The men rushed Manfield. For an instant he considered running. Instead, he shot the first man in the chest. The group didn't hesitate, their liquored minds not grasping the significance of what was occurring. He shot another. This whole thing was senseless. Why didn't the men run away? Or fall down to beg for mercy?

But the second bullet had the effect Manfield was after. The other three came to their senses, stopped, reached for the two staggering men who were shot, one collapsing to the floor. The others scrambled to get away from Manfield, pulling the second wounded man with them, shouting obscenities at him. In all the tumult they blocked the assassin's view of his targets though, so Manfield moved forward and to the side of them.

The Russian woman, he realized, had been hit, but not fatally. She was on her feet, one hand to her bleeding head, swaying to stay upright, looking like a drunk who'd just been in a bar fight. The two Americans were moving quickly away from him down the hallway, their backs turned. Manfield pointed the pistol to kill them when one of the now fallen Russian men tried to rise up. From the floor a powerful hand seized his arm. He'd put the men completely out of his thoughts in his single-minded desire to kill and had moved too close to them. One of those he'd shot, half-sitting, half-lying on the floor, had hold of his arm and was twisting it down and out of its socket in a practiced move, forcing Manfield to bend nearly to the floor. He screamed in pain as the Makarov dropped from his hand. He let out a cry, the words springing from his childhood, coming out in Chechen. "Help me!"

The other man he'd shot grabbed for the gun, aimed at the assassin, then emptied the clip into his body. As Manfield crumbled to the floor with a look of disbelief, the one who'd grabbed his arm spit on him, then said in Russian, "Chechen scum!"

Outside, in his idling taxi, Vakha saw none of this. Instead, he spotted the young Russian woman stagger out of the building, holding one hand to her head, blood streaming down her clothes. She managed to get into her car and drive off quickly just as the American couple exited the building. They paused, looked for the car, spotted his taxi, and ran toward him.

"Do you speak English?" the woman said.

"A bit," Vakha answered, watching the building for the Englishman out of the corner of his eye.

"Take us to the Metropol Hotel. Hurry!" The couple scrambled into the rear seat.

Vakha hesitated, still waiting, but no one else emerged from the building. Then he heard the wail of militia cars and engaged the clutch. By the time the police arrived, he was well clear of the area and had decided he'd done enough for the Cause for one night. If the Englishman was still alive, he was on his own.

O O O O O O O O O O O 6 2

MOSCOW, RUSSIAN FEDERATION
METROPOL HOTEL
TUESDAY, SEPTEMBER 5
9:06 A.M.

Jeff climbed from the shower, his skin dripping with hot water, and angled his body so he could see the wound without its bandage. It was an angry red, but had stopped bleeding. Since it hadn't been stitched, there'd be an ugly scar, but they'd not risked a doctor. Instead, when they'd arrived back at the hotel Sunday night, Daryl had retrieved their key from the desk and taken him directly to the room.

Leaving him alone, she'd gone to the hotel shop, where she bought cotton, bandages, and tape. Back in the room she used an airplane-size bottle of vodka from the minibar in the room to sanitize the wound, then bandaged it. "It doesn't look serious," she'd said, "but I'm no expert. It's up to you."

"No doctor. We can't risk it."

"Here," she said, handing him two pills. "Take these. They'll help with the pain and let you sleep."

Jeff hadn't asked what they were. He'd taken them with gratitude, cleaned up in the bathroom, then stretched on the bed. Eighteen hours later he awoke. Daryl ordered room service for him, gave him two more pills, and he'd promptly slept all night again. Only now, after he dried himself and left the bathroom, was he beginning to feel normal. He'd had no idea how exhausted he'd been.

He opened the curtains to reveal brilliant morning light. He couldn't say that Moscow had much of a view, but he could make out the onion-shaped domes of the Kremlin. He lifted the note Daryl had left for him. It said not to worry, that she expected to be back with good news. He'd had no idea what she meant, but tamped down the initial flutter of worry he felt and relaxed, knowing he could trust her. He ordered breakfast, then turned the television to International CNN. He wasn't expecting to come across any mention of the shoot-out in the apartment-building hallway, but wasn't sure he was relieved or frustrated when he didn't. He lay on the bed to wait for Daryl, for breakfast. Room service woke him. He'd dozed off. He was just finishing breakfast when he heard the key in the door and looked up to see Daryl enter carrying packages, her face aglow with excitement.

"I see Rip van Winkle has decided to join me. Good for you. Ready for some news?"

"We're about to be arrested and thrown into a gulag."

"Cynic," she joked. "No, I think that was the one bullet we did manage to dodge." She laid the packages on the unmade bed and took a chair opposite him. "I know where Ivana Koskov is."

"How'd you manage that?" They'd discussed the problem briefly Sunday night. Thanks to shootings at both locations, neither of them could return to the apartments to try to learn where Ivana was. She had the drive. But before they could come up with a solution, Jeff had nodded off, the pain and fear caused by his wound finally catching up with him.

"I called colleagues at NSA," Daryl said, her face shining with excitement. "As luck had it, one of the attachés here actually works for the NSA. My contact spoke with him yesterday and he sent one of their Russian-speaking operatives out to make inquiries. I don't know how he did it, but he reached Ivana's mother. Ivana is in Milan, Italy, staying with a friend. I have the address and a telephone number. We're booked out of here in about four hours."

"Amazing!" Jeff looked at his companion with continued admiration. "I never would have thought it possible."

"I've also got some pain pills here if you need them, along with Band-Aids, which should be all you need now. And"—she rose to go to the bed, where she removed something with a flourish, then brandished it like a toreador's cape—"I found this in your size." It was a leather coat.

"I had to trash the other one. You look very sharp in leather, I might add."

Jeff was amazed at her efficiency. "You're just full of surprises. Any word from your team?"

Daryl's face, which had been alive with pleasure, fell. "Nothing good, no. I spoke to them a few hours ago. Microsoft and Symantec finally got fully on board, but it's probably too late."

"What about DHS?"

"I'd almost forgotten. Are you ready for this? George Carlton was murdered in Paris."

"Murdered?" Jeff said, shocked. "How?"

"Stabbed to death. In broad daylight. DHS is stumped over it. He was there on a spur-of-the-moment thing, supposedly to meet with a counterpart, but she knew nothing about a meeting. They don't really know why he was in Paris."

Jeff wrinkled his brow in thought. "Do you think it's connected to what's been happening to us?"

Daryl shrugged. "It does seem odd. Not at all something that would happen to George."

"Dead! It's hard to grasp." Jeff despised the man, but he'd never thought of killing him. Disgraced, held to account, yes, those he could imagine—but dead?

Daryl broke into his thoughts. "We should get going. It's a direct flight and we'll be in Milan later today. With luck we should see Ivana tonight and get the external drive."

"If she took it with her."

OOOOOOOOOOOO 6 3

The Lufthansa flight from Moscow to Milan was just under four hours. From the moment he'd stepped on the German plane, Jeff had felt as if he were already out of Russia.

He'd slept so much since being shot he couldn't nod off during the afternoon flight. Daryl spent her time on her laptop working on Superphreak, but Jeff was too mentally spent to give it any thought.

If someone had told him a month ago that he'd be on the run from assassins with a beautiful new lover, that he'd be shot at and wounded, that the fate of the Western world lay with him, he'd have told them they were crazy. But here he was and he had to admit there was something to be said for it. He recalled that the young Winston Churchill, upon being sent to South Africa to cover the Boer War for a newspaper, had written after his first combat experience, "Nothing in life is so exhilarating as to be shot at without result."

Well, he'd been winged, if that was the word for it, but he understood what Churchill had meant. It *was* exhilarating and he'd never felt more alive. He'd had no idea that "saving the world" could be so exciting. On the other hand, he knew, had he been seriously injured, he'd feel very differently.

Daryl folded her laptop, then slipped it into its case. "You're staring at the back of the seat in front of you," she said. "You do know there's no television screen there, don't you?"

"I'm thinking."

"About what?"

"My life has been pretty exciting these last few days."

She laughed. "That's excitement I could do without. Or don't you think so?"

Jeff grunted. "I wouldn't change a thing, actually." He looked at her with open affection, and she returned it. "Learn anything?"

"Superphreak?" The warm expression faded from her face. "Not much. The viruses we've got are nothing special. The rootkits and encryption's a bitch, though. I don't know why I wasted my time on it. Do you think there'll be enough on this external drive to be any help?"

"It's a long shot," Jeff said, taking her hand. "But what else is there?"

Deciding to skip registering at a hotel, Daryl and Jeff took a taxi directly from Milan's Malpensa Airport to the address they had for Ivana in the central part of the city. It was nearly an hour before they stepped out with their luggage and paid the driver.

The street was wider than was typical for an Italian city, though still cobblestoned. A row of graceful trees flanked the sides, bordered by narrow sidewalks. The buildings were of a rough brownstone and, from the weathering Jeff could see, were at least two hundred years old. "Is this it?" he asked, every door looking the same to him.

"Yes. Number 346." Daryl stepped up and knocked on the aged wooden door.

After a long pause, they heard footsteps approaching. The door opened six inches and the plain face of a woman in her middle years showed itself. Daryl spoke in Italian, but before she finished, the women interrupted, saying, "I'm sorry, but I don't speak Italian."

"English?" Daryl said.

"Yes." The woman looked them over. "My guess is you're the American couple from Moscow, come to see Ivana. Am I right?"

"Yes," Daryl said, her face reflecting her surprise. "How did you know?"

The woman shrugged. "Ivana's mother called after she spoke with the man from the embassy. She was afraid she'd made a mistake and wanted to alert her daughter. And, of course, Ivana told me about you. Let me see the wound, please," she said to Jeff, who stood surrounded by their luggage.

Jeff didn't understand what she meant at first, then he pushed his jacket and shirt off his shoulder and exposed the bandages to the woman.

"That's good enough for me. Come on in. I just put on a pot of coffee. My name's Annie, by the way. What are yours?"

Annie led them through the entryway, telling them to put their things down near the front door, then showed them into a sitting room. "Have a seat," she said. "I'll be right back."

They sat side by side on matching chairs and glanced about the ornate room. It had high ceilings and rough-plastered walls that gave a sense of strength and restfulness. The ceiling was decorated with a lavish painting now long faded. The furniture was of dark woods, mostly carved, and brightened with colorful fabrics. On the floor was a Persian rug.

"Very nice," Daryl said, and Jeff nodded his agreement.

Annie returned a few minutes later with coffee and cookies on a tray, which she placed on a nearby table. She took her seat and poured, offering sugar or milk as they liked. Annie was perhaps forty-five years old, stout, and with plenty of short gray hair that showed no sign of being colored. A self-assured woman, she was dressed simply in gray slacks and a light blue sweater, with no jewelry of any kind.

"The cookies are delicious," she said, referring to the tray. "When I'm alone, I dip them in the coffee. Marvelous." She took a bite, glancing at the coffee as she did. "I'm spending some time here with my brother before returning to America. He's retired from the U.S. army. It's my first visit to Italy. I'm tempted to stay longer. It's lovely. But you don't want to hear that." She shrugged. "Let's see, where to begin. Ivana arrived here yesterday. She had no idea you were alive until her mother called. She was sure the gunman had killed you."

"He's dead. Those men in the hallway killed him," Jeff said.

Annie nodded in approval. "Ahh. She'll be glad to hear that. When

I first met her, I never could have imagined she could be so tough. These Russian women . . ."

"How is Ivana?" Daryl asked. "I saw her go down and there was a lot of blood before she fled."

"She's fine. The wound wasn't serious, though there was initially some bleeding. She had a terrible headache when she arrived. But she's okay. Physically, anyway." Annie sighed. "She spent a lot of time on my computer and didn't want to be bothered. She's very good with them."

"When might we see her?" Daryl asked.

Annie folded her arms. "What do you want with Ivana? Don't you think she's suffered enough?"

"To be frank," Daryl said, "what we really want is the external drive she took with her."

"And why would you want that?"

Leaning forward, Jeff told Annie who they were and what they did. He explained about the concentrated virus attack and how Ivana's husband had provided the essential cloaking portion of the virus. "If we can get his information, we still have five or six days to get it into the hands of experts who can prepare signatures and patches and distribute them while there's still time."

Annie looked stunned. "Do you really think it's as catastrophic as all that?"

"They tried to kill us in New York City and again in Moscow," Jeff said. "They killed the woman I was working with on the virus and her boss and even sent the same gunman to Moscow to kill Ivana's husband. He tried to kill Ivana and us as well. I'd say that *they* certainly think they have something to protect."

"Yes, I understand," Annie said, turning quite sober.

"It's important we speak with her," Jeff said.

Annie set her cup down. "I understand and I believe you. But Ivana isn't here, and neither is the external drive you want."

Dufour checked the front door to the offices to be certain it was unlocked. The visitor could arrive at any time. Dufour stood at the entrance and scanned the room. The employees had been gone for more than an hour, leaving behind their usual mess. It looked like what it was, a busy graphics company. It would arouse no suspicion.

He returned to the back office, leaving the doors between the rooms open, something he'd never before done. In the room from which he and Labib had launched the cyber jihad against the West, Dufour said to the two men, "I'm going to stay up front. She could come any minute. Are you ready?"

Labib was seated at his usual computer, but this evening he was ashen. He merely nodded. Fajer was half-sitting, half-leaning against a table. He was calm and, as always, in command. "Yes. We are ready. Be certain she is alone and lock the door behind her before she sees us so she has no escape."

"It will be done."

The e-mail had arrived early that morning. Someone claiming to be the wife of the Russian, Superphreak, said he had been murdered and demanded to know what Dufour had involved him in.

At first he'd been startled by the message. He'd forwarded it to Labib, busy on the computer behind him. "Read this. What should I do?"

Labib read the message, then picked up his cell phone and called his
brother, explaining about the e-mail. Fajer listened, then told him,
"Ask what she wants. Get more information from her."

Dufour had rapidly typed and sent a message. It became apparent
that the woman knew little about what her husband had been doing.
He told Labib as much.

"Assure her we are on her side."

Dufour wrote that they themselves had been in danger. They deeply
regretted her loss. Was there anything they could do for her? How did
she get his e-mail address? Her reply was electric:

Date: Tues, 5 September 08:25 — 0700
To: Xhugo49 <xhugo1101@msn.com>
From: IvanaK434 <IvanaK434@au.com.ru>
Subject: help

The people who killed my husband are after me. I have the external
drive of his work and they want it. I found your email on it along
with a lot of other information I don't understand. I want to warn
you.

"Read this," Dufour said without bothering to forward the message
to Labib, who came and read it over his shoulder.

"What do you think she has?" Labib asked, his voice rising a bit in
excitement.

"That crazy Russian might have backed up everything on an external drive. It could be all the work he did for us, every rootkit we're using, even some of the viruses."

Labib didn't have to stop and think. "Try and get her to come to
Paris with the drive. Or at least tell us where she is."

Dufour and Ivana exchange several more e-mails. She refused to say
where she was and seemed hesitant about coming to Paris. By that time
Fajer had arrived and Labib showed him the messages. He grunted.
"Looks as if the Chechen did the job. I wonder if he's still after her."

"Haven't you talked to him?"

"No. No one's answering the cell phone he got in Moscow. I don't know what to make of it. If you can get her here with the drive, though, that threat will be finished. The Chechen won't matter. We'll see to her. Dufour?"

"I've told her she is in great danger, that it is essential we see the information she has, that we can protect her." He looked up for approval. "I also told her that her husband was a great man and we were honored to work with him. I suggested we meet in a park or somewhere neutral, but she refuses. She says if she comes, she'll come right here, so I've given the name of the company and our address. It was the only way. She's just a woman. There will be no problem."

Fajer agreed. "Any reply?"

The computer pinged. The three men gathered before the monitor and read:

Date: Tues, 5 September 09:08 —0700
To: Xhugo49 <xhugo1101@msn.com>
From: IvanaK434 <IvanaK434@au.com.ru>
Subject: help

I'm afraid and confused. I am taking the train and will be in Paris
sometime tonight. I will come straight to your address. Please
help me.

Fajer straightened up and smiled. "Excellent. We'll have a reception waiting for her."

MILAN, ITALY
TICINESE-NAVIGLI DISTRICT
VIA CHIESA ROSSA
TUESDAY, SEPTEMBER 5
6:52 P.M.

She isn't here? But her mother told us she was staying with you," Daryl said.

"She *was* here until lunch. But she's gone now."

"What happened?" Jeff asked. "Did she think she was in danger?"

"No, not that." Annie shook her head. "She used my computer to access the external drive. Apparently Vlad even ran his e-mail from there. She contacted one of his Internet friends and told him her husband was dead."

"Which friend?" Jeff asked, trying to recall all the cyber handles he'd seen. *My God*, he thought, *just when I thought things couldn't get any worse.* He and Daryl exchanged a worried glance.

"I'm not even certain she told me the friend's name," Annie said. "I know I didn't think it was my place to ask."

"What did she learn?" Daryl asked, ignoring Annie's attitude.

"She was told that Vlad had been working for a company in Paris, possibly run by Arabs. That it must have been them who had her husband killed."

"Did she give you any names, or an address?" Daryl asked.

"No." Annie's expression remained unyielding.

"What's Ivana up to?" Jeff asked, raking his hand through his hair, desperate to find a way to recover the disk.

"It was all crazy," Annie said, shrugging. "She was writing these e-mails, pacing back and forth waiting for answers, drinking coffee. Then her mother called and they talked. Not long after that she was back on the computer. Then she packed and left."

"For where?" Daryl asked.

"Paris, of course."

"Why go there?" Jeff said, recalling for an instant that Paris was where Carlton had been murdered.

"She told me she had the address where the men worked. They told her if she brought them the external drive, they could protect her."

"She believed them?" Jeff said, stunned at the thought.

"No, she didn't," Annie said, sitting back in her chair, eyeing them both evenly. "I don't think you understand what's going on."

"Doesn't she realize this is probably a trap?" Daryl asked incredulously.

"I think she knows that. She's planning on it. I tried to stop her, but she wouldn't listen. She can be very, very determined once she sets her mind on something." Annie paused. "She took my brother's gun with her."

Jeff looked at Daryl, then back to Annie. "We need to see that computer."

PARIS, FRANCE
5ÈME ARRONDISSEMENT
GRAPHISME COURAGEUX
WEDNESDAY, SEPTEMBER 6
1:56 A.M.

It was nearly two in the morning when the airplane from Milan landed at Charles de Gaulle Airport outside Paris. Jeff and Daryl took a taxi from the stand and gave the driver the address for Graphisme Courageux.

The driver looked at it, then in French said, "This is a business. It will be closed."

Daryl answered. "We know. Go there anyway."

The man gave a very Gallic shrug, then put the car into gear.

"Do you think we're in time?" Jeff asked.

"Annie said she took the TGV train to avoid airport inspection, for obvious reasons. I looked at the schedules, and we're arriving at about the same time."

"Do you really think she means to try and do it?" Jeff asked.

Daryl recalled Ivana and tried to see the angry Russian as an avenging angel. "Annie does—and after what they did to her family, I don't doubt it."

Ivana Koskov stepped from the taxi two blocks from the Graphisme Courageux office. She had the driver point the way for her, paid him, then stood watching as he drove off and was well away. She lit a ciga-rette.

The streets were quiet at this time of the morning. She'd always imagined coming to Paris, but never like this. All she'd brought with her from Milan was a shoulder bag with a change of underwear, some toiletries, the external drive, and, of course, the heavy gun.

On the speeding train locked in the restroom, she'd hefted the weapon several times. It was a revolver so she'd had no difficulty seeing that the gun was loaded. She'd looked but she could find no safety. She was certain all she had to do was point the thing and pull the trigger.

Ivana did not doubt her ability to kill these men. She just wished she could be certain that she'd hit what she aimed at. If she knew she'd killed them, whatever happened to her afterward didn't matter.

For a fleeting second she thought of the baby growing inside her. If she lived, she hoped the French authorities would let her mother raise the child. If they didn't, it would grow up in France, and that had to be better than living in what Russia was and was becoming. And if, as she feared, she died? She pushed that thought from her mind.

Dufour fell asleep about midnight. Labib had joined him in the front office, keeping a silent vigil through the windows. Behind both men, sitting in the hallway in a chair he'd pulled from the back office, sat Fajer, fingering the *shafra*.

Fajer had considered using a gun, but such a weapon would be loud and the Paris police were notoriously efficient. No, a knife would do. There was no reason to be suspicious of the ease with which they had drawn her to them. She was, after all, only a woman.

A light shower had fallen in Paris shortly after midnight. Couples had scurried from doorstep to doorstep on their way home. Now the streets on the Left Bank were nearly clear of life. The rain had left the cobblestones slick with patches of water that reflected the streetlights.

Ivana drew a deep breath, walked toward the shadows on the right side of the street, then moved slowly toward the address she had for Graphisme Courageux. She shifted her shoulder bag well back behind her left arm and firmly gripped the revolver in the pocket of her light jacket.

For a second she realized she was likely walking to her death, but she pushed the thought back. Some things you had to do, and this was one of them.

As she crossed a narrow street to the block where the address was, a taxi came up behind her. She turned and watched as it slowed, then stopped about twenty feet from where she was standing. The American couple she'd last seen in Moscow, the handsome young couple she'd thought dead, emerged from the vehicle. The taxi drove off, and the couple, spotting her, ran toward her, the man holding the shoulder where he'd been shot.

"Ivana," the woman shouted. "Don't do this."

"Stay back," Ivana warned. "I have a gun. I don't want to hurt you, but you aren't going to stop me."

"It won't bring your husband back," Daryl said. Ivana looked frail for such determination. A large bandage covered one side of her head, and her face was pale.

"You have to be Russian to understand why I must do this."

"The external drive. Do you have it with you?" Jeff asked, thinking of the hundreds of thousands, even millions, of lives that might be at stake.

"Of course. I may need to show it to them to get close. Now go away from here."

"Give us the drive and then we can all talk about what to do next. Please," Jeff pleaded.

"No. I need it. Walk away."

"Let us call the police," Daryl said

"Why?" Ivana said, seeming genuinely perplexed. "How do I prove these men killed Vlad and my father? Think about it. Everything was done by computer. It was a virtual killing, except for the blood of my family."

"The assassin is dead," Jeff said.

"How do you know?"

"We saw it," Daryl said. "Those men in the hallway managed to kill him."

"Good. Very good." Ivana's voice was hard, and bitter.

"Ivana, please . . . ," Daryl begged.

"Enough! Turn and leave, or I will shoot you too. I mean it!" Ivana drew the pistol from her pocket and pointed it at them. "Go!"

Jeff took Daryl's sleeve and drew her back. "We'll wait," he said.

"Good. If I miss one, you can kill him." Then Ivana turned and walked briskly away from them, returning the revolver to her pocket.

Jeff and Daryl watched as the slim woman paused at a door, tried the handle, then entered without hesitation.

"Keep an eye on that door," Jeff shouted at Daryl before running toward it, then turning right down the alley.

Daryl moved toward the door herself, uncertain what she should do. A long minute passed. Then she heard a gunshot.

Dufour was startled from his sleep when the bell over the front door chimed. He jumped to his feet, nearly losing his balance. They had left the night-light on so as not to attract the attention of the police patrol, who were used to it. The front office was almost entirely in shadows.

Only then did he see the woman, standing just inside the door.

Labib also rose from his chair. "You startled us," he said.

"I'm sorry, I don't speak French," Ivana said.

"English, perhaps?" Labib said, switching languages, moving slowly toward her.

"Yes, English is fine. My name is Ivana. Are you the men I e-mailed earlier today?"

Dufour had gathered himself by now. "Yes, I am Xhugo. It is a pleasure to meet you in person," he said in heavily accented English. "Allow me." He moved toward her, closed the door, then locked it, all the while smiling.

Ivana shifted her place slightly so he could not reach her, pretending to look scared. Could these men really be the killers of her husband and father? It didn't seem possible. The man nearest her appeared to be a teenager, while the other, though older and clearly an Arab, looked as if violence was far beyond him.

"We are sorry for the loss of your husband. But you are safe now, here with friends. We greatly respected his work. You have the external drive?" Labib asked, coming from around the desk into the waiting area where Ivana stood.

"Yes. I have it."

"Show us," another voice said from behind the Arab. Ivana looked and a taller Arab stepped from the shadows. Though the office was darkened, a light from outside caught his face fully for just an instant.

Yes, she thought, *here is the killer.* "I have it right here." From her pocket she drew the weapon.

Jeff ran down the alley, then turned left at the next opening. He found a series of back doors; all the public entrances and exits to the businesses faced the street. These were unmarked, from what he could see, in an alley with almost no artificial light. He moved urgently along the doors as quickly as he could, listening, looking in where possible. His sense had been that Ivana had entered not quite halfway down the block; he rushed past the first doors, then slowed as he estimated the location.

Then he heard the gunshot. Running to the next door, he heard a second, then a third, shot from behind it. He tried the handle but the door was locked. Pressing his shoulder against the door, he pushed as hard as he could. Stepping back, he heard a fourth, then a fifth shot. He rushed the door. As he struck it with his good shoulder, the lock gave and he tumbled into the back office.

"Gun!" Dufour shouted in Arabic when he saw the weapon clearing her hand. He pulled away from Ivana, though part of him said he should rush her before she could fire. The young woman pointed the gun at him and shot once, striking Dufour squarely in his chest.

It was as if he'd been hit with a heavy hammer. The air rushed from his lungs as Dufour fell back and toppled to the floor.

"Get her!" Fajer shouted in Arabic as he moved forward. Labib rushed Ivana, reaching her just as she swung the gun toward him and fired, the shot winging over his left shoulder. He grabbed her in a sort of tackle and the two of them struck the wall beside the door heavily. Ivana moved the gun against the man's side and pulled the trigger. The explosion was loud and Labib screamed as he released her and began to fall, clutching at her clothing as he did.

Across the entryway Fajer was cursing his own stupidity as he launched himself at the Russian woman. He should have brought a gun. With a sinking heart he saw Labib fall, but by then he was only two short steps away, the *shafra* held aloft, ready to slash across the woman's throat.

Labib was gripping Ivana's jacket as if clinging to a lifeline. She pulled the trigger a fourth time, the bullet striking the Arab in the side of his head. He fell to the floor, a loud gurgling sound coming from deep in his throat.

Ivana could see the third man, the one with the killer's face, almost on top of her. She managed to raise the revolver and fire the final two shots. One went into the floor, the other missed him widely to the left. She saw the flash of the blade and knew she was dead.

Jeff rushed through the back office, down the short hallway, and entered the front office as Ivana fired the sixth and final shot from her gun. He sensed one man lying to his left, a second moaning, lying almost at the woman's feet, and saw the motion of the third man as he stabbed at Ivana.

"Stop!" he shouted as he rushed at the man. Instinctively, Fajer turned toward the sound, causing his knife to strike Ivana on the shoulder. She screamed.

Daryl heard the shots in rapid succession. Hesitating at the entrance, not sure what to do, she had no idea if Jeff had found the back way in. Then she heard the struggle at the door and Jeff's voice shout, "Stop!"

Without thinking, she ran the few short steps to the door and threw herself against it. The door flew open and she sprawled into the entryway, just beside the startled Fajer and screaming Ivana. When she saw Jeff leaping across the short distance from the desk at the fair-skinned Arab, Daryl threw herself at him as well.

Where had the devils come from? Fajer wanted to know.

One moment it was the three of them against the little woman, the next Dufour was dead, his brother dying. His own attack had been thwarted, but he could not return to the woman until he had killed the man. But as he whipped his blade in front of him, the front door exploded open. In rushed a blond apparition that threw itself at him, too. He didn't know which threat to respond to, and in that moment of indecision, Jeff flew into him, bowling the man over, crashing hard with him into the wall.

Ivana grabbed her shoulder. The pain seared her flesh. She let herself fall to the floor, where she curled into a tight ball as she felt the bodies struggling above her.

Jeff smelled the fear as he struck the man. The pair of them grappled for the knife. All the while the man was swearing in Arabic. Determined as he was, Jeff was stronger; if he could avoid getting disemboweled, he'd have the better of the Arab in seconds. He twisted the man's wrist again, so hard he expected to hear the snap of bone. The Arab grunted in pain. Jeff heard the knife clatter to the floor and a moment later felt hands seize his throat and begin to squeeze like a vise.

Daryl was grabbing at the Arab, trying to find some way to help Jeff, when she saw him put his hands around Jeff's throat. At her feet lay the knife he'd had. She reached down and picked up the strange-looking weapon.

Beside her, Jeff grunted. Daryl grimaced, then plunged the knife into the Arab's stomach.

Fajer had never before experienced such pain. Releasing the man, he clutched at his side, pulling away from everyone. The blond woman held in her hand his knife, the one that he realized had taken his life.

Blood flowed from him in a torrent. He prayed in Arabic as he attempted to stanch it. Within moments he became lightheaded, then sleepy.

The jihad, he thought. *It is unleashed whether I live or not. This is Allah's will.*

He swayed on his feet, then toppled over, falling across the dead body of his brother Labib.

PARIS, FRANCE
HILTON HOTEL
CHARLES DE GAULLE AIRPORT
THURSDAY, SEPTEMBER 7
2:43 P.M.

Jeff watched the Arab die without emotion, then checked on the other Arab lying on the floor. He was dead as well. The third man was also lifeless.

"Jeff!" Daryl said. "Are you all right?"

"Yes. I'm fine. You?"

"Me too. I think he stabbed Ivana, though." She squatted down beside the Russian woman, who was still curled in a ball. "Let me help," Daryl whispered.

"We have to get out of here," Jeff interrupted her. "The police will arrive any second." He checked the floor, slippery with blood. Spotting the external drive, he grabbed it and thrust it into his pants pocket. "Let's go. Now!"

Already they could hear the siren of a Paris police car. He helped lift Ivana, who moaned and winced at the touch of his arm around her. "I can walk," she murmured in halting English.

The three of them hurried out the back and into the alley. "Wait a minute," Jeff said. "Daryl, put pressure on the wound. I'll be right back." He rushed off. When he returned, he was carrying their two travel bags, which they'd left on the street. Moving as quickly as they could, they fled the death and chaos.

Five blocks away, they stopped at a fountain and washed as well as they were able to. Daryl removed Ivana's bloody jacket and threw it away. Jeff reached for his undershirt, tore most of it off, and tied it against her wound to stem the bleeding. Then Daryl took her jacket off and slipped it over the Russian.

"Let's flag a taxi while we can," Daryl said. "We look presentable enough. It will take the police a few minutes to figure out what happened."

Jeff moved to a wider street, where he spotted a taxi stand and waved.

"Act like we've been nightclubbing," he said. "We don't want to be especially memorable, at least not for the wrong reason."

A moment later the car approached and the three entered, all laughing. Despite her pain, Ivana put a smile on her face.

"Where to?" the driver asked in French.

Daryl thought for a moment. "The Hilton." She looked at Jeff and shrugged. They must have a Hilton somewhere.

"There are five," the driver said. "Which one?"

Daryl thought for a moment again. "The one by the airport."

The driver audibly sighed. "Which airport? There are two with Hiltons."

"Charles de Gaulle." That, Daryl decided, should be far enough away.

Daryl checked them into a suite, then helped Jeff bring Ivana to their room. Removing the shower curtain, Jeff spread it across one of the two beds and helped Daryl lay the Russian there.

As Daryl began removing Ivana's clothing, Jeff went back downstairs, asked the desk clerk where he might find an all-night pharmacy, and walked the two blocks to it. There an Arab clerk rang up his collection of bandages, Tylenol, and tape.

"Here," Jeff said as he entered their room. The wound was still oozing blood from around the wet towel Ivana had pressed to her shoulder. "I'll be in the business suite if you need me," he said, to give the women privacy as Daryl closed and taped the wound.

The business suite was open twenty-four hours a day. A sleepy young woman smiled and asked him to enter his room number and name on the sign-in sheet as she gestured toward any of the free computers. Jeff had the room to himself. At one of the computers he connected the precious hard drive and scanned it for content. Separating the source code and executable files, he zipped them, then uploaded the files by FTP to a secure drop site. He sent an e-mail to Daryl's office alerting them to its presence, even though she'd be calling in a few minutes. The simple process seemed anticlimactic to him after so much running and so many deaths. He felt let down and stupefied, didn't move from his seat for a few minutes.

When he returned to the room, Daryl had finished. Ivana was sipping from a cup and gave Jeff a weak smile before collapsing onto the pillows. Within minutes she was asleep.

"It's off," he said. He still couldn't believe that part had come so easily. After all the blood, there should have been more to it. He was exhausted and imagined Daryl must be too. He tentatively examined his shoulder. The wound had bled a little again, but otherwise didn't feel too bad.

Daryl nodded. "I'll call the office, then take a shower."

Later, Daryl and Jeff lay in bed, speaking in whispers. "Does she need a doctor?" he asked.

"I don't think so. She wasn't cut very deeply, and the bleeding's stopped. She won't go to one, anyway."

Jeff said nothing for a long time. He felt Daryl's deep, steady breathing and decided she'd fallen asleep. Almost to himself he said, "We were very lucky."

"Yes, we were," she murmured.

"You don't have to leave just yet," Jeff said at the airport the next day. Daryl was back at the hotel, in contact with her office.

"I do," Ivana said. "I have a father and husband to bury." She was dressed in clothes Daryl had bought that morning and looked exhausted. "And my mother needs me."

Jeff took her arm and drifted with her to a wall away from the busy concourse. "I'm sorry for everything that's happened."

"It was not your fault. It is fate. You helped kill the assassins. I am in your debt." She looked at this American and wondered how he could have done such things. He seemed so gentle.

"Is there anything else I can do?" Jeff didn't want to let Ivana go, for reasons he couldn't fathom. She'd shown a toughness he'd never imagined possible for someone who was so clearly not usually a violent person. He wondered for a moment what the world would think if they knew the whole story. Would they condemn her husband for what he'd done? Or laud her for risking everything to undo it? He doubted that in all his life he'd ever meet someone like her again.

"Nothing." Ivana leaned forward and kissed him lightly on the cheek. "God bless you both."

"Did she get off?" Daryl asked as Jeff entered the suite.

"Yes. She hid the pain very well, I think."

"She's a tough lady."

"That would describe her. For sure . . ." Jeff's voice trailed off. "Any progress with saving the world?"

Daryl looked tired, but had that determined look he'd grown to know when she was on a mission. "The code is encrypted, but NSA's working on cracking it full-time, I'm proud to say. My team at US-CERT is spreading the word to the security vendors. When NSA has clean code for us, we'll disseminate it to the vendors, then they'll get the signatures ready and released, in quick time."

Jeff thought back to the small space where, for all he knew, three dead bodies still lay soaking in blood on the floor. "Did you get a look at that office?"

"Not really." Daryl shook her head. "It all happened so fast. It was terrible, just terrible."

For the first time since all this had started, Jeff saw Daryl's face start to crumble. He took her into his arms and held her as close as he could. After a moment he said, "I was thinking about the virus attack. Altogether it was just three men, and perhaps four computers. That's all it took." He paused. "There's only four days to go."

"I know," she said softly against his chest.

Jeff thought back to the day he'd first walked into the law firm and met with Sue Tabor and Joshua Greene. It was as if a lifetime had passed since then. For years he'd focused on Internet and computer security, for years he'd anticipated just such a coordinated attack against the fragile infrastructure of the West. When it came, it hadn't originated from a rogue nation nor had it taken substantial resources. It had come from a small back office in Paris. And it had not been stopped by a firewall or antivirus software. In the end it had taken the two of them, risking everything and nearly coming up short. It seemed incredible to him.

How long could they stay lucky? This very minute in Singapore, or China, or at any American college campus, some geek could be developing or releasing a destructive virus that used a newly discovered zero-day vulnerability to spread—a new virus for which by definition they had no protection on the always-lagging antivirus signatures, one against which no superheroics could save them.

In the end the Arabs had been unlucky, nothing more. No great feats of software engineering had saved the West. And if it hadn't been for Ivana's single-mindedness, he and Daryl would never have found the Arabs or would have been too late. Even now they might not have done enough.

He held Daryl more tightly. At least, finally, he'd found this. The coming days were uncertain. There'd be little time to think about the two of them. But whatever happened from here on, he believed, nothing would change that it was now *we* instead of *I*, and some consolation was to be found in that.

"Will this do enough good, do you think?" she asked.

"Some. Better than nothing." He met her eyes. "All we can really do now is wait. Together." Daryl nodded. "Wait," he said, his voice flat. "But know that if not this time, then next."

ZERO DAY

DHS ASSURES NO THREAT OF CYBER-ATTACK

By Isidro Lama
Internet News Service
September 10

A report released Friday assures that neither Al Qaeda nor any other terrorist organization possesses the ability to significantly harm American computers or the infrastructure of the Internet.

"Statements that we are vulnerable to a so-called cyber-attack are simply unfounded," said the executive assistant director of the Department of Homeland Security, Roger Witherspoon, in a press release Friday. "Security has never been higher and such groups lack the sophistication and expertise to exploit what vulnerabilities remain, ones we are in the process of closing."

The increasing use of viruses for financial scams is the major concern now facing the industry, said Witherspoon, responsible for the overall security of the network, which connects millions of computers worldwide. He dismissed recent assertions that the nation is vulnerable to even a modest attack because so many computers and computer networks lack even basic security software.

"Such talk is counterproductive," he said. "The various security-software vendors are cooperating completely with DHS and we can be assured that we are secure."

PATERSON, NEW JERSEY
CONSOLIDATED BANKING SERVICES CENTER
MONDAY, SEPTEMBER 11
12:01 A.M.

From her perch above the rest of the employees, Margaret Harper glanced across the darkened room, taking in the screens of eighty-three computers in a glance.

Everything was normal, as it usually was this time of night. One shift was leaving as another arrived. Forty-eight personnel, mostly women, had just eased away from their stations, to be replaced by just thirteen until six in the morning, when the room would go to full complement.

Margaret's part of CBSC was to handle the few customer-service needs for those banking customers with problems who managed to clear the numerous hurdles their local bank had created to keep them from actually talking to a real live human being. More than a dozen banks outsourced their customer service to CBSC from 9:00 p.m. until 6:00 a.m., Monday through Friday, and Margaret was responsible for making it all work.

It was not an especially demanding job, and given her hours, none of the other supervisors were clamoring for it. The 10 percent differential made it worth her while. She couldn't sleep nights anyway.

"Maggie?" one of the representatives who'd been stuck on a call said into her headset.

"Yes?"

"I've got a live one. He insists his statement is off three cents. I'm afraid I was a little testy with him and offered to give him the three cents myself. He says that's not the point and wants to talk to my supervisor. Sorry."

Margaret chuckled. "I'll take him." But just as she heard the unpleasant voice of the customer on the line, the screens across the room flickered, turned blue, then read:

Rebooting...

After a few seconds, the screens flickered again, and read:

NO OPERATING SYSTEM FOUND.

Then the screens turned black.

Margaret disconnected the call without comment. "I'm calling tech support!" she shouted over the sudden chatter that filled the room.

SUBMARINE GROUP 10
NAVAL SUBMARINE BASE KING'S BAY
SOUTHEAST GEORGIA
MONDAY, SEPTEMBER 11
12:01 A.M.

Petty Officer Third Class Russell Winters leaned back in his swivel chair and yawned. As always, day or night, the lights in the communications room were subdued with a certain surreal quality he had some difficulty adjusting to. He'd just come on duty and was already ready for a nap. That wouldn't do. He took a long sip of the strong black coffee with which he began every shift and turned back to his computer screen.

This was a quiet time for the submarine net spread across the Atlantic. Winters manned the very low frequency, or VLF, radio for the ballistic-missile submarines known as boomers. The screen placed each boomer by location, while the silence in his earphones told him no one was calling home. No one was expected to be calling in, so in this case silence was golden.

Six communications specialists were on duty, along with Lieuten-
ant Commander Danielle Alvarado. She ran a quiet station, which was
just as well with Winters. His personal life had all the drama he could
manage for now.

He took another sip of coffee as every computer screen blinked.

"What was that?" Alvarado asked from her desk, alert.

"Some kind of hiccup, ma'am," Winters said. His screen turned
blue, then went black. They were down.

"What's going on?" Alvarado demanded, standing in place.

Winters clicked his mouse. "I don't know, ma'am. But we're out of
contact."

Alvarado was already on the telephone. "I need every tech you've
got, now! We're down. There's no way we can give an order or receive a
message. You understand? We're naked right now. We'll be waiting."
She looked up at her confused staff. "Everybody reboot. We need to get
back up."

"Ma'am," Winters said, "I just noticed that our satellite uplink is
down as well."

COLUMBUS, OHIO
MONDAY, SEPTEMBER 11
12:01 A.M.

James Black ran the numbers one more time. Maybe, just maybe, they
were finally turning the corner. The fall season the previous year had
been good for the family company, and they'd just come out of the tra-
ditionally slow summer with a positive cash flow, a first. If the economy
stayed healthy through the holidays, they'd be in the best shape ever
since mortgaging their house three years before to finance the company.

Working from home had been their dream. Black had to admit it
was pretty good. It sure beat the daily commute and that boss he'd had.
What a jerk! But now it was all in their hands, though if these numbers
were correct, it was looking as if they'd made the right call. The key to
the company's success was the lack of an inventory and all the associated costs. It had taken him an entire year to figure that part out. Now
he took the orders online, placed his own order with the wholesaler for

direct shipment to the customer, then processed the charge. Smooth. The computer made it all possible.

Not that it had been as easy as that in the beginning. He'd had to make many modifications to the software to get it to do what their novelty business required, but that speed bump was behind them. Everything was going to be just fine. Black sat back with a sense of satisfaction.

His computer screen flickered, then turned blue and read:

Rebooting ...

A moment later the screen blinked again, read:

NO OPERATING SYSTEM FOUND.

Then turned dark.

Black stared in amazement. He'd never seen anything like it. He killed the power bar, waited, then turned it back on. His attempt at rebooting went nowhere. He tried it repeatedly with no luck. His computer was dead.

Jeez, he thought, *what am I going to do tomorrow? I won't receive, let alone be able to process, any orders. And what about the family photos?* "Hell," he said aloud with sudden comprehension, "what about our financial records and the software?"

He stared at the screen again, as if seeking an answer, his chest beginning to constrict with panic.

CHICAGO-O'HARE INTERNATIONAL AIRPORT
CHICAGO, ILLINOIS
MONDAY, SEPTEMBER 11
12:01 A.M.

Air traffic controller Byron Smith took in the screen with a single practiced sweep. He could close his eyes and place every airplane on the screen exactly. What's more, he could tell you where'd they'd all be in one minute. As he often told Carla at home, his mind was the best computer of all.

Chicago-O'Hare was one of the busiest airports in the world, and the second busiest in the United States, with more than twenty-six hundred flights daily. Frankly, with their antiquated software, Smith thought it amazing they could juggle so many flights. Still, he enjoyed the challenge and had more than once been called upon to exercise his considerable mental dexterity when the system had become overloaded and sluggish.

This was not an especially busy time for the airport. He didn't like working nights anyway, and the undemanding work only caused the hours to drag. This was also the time when the techs tended to update the software, and that did not always go without a hitch.

"Stand by!" their supervisor called out. "Any second now."

Smith had been told this was a minor update. He shouldn't even notice it, so when the screen blinked, he smiled. So much for techs and their so-called expertise. Then the screen went blue, then black. They were down.

Others shouted while Smith waited. Nothing. He closed his eyes and visualized the planes he'd been monitoring, placing them in their ever-changing locations. The other controllers were now screaming at the supervisor, who was on the telephone, cursing.

"Send them elsewhere!" he shouted. "Emergency landings only. They have no idea what's going on. Careful now. But clear the sky."

Calmly, Smith hit the SEND button and began speaking. "United Flight 145, this is O'Hare. Please divert to another airport. We cannot land you. Thank you. American Airlines Flight 334, this is O'Hare. Please divert to another airport."

Throughout the control room the other controllers were talking to their planes as the supervisor continued screaming into his headset.

DETROIT, MICHIGAN
MONDAY, SEPTEMBER 11
12:01 A.M.

Mike Ruiz glanced at his wristwatch, then looked up at the fourteen robots doing their awkward dance. He'd taken over for the recently deceased Buddy once the line was declared ready, and for the last two weeks assembly had gone off without a hitch.

Mike didn't like the idea of sitting in a dead man's chair, though. He'd never known anyone who was killed on the job before, and the whole thing made him queasy. But he couldn't see passing up a good slot like this just because Buddy had been careless enough to get his head cut off.

Mike and his aging coworkers had talked a lot about the accident, and nobody could really figure out just how it happened. The line moved so slowly it seemed impossible that anyone could lie still long enough for that to happen, but apparently it had. Mike had given this a lot of thought, even talked to his wife about it. If the robots ever acted up again, he knew exactly what he was going to do.

Shortly before midnight, Mike Ruiz left his workstation with a clean rag and lubricant can. At the first robot he pressed the large blue plastic button that caused the machine to retreat from the assembly line five feet. Once in place Mike lubricated six points, then wiped them down. Finished, he pressed the button and watched the robot move back into place and resume operation.

Mike was halfway through the chore when the robots stopped doing whatever they'd each been up to. They then moved, as if standing to attention. Mike stepped back and gawked at the machines. He'd never seen them act like this before.

Then, without warning, all fourteen of them moved to their left and dropped down low. For just an instant, Mike was frozen in place. Then he understood how Buddy Morgan got his head chopped off. With a loud grunt, he dropped to the floor, pressing himself as hard to the vinyl surface as he could. Over his head, the nearest machine swung its arm violently forward as if swinging at a ball, just brushing Mike's pants.

Never more terrified in his life, Mike crawled away as fast as he could, just as they'd taught him in the army. Finally, away from the robots, he rose, then raced over to the shift supervisor.

"Did you see that?" Mike asked breathlessly, looking back at the machines, which were now performing some macabre dance in unison.

"See what?"

"Those . . . those . . . things! They just tried to kill me, like they did Buddy!"

MEMORANDUM

NS rated 10

DATE: April 18
FROM: Dr. Daryl Haugen
             Assistant Director
             Computer Infrastructure Security Unit, DHS
TO: Leonard A. Hayes
             Senior Deputy Director, NSA
RE: Interim Report, Summary of Events Related to Superphreak
             Virus and Resignation

Forgive me for wrapping up so many subjects in a single memo, but in my mind these are all intimately interconnected. First, as you requested, following is a summary of certain events related to the recent disruption in Internet service and the destruction of computers in the United States and Europe.

- We estimate that 800,000 computers were struck and suffered significant damage of one kind or another.
- To date, 23 deaths have been directly attributed to the various viruses.
- Three nuclear power plants shut down and took more than one month to come back online.
- The air traffic control system crashed in 11 airports, the largest of which was Chicago-O'Hare. No incidents occurred.
- The Navy lost contact with its ballistic missile submarine fleet for eight days. Emergency measures in place prevented any incident.
- The electric power grid in the Pacific Northwest was down for 3 days.
- We estimate a loss of $4 billion in the private sector and an additional $1 billion in government loss.

- Our efforts to portray this as a financial attack by the Russian mob have so far met with success. No credible source has linked this to any terrorist group.

Next, are the related subjects in which you expressed interest.

The law firm of Fischerman, Platt & Cohen went out of business. As I understand it, the death of the managing partner was the last in a series of unfortunate events leading to the demise of the once well-regarded firm. Its office space has been assumed by a branch office of the Department of Homeland Security, Manhattan District.

The murders of Sue Tabor and Joshua Greene remain unsolved. The murders of Michel Dufour, Labib al Dawar, and Fajer al Dawar have also not been solved, though a confidential report to the President of the Republic offered the opinion that it was a reprisal attack by another Arab group or a Mossad operation.

The murder of George Carlton was resolved by the charging of a local pimp and extortionist.

The woman who proved so instrumental in all this, Ivana Koskov, returned to Moscow. She has been sponsored into the United States by Interport, Inc.

I believe that is it. As we discussed, please accept this as my letter of resignation effective in 30 days. I will be joining Jeff Aiken in his company and look forward to working with you in that capacity in the future.

Acknowledgments

I'd like to thank Chris Corio, Scott Field, John Lambert, and Matt Thomlinson, colleagues of mine at Microsoft, for reviewing drafts of *Zero Day* and providing valuable input. Thanks also to David Solomon for his multiple reviews and many conversations discussing the technical aspects of the book. Ron Watkins provided me helpful advice and coaching on the plot, structure, character development, and other aspects of the book. *Zero Day* is a better book than it would have been because of the feedback I received from these friends.

I owe a special thanks to Howard Schmidt for the foreword and to Bill Gates for providing a promotional blurb and for the many discussions we had on cyber security. I'm grateful to Scott Stein for introducing me to Howard.

I might have given up getting the book published if it were not for the dogged persistence of my agent, Ann Collette, from the Helen Rees Literary Agency. She also reviewed numerous versions of the book, editing and making suggestions that helped tighten the plot.

Thanks to Peter Joseph, my editor at Thomas Dunne Books, for his reviews and for ushering the book through publication, and Thomas Dunne for taking a chance on a first-time novelist.

Finally, I want to thank my wife, the real-life Daryl, for her incredible support on this and everything else I do.